A Ladder to the Sky

www.penguin.co.uk

A
Ladder
to the Sky

JOHN BOYNE

Doubleday

LONDON · TORONTO · SYDNEY · AUCKLAND · JOHANNESBURG

TRANSWORLD PUBLISHERS
61–63 Uxbridge Road, London W5 5SA
www.penguin.co.uk

Transworld is part of the Penguin Random House group of companies
whose addresses can be found at global.penguinrandomhouse.com

First published in Great Britain in 2018 by Doubleday
an imprint of Transworld Publishers

A CIP catalogue record for this book
is available from the British Library.

ISBNs 9780857523495 (hb)
9780857523501 (tpb)

Typeset in 12/15.5 pt Dante MT by Jouve (UK), Milton Keynes
Printed and bound in Great Britain by Clays Ltd, Elcograf S.p.A.

Penguin Random House is committed to a sustainable
future for our business, our readers and our planet. This book
is made from Forest Stewardship Council® certified paper.

MIX
Paper from
responsible sources
FSC® C018179
www.fsc.org

1 3 5 7 9 10 8 6 4 2

For Stephen Walsh

Contents

PART I

BEFORE THE
WALL CAME DOWN

'All things which take place in the sexual sphere are not the private affair of the individual, but signify the life and death of the nation.'

– Heinrich Himmler

1. West Berlin

From the moment I accepted the invitation, I was nervous about returning to Germany. It had been so many years since I'd last been there, after all, that it was difficult to know what memories might be stirred up by my return.

It was the spring of 1988, the year the word 'perestroika' entered the language, and I was seated in the bar of the Savoy Hotel on Fasanenstraße, contemplating my sixty-sixth birthday, which was only a few weeks away. On the table before me, a bottle of Riesling had been decanted into a coupe glass that, a note in the menu revealed, had been modelled on the left breast of Marie-Antoinette. It was very good, one of the costlier wines on the hotel's expansive list, but I felt no guilt in ordering it for my publisher had assured me that they were content to cover all my expenses. This level of generosity was something new to me. My writing career, which had begun more than thirty-five years earlier and produced six short novels and an ill-advised collection of poetry, had never been successful. None of my books had attracted many readers, despite generally positive reviews, nor had they garnered much international attention. However, to my great surprise, I had won an important literary award the previous autumn for my sixth novel, *Dread*. In the wake of The Prize, the book sold rather well and was translated into numerous languages. The disinterest that had generally greeted my work was soon replaced by admiration and critical study, while the literary pages argued over who could claim credit for my renaissance. Suddenly I found myself invited to literary festivals and being asked to undertake book tours in foreign countries. Berlin was the location for one such event, a monthly reading series at the Literaturhaus, and although I had been born there, it did not feel like home.

I grew up close to the Tiergarten, where I played in the shadow of statues of Prussian aristocrats. As a small child, I was a regular visitor to the zoo and fantasized about being a keeper there some day. At the age of sixteen, I stood with some friends from the Hitlerjugend, each of us wearing our swastika armbands, and we cheered as Begas's Memorial to Bismarck arrived in the heart of the park from outside the Reichstag as part of Hitler's plans for a Welthaupstadt Germania. A year later, I stood alone on Unter den Linden as thousands of Wehrmacht soldiers paraded before us following the successful annexation of Poland. Ten months after that I found myself in the third row of a rally at the Lustgarten, surrounded by soldiers my own age, saluting and swearing our fealty to the Führer, who roared at us from a platform erected in front of the Dom of a Thousand-year Reich.

Finally leaving the Fatherland in 1946, I was accepted as an undergraduate student at the University of Cambridge, where I read English Literature, before spending several uneasy years as a teacher at a local grammar school, my accent the source of much derision by boys whose families had been traumatized and depleted by four decades of armed conflicts and unstable reconciliations between our two countries. Upon completion of my doctorate, however, I won a place on the faculty of King's College, where I was treated as something of a curiosity, a fellow who had been dragged from the ranks of a murderous Teutonic generation and adopted by a noble British institution that, in victory, was prepared to be magnanimous. Within a decade I was rewarded with a professorship and the security and respectability attached to that title made me feel safe for the first time since childhood, assured of a home and a position for the remainder of my days.

When being introduced to new people, however, the parents of my students, say, or some visiting benefactor, it was often remarked that I was 'also a novelist', the addendum both discomfiting and embarrassing to me. Of course, I hoped that I had some modicum of talent and longed for a wider readership but my standard reply to the inevitable question *Would I know any of your books?* was *Probably not.* Typically, new acquaintances might ask me to name some of my novels and I would do so in anticipation of humiliation, observing the blank expressions on their faces as I listed them in chronological order.

That night, the night of which I speak, I had endured a difficult evening at the Literaturhaus, where I had taken part in a public interview with a journalist from *Die Zeit.* Uncomfortable with speaking German, a language I had all but abandoned upon my arrival in England more than forty years earlier, an actor had been hired to read a chapter of my novel aloud to the audience and, when I told him the particular section that I'd chosen, he shook his head and demanded to be allowed to read from the penultimate chapter instead. Of course, I argued with him, for the piece he suggested contained revelations that were intended to come as a surprise to the reader. No, I insisted, growing irritated by the arrogance of this disenfranchised Hamlet, who, after all, had been hired simply to stand up, read aloud and then depart by the back door. No, I told him, raising my voice. Not that one. *This* one.

The actor took great offence. It seemed that he had a process when reading to an audience and it was as rigorous as his preparations might be for an evening on the stage of the Schaubühne. I thought he was being precious and said so and there were raised voices, which upset me. Finally, he acquiesced, but without grace, and I retained enough German to know that his reading was half-hearted, lacking the theatricality required to engage an audience. As I walked the short distance back to the hotel afterwards, I felt disillusioned with the whole business and longed for home.

I had noticed the boy earlier, a young man of about twenty-two carrying drinks to the tables, for he was very beautiful and it seemed that he had been glancing in my direction as I drank my wine. A startling idea formed in my mind that he was drawn to me physically, even though I knew that such a notion was absurd. I was old, after all, and had never been particularly attractive, not even at his age, when most people have the magnetism of youth to compensate for any physical inadequacies. Since the success of *Dread* and my subsequent elevation to the ranks of literary celebrity, newspaper portraits had invariably described my face as 'lived in' or as 'one that has seen its share of troubles', although thankfully they did not know just how deep those troubles ran. I felt no sting from such remarks, however, for I had no personal vanity and had long ago given up on the idea of romance. The yearnings that had threatened to annihilate me throughout my youth had diminished over the years, my virginity never conquered, and the relief that accompanied lust's exile was akin to how one might feel having been unshackled from a wild horse let loose on prairie ground. This proved a great benefit to me, for, confronted by an endless stream of handsome youths year after year in the lecture halls of King's College, some of whom flirted shamelessly with me in the hope of receiving better grades, I found myself indifferent to their charms, eschewing vulgar fantasies or embarrassing attachments for a sort of distant avuncularism. I played no favourites, adopted no protégés, and gave no one cause to suspect impure motives within my pedagogical activities. And so it came as something of a surprise to find myself staring at the young waiter and feeling such intense desire for him.

Pouring another glass of wine, I reached for the bag that I'd left next to my chair, a leather satchel that contained my diary and two books, an English-language edition of *Dread* and an advance copy of a novel by an old friend that was due to be published a few months later. I picked up where I had left off, perhaps a third of the way through the book, but found myself unable to concentrate. This was not a problem that I normally faced and I looked up from the pages to ask myself why. The bar was not particularly noisy. There was really no reason that I could think of to explain my lack of focus. And then, as the young waiter passed me, the sweet and intoxicating scent of boyish perspiration infusing the air, I realized that he was the cause of my distraction. He had stolen into my consciousness, nefarious fellow, and was refusing to surrender his place. I set the novel to one side and watched as he cleared a nearby table before wiping it down with a damp towel, replacing the coasters and relighting the votive candle.

He wore the standard Savoy uniform of dark trousers, white shirt and an elegant maroon waistcoat emblazoned with the hotel's insignia. He was of average height and regular build, and his skin was smooth, as if it rarely knew the pull of a razor. He had full red lips, strong eyebrows and a mop of unruly dark hair that looked as if it would fight with all the resolve of three hundred Spartans at the Pass of Thermopylae against any comb that attempted to tame it. He recalled to me Caravaggio's portrait of the young Minniti, a painting I had always admired. Above all else, however, there was that unmistakable spark of youth about him, a powerful blend of vitality and impulsive sexuality, and I wondered how he spent his time when he was not on duty at the Savoy. I believed him to be good and decent and kind. And all this despite the fact that we had not, as yet, exchanged a single word.

I tried to return to my book but it was lost to me now and so I reached for my diary to remind myself of what the following months held in store. There was a publicity trip to Copenhagen and another to Rome. A festival in Madrid and a series of interviews in Paris. An invitation to New York and a request for me to take part in a series of curated readings in Amsterdam. Between each visit, of course, I would return to Cambridge, where I had been granted a year's leave of absence to pursue my unexpected promotional opportunities.

A bored voice interrupted my fantasies, an insolent noise

enquiring whether there was anything else that I needed, and I looked up irritably as the young man's older colleague, overweight and with dark bags beneath his eyes, stood before me. I glanced at the Riesling, which was almost empty – had I really drunk an entire bottle of wine alone? – and shook my head, certain that it was time for bed.

'But tell me,' I said, hoping that my eagerness would not be a cause for humiliation. 'The boy who was serving earlier. Is he still here? I wanted to thank him.'

'His shift ended ten minutes ago,' he replied. 'I expect he's gone home by now.'

I tried not to let my disappointment show. It had been so long since I'd felt such a powerful and unexpected attraction to anyone that I didn't know how to act when thwarted. I was uncertain what I wanted from him but then what does one want from the *Mona Lisa* or the statue of *David* other than to sit silently in their presence and appreciate their enigmatic beauty? I was due to return home the following afternoon so could not even plan a surreptitious visit to the bar the following night. It was over; I would not see him again.

Something like a sigh escaped me and I might have laughed at my own foolishness but there was no laughter inside me now, just longing and regret. The solitude I'd endured throughout my life had stopped being painful many years before but now, without warning, it had reared its head again and old, forgotten heartaches sought my attention. My thoughts turned to Oskar Gött and the single year of our acquaintance. If I closed my eyes I could see his face before me still, his complicit smile, his deep blue eyes, and the arch of his back as he lay asleep in the guesthouse in Potsdam on the weekend of our bicycling holiday. If I concentrated I could recall the anxiety I'd felt that he should wake and discover my indecency.

And then, to my surprise, I was interrupted once again. I looked up and there was the young waiter, now changed into a pair of dark jeans, a casual shirt with two buttons undone at the neck and a leather jacket with a fur trim around the collar. He carried a woollen hat in his hands.

'I'm sorry to disturb you,' he said, and I knew immediately that he was not German as I'd assumed but English, his voice betraying echoes of Yorkshire or the Lake District. 'It's Mr Erich Ackermann, isn't it?'

'That's right,' I said, surprised that he should know my name.

'May I shake your hand?'

He reached out. The skin on his palm looked soft and I noticed how neatly trimmed were his nails. A fastidious creature, I thought. He wore a plain silver band on the middle finger of his right hand.

'Certainly,' I said, a little bewildered by this turn of events. 'We don't know each other, though, do we?'

'No, but I'm a great admirer,' he said. 'I've read all your books. I read them before *Dread* came out too so I'm not just jumping on the bandwagon.'

'That's very kind of you,' I said, trying to conceal my delight. 'Very few people have.'

'Very few people are interested in art,' he replied.

'That's true,' I agreed. 'But the lack of an audience should never be a deterrent to the artist.'

'I've even read your book of poems,' he added, and I grimaced.

'They were ill advised,' I said.

'I disagree,' he said, quoting a line from one that made me hold my hands in the air, pleading with him to stop. He beamed then, and laughed, displaying wonderfully white teeth. As he did so, a slight crinkle appeared beneath his eyes. He was so very beautiful.

'And your name?' I asked, pleased to have an opportunity to stare at him.

'Maurice,' he replied. 'Maurice Swift.'

'It's a pleasure to meet you, Maurice,' I replied. 'It's nice to know that there are still some young people who are interested in literature.'

'I wanted to study it at university,' he said. 'But my parents couldn't afford to send me. That's why I came to Berlin. To get away from them and earn my own money.'

He spoke with a certain bitterness in his tone but stopped himself before he could say anything more. I was surprised by how dramatic he had become, and how quickly.

'I wonder whether you might let me buy you a drink,' he continued. 'I'd love to ask you some questions about your work.'

'I'd be delighted,' I said, thrilled by the opportunity to spend some time with him. 'Please, Maurice, take a seat. But I'll have to insist that they're charged to my room. I couldn't possibly allow you to pay.'

He looked around and shook his head. 'I'm not allowed to drink here,' he said. 'Employees aren't permitted to socialize on the premises. If they catch me, I'll get fired. I shouldn't even be talking to you, in fact.'

'Ah,' I said, putting my glass down and checking my watch. It was only ten o'clock; there was plenty of time until the bars closed. 'Well, perhaps we could go somewhere else, then? I'd hate to get you into trouble.'

'I would love that,' he said. 'I slipped into your interview earlier for about twenty minutes when I was on my break. I was hoping to hear you talk but an actor was reading from *Dread* and not doing a very good job of it, I thought.'

'He was annoyed that I'd chosen a section for him to read that he didn't like.'

'But it's your novel,' said Maurice, frowning. 'What business was it of his?'

'That's what I thought,' I replied. 'But he had different ideas.'

'Well, by the time I had to come back here he was still reading so I didn't get to hear you answer any questions and there were so many that I would have liked to ask. You did have something of a scowl on your face all the way through, Mr Ackermann.'

I laughed. 'Let's just say it was not an entirely pleasant evening,' I said. 'Although it has brightened up considerably now. And please, call me Erich.'

'I couldn't.'

'But I insist.'

'Erich, then,' he said quietly, testing out the word on his tongue and looking, I thought, a little nervous. Perhaps it was my ego or my awoken desires or a combination of the two that made me happy to feel the stream of veneration making its delicate journey from his lips to my ears. 'You're sure that you want to go out?' he asked me. 'I don't want to intrude upon your time. You're not too tired?'

'I'm not tired at all,' I said, even though I was quite exhausted from an early flight and the disappointing event. 'Please, lead the way. I daresay you know the city better than I do.'

Standing up, I cursed myself for the slight groan that emerged from my mouth as my limbs adjusted to being erect once again and, without planning to do so, reached across and held on to him by the upper arm for a moment. The muscle was hard and tightened beneath my grip.

'Where shall we go?' I asked, and he named a bar on the other side of the Tiergarten, close to the Brandenburg Gate. I felt a momentary hesitation, as this would bring us close to the ruined Reichstag, a place I did not particularly care to revisit, but nodded. I could not risk him changing his mind.

'It's not far,' he said, perhaps sensing my reluctance. 'Ten minutes if we take a taxi. And it's usually pretty quiet at this time of night. We can talk without having to shout over the noise.'

'Splendid,' I said. 'Lead on.'

And as we made our way through the hotel doors he uttered the phrase that I usually dreaded but which now, inexplicably, sent waves of excitement through my body.

13

'I'm a writer too,' he said, sounding a little embarrassed at the revelation, as if he'd admitted to a desire to fly to the moon. 'Or I'm trying to be, anyway.'

2. Copenhagen

My visit to Denmark was scheduled for three days in early April; press interviews followed by a public reading at the Royal Library the following evening. I was offered an extra night's accommodation by my Danish publisher so that I could see something of the city and I accepted, booking a second room at my own expense for Maurice, who had agreed to accompany me in the slightly nebulous role of personal assistant. Anxious that our rooms be located adjacent to each other, I sent a carefully worded request to the hotel two weeks in advance. This, I told myself, was so that my young friend would be nearby should I need him. It was one of many lies I told myself during the year of our acquaintance.

At the end of our shared evening in Berlin six weeks earlier, I had given Maurice my address, inviting him to stay in touch, and upon my return to College I waited hopefully for a letter, but none came. I began to wonder whether he'd misplaced the piece of paper on which I'd written it or perhaps he had sent me something and it had got lost in the post. I considered initiating a correspondence myself, writing to him care of the Savoy, but every letter I wrote seemed more tragic than the last and so I gave the whole thing up as a bad job. Finally, after almost a month of silence, I assumed I wouldn't hear from him but with poetic timing a large envelope arrived that same day with the name 'Maurice Swift' and a Berlin return address inscribed across the back.

In his letter, he apologized for taking so long to get in touch, claiming to have been uncertain whether he should take advantage of my proposal to read his work or whether it was simply a polite offer on my part after too many glasses of wine. Nevertheless, he enclosed a short story, titled 'The Mirror', and asked whether I might take a look, begging me not to spare his feelings.

Of course, I had no intention of going back on my word but to my disappointment his story proved to be nothing special. The central character, an obvious fictional representation of himself, was presented as shy and self-deprecating, amusingly inept in his relations with girls, and prone to finding himself in disastrous sexual encounters. And yet there was a touch of vanity to the exercise, for it was clear that he was considered utterly charming by everyone who crossed his path. But for all the mundaneness of the plot, the writing was impressive. He'd clearly worked hard on his sentences and I seized on this as evidence of a dormant talent. If only the story itself were not so boring, I decided, then it might even have been publishable.

Anxious not to appear too eager, however, and recalling how long it had taken him to write to me, I waited three interminable days before replying, sending a carefully considered critical analysis of the piece, during which I tended towards praise while noting the occasional moment that I felt could benefit from a little more attention. In a postscript, I mentioned the Copenhagen trip and suggested that, as I was getting older and these journeys could be tiring, he might be interested in accompanying me. *It would give you a sense of a writer's life*, I told him, hoping that this would prove incentive enough. *Naturally I will pay all your expenses and offer a stipend in exchange for whatever small duties I might require of you while we're away.*

This time, he responded almost immediately with an excited 'yes' and plans were duly drawn up. In the week leading up to our departure, however, I became increasingly fretful of meeting him again, worried that an enjoyable evening in Berlin would turn into something awkward when we tried to replicate it over a longer period in Denmark. But no, Maurice proved amenable and friendly from the moment of our reunion and, if he noticed how intensely I stared at him, then he was kind enough not to remark upon the fact. The slightest thing caught my eye: a shirt with its top buttons undone offering a glimpse of bare skin beneath the fabric and the grooved cavity at the centre of his chest where the muscles separated, a gully I longed to explore; the manner in which his trousers would ride up slightly when he crossed his legs and the intoxicating ankle that appeared at such moments, for Maurice never wore socks, an affectation I found ridiculous and erotic in equal measure; the manner in which his tongue darted from his mouth to lick his lips whenever food arrived and how his appetite was never satisfied, like a farmhand at the end of a long day's harvesting. I took note of all these observations and more. I wrote them down, I memorized them, I allowed the negatives to rest in my brain for later development, and as he talked I simply watched him, feeling rejuvenated by the presence of this boy in my life while all the time trying not to think about how painful it would be when he inevitably departed it again.

On our last day, I suggested a trip to Frederiksborg Castle on the vague pretence that I was considering a historical novel based around the fire of 1859 and the role of the Carlsberg brewer in the building's reconstruction. He agreed and, fulfilling the role of assistant beautifully, booked two first-class train tickets and made some notes on the history and architecture of the palace, which he shared with me on the journey. After a few pleasant hours spent examining its treasures and walking the gardens, we found a small restaurant nearby where we sat at a corner table and ordered pints of local beer with plates of meatballs.

'This is what I've always dreamed about,' Maurice announced, looking around enthusiastically, his blue eyes lively and alert. 'Being a professional writer and travelling to other countries to promote my work or undertake research for the next novel. Wouldn't you like to give up teaching and write full time? You probably could now, I suppose, after the success of *Dread*.'

'No,' I said, shaking my head. 'Cambridge has given me a home and a routine for more than forty years and I value that enormously. I could never stop writing, it's an intrinsic part of who I am, but I don't look forward to the day when I'm forced to retire from teaching.'

He took a notebook from his bag, a pale blue Leuchtturm 1917 with numbered pages and a ribbon band, and began to make some notes; he'd been doing this since our first conversations in Copenhagen and it flattered me enormously.

'What?' I asked, smiling at him. 'Did I say something particularly wise?'

'A home and a routine,' he said, not looking up but scribbling away furiously. 'And I'm writing something down about balance. You seem to have struck a good equilibrium between your work life and your artistic life. Perhaps I need that too. Waiting tables doesn't provide much intellectual stimulation.'

'But I daresay it pays the rent,' I replied. 'Anyway, you can't write all the time. There's more to life than words and stories.'

'Not for me there isn't,' he said.

'That's because you're young and this is the life that you dream of. But once you have it, you might find that there are other things of equal importance. Companionship, for example. Love.'

'Did you always want to write?' he asked.

'Yes,' I replied. 'As a boy, I had a peculiar obsession with stationery. There was a wonderful shop near where I grew up and I used to save my pennies to buy beautiful paper, and ink for my fountain pens. My grandfather was a historian and, from my fifth birthday onwards, he presented me with a different fountain pen every year, and they were treasures to me. I still have all but one.'

'Did you lose the other?' he asked.

'No,' I said. 'I gave it as a gift to a friend of mine many years ago. I keep the rest now in my rooms in College. They remind me of my childhood, before the war, which I think was the happiest time in my life.'

'And where was this?' he asked. 'Where did you grow up?'

'Where we met. In Berlin.'

'Forgive me,' said Maurice, frowning a little. 'But aren't you Jewish?'

'It depends on your definition of the word,' I told him.

'But you fought in the war?'

'Not quite,' I said. 'I was a clerk at a Wehrmacht headquarters in the city. I've been quite open about that.'

'Yes, but still I don't understand.'

I glanced out the window at the tourists making their way across Møntportvejen Bridge towards the castle. 'Both my parents were German,' I explained, turning back to him. 'My mother's father, however, was Jewish. So, by blood, you could say that I am a quarter Jewish but of course the Jews don't deal in fractions. There was a word used back then. *Mischling*. I first learned of it when the Nuremberg Laws were introduced in 1935. They stated that those with only one Jewish grandparent were a second-degree *Mischling* – or of mixed-birth – and approved for citizenship of the Reich. For the most part, second-degree *Mischlings* were safe from any form of persecution.'

'And a first-degree *Mischling*?' he asked.

'Two Jewish grandparents. Much more dangerous.'

'You must have known some of these.'

I felt a sharp pain across my chest. 'One,' I said. 'One that I knew of, anyway. A girl.'

'A friend of yours?'

I shook my head. 'Not really, no. An acquaintance.'

'But if you don't mind my asking, if you were a quarter Jewish, did you not feel any sense of shame at working with the Nazis?'

'Of course I did,' I said. 'But what else could I have done? Refused? I would have been shot. Or sent to the camps. And, like you, I wanted to be a writer, and in order to be a writer I needed to stay alive. My brother, Georg, worked for them too. Tell me, Maurice, in my situation, what would you have done?'

'You have a brother?'

I shook my head. 'He died very young,' I told him. 'We lost touch after the war, when I left Germany. A few years later I had a rather abrupt letter from his wife to say that he'd been killed in a tram accident and that was the end of that. Look, the truth is, who can have lived through those times and not feel some degree of shame over his actions?'

'And yet you've never written about it,' he said. 'Or spoken of it in interviews.'

'No,' I admitted. 'But please, let's talk about something else. I prefer not to dwell on the past. Tell me about you instead. About your family.'

'There's not much to tell,' he said with a sigh, and I could tell that he would have preferred to keep the focus on me. 'My father is a pig farmer and my mother keeps house. I have five sisters and an older brother. I'm the youngest of the lot and the black sheep.'

'Why so?' I asked.

'Because everyone else stayed at home and found a local to marry. And they've all done exactly what was expected of them. They're farmers, coalminers, teachers. None of them has ever travelled, they haven't even left Yorkshire. But I always wanted more. I wanted to see the world and to meet interesting people. My father said I had ideas above my station but I don't believe in such things. I want to be—'

He stopped and looked down at his drink, shaking his head.

'Finish that thought,' I said, leaning forward. Had I been braver, I might have taken his hand. 'You want to be what?'

'I want to be a success,' he replied, and perhaps I should have heard the deep intent in his tone and been frightened by it. 'It's all that matters to me. I'll do whatever it takes to succeed.'

'But of course,' I told him, sitting back again. 'A young man will always want to conquer the world. It's the Alexandrian impulse.'

'Some people think ambition is wrong,' he said. 'My father says dreaming of better things only sets you up for disappointment. But your work has made you happy, hasn't it?'

'It has,' I agreed. 'Immensely so.'

'And did you never . . .' He paused for a moment, an expression on his face that suggested he was uncertain how personal he could get. 'Did you never marry?'

I took a sip from my glass and decided there was no reason to be disingenuous. If we were to have a friendship, then it was important that I should be honest with him from the start.

'Of course, you realize that I'm homosexual,' I said, looking him in the eye, and to his credit he didn't look away.

'I thought as much,' he said. 'I wasn't certain. It's not a theme that you explore in any of your books. And you've never addressed it publicly.'

'I don't care to talk about my private life to the press or in a room full of strangers,' I said. 'And as you know, I don't write about love. It's a subject that I've avoided scrupulously throughout my career.'

'No, you've always written about loneliness.'

'Exactly. But you mustn't think that my writing is in any way autobiographical. Just because one is homosexual does not mean that one is lonely.' He said nothing and I sensed an awkwardness in the air that discomfited me. 'I hope it doesn't make you uncomfortable to hear me speak of this.'

'Not in the least,' he said. 'It's 1988, after all. I don't care about things like that. My best friend in Harrogate, Henry Rowe, was gay. I wrote one of my earliest stories about him, in fact. These labels mean nothing to me.'

'I see,' I said, uncertain what he meant by this. Was he suggesting that he did not discriminate between his friends on the basis of their sexuality or that he himself was prepared to have intimate relations with people of either gender? 'And was your friend in love with you, do you think? It's possible, of course. You are very beautiful.'

He blushed a little but ignored the question. 'Did you ever try?' he asked me. 'With a girl, I mean? Actually, I shouldn't have asked, should I? It's none of my business.'

'It's fine,' I said. 'And no, I never did. It wasn't something that would have worked at all. Perhaps you feel the same way about boys?'

He shrugged, and I knew that I was pushing too hard; I should pull back if I was not to frighten him away. 'It's not something I've ever given much thought to, if I'm honest,' he said. 'I want to live a life that's open to anything. The only thing I know for sure in that regard is that I want to be a father someday.'

'Really?' I asked, surprised by this revelation. 'That's a curious desire in one so young.' F9bf832

'It's something I've always wanted,' he told me. 'I think I'd be a good father. And speaking of my stories,' he added then, sounding a little embarrassed to be bringing the subject up, but it was inevitable that we'd have to discuss them at some point. I'd read two or three more since our arrival in Copenhagen and, to my disappointment, had felt the same way towards them as I had towards 'The Mirror'. Well written, certainly, but dull. 'They're amateur, I know, but—'

'No,' I said, interrupting him. ' "Amateur" would be the wrong word. But they are clearly the work of someone who has yet to discover his voice. If you were to read some of the stories that I wrote at your age, you'd wonder why I ever bothered trying for a literary career.' I paused, demanding honesty of myself. Already there was a degree of deceit in our relationship but on this subject, on the subject of writing, I felt honour bound to be truthful. 'The fact is, you have skill, Maurice.'

'Thank you.'

'I can tell that you think about every word before committing it to the page and I'm impressed by your use of language. But it's the stories themselves, you see. The subject matter. Therein lies the problem.'

'You mean they're boring?'

'That would be too harsh,' I replied. 'But at times, they feel like stories I've read before. As if I can picture the books on your shelves. The ghosts of the writers you admire seem to slip into the cracks between the scenes. It takes a great deal of talent to write as well as you do but, ultimately, if your story is not engaging, if the reader doesn't feel that it's entirely yours, then it simply won't work.'

He looked down at the table and nodded. I could see that he was crestfallen but what I had said was the truth and he needed to hear it; I owed him that much at least.

'You're right, of course,' he said finally. 'I'm not very good at thinking up plots, that's the problem. I feel like all the stories in the universe have already been told.'

'But that's just not true,' I insisted. 'There's an infinite supply for anyone with an imagination.'

'Sometimes I think I would be better as a musician. The type who writes the words but lets someone else come up with the melody. Perhaps I'm simply tone deaf.'

'You're too young to write off your weaknesses as failures,' I said. 'The more you read, the more you write, the more the ideas will appear. They'll fall like confetti around your head and your only difficulty will be deciding which ones to catch and which to let fall to the floor.'

'And you,' he asked, looking up again. 'How do you do it? Your stories are always so original.'

'I'm not sure,' I admitted. 'The truth is that I just make them up as I go along.'

'Really?' he asked, laughing. 'Can it be that simple?'

'It can be,' I said. 'Look, here we are in Copenhagen. There are stories everywhere. Think of that castle. Think of the people visiting it. Think of us, two relative strangers sitting here talking to each other. Your writing is exceptional and will only get stronger over time. So it's your stories that you need to focus on. When you find one, when you hear one, make it your own and then the world will come to you. That's the best advice I can give you. Even in that hotel of yours in Berlin. All those people coming to and fro. Who are they? Where have they been? Where are they going? What secrets are they hiding?'

'Most of them are just rich people on holiday,' he said.

'No,' I insisted. 'Everyone has secrets. There's something in all our pasts that we wouldn't want to be revealed. Look around the foyer the next time you're there and ask yourself, *What would each of these people prefer that I didn't know about them?* And that's where you'll find your story. A hotel can be a fascinating place. Hundreds of people gathered together in one building, yet each one desperate to maintain their privacy.'

'There are worse jobs for an aspiring writer, that's true,' he said. 'But I get so tired, and I'm not writing as much as I should. I'm desperate to move away from short stories and begin a novel. I just need to find the subject.'

'Love,' I said. 'Love is always the subject.'

'Not for you,' he replied.

'But what is loneliness,' I pointed out, 'other than the lack of love? I wonder . . .' I added after a brief pause, uncertain whether it was too early to raise a subject that I'd been considering ever since our first night together in Copenhagen. There were moments when I thought it a wonderful idea and others when I thought I could only humiliate myself by asking. 'I've mentioned that I have quite a number of trips to make over the coming months,' I said.

'Yes.'

'And the thing is, Maurice, I find all this travelling quite exhausting and hate the idea of dining with strangers every night. Also,

JOHN BOYNE

hotels and trains can be difficult for me to negotiate at times. And then there's the issue of laundry and keeping track of refundable expenses, and so on. It occurred to me that over the time ahead I could very well benefit from having a companion of some description. An assistant, if you will. Someone to do the work that you've been doing for me over these last few days.'

'I see,' he replied, and I could see that he was excited by the turn the conversation was taking.

'Is that something you might consider?' I asked.

'I'd like nothing more!'

'Of course,' I said, 'between each trip you could return to Berlin, but if we were to say a six-month period of employment, then I could give you a stipend that would offer you some financial security for the entire time. You could leave the Savoy or, if you preferred, stay there and find better accommodation. That would be for you to decide.'

I named a figure; it was beyond generous and more than I could reasonably afford, but I was desperate for him to say yes. And when we shook hands on the deal I felt as happy as I had felt in years. It was as if I'd won The Prize for a second time.

'Thank you,' he said, utterly delighted. 'You're very kind.'

'It's my pleasure,' I told him, which was as truthful a remark as I had made since disembarking the plane.

3. Rome

In Rome, of course, we spoke about God when Maurice remarked that he had been brought up Anglican and maintained a sentimental attachment to his faith.

'And you?' he asked. 'Are you religious at all?'

'Well, you must remember, I lived in Europe during the thirties and forties,' I told him. 'So I have little choice but to be an atheist.'

24

'And before then?'

'That's too long ago for me to recall. But if you have a spiritual bent, then I suppose Rome is the place to be.' I took a deep breath and debated whether to introduce a new character into our dialogue, a person whose importance in my life could not have been overestimated. 'I had a friend once,' I told him. 'Oskar Gött. His great ambition in life was to come here. He read a book about the catacombs and wanted to visit them.'

'And did he make it?'

'No,' I said, shaking my head. 'He died shortly before the war began.'

'How did he die?'

'He was shot.'

Maurice nodded, and I stopped at a bench, sitting down and closing my eyes as I tilted my head back, allowing the late-morning sunshine to warm my skin. I felt him sit down next to me and the slight connection between his leg and my own. A passer-by might have taken us for father and son, a misunderstanding which had in fact taken place a few nights earlier when we'd checked into our rooms at the hotel, adjacent once again at my insistence, and it had upset me more than I'd expected, although Maurice had simply laughed.

'You remind me of him,' I said finally. 'Of Oskar, I mean. You have similar features. Round, cheerful faces, bright blue eyes and that untameable dark hair that falls over your forehead.'

'Tell me about him,' he said. 'Was he a good friend of yours?'

I hesitated. This was a part of my life that I'd locked away for many decades, never confiding the story in a single person. And yet sitting there that day on a bench in Caffarella Park, this twenty-two-year-old boy made me long to reveal my secrets in the most self-destructive way imaginable. I wanted to confide in him, to tell him my story.

Oskar and I, I told him, had met in early 1939, shortly after my seventeenth birthday, in the Nachmittag Café near the Volkspark am Weinbergsweg in Berlin. Like Maurice, Oskar, who was a few months younger than me, was a waiter, working for his parents in this small restaurant they had run for many years in the north of the city. It was not my usual custom to wander into such places alone but on the day in question it had begun to rain while I was on my way home and I took shelter inside, choosing a seat by the window and ordering a cup of coffee with a slice of Stollen. I noticed a book sitting on the window ledge, an adventure story that I had read and enjoyed several times. This volume, however, was considerably thicker than the one I had at home, more than three times its length in fact, and so I picked it up and turned to the title page, only to discover that it was a deceit, for the book's jacket had been removed and another, a less controversial one, pasted in its place.

Before I could consider why someone might have done such a bizarre thing, a boy came running out from the kitchen area with an exaggerated sense of urgency and I looked up when he stopped before my table, one hand pushing the hair back from his forehead as he stared at me in dismay. I was aware of the anxious expression on his face but, more than this, I experienced a stirring at the pit of my stomach unlike any I had felt before. Of course, I had known for some years that I was homosexual and, at seventeen, was no stranger to physical attraction. For a time, I had tried to force myself to be attracted to girls but it was no good and I had little interest in pursuing so fruitless a goal. My homosexuality, I knew, was something that I could never change but also something that I could never indulge. Himmler, after all, had given a speech only a year earlier in which he had denounced the personal for the public and I had listened to his words on our wireless, uncertain why such a curse had been placed upon my head. He declared that the homosexual had to be got rid of – 'Just as we pull out weeds, throw them on a heap and burn them' – and there were rumours that known homosexuals were being sent to concentration camps or shot.

Naturally, such ideas terrified me. And so my plan had been to feign a disinterest in all sexual matters, to become a eunuch around my friends, betraying no hint of desire and never indulging in or even pretending to understand crude jokes. Should it prove necessary, I imagined that I might one day take a wife and perform as husbands do but promised myself that this would only be a last resort for self-preservation.

'My book,' said the boy, reaching a hand out towards me. 'I was searching for it.'

'You changed the jacket,' I replied. 'Might I ask why?'

He bit his lip nervously and glanced around the room. Despite the inclement weather, the tables near mine were quite empty.

'Give it to me, please,' he said, lowering his voice. I nodded and handed it across. 'You won't tell anyone what you saw, will you?'

'No,' I said. 'It's none of my business and, anyway, I've read that book myself. At home, in my bedroom. With the curtains closed. Aren't you frightened of reading it in public?'

'Of course, that's why I made it look like something else. When I realized I'd left it out here, I thought I was going to faint. If the wrong person had found it, I might have been in trouble.'

The book was *Buddenbrooks*, by Thomas Mann, and I was aware, as was Oskar, that its author had fled Germany for Switzerland some six years earlier and that his books had subsequently been banned when he had been declared an enemy of the Reich. From his home in Zürich he had written at length about his contempt for the Führer and the Nazi Party and although the majority of his articles had been suppressed, some had appeared in underground papers and his views had been disseminated among a largely apathetic populace.

'Join me if you like,' I said, indicating the seat opposite me. 'I'd be interested to know what you thought of it.'

'I can't,' he said, glancing back towards the counter, where an older man I took to be his father was watching us warily. 'My shift

27

doesn't finish for a couple of hours yet. I haven't seen you in here before, have I?'

'I came in to escape the rain.'

He nodded and seemed lost for what to say next, finally raising the novel in the air in appreciation and smiling at me. 'Thank you for this,' he said, turning around, and a moment later he disappeared back into the kitchen.

It had been a short conversation but afterwards I found myself unable to get him out of my mind and so, three days after this, I returned to the café, this time arriving almost two hours later in the hope that he might be finishing work. When he emerged from the kitchen, he noticed me sitting there and offered a wave, apparently happy to see me again.

'Have you finished your book yet?' I asked, when he came over to say hello.

'Last night,' he said. 'And now I'm reading Dickens. *A Tale of Two Cities*. No one can object to Dickens, surely.'

'I wouldn't be so sure,' I replied, attempting a casual tone. 'These days, anyone can object to anything. Will you join me now?' I added, but once again, to my great disappointment, he shook his head.

'My father doesn't like me to sit here with friends,' he said. 'He resents the idea of waiting on us. But what if we were to go somewhere else? Do you know the Böttcher Tavern? It's not far from here. A few streets over.'

'Of course,' I said. 'What's your name, anyway?'

'Oskar Gött,' he said. 'And yours?'

'Erich Ackermann.'

'I'll meet you at the Böttcher at five o'clock. Do you drink beer, Erich?'

'Yes,' I said.

'Then I will buy you a beer. It will be my way of thanking you for keeping my secret.'

I left the Nachmittag, taking a stroll around the neighbourhood as I watched the hands of my watch move sluggishly
towards the hour. When it was finally time to return, I walked in
great excitement towards the bar, which stood opposite the
Schutzstaffel headquarters, where a tall, thin, red-haired guard,
distinctly different from the typical Aryan type, stood with a rifle
slung over his shoulder. I could feel his eyes on me as I ran across
the road and pushed open the doors, looking around and smiling
when I saw Oskar sitting at a table in the corner, drawing in a
notebook.

At this time, in the early months of 1939, there was a general
assumption that war was coming. No matter what the British said
or did, it seemed clear that the Führer wanted armed conflict,
knowing that only a full-scale international engagement could
establish Germany as the world's leading power. For young men of
my age, this was a frightening thought. We had seen the effect the
last war had had on our fathers – those of us who still had fathers,
that is – and did not relish the idea of our lives following a similar
pattern. And so perhaps it is not so strange that the first thought I
had upon laying eyes on Oskar in the Böttcher was that war must be
avoided at all costs lest someone as beautiful as him fall to the indis-
criminate brutality of the battlefield.

'Oskar,' I said, sitting down, and as I did so he closed his notebook and placed the charcoal pencil on top of it.

'My friend!' he replied, smiling at me, and I swallowed nervously. I had never before known someone whose sheer physicality
could hypnotize me to this extent. We ordered two beers and
clinked our glasses together. He told me that he hated working in
the café because his father was a brute but his plan was to save
enough money so that he could travel and see the world. 'I'd like to
be an artist,' he said. 'And Paris is the place for that. Have you ever
been?'

'No,' I said. 'I've never left Berlin.'

'I'd like to see London too,' he added. 'And Rome. I read a book about the catacombs once and they've fascinated me ever since.'

Neither of us mentioned the possibility of war. There were two types of youth in Germany then: those who could barely wait for it to begin and those who pretended that it was not coming at all, as if by ignoring the fact we could smother the bellicose infant in the crib.

'You were drawing when I came in,' I said, nodding towards his sketchbook. 'Will you let me see your work?'

He shook his head and smiled, his cheeks flushing a little. 'No,' he said. 'Anyway, that wasn't drawing, it was just doodling. You know this word, yes? Something to pass the time. I have some canvases at home and that's where my real work is. I paint with oils, mostly. At the moment, however, I can't seem to find the proper inspiration. I paint landscapes, bowls of fruit and portraits of great buildings simply because I can and I'm able to sell them at the street markets. But what I really want is to paint something that no one else has ever painted before. Either that or paint something familiar in an unfamiliar way and allow the viewer to consider it from an unexpected angle. Does that make sense, Erich? I hear myself speak and worry that I might sound ridiculous to you.'

'Not at all,' I said, drawn to the idea of Oskar as a great painter. 'I would like to be an artist too someday.'

'You paint?' he asked.

'No, I can barely draw a straight line,' I replied with a laugh. 'But I write a little. Stories, that's all. Perhaps one day a novel. Like you, I have not yet found my subject but I hope it will appear one day.'

'Would you let me read one of your stories?'

'Only if you show me one of your paintings.'

We talked of other things then. Of our schools and our classmates, of the subjects that interested us and the ones that didn't. And – because all conversations then turned to this subject eventually – we spoke of the Führer and our weekly meetings of the Hitlerjugend. We were members of different corps and shared an enjoyment of field exercises while agreeing that doctrinal classes bored us to the point of paralysis. We had both attended the Nuremberg Youth Rallies since graduating from the Deutsches Jungvolk and found the atmosphere oppressive with the extraordinary numbers gathered there and the terrifying noise of unenlightened patriotism.

'I saw him once,' Oskar told me, leaning forward a little and lowering his voice. 'A year ago, perhaps a little less. I was coming out of the Hauptbahnhof when a convoy of cars appeared along Lüneburg-erstraße and everyone stopped and stared. His car, a black Grosser Mercedes, drove past me, and he turned his head just as I looked in his direction and our eyes met. I clicked my heels together and saluted him and despised myself for it afterwards.'

I sat back in disbelief when he said these words. Had I heard him correctly? Had he told me that he despised himself for saluting the Führer?

'I think perhaps I have shocked you,' he said, and there was anxiety in his tone now. Fear. This was not an opinion that people voiced out loud, even if they felt it, and especially not to a new acquaintance whose trustworthiness had yet to be established.

'A little,' I said. 'You don't believe in him, then?'

'He frightens me,' said Oskar, and I understood this because he frightened me too. But then of course my younger brother and I were Jewish, or a quarter Jewish anyway, and the purges against the Jews had already begun. By now it had been more than three years since Jews had been stripped of their citizenship entirely and I knew of at least two couples whose engagements had been cancelled after the law had come into place banning Jews from marrying non-Jewish Germans. Only four months earlier, the city had descended into chaos after a boy my own age, a Jew, had shot a Nazi diplomat in the German embassy in Paris. Days later the SS had run riot through the city, destroying Jewish shops and synagogues, desecrating graveyards and arresting tens of thousands for deportation to the camps. Running home that night, desperate to escape the violence, I witnessed an elderly man being beaten to death by an officer some forty years his junior, another emerging from a jewellery store with blood pouring down his face after the glass in his shop window had been shattered and, near my home, I saw a girl being raped by an SS Sturmbannführer in a side-street while his colleague pinned her father to the wall and forced him to watch. I had not been a victim of any of this for I did not share any of the typical physical characteristics of the Jew, nor were we an observant family so we did not live with other Jews or attend synagogue. But the fact remained: I, and my brother, were *Mischlings*.

'They say that he will restore Germany's power,' I remarked carefully.

'And he may succeed,' said Oskar. 'He has charisma, it's true, and his oratorical skills incite the crowds. The people are behind him for now. He has infected them with his hatred. He demands absolute loyalty, and when anyone dares to criticize him, they lose their position. I think he will lead a great army, but what will be the result?'

'A thousand-year Reich,' I said. 'At least that is what he says.'

'And is that what you want?'

'All I want is to live in peace,' I told him. 'I want to read books and perhaps one day write some of my own. The future of the Fatherland is not something that concerns me.'

He smiled and reached a hand across the table, placing his atop mine in what was certainly intended as a fraternal gesture but sent sparks of electricity through me nevertheless. No boy had ever touched me like that before. 'I want the same,' he said. 'Only with my paintings.'

'Do you think I might find inspiration in Paris too?' I asked.

'For your novel? Of course! Great writers have lived there. Hugo, Hemingway, Fitzgerald. Many classics of literature have been written in the city. It encourages creativity, or so I've heard.'

An image came into my mind of the two of us sharing a flat on the top floor of some decrepit old building near Notre-Dame, he painting in his studio, me writing in my study, the two of us coming together as one in our shared bedroom at night. The idea was almost too glorious to imagine. Before I could embarrass myself by suggesting it, however, he stood up and excused himself to use the bathroom and while he was gone I looked across at his sketchbook, telling myself to leave it alone, not to intrude on his privacy, but I could not resist and pulled it towards me, opening it at the first page. It was brand new, containing only one drawing so far, and as I stared at it my heart sank in my chest as waves of disappointment poured over me. The sketch was of a young girl with long black hair, very beautiful, turned to a left profile but with her back to the artist as she sat on an ottoman. Her right hand was touching her cheek and she was naked. A hint of her breast was given towards the left of the picture and there was something in her eye that suggested desire. I wondered whether she was a creature from his imagination or a girl who had posed shamelessly for him and, if the latter, did that mean that she was his lover? Closing the sketchbook, I returned it to his side of the table, placing the charcoal pencil on top of it, and when he returned a moment later he told me I had a sad expression on my face and the only way to conquer that was for the two of us to stay there and drink until our money ran out, a suggestion I agreed to immediately.

'Did he know that you had looked at his drawing?' asked Maurice, and I turned to him, shivering a little as I dragged myself back from a lost Berlin to a living Rome.

'No,' I said. 'I think it would have disappointed him if he'd caught me and perhaps our incipient friendship would have ended at that moment. Anyway, we got very merry and by the end of the evening I was certain that I was in love with him, but every time my eyes fell to that sketchbook I felt the impossibility of a romance and then I would drink some more to numb the pain.'

I glanced at my watch, it was time for us to move on, and we stood up, talking of other things as we made our way back to the hotel. I sat alone in the bar later, lost in my thoughts, and when Maurice rejoined me he had taken a shower and smelled of soap, his hair a little damp on his head, and this was exhilarating to me. We spoke some more of Maurice's own writing and he told me how much my stipend had meant to him for he had moved to a small flat closer to the Savoy where he found it easier to write.

Later, as we walked along the corridors towards our bedrooms, he paused outside my door and I reached for his hand, to wish him goodnight, but to my surprise he leaned forward and offered me a hug. Like an inexperienced performer on a stage, I was uncertain what to do with my arms, whether I should leave them hanging by my side or wrap them around him too. I breathed in the musk of his scent, and my lips, so close to his neck, longed to find a place to call their own. But before I could embarrass myself any further, he pulled away.

'Your advice is so helpful to me, Erich,' he said. 'I'm lucky to be able to learn from you. I hope you know how grateful I am.'

And with that he was gone and I let myself into my room, knowing that I would lie awake for hours yet.

4. Madrid

I didn't see Maurice again for more than a month after this. He returned to Berlin and I to Cambridge. I longed for the trip to Madrid and, when it came, I waited for him in the foyer of the Hotel Atlántico, pretending to read while keeping a close eye on the door for his arrival. I did my best not to look in the direction of the receptionist, with whom I had engaged in an earlier altercation upon discovering that Maurice's room would not be adjacent to mine but located on the floor below. I had pleaded with her to make the necessary changes but she had proved intractable and I may have disgraced myself with a childish tantrum. When he finally appeared, however, my spirits lifted and we embraced like old friends, before repairing to a local tapas bar, where he ate like a healthy young horse and I simply sat and watched him.

The following day, a lunch was held in my honour in a private room at the Museo del Prado and, although we arrived early to immerse ourselves in the Titians, I lost track of him at some point and was forced to make my way alone to the reception, where I found myself standing next to the American writer Dash Hardy, with whom I shared a Spanish publisher. As he was spending a semester in the city, teaching at the university, he had been invited to attend the gathering but, anxious about Maurice's disappearance, I found it difficult to concentrate on his conversation. I remember, however, that he congratulated me on my recent success while informing me that, while he had not read my book – because he did not read non-American writers – he had been assured by our mutual editor that it was a work of some merit.

'Please don't be offended,' he drawled, reaching his chubby fingers into his mouth, removing a morsel from one of the canapés that had lodged itself between his teeth and examining it for a moment with the intensity of a forensic scientist before flicking it to the carpet. 'I don't read women either and I make sure to say so in every interview as it always ensures that I receive the maximum amount of publicity. The politically correct brigade loses their collective mind and before I know it I'm on the front of all the literary pages.'

'You're a controversialist, then,' I said.

'No,' he replied. 'I'm a fiction writer with an expensive apartment overlooking Central Park West. And I need to sell books in order to pay the co-op fees.'

We talked for ten minutes or more but I struggled to find common ground with him. I recalled a memoir of his that I had read

some years earlier where he listed in graphic detail the many homosexual encounters of his youth and young adulthood, meetings that
seemed almost sordid in his perfect recall. He was the type of writer
I thought of as a professional queer, one whose nature defined both
his public persona and his work, and that was something that had
always made me uncomfortable.

'And I see you have a handsome young friend travelling with
you,' Dash said finally, smiling lasciviously and winking at me. 'I
noticed him earlier staring by the El Grecos and I simply had to go
over to introduce myself. He was too beautiful to ignore. He recognized me immediately, which of course made my day, and told me
that he was your assistant. Lucky old you.'

Before I could reply, I caught sight of Maurice entering the room
at last, locked deep in conversation with a lady novelist, a previous
winner of The Prize, and as they stood there, she squeezing his
hand tightly as they conversed with passionate intent, I felt a surge
of jealousy. I longed to grab him by the arm and make a quick exit
from the Prado but of course such a thing would have insulted my
hosts.

'There he is,' said Dash, turning around now and following the
direction of my eyes. 'Where did you pick him up, anyway? He's
pretty as a peach but also very *street*, don't you think?'

'I didn't pick him up anywhere,' I replied, trying to control my
irritation at his vulgarity. 'He's simply a young writer who helps me
out from time to time, that's all.'

He seemed to enjoy my discomfort. 'You remind me of my Aunt
Gloria,' he said. 'She's long dead now, of course. The poor dear
couldn't bear any talk of sex. She had a stroke halfway through
reading my first novel and ended up in hospital for the rest of her
life. I don't know if it was the book that brought it on but I've always
rather hoped that it was. But tell me, Erich, is he submissive, this
young assistant of yours, or dominant?'

I looked at him again, longing for the lunch to begin in order that it might sooner come to an end, and claimed not to understand what he meant.

'Oh, don't be disingenuous,' he said. 'You know perfectly well what I'm talking about. What's his name?'

'Maurice,' I said, and he threw back his head and laughed.

'Of course it is! You couldn't make it up! What a shame your name isn't Clive. And does he charge you by the day or is he one of those agreeable boys who's happy to give you everything he has as long as you open enough doors for him? You've certainly brought him to the right place, that's for sure,' he added, looking around at a room that had by now filled with writers, editors and literary taste-makers. 'I imagine he'll be *very* grateful tonight.'

'You couldn't be more wrong,' I told him. 'For heaven's sake, he's just a boy. We're friends, that's all.'

'Don't be ridiculous,' he said. 'You're at least forty years older than him. You can't possibly be friends. If he's not giving you what you want, then you should throw him back where you found him and find someone who will. Creative-writing courses are full of accommodating boys who have no scruples when it comes to such things. Believe me, I should know.'

A moment later, lunch was called and to my further annoyance I found myself seated at some distance from Maurice, sandwiched instead between the marketing director from my publishing house and the editor of a literary magazine. He, on the other hand, was placed next to a handsome young Spanish writer who had published three novels in three years, the most recent of which had been a major international success. They spent almost the entire meal locked in conversation, laughing fitfully from time to time, but he never turned in my direction once. And when he took his ever-present notebook from his bag and started to scribble something down that his companion had said, it was all I could do not to pick up the salt cellar and fling it in his direction.

Later that evening, as was our custom, we spent an hour in the hotel bar, where I tried not to allow my dark mood to overshadow our time together, although perhaps it was obvious that I was annoyed for he asked whether anything was wrong.

'Why should it be?' I said. 'It's been a perfectly pleasant day.'

'You just seem a little out of sorts, that's all.'

'It's tiredness, nothing more. You enjoyed yourself, though? You seemed to be having a wonderful time at lunch.'

'I loved it,' he said enthusiastically. 'All those writers! I felt like I was one myself.'

'You are one,' I insisted, despite the fact that he had given me nothing new to read in some time.

'I'm not,' he said. 'Not until I finish my novel. Actually, not until I *publish* my novel.'

'Well, you have to start one to finish one,' I said.

'Oh, but I have!' he told me. 'Didn't I mention it? An idea came at last. A plot. And I just sat down and began writing.'

'I see,' I replied. 'And are you going to tell me what it's about?'

'Not just yet,' he said, shaking his head. 'The thing is, I'm superstitious about things like that. Do you mind if I just keep going and don't say too much about it for now?'

'I don't mind at all,' I said, even though I minded a great deal. 'Do whatever makes you happy. And your companion at lunch, the Spanish novelist. Did he offer you any advice?'

'We weren't really talking about books,' he said.

'Then what were you talking about?'

'His wife, mostly. And his mistresses. He has a number of them.'

'I'm surprised you could bear to listen to all of that.'

'He gave me his card and told me to look him up if I'm ever back here.'

'You certainly know how to collect us, don't you?' I asked. 'Writers, I mean. Don't you ever long for someone a little less accomplished? A friend your own age, perhaps? Although I suppose it would be unwise to let yourself be distracted from your work.'

'I'm happiest on my own,' he told me. 'And if I wanted companionship—' He broke off and pointed over my shoulder towards the foyer. 'Oh!' he said. 'Look who's just walked in.'

I turned around and saw Dash Hardy standing in the lobby, looking around in search of someone who might recognize him and pay him the requisite adoration. He must have been staying in the same hotel as us and my heart sank, sure that he would notice us too and spoil our evening by insisting on joining our table, then flirting shamelessly with Maurice while making the offensive *double entendres* that seemed specifically designed to discomfit me. Indeed, I was certain that he did see us for he smiled in our direction, raising a hand in a half-wave, but then, to my surprise and relief, he turned away and walked towards the elevators.

'Thank God for that,' I said. 'I can't bear that man.'

'You said my attention should be solely devoted to my work,' said Maurice, ignoring this remark. 'But you allowed yourself to get distracted at the start of your career, didn't you? By Oskar, I mean. So perhaps a little distraction is a good thing.'

'I don't understand,' I said.

'When we were in Rome you told me how you two met. You weren't focussed on your writing then but on your desires, right? How did they develop after that, anyway?'

They developed as these things do, I told him. Two teenage boys with much in common, living in dread of war, feigning a loyalty to a Fatherland towards which we felt no particular attachment. Something struck between Oskar and me that evening in the Böttcher Tavern, perhaps because we got so drunk, perhaps because we both had artistic ambitions, but whatever the reason, we very quickly became fast friends. Outside those times when he was in his father's café, at home painting or we were attending meetings of the Hitlerjugend we were mostly together, sharing ideas with

39

each other, discussing novels and painters, planning what we hoped would be our extraordinary futures. His own work developed considerably during this period and he trusted me now with studies of the girl I had seen in his sketchbook on that first evening. In his drawings, she was always looking away from him and always nude, but there was nothing prurient about the manner in which he drew or talked about her. Certain that I could not bear for him to tell me whether she was real or imagined, I never asked her name, nor did he offer it, but it was obvious that if she *was* real, then whatever intimacy he shared with her had been recreated in his work, which just got better and better. Mine, on the other hand, was suffering, as I found myself unable to concentrate on fiction when my thoughts were devoted to him. Perhaps it seems unusual, I told Maurice, that we never talked of romance, either of us, but boys were different in those days than they are today. I did not pry into his *affaires de cœur* and he did not enquire into mine. To do so would have served only to embarrass us both.

A few months after we met, to coincide with Oskar's seventeenth birthday, we decided to take a bicycling holiday over a weekend towards the Havel Lakes and travel on from there towards Potsdam, a distance of some forty kilometres. We left on a Saturday morning, displaying our papers to the soldiers on guard at the gates of the city, and cycled westward in the direction of the Olympic Stadium, arriving at the mouth of the Scharfe Lanke around lunchtime, where we sat at the lake's edge, eating our sandwiches and drinking warm bottles of beer that spilled over the sides when we uncorked them, causing us to rush to lick our fingers to capture every drop. It was a warm day and, soaked in perspiration from our exercise, Oskar suggested a swim.

'But we have no costumes,' I said.

'Oh, we don't need any.' He laughed, standing up and slipping the braces from his shoulders as he started to unbutton his shirt. 'There's no one around for miles. We won't get caught.'

He was stripping so quickly, his boots and socks already thrown to one side, his trousers pulled off in a moment, that there seemed to be no point in arguing with him, but if I were to follow his lead I knew that my desire would be all too visible.

'What's the matter?' he asked, turning to me with a frown on his face as he slipped out of his shorts and threw them on the pile of discarded clothes by his feet. He was fully revealed to me now at last, all my imaginings brought to life in a matter of moments, and it stunned me how casual he could be in his nakedness. I tried not to look at his sex, which lay dormant, hanging shamelessly from a thick patch of dark pubic hair. 'You're not shy, are you, Erich? There's no reason to be.'

'It's not that,' I said, uncertain whether to look directly at him or turn away. 'The truth is that I can't swim.' A lie that felt to me like a satisfactory excuse.

'Can't swim?' he said, bursting out laughing as he pulled one foot behind him, bringing it up to his backside and stretching the muscles of the leg with a satisfied groan before performing the same operation on the other. 'Whoever heard of such a thing? Swimming's easy. Anyway, the water is quite shallow here, I think. You don't need to go out any further than feels safe. Just keep the sand beneath your feet and splash around. It will cool you off.'

'No,' I said, and he simply shrugged his shoulders and made his way down towards the water. I watched his retreating back, my entire body pulsating with lust. His revealed shape was so over-whelming that I might have groaned aloud as he waded into the water and submerged himself quickly before jumping up again with a roar of delight. I longed to be in there with him so turned away, focussing on other things until my ardour had subsided a little, then quickly threw off my clothes and ran in, caring little for the coldness of the water as I plunged down in order to hide myself as soon as possible. In the distance, Oskar waved in my direction and I waved back.

'You see?' he said, swimming over towards me now. 'I told you it's easy. You're a natural!'

'I suppose I've never tried before,' I replied, grinning at him and watching as he flipped over on to his back and stretched his arms out to swim away from me, gliding along with the confidence of a shark. I started to swim too, enjoying myself at last, but quite soon I heard the sound of furious splashing in the distance and looked towards my friend, whose arms were flailing uselessly as he disappeared beneath the water and rose from it again, and I realized that he was in distress. I swam over, throwing my body towards him, and although he struggled against me, as a drowning man always will, he soon submitted and I turned him in such a way that his head was above the lake while my hand held steady beneath his chin, using my other arm to direct us back towards the shore. When I dragged us both out we lay next to each other for several minutes, exhausted and gasping for air, until Oskar rolled over on to one side, coughing feverishly as the water rose from his lungs, and I put a hand on his shoulder, telling him that he was all right, that he was alive and had nothing more to fear. We lay there for a long time, the sun beating down on our bodies, and when he dozed off it was with my arm across his chest, a hand stretching low across his abdomen, resting in a spot just below his navel. I was still lying like this some minutes later when he awoke with a start, pulling himself away from me in embarrassment as I sat up. I covered myself quickly with one hand, although it was obvious that he had noticed my tumescence for he turned away with a confused expression on his face and said nothing before standing up and making his way over to his clothes and dressing once again. He kept his back to me throughout all of this and only when I was fully clothed did he speak.

'I don't know what happened,' he said, looking a little embarrassed. 'I suppose I went in too soon after eating. I got cramp, you see, and my legs wouldn't work.'

'It's over, anyway,' I said. 'No harm done.'

'You told me that you couldn't swim. But actually, you're an excellent swimmer. I could tell as you were bringing me to the shore. Why did you lie?'

'I didn't lie. I was focussed on helping you, that's all, and I suppose my natural instincts simply took over.'

He thought about this and I could tell that he was unconvinced. 'Well, thank you, Erich,' he said at last, his forehead wrinkling into deep furrows as he considered his brush with mortality. 'I would have drowned if it wasn't for you.'

I turned to look at him and we stared at each other, the shared awkwardness unsettling me. 'We should continue on our way,' I said finally. The afternoon had been peculiar and disconcerting and I longed to be back on my bicycle, working off my desires through exercise. 'We still have about twenty kilometres to Potsdam.'

Later, it seemed that we had made a silent agreement not to mention the incident again and we enjoyed a good dinner and more beer, but eventually, tired from the exertions of the day, we retired to bed earlier than usual. I found it hard to sleep, though, disturbed by the unfamiliar sound of his breathing in the next bed, and eventually rose, sitting by the window and opening the curtain a little to stare out towards the fields beyond. The moon was almost full and as the light slipped into the room I turned around to observe the arch of Oskar's bare back as he slept, appreciating the gift the sheets had given me as they fell from his body. I grew aroused again, laying hands upon myself as quietly as possible, recalling all the things that I had seen that afternoon and what I could see now, climaxing so quickly into a handkerchief that my accompanying cry of pleasure seemed loud enough to wake him. And then, simultaneously satisfied and frustrated, I climbed back into bed and fell quickly asleep.

'What would you have done had he woken up?' asked Maurice, looking at me with wide eyes but no trace of embarrassment, despite the crude nature of these memories.

'I don't know,' I said, shaking my head. 'Laughed it off, I suppose. Died of humiliation. One or the other.'

He quizzed me on more aspects of the day, and the conversations that we'd had the following morning, but the recollections, along with the wine, had tired me out and finally I confessed that I could stay up no longer. We finished what was left in our glasses before saying goodnight and retiring to our rooms.

Just before I fell asleep, however, it occurred to me that I had forgotten to tell him what time we should meet the following morning and, as there was no telephone by the bed, I had no choice but to get up, don my clothes and go out into the corridor, making my way down the staircase towards his room, where I tapped cautiously on his door in the contradictory way that one does when one wants to get the attention of the occupant but is also wary of disturbing him. He didn't answer, so I knocked louder, pressing my face to the wood this time as I half whispered, half called his name. Again, there was no reply and I assumed that he had fallen into a deep sleep from which it would be impossible to wake him. And so I returned to my room and scribbled a note on some hotel notepaper before returning to the lower floor and sliding it beneath his door, having knocked one more time but again been frustrated by the silence from within.

As I made my way back towards the staircase, however, I saw Dash Hardy ascending from the foyer holding a bottle of champagne. He turned in my direction and stopped immediately, as if he had seen a ghost, before pulling himself together and asking whether I had enjoyed my evening. I replied in the affirmative before adding that I was tired, that it had been a pleasure to meet him – which it had not – and continuing on my way.

'Goodnight, Erich,' he called after me, before adding in a sing-song voice, 'Sweet dreams!'

I rolled my eyes impatiently, and it was only as I fell asleep that I began to wonder why he had been carrying two glasses in his hand.

5. Paris

In July, I found myself drinking a glass of rosé outside a bar in Montmartre, a chestnut tree shading me from the late summer sunlight, while I observed the closing moments of a marriage. A woman in her late forties, very beautiful, with short black hair and expensive sunglasses, had been sitting alone since my arrival with a large glass of white wine and an envelope on the table before her. She had already smoked three cigarettes and was lighting a fourth when a man appeared, perhaps a little older than her but dressed just as smartly, holding his hands in the air in apology for his tardiness, and she stood to allow him to kiss her on both cheeks. The waitress brought a second glass and she poured some wine for him as he reached into his bag and removed a similar envelope to hers. They spoke for some time and at one point he laughed and put an arm around her shoulders before they picked up the envelopes and took out two lengthy documents. Turning to the last page of each they allowed their pens to hover over the paper for only a moment before signing simultaneously, then passed each one to the other, whereupon they signed again. Finally, the man returned both forms to his bag and the couple removed their wedding rings, dropping each one into their glasses before standing up, kissing on the lips and walking off in opposite directions, their hands drifting out behind them, their fingers touching momentarily before they disappeared from my sight and, presumably, from each other's lives.

I was still staring at the empty glasses and their expensive additions when Maurice appeared from around the corner, raising a hand in greeting as he sat down to join me. It was a warm afternoon, and when his beer arrived, he drank a third of it without pausing for breath, sitting back with a satisfied sigh.

'I visited the Père Lachaise Cemetery while you were doing your interviews,' he told me. 'Placed my hand on top of Oscar Wilde's grave.'

'And I daresay you'll never wash it again,' I said.

'I want to be entombed when I'm gone,' he said, sitting up straight now. 'Or have a memorial in Poets' Corner in Westminster Abbey.'

'I hope you're joking,' I said.

'Of course I am,' he replied, bursting into laughter. 'I'm not that arrogant. No, I don't care what happens to me as long as my books survive.'

'That's important to you?' I asked.

'Yes,' he said. 'It's the only thing. Well, that and, as I told you before, becoming a father.'

'You're still intent on that?'

'Absolutely.'

'But you're so young.'

He shrugged. 'I don't see what that has to do with anything,' he said. 'Did you never want one? A child, I mean.'

'Well, it would have been—' I began, but he cut me off.

'Just because you're gay doesn't mean you wouldn't have enjoyed being a father.'

'True,' I said. 'But I never gave it much consideration, to be honest. I knew it was never going to happen so it wasn't something that preyed on my mind.'

I glanced out towards the street, where a pair of schoolgirls were walking past in short skirts. I watched to see whether Maurice's eyes would follow them and they did for a few moments, but without any particular interest, as he finished his beer and ordered another.

'By the way,' he said, reaching into his satchel and pulling out a magazine that he handed across. 'I have a present for you.' The publication was titled *Coney Island* and I felt an immediate aversion to the cover image, a close-up of a clown vomiting letters on the heads of George Bush and Michael Dukakis.

'Thank you,' I said, uncertain why he thought I would be interested in such a thing.

'Turn to page sixteen,' he said, and I did as instructed, where-upon I discovered a title, 'Red', with the words 'by Maurice Swift' printed in large letters underneath. 'My first published story,' he said, grinning from ear to ear.

'Maurice!' I said, truly delighted for him. 'Congratulations!'

'Thank you.'

'I didn't know that you were even submitting to magazines.'

'Well, I haven't been, to be honest,' he told me. 'But I happen to know one of the editors there and he asked whether I might have something that would work for them. So I sent this along and he liked it.'

'Well, I'm very happy for you,' I said. 'You must feel very encouraged.'

'I do.'

'And your novel? How is that coming along?'

'Ah,' he said, pulling a face. 'Slowly. I have the opening chapters and a good hold on my characters but I'm not sure where it's going as yet.'

'You haven't plotted it out?' I asked.

'Oh no,' he said, looking at me as if I'd just accused him of spending his days watching television. 'I could never do something like that. Doesn't it all become a little boring if you know everything that happens in advance?'

'I don't think so,' I said, and I might have challenged him further on it were it not for an interruption by our waitress, who came over holding a tray that carried the two glasses from the divorcing couple's table and looking inside them with an astonished expression on her face. She asked whether I had seen who had left them there and I related the events as I'd observed them earlier and she shook her head in disbelief before making her way back indoors. A moment later, Maurice's trusty notebook was on the table again and he was scribbling away.

'What are you writing?' I asked him.

'The story you just told her,' he said. 'It's a good one. I thought I might use it for something.'

'As it happens,' I said, 'after they left I thought the same thing. That it might make for an interesting opening for a novel. I was working through some possibilities in my mind.'

He lifted his notebook and waved it in the air triumphantly. 'Sorry, Erich,' he said. 'It's mine now. I wrote it down first!'

'All right.'

'You don't mind, do you?'

'No, of course not,' I said, a little surprised by his literary larceny. 'You're still coming to Shakespeare & Company tonight, I hope?'

'Of course,' he said. 'What time is your reading?'

'Seven o'clock.'

'And after that?'

'Dinner with the publishers.'

'Ah,' he said. 'Do you mind if I skip that one? I have a friend in Paris. We were thinking of meeting for a drink, that's all. Of course, I'll join you if you really want me to but—'

'It's entirely your decision,' I said. 'Don't bother if you're not interested.'

'Of course I'm interested,' he said. 'And normally I'd love to come. It's just that I haven't seen her in some time. She was a colleague of mine in the Savoy.'

'And you were friends?'

'Yes. Good friends.'

'What's her name?' I asked.

'Clémence. She hopes to be a photographer someday. She photographs nudes.'

'I hope she hasn't photographed you,' I said, laughing.

'She has, yes.'

'Oh.' I found myself blushing scarlet, a mixture of embarrassment and envy coursing through my body. 'Aren't you worried about them getting out?'

'Not in the slightest. I'd be happy for people to see them. They're very artistic. She's photographed many other people too, not just me. I daresay she'll have an exhibition one day. Would you like one? I could bring one back for you if you like.'

He smiled. Was he taunting me? Deliberately twisting the levers of power between us? 'No thank you,' I said primly.

'Suit yourself. But I'll find a pay phone and call her to say that I can't make it if—'

'No,' I said, shaking my head. 'Of course you must meet her. I wouldn't dream of spoiling your evening.' I hesitated slightly. 'Will you be in the hotel bar later, do you think? After I return? We could have our usual nightcap.'

'What time will you be back?'

'Around ten?'

'Let's say that if I'm there, I'm there, and if I'm not, then I'm either still out with Clémence or I've gone to bed early. Don't bother waiting up for me.'

'All right,' I said, feeling a sense of bitter disappointment. The waitress reappeared and I reached into my satchel for a Polaroid camera that I had brought with me to France. I'd bought it only recently and had been trying to find an opportunity to get a photograph of Maurice and me together.

'Shall we have a picture?' I asked.

'Really?' he said, his face frowning a little. 'For what?'

'For nothing,' I replied. 'For friendship.'

He shrugged. 'All right,' he said, pulling his chair closer to mine and, to my delight, throwing his arm around my shoulders and grinning at the young woman, who stood back a little and pressed the shutter button. She handed it back to me and, a moment later, the camera released its prize and I stared at it, enraptured, as our images began to appear. He was looking directly into the lens; I had turned my head at the crucial moment and was looking at him.

He moved back to where he had been and an uncomfortable

silence ensued, but not wanting any further awkwardness to develop between us, I ordered some more drinks and when they arrived he mentioned that, since Madrid, he'd been thinking a lot about my friendship with Oskar and it saddened him to think of us growing up in Nazi Germany, the shadow of war across our future.

Of course, I told him, when I thought of those days I realized that I had been more focussed on my desire to possess Oskar than on the extraordinary events taking place around us. We knew that it would not be long before we were conscripted into the army and I dreaded that day, not because I feared death but because I didn't want us to be separated. This was something we finally discussed one evening in Berlin, when I realized that Oskar was just as anxious about the future as I was.

'I had hoped that some type of resolution would be reached,' he said as we sat drinking beer in the Böttcher Tavern. Through the window I could see the red-haired guard standing outside the SS headquarters once again, scanning the street. The poor boy seemed as if he was always on duty but never got beyond the front gates. 'But that's not looking likely now, is it?'

'My father says that the English don't have the stomach for another war so they'll allow the Führer to take whatever he wants as long as he leaves them alone.'

'Then your father is wrong. Hitler will occupy the Low Countries and sail across the North Sea to invade. If he takes France, then it becomes even easier. Still,' he added, 'I think I'd rather be a sailor than a soldier. Have you decided which branch you'll join?'

'The Luftwaffe,' I said, the first answer that sprang to mind.

'Not for me,' he replied, shaking his head. 'I don't want to get shot out of the skies.'

'You're right,' I said, too quickly. 'Then perhaps I'll be a sailor too.'

He offered me a look of displeasure and I blushed, knowing that flattery by imitation irritated him. Ever since that afternoon by the

Scharfe Lanke I had felt a certain suspicion on his part towards my intentions.

'The thing that worries me most,' I said, 'is the idea of dying without having achieved anything in my life. A writer is supposed to get better as they age but what can I possibly accomplish if I'm killed before I turn twenty?'

'You need to get started on that novel right away,' he said with a bittersweet smile. 'The future doesn't look good for our generation.'

'But how can I when I have nothing to write about? I've seen nothing, I've done nothing. A writer needs experiences to draw upon. Love affairs,' I added tentatively. 'A painter does too, I'm sure.'

'True,' he said, reaching for his bag. 'Actually, there was something I wanted to show you. Do you mind?'

'Of course not,' I said.

'I've been painting a lot lately,' he told me. 'Into the nights and the early mornings, and I feel that I've finally hit on something. Take a look at this.' He handed me a rolled-up canvas and I untied the string, unravelling it slowly while being careful not to allow any part of the painting to touch the damp tabletop. The picture revealed itself to me in stages. First a toe, then a foot. A bare leg. A torso. A pair of full breasts with dark nipples. And then a girl's face, the same face I had seen in all of his sketches to date but for once not hidden in profile but staring out at me, a challenge in her eyes. Her left hand was stretched across her naked body, her fingers resting between her legs, which were parted just enough to offer a glimpse of her sex. There was nothing pornographic to the painting but there was an erotic charge to both the brushwork and the girl's smile that left me disoriented. I looked across at my friend, whose expression was one of hope mixed with excitement.

'Well?' he asked. 'What do you think?'

'I'm not sure,' I said. 'It's quite shocking, don't you think?'

'Shocking?' he said, sitting back in his chair, and I realized that what I, in my prudishness, might consider scandalous, he might define as art. 'Do you mean the use of shade across her shoulders? Yes, I wasn't certain about that myself, whether or not I'd overdone it. I think it works but I'm not sure. I'm happy with her hands, though, because I always struggle with hands, but they came out well, don't you think? And the way she holds her fingers above her cunt? I really feel that I've captured her spirit as well as her physicality.'

I took a breath in surprise. We might have been discussing anything mundane – the weather, the time, the price of bread – for all the concern he had for his choice of words.

'Of course, as you know, this is the most recent in a long series,' he added. 'But by abandoning my commitment to her profile, I really feel I've hit on something important.'

'Simply by getting her to turn around?' I asked. 'That's your big breakthrough?'

'No, it's more than that,' he said, a wounded tone creeping into his voice. 'It's the defiance in her eyes. The manner in which she both conceals herself while, at the same time, inviting us to observe her most private moment.'

'But it's just a naked girl lying on a couch,' I said, aware of how critical I sounded and trying to keep my discontent under control. 'It's hardly an original conceit. Haven't artists been doing that sort of thing for centuries?'

'Yes, of course,' he replied, his confidence fading a little now. 'But I'm trying to bring something new to it. Painters search for beauty, and where else should we find it other than in the female form, the most beautiful of God's creations?'

'Really?' I asked. 'More beautiful than a sunrise? Or an ocean? Or a sky full of stars?'

'Yes, so much more beautiful!' he cried, growing enthusiastic again as he raised his hands in the air. 'Whenever I'm alone with a girl, whenever I make love to one, I find myself consumed by her in a way that I have never been by nature. You must have felt that too, surely?'

I stared at him, uncertain how to reply. Did he assume that I, like him, was experienced in matters of sex?

'Of course,' I said hesitantly. 'But there's more to art than—'

'And every painter brings something new to the nude,' he continued. 'Just as if you were to write about, I don't know, let's say the Great War, then you would try to find a fresh perspective on it, a different point of view. That's what I'm attempting with this portrait. Do you remember I said to you once that I wanted to paint the familiar in an unfamiliar way? I'm not there yet, of course. I still have a long way to go and much to learn. But I'm getting closer, don't you think?'

I said nothing but rolled the painting up again and re-tied the string before handing it back to him.

'Have you shown this to anyone else?' I asked, and he shook his head. I took a long draught of my beer before speaking again. 'Oskar,' I said. 'I'm your friend, I hope you know that. And I care about you a great deal. So, what I say to you now, I say out of comradeship and loyalty.'

He sat back and frowned. 'All right,' he said. 'Go on.'

'I believe that this painting is both unsophisticated and obscene,' I said. 'I know that you think there is beauty here, and style and elegance and originality, but I'm afraid that it's a failure. You're too close to it to recognize its essential vulgarity. The hands that you mentioned are well drawn, yes, but their action borders on the pornographic. Can you not see that? It's as if you have painted this to titillate the viewer, or – worse – to titillate yourself.'

'No!' he cried, looking hurt. 'How can you think that?'

'Your subject does not seem lost in her own desires but anxious that we should desire her instead, which makes the painting manipulative. It's the type of thing that a fifteen-year-old boy might hide under lock and key but that could never hang in a gallery. I say this not to hurt you, my friend, but to help. I believe that if you were to show this to anyone else then you would find yourself a figure of mockery. Perhaps even worse. And you know that the Reich has little time for pornography.'

He said nothing for a long time, bowing his head over the table as he considered my words. When he spoke again, all the pleasure had gone from his tone, and there was a look of humiliation on his face.

'I thought I had captured something new,' he said quietly. 'I've worked so hard on it.'

'Of course, I know nothing about painting,' I said, attempting to sound casual now. 'And I could be wrong. But I would not be a true friend if I did not share my honest feelings with you. Do you remember the weekend that we went to Potsdam?'

'Yes, of course,' he said. 'What of it?'

'There was so much to capture there. The landscapes. The lake where we swam. The cows. Couldn't you focus on something like that for a change?'

'Cows?' he asked, looking at me as if I were crazy. 'You think I want to paint cows? Cows have no soul. Alysse, at least, has a soul.'

'Alysse?' I asked. 'And who is Alysse?'

He nodded towards the canvas. 'My model,' he said.

'So, she is a real person then, not a fantasy?'

'Of course she's real! I could never paint something like this from my imagination. I'm not that creative.'

I could bear it no longer; I had to ask. 'And are you in love with her?' I asked.

'Very much so,' he said, as if it were the most obvious thing in the world. 'We are in love with each other.'

I sat back in the seat, staring at him in dismay. 'If that's the case,' I asked, 'then why have you never mentioned her until now?'

'Well, I didn't think—'

54

'We're friends, I thought? Although if it's just a silly summer romance—'

'But it's not,' he insisted. 'It's a lot more than that.'

'How can you be sure?'

'I just am.'

I shook my head. 'If you loved her that much,' I said, 'then you would have talked about her to me.'

'If these were normal times, perhaps yes,' he replied. 'But they're not normal times, are they? I have to be careful. We all do.'

'Of what?'

'Of everything. And everyone.'

I looked around. Suddenly it seemed to me that the entire tavern was listening in on us, watching us, aware of Oskar's feelings for this girl and my feelings for him. In my heart, I had always known that Oskar did not share my romantic longings but it wounded me deeply to think of his being intimate with another.

'I'm not certain that you're right,' he said. 'Shouldn't the artist remain true to his own instinct?'

'I can't tell you what you should think, Oskar,' I said. 'I can only tell you what I feel.'

'And you believe that I should destroy it?' he asked.

'I do. Not only that, but I don't think that you should paint Alysse any more. Perhaps you're too close to her. You should reserve your talent for something more appropriate.'

He blanched but I felt no remorse. I wanted him to burn the painting, to feel that it was so worthless he would abandon the concept entirely and, with it, the girl. Paint cows, I thought. Paint all the cows you like. Diversify into sheep if it satisfies your artistic needs.

'And did he?' asked Maurice, who had remained silent as I told him this story. 'Did he destroy it?'

'Yes, he did,' I replied, unable to meet his eye. 'We stayed in the Böttcher late into the night, becoming very drunk, and, as was his way at such moments, he turned maudlin, hanging his head and weeping for what he considered his lack of talent. And then, finally, he reached for the painting and ripped it in half, and then in half once again, and again and again.'

Maurice said nothing, but finished his drink while looking out towards the street.

'I hope you don't think less of me now,' I said finally, and he shook his head, reaching over and placing his hand on mine, just as Oskar had done some fifty years earlier in Berlin.

'Of course not,' he said. 'What you did, you did out of jealousy but also out of love. And you were just a boy at the time. None of us is in control of our emotions at that age.'

I glanced at my watch and sighed. 'Anyway, we should get back to the hotel,' I said. 'I need to change.'

He didn't show up in the bar that night after I returned from the publishers' dinner. And, despite his instructions, I did stay up, hoping he might arrive later. But as the clock reached midnight I finally gave up on him and decided to return to my room, a little the worse for wear, pressing my ear against his door for any sounds from within, but it was silent. When I climbed into bed I was tired and ready for sleep but, before I turned the light off, I noticed the magazine that he had given me earlier sitting on the night stand and picked it up to turn to his story. It was not good. Not good at all. So bad, in fact, that I began to question whether he had sufficient talent to be a writer and if I was doing him a disservice by encouraging him. I flicked through the rest of the magazine and my heart sank as I noticed the credits on the final page, for the Editor-at-Large was none other than Dash Hardy, the American writer we had met in Madrid. It was he who had commissioned the piece, he who had seen merit in it and he who had published it.

Of course, looking back, I can see that I had used the wrong words to describe Oskar's painting of Alysse. Despite my youth and ignorance of art, I knew it was the furthest thing in the world from unsophisticated or obscene. In fact, it was magnificent. The irony was that, in 1939, I had seen something beautiful and told its creator that it was a travesty. And now, almost fifty years later, I had read something terrible and, when asked, would surely praise it.

Really, it was unconscionable behaviour.

6. New York

The flight to New York was the first occasion that we actually travelled together and, while on the plane, we planned our itinerary. I was to give a reading at the 92nd Street Y, another as part of a panel of novelists at New York University and a third in a Brooklyn library, along with the usual interviews, signing sessions and radio broadcasts, and Maurice agreed to accompany me to all of these as long as he could keep one evening free to catch up with some friends who lived in the city.

The readings themselves went well, except for the panel event, where I was teamed with a much-praised novelist from Park Slope some twenty years my junior who looked as if he'd spent the entire day shooting a fashion commercial for a high-class designer label and a young woman whose debut had been published six years earlier but showed no sign of committing to a second book. For some reason, she insisted on calling me Herr Ackermann, despite repeated pleas on my part for her to call me Erich. ('I couldn't,' she said backstage, as she demanded a glass of wine from a volunteer. 'You're, like, old enough to be my grandfather.') The woman (let's call her Susan) and the middle-aged man (we'll try Andrew) sat on either side of me on the stage and, as Susan's novel drew artificial and deeply contrived parallels between the political tensions in Germany during the thirties and American opposition to the Vietnam War some thirty years later, the moderator asked me whether

I found that her writing accurately reflected my experience of the city during those days.

'It's so long ago that it's difficult for me to remember,' I said, looking out at an audience whose attention seemed entirely focussed on the younger man to my left. 'You must remember that I was just a teenager then and my mind wasn't particularly concerned with politics. I was thinking about my future and hoping for a career as a writer. However, while I think Susan's book is very well researched – she certainly captures the geography of the city well – my concern would be for the lack of a moral compass among the German characters.'

This was a considerable understatement on my part for I had read the novel a few weeks earlier upon receiving my schedule and found it to be not only trite in its depiction of racial conflict but deeply naïve in its thinking, while her research seemed to have been conducted exclusively from watching old Second World War movies. At even the merest hint of criticism, however, she turned to me, instantly defensive. 'A moral compass?' she said. 'Could you clarify what you mean by that, Herr Ackermann?'

'The fact is,' I replied, impressed by how she could use a form of address to suggest a lack of balance on my part, 'there were some Germans during those days who were quite vocal in their dissent to the policies of Hitler and many who sought to escape the country entirely. It seems unfortunate to me that their presence is so rarely represented in war fiction.'

'I don't write *war fiction*,' she said, making inverted comma signs in the air with her fingers. 'Please don't compartmentalize my work.'

'I think you want to be very careful how you tread here, pal,' said Andrew, who was sitting forward in his chair now, amusement and outrage competing for dominance in his tone. 'Susan's something of an expert on that period of history.'

'And I actually lived it,' I replied.

'But like you said, you were just a kid.'

'Yes, but people often assume that, after the rise of National Socialism, the entire nation turned, overnight, into a horde of anti-Semitic barbarians. Surely as writers of fiction we should look for the stories that are less often told? And some can be found in the lives of those who both took a stand against the Nazis and died for their troubles.'

'I'm sorry,' said Susan, holding her hands in the air and looking as though she might need a tranquillizer if I were to continue speaking. 'My best friend's husband's entire family was killed in the camps. So this is a very emotive issue for me. For you even to suggest, Herr Ackermann—'

'I'm simply saying—' I began, but was immediately cut off by Andrew, who placed a hand on my knee to silence me.

'Am I right in thinking, Erich,' he asked, 'that you were a member of the Hitler Youth?'

'Well, yes,' I said, feeling a prickle of perspiration creeping along my back. 'That's been well documented. All boys my age had no choice but to sign up. Just as all girls had to be members of the Bund Deutscher Mädel.'

'Women don't fight wars,' insisted Susan. 'And they never start them.'

'Tell that to Mrs Thatcher,' I said. 'Tell it to Helen of Troy.'

'And you were a soldier in the German army?' continued Andrew.

'In the Wehrmacht, yes,' I admitted. 'I've never denied it. Although I didn't see any action, of course. I was part of a clerical team in Berlin during—'

'Then perhaps, before you tell us your stories about all the good Germans who tried to stop Hitler,' he said, 'you might just pause for a moment and give a thought to the families of those who lost their lives bringing freedom to the world.'

'Hear, hear,' agreed Susan, at which point the audience burst into tumultuous applause at such cod-patriotism, such crowd-pleasing cliché, offering Andrew a standing ovation that he pretended not to notice as he sipped his water and toyed with his wedding ring. From that point on, both novelists and the moderator ignored me entirely and yet afterwards, backstage, they each asked me to sign a copy of *Dread* and to pose for photographs, shaking hands as we said goodbye as if we were old friends.

'Fucking arsehole,' said Maurice, as we took a cab back to the hotel afterwards, referring to the male model in writer's garb. 'He was just playing to the gallery, that's all. And did you see how people were congratulating him afterwards in the signing queue? As if he'd single-handedly led the charge on the beaches at Dunkirk? I mean, it's not as if *you* actually killed anyone, is it? Like you said, you were just clerical staff.'

'I suppose I can hardly sermonize about a Nazi resistance when I wasn't part of it, though.'

'You were following orders. If you hadn't, you'd have been shot.'

I didn't respond but stared out of the window at the passing streets and, for the first time in our acquaintance, declined a nightcap at the hotel, retiring to my room instead, where I took a long, hot bath and drank alone long into the night.

The next day passed with little incident and the morning after that I woke early, looking forward to meeting Maurice for breakfast. I had missed him the previous evening when he had been out with his friends but we had arranged to meet at ten o'clock in the foyer of the hotel. He didn't show up and, hours later when I came downstairs for lunch, I saw him strolling through the doors behind me, wearing the same clothes he'd been wearing the night before, and looking rather dishevelled. The relief must have been evident on my face, however, for he looked a little guilty, claiming that he had over-indulged and decided to spend the night at the apartment of a friend.

'You might have got in touch,' I said. 'I didn't know whether you were alive or dead.'

'Don't be so melodramatic, Erich,' he said, waving my concern away, and his disdain hit me like a punch to the guts. It seemed as if our relationship had begun to change and that he no longer felt the need to be quite as respectful as he once had.

'Come on,' he said. 'I'm starving. Come upstairs while I order some food.'

I wanted to tell him no, that I had better things to do than to trail around after him all day, but he was already making his way towards the elevators and, knowing that I might not see him again for hours if I did not follow, I swallowed my pride and slipped between the doors as they closed and we rode silently up to our adjacent rooms on the eleventh floor.

I felt something of an erotic thrill entering his bedroom. His suitcase was lying open on a table and his bed was still unmade from a nap he'd taken the previous afternoon, the sheets in disarray. I could see underwear and socks scattered haphazardly around the floor and the intimacy of the scene was intensely arousing.

'Have you had lunch?' he asked, kicking his shoes off.

'Of course,' I said. 'It's gone two o'clock.'

'Well, I'm starving. Do me a favour, would you, and order me some room service? A cheeseburger and fries. Something like that. I need a shower.'

I reached for the leather-bound folder by the desk and flicked through it.

'Would you like something to drink with that?' I asked.

'A Diet Coke. Lots of ice.'

As I dialled the appropriate number and placed the order, he sat down and peeled his socks off, examining his toes for a moment, before pulling his T-shirt over his head to reveal his body to me for the first time. He was well muscled and hairless and, as he leaned over, the deep grooves of his abdominal muscles became sharply defined. A scar ran across his lower right-hand side. It was impossible not to stare and even when I knew that he was looking directly at me I could not avert my eyes.

'I had an appendix operation when I was twelve,' he told me as he stood up again. 'The surgeon botched it, which is why the scar is so noticeable. If you touch it, it turns bright red. Try, if you like.'

I walked over to him and reached out, allowing the tip of my index finger to track its way along the wound, and sure enough it became slightly inflamed at my touch. When I arrived at the place where the redness blended back into his natural colouring I placed my palm flat across his stomach, feeling the warmth of his tight, young skin against my aged hand.

'See?' he said, stepping back and unbuckling his jeans before pulling them off and throwing them on the bed without any cere-mony. He stood before me now in his boxer shorts and I forced myself to look away, catching a hint of a smile on his face as I did so.

'I should go,' I said.

'No, stay here, if you don't mind. The room-service guy might come while I'm in the shower and I'll need you to let him in.'

He went into the bathroom, leaving the door slightly ajar, and after a moment I heard the water pounding down on the floor of the stall and then the more muffled sound as he stepped beneath the spray. Had he been flirting with me, I asked myself, or did he just lack any sense of self-consciousness? There was something knowing in Maurice's actions. I stepped over towards the bath-room door and peered inside at his naked form, hidden by the glass of the shower stall and the steam that surrounded him, and when he turned I walked back towards the bed, feeling an erotic desire that was almost overwhelming. It embarrasses me to recall how I buried my face in his pillow, hoping to catch some-thing of his scent, but there was nothing there. Before I could embarrass myself any further, there was a knock at the door and his lunch arrived.

Emerging from the bathroom a few minutes later with a white

towelling robe tied loosely around his waist, he invited me to share some of his food, but I declined, saying that I would return to my room.

'No, stay,' he insisted. 'I hate eating alone. Tell me more about your friend Oskar.'

'Some other time, Maurice,' I said, shaking my head. 'I'm not in the mood for storytelling today.'

'But I want to know. Sit down. Continue your story. Erich, *sit*.'

And of course, it was outside my capabilities to disappoint him so I did as instructed and began to talk.

It was the summer of 1939, only a couple of months before the war began, and I had arranged to meet my friend in our usual place to celebrate his seventeenth birthday. He was seated alone in the window as I crossed the road and when I knocked on the glass, waving at him, he broke into a wide smile and beckoned me inside. I felt such happiness as I entered and, when the waitress brought over our beers, we raised our glasses in salute.

'Happy birthday,' I said, reaching into my bag and taking out a present that I had carefully gift-wrapped earlier in the day. He sat back in some surprise as I placed it on the table between us. He ripped off the packaging and lifted the lid on the box inside. My gift to him was a fountain pen, one that my grandfather had given me for my own birthday a few years before. The finest of them all and the one that I treasured the most. I wanted him to have it.

'Ah,' he said, frowning a little, and his expression confused me for he did not look as pleased as I had expected. 'This is very kind of you.'

'Do you like it?'

'I do,' he said. 'Very much.'

'What's wrong?' I asked.

'Nothing, why do you ask?'

'I don't know. There's something, though. I can tell from your face.'

Before he could reply, a girl slipped into the seat next to him and looked back and forth between the two of us.

'Alysse,' said Oskar, turning to her. 'This is Erich, who I've told you about.'

'At last,' she said, extending a hand to me. I recognized her immediately from Oskar's sketchbooks and paintings. She seemed anxious, glancing around the bar and trying to make herself small in the seat, as if by doing so she might avoid attention. 'I thought Oskar was making you up. He mentions you so often but has never introduced us.'

'It's because I don't trust him,' said Oskar.

'What?' I asked, turning to him in dismay. 'Why not?'

'I thought you might steal her away from me,' he continued, laughing. 'I'm joking, Erich. Don't look so horrified!'

'No one could take me away from you,' she said quietly, and they smiled at each other for a moment before leaning forward and allowing their lips to meet. When they separated again, they continued to grin like fools, giddy with love.

'And what's this?' she asked, looking down at my grandfather's fountain pen. 'How beautiful.'

'It's Erich's,' said Oskar. 'Or rather, it's mine. He gave it to me for my birthday.'

She lifted it up and examined it from all sides. The light through the window sent a gleam sparkling off the gold inlay. 'Erich,' she said, her eyes wide as she looked at me, 'what a thoughtful gift. It's so beautiful.'

'I don't think Oskar likes it,' I said.

'He's just embarrassed,' she said with a shrug. 'Show him,' she added, turning to my friend.

'No, it doesn't matter,' he said.

'Show him,' she insisted. 'I don't mind.'

He sighed and reached into his bag, removing another fountain pen, a far less expensive one, the type that could be purchased in any stationery shop, although it had been engraved with his initials, *OG*. 'It was Alysse's gift to me,' he said. 'A coincidence, that's all.'

'I'm defeated,' she said, laughing. 'Yours is so much better, Erich.'

'Yes, it is,' I agreed. 'How long have you two known each other, anyway?'

'About eighteen months,' she said, ignoring my rudeness. 'We were just friends at first and then, finally, things changed. He was too shy to kiss me for a long time.'

'But not too shy to paint you?' I asked.

She laughed but, to my disappointment, didn't seem particularly embarrassed. 'You mustn't think I'm the type of girl who takes her clothes off for just anyone, Erich,' she said. 'I'm his muse. Oskar is going to be a great painter one day, I'm certain of it. My image might hang in the Louvre, like the *Mona Lisa*.'

'Are you comparing yourself to her or Oskar to Leonardo da Vinci?' I asked, trying to keep the sarcasm out of my tone.

'Neither,' she said. 'I only meant—'

'If you had a girlfriend as beautiful as Alysse,' said Oskar, 'wouldn't you want to paint her too?'

'I wouldn't know,' I said. 'I've never had a girlfriend.'

'That can't be!'

'But it is.'

'Then perhaps I should introduce you to some of my friends,' said Alysse.

'Why bother?' I asked. 'Oskar and I will be off to war soon. We'll be lucky if we're still alive to see 1940. I don't want to waste whatever time I have left trying to impress some tart.'

A silence descended on the table. Alysse's smile faded completely and Oskar stared at me as if he could hardly believe that I'd said such a thing.

'I'm just being realistic,' I said, unable to look either of them in the eye. 'They're setting up more and more recruiting stations around Berlin as it is. A year from now, we'll be eighteen, and what hope do we have then?'

'They can set them up wherever they like,' he said. 'I won't be entering any of them.'

'Oskar!' said Alysse.

'But it's true.'

'Oskar,' she repeated, quieter now, a note of warning in her tone.

'What are you talking about?' I asked.

They looked at each other and finally Alysse shrugged her shoulders. 'You must keep this to yourself, Erich,' she said.

'Keep what to myself? What's going on?'

'We're going to get out of here soon,' he said. 'We plan on living somewhere else.'

'But where? Another part of Germany?'

'Of course not. Away from Europe altogether.'

Alysse glanced at her watch and shook her head. 'I should go,' she said. 'I have to collect my brother from school. I'll see you later, Oskar, yes? You're coming for dinner?'

'Of course,' he said. 'I'll be there at six.'

'Erich, it was nice to meet you,' she added as she stood up and put her coat on. 'But please talk about something else, all right? Something cheerful. It's Oskar's birthday, after all.'

I nodded and watched her leave.

A sound from outside made us both look out the window. Alysse had been stopped by the tall, red-haired SS guard and he was beckoning her towards him.

'What's going on?' asked Oskar, frowning.

The guard said something to her and she reached into her pocket for her papers, handing them across, and he took them from her, staring at her for a long time before directing his attention to the pages themselves.

'I'm going out there,' said Oskar, standing up, but I grabbed his arm immediately.

'No,' I said. 'Just wait. Let it play out as it will.'

He paused and we watched as the guard flicked through the papers, then removed his gloves and slowly reached up to run a finger across Alysse's face. I could see him smiling and recognized the desire in his eyes.

'That fucker,' hissed Oskar, and it took all of my strength to hold him back.

'If you march out there now, it will only cause trouble for you both,' I told him, my lips close to his right ear. 'Give it another minute and he'll probably let her go.'

He relaxed a little and, as I had predicted, the guard eventually handed back her papers and she continued on her way, only turning around once to glance anxiously in our direction.

'Well?' I asked, when she was gone and we'd sat down again. I could tell how incensed my friend had grown; I had never seen such strong emotion on his face before. 'What's going on? You can't possibly leave Germany.'

'I have to,' he said.

'But why?'

'Because of Alysse.'

'What about her?'

He looked around nervously and, although the tables nearby were empty, he lowered his voice as he spoke. 'I'm only telling you this because you're my friend,' he said. 'You must promise not to breathe a word to anyone.'

'You have my word,' I said.

'Alysse isn't like you and me,' he said. 'You've read the Nuremberg Laws, haven't you?'

'Of course.'

'She's a first-degree *Mischling*. She has two Jewish grandparents,' he added for clarification. 'And two German.'

'But so what? The Führer himself has said that first-degree *Mischlings* will not be arrested.'

'No, Erich, he's said that they will not be arrested "at this time" but that he will decide their fate after we win the war. Which might be only months after it begins. And who knows if he will even stick to his word? He could change his mind in a moment and Alysse would be taken from me. As would her entire family. Jews are already being deported and sent to work camps. I've heard that some are even being shot.'

'And because of that you're going to abandon both your duty and the Fatherland?'

'Don't you ever feel,' he asked, leaning forward now so our faces were practically touching, 'that the Fatherland has abandoned us?'

'No,' I told him, retreating a little, feeling a mixture of anger, devastation and hatred. 'No, I don't feel that at all.'

'You felt hatred?' asked Maurice from a distance of some fifty years, sitting in that hotel room in New York as I told him this part of my story. His hair was lying flat on his head, dry now. His plate was empty, his knife and fork thrown to one side, and he was look-ing directly at me as I stared through the window at the skyline of the city. 'But hatred towards whom?'

'Towards Alysse, of course,' I said, turning back to him. 'I hated that girl with every fibre of my being. I don't think I have ever felt such hatred for anyone, before or since. She was going to take Oskar away from me.'

'But he loved her. And he could sense the danger that she was in.'

I shook my head. 'I didn't care,' I said. 'All I could see was the loss that I was going to suffer.'

We said nothing for a few moments and then Maurice rose, tak-ing some clothes from his wardrobe and saying that he was going into the bathroom to change. I stood up and told him that I would see him later, perhaps for dinner. I heard the taps in the sink run-ning as I left and noticed his satchel on the floor, lying where he had discarded it earlier. I reached down to pick it up and lay it on the bed and as I did so a book fell out and I glanced at the title.

It was the latest novel by Dash Hardy and I rolled my eyes in irritation. Why was he reading such rubbish? I asked myself. On a whim, I turned to the title page and somehow wasn't surprised by the inscription I found there. *For Maurice*, it said, *with my fondest love.*

He had dated it too. He must have signed it earlier that morning before Maurice left his apartment.

7. Amsterdam

There was only one city left on my promotional schedule but I was in two minds about inviting Maurice to accompany me. His increasing arrogance was becoming tiresome to me but more wounding still was the knowledge that he'd established some type of connection with Dash. And yet, despite my sense of grievance, he was on my mind as much as ever and I desperately wanted to see him again, particularly since this would mark the end of our time together. So I booked his ticket and, although I received neither a phone call nor a letter in reply, he showed up at the Amstel Hotel on the appointed evening in high spirits.

My publisher had booked me a suite with a view of the canals but once again the hotel had let me down and Maurice's more basic room was on the other side of the corridor, overlooking Professor Tulpplein. I was not as desperate for us to be next to each other any more but when he saw where I was situated he seemed so entranced by the vista that I offered to switch with him and he accepted immediately, moving his belongings into the suite while I took mine to what was known as a 'classic room'.

Having undertaken all the usual interviews and given a reading in a city-centre bookshop, our final evening in Amsterdam was free of promotional duties and we found a cosy bar overlooking Blauwbrug Bridge, where we sat at a small table near the rear, surrounded by cushions and candlelight.

'Our last night together,' he said as we clinked glasses. 'The last six months have been a great experience, Erich. I'm very grateful.'

'Well, you've been a terrific help,' I told him. 'Not just because of your efficiency but also your companionship. I don't know how I would have got through all these trips without you. I imagine successful novelists must have a terrible time of it.'

'But you *are* a successful novelist,' he said, laughing. 'At least you have been since you won The Prize.'

'I mean the very rich and famous ones,' I said, correcting myself. 'Those who have readers, not those who win awards.'

'Do the two have to be mutually exclusive?'

'In a perfect world, no. But in the real world, they generally are.'

'I'm going to be different,' he said, nodding confidently.

'Oh really? In what way?'

'I'm going to have readers *and* win prizes.'

'You don't want much, do you?' I said, smiling a little.

'My agent thinks I can combine commerce with art.'

I looked up, taken aback by this latest revelation. 'Your agent?' I said. 'Since when have you had an agent?'

'Didn't I tell you? It hasn't been long. I met her when we were in New York and she asked to read my novel.'

'How did you even find her?'

'Do you remember when we were in Madrid and a lunch was thrown for you in the Prado?'

'Yes,' I said.

'The Spanish novelist seated next to me. He put me in touch with her. She's his agent too, you see.'

I took a long sip from my glass, trying not to allow my thoughts to get the better of me. 'And your novel,' I asked finally. 'You can't have finished it already?'

'No, but it's almost there. I gave her a few sample chapters. She's waiting to read the entire thing but she liked what she saw so much that she signed me up as a client.'

'I see,' I said, trying not to make my irritation too obvious. 'You do realize that I have an agent too, don't you?'

'Yes, but you never offered an introduction.'

'Because you hadn't finished anything yet!'

'Well, I suppose my friend in Madrid felt that, on the basis of what I'd already written, I had something special.'

'How prescient of him,' I said. 'So when will this masterpiece be ready?'

'Over the next couple of weeks, I hope. And there's no need for sarcasm, Erich, it's unbecoming in a man of your years. She hopes to start submitting it to editors in the spring.'

'Well, I look forward to reading it,' I said. 'Did you bring the chapters for me?'

'Oh no,' he replied, shaking his head. 'No, I'm sorry but I don't want anyone to read it until it's published.'

'Don't you mean *unless* it's published?'

'No, I mean *until*. I choose to look on the positive side of things.'

'I just don't want you to feel upset if—'

'Why aren't you supporting me in this?' he asked, putting his glass down and giving me a quizzical look.

'I am,' I said, my face flushing a little. 'I just happen to know how unkind this business can be, that's all, and I'd hate to see you disappointed. Some young writers have to write two or three novels before they produce one that's good enough to find a publisher.'

'You sound as if you're jealous.'

'Why on earth would I be jealous?'

'No reason that I can think of, which is what makes your attitude so peculiar. I can't decide whether you don't think I'm good enough to succeed or whether you'd just prefer me to fail. I can't be your protégé for ever, you know. Nor will I always need a mentor.'

'That's unkind,' I said. 'Surely you must know by now that I'm on your side.'

'I've always assumed that you were.'

'I am, Maurice, I am,' I insisted, reaching across and attempting to place my hand atop his, but he pulled away from me, as if my touch might burn him. 'Perhaps I expressed myself wrongly, that's all,' I said quietly. 'I'm sure you're right and your novel will be a great success.'

'Thanks,' he said, without any great enthusiasm.

'I suppose that means you won't be available next year?'

'Next year?' he asked. 'For what?'

'For the paperback publication of *Dread*. I imagine that I'll be invited to other countries, other cities and other literary festivals. You could always join me again if you wanted to? We could see—'

'I don't think so, Erich,' he said. 'It's probably time for me to focus on my own career now and not yours.'

'Of course,' I said, feeling humiliated, and as I lifted my glass I could see that my hand was shaking a little.

'Anyway, as this *is* our last night together,' he said, smiling again, looking as if he wanted to restore our equanimity, 'then I'd like to know how things turned out between Oskar and Alysse. Did they escape Germany in time?'

'Oh, that's all so long ago,' I muttered, in no mood now to return to those dark days, wishing instead that we could simply go back to the hotel and retire for the night. I felt very low, close to tears. *Was* I jealous? I asked myself. And if so, of what?

'But I have to know how it ended,' he insisted. 'Come on, you're a storyteller. You can't walk away without revealing the final chapter.'

'There's not that much more to tell,' I said with a sigh.

'There must be. When we were in Madrid, you said that Oskar and Alysse had decided to leave Berlin. That she was a . . . what was the word you used again?'

'A *Mischling*,' I said. 'And it wasn't Madrid, it was New York.'

'Of course,' he said. 'I'm so well travelled now that I get confused.'

I knew that I had no choice. I had got this far, after all. In the fifty years since the start of the war, those events had stayed with me, a shadow across any possibility I might have had for happiness. In fact, as I had walked to the stage on that evening in London to collect The Prize, I had thought of them both, had even imagined that I saw them seated in the audience near the front, a small boy between them, the only three people not applauding or standing in an ovation but sitting side by side, looking exactly as they did in 1939, all the time staring at me and wondering how such extraordinary success could be visited upon a man who had committed such a heinous and unforgivable act.

The fact was, there was no way that I could have permitted Oskar and Alysse to leave Berlin together. My feelings for him were too strong and in my sexual confusion I had allowed myself to become so overwhelmed that I simply could no longer think straight. I had convinced myself that if I could somehow persuade him to stay, then our friendship would transform into something more intimate. Two days after his birthday he left a note for me at my home, asking me to meet him in the late afternoon by the entrance to the Tiergarten Zoo and, as we walked back towards Maxingstraße, I begged him to reconsider his decision.

'I can't,' he told me with utter certainty. 'For heaven's sake, Erich, you live in this city. You've seen what's happening. I won't stand by and wait for them to take Alysse away.'

'Oh, just listen to yourself,' I said, raising my voice in frustration. 'They're Jews, Oskar. I know you think that you love her but—'

'Erich, you're a Jew,' he pointed out.

'I'm not,' I insisted. 'Not really.'

'If either of us needs to be worried about how things are changing here, then it should be you, not me. Anyway, it's all been decided so there's no point in trying to change my mind. We're going to America, her entire family and me. That's why I wanted to meet you this afternoon. To say goodbye.'

I stared at him, feeling a sickness build at the pit of my stomach. 'You'll need tickets,' I said, when I could find my voice again.

'Her father has them already. We're going to take a train to Paris and travel from there to Calais. Then we'll take the ferry across the Channel to Southampton and, in time, journey on to New York.'

'And what will you do when you get there?'

'I'm not sure, but Alysse's father is a resourceful man. He knows a lot of people in the city. Perhaps we'll start a business, I don't know. All that matters is that we'll be safe.'

'And the checkpoints?' I asked. 'You know that you'll never get through them, don't you? Your papers won't be in order.'

'You'd be surprised the work that forgers can do these days, Erich. In this climate, they're making a fortune.'

'And I suppose her father paid for that too?'

'He has a little money.'

'Of course he does,' I said bitterly. 'They all do. The fucking Jews have more money than the rest of us combined. Perhaps Hitler is right in what he says. Perhaps we'll all be better off when they disappear from Germany.'

His smile faded now a little. 'They don't have anything,' he said. 'You know as well as I do that they've all been shipped off to God knows where over the last year. How many Jews have you even seen on the streets in recent months? They're all gone. It's the same all across Europe. First degree, second degree, none of these distinctions will matter if Hitler gets his way. The Nuremberg Laws will be ripped up. The time to leave is right now.'

'When will you go?' I asked finally.

'Tonight. At nightfall.'

'But that's too soon!'

'We're ready. There's no reason for us to stay any longer. I'll write to you when we reach England. In the meantime, we must pray that, if there is a war, Germany loses.'

Without thinking, I grabbed him by the arm and pulled him into a side lane empty of people, pushing him up against the wall.

'Don't say things like that,' I said. 'If you're overheard you will be shot.'

'All right, Erich. Let go of me.'

'Not until you promise not to leave. The day will come when you'll regret this decision. You'll realize that you deserted the Fatherland at the moment of its greatest need and hate yourself for it. And for what? For some girl?'

'But she's not some girl,' said Oskar. 'Don't you understand that I'm in love with her?'

'You're seventeen years old,' I said. 'You'd say you were in love with a wild boar if it let you have your way with it.'

His smile faded and I could see his face grow dark. 'Be careful, Erich,' he warned. 'I care about you but there's a line that I won't allow you to cross.'

'You're confusing loyalty with love, that's what's wrong here.'

'I'm not,' he said. 'And one day, when you fall for someone, you'll understand that.'

'You think I don't know what it is to be in love?' I asked.

'I'm not being cruel but there's no girl in your life, is there? And there never has been. At least none that you've told me about, anyway.'

'I don't need a girl to understand love,' I said, taking his face in my hands and pressing my lips against his. For a moment, perhaps in surprise at what I was doing, I could feel his lips part a little and a certain lack of resistance from him. But then, just as quickly as it had started, the only kiss of my life came to an end. He pulled away from me, wiping his hand across his mouth and shaking his head. I didn't turn away. I felt no shame and looked directly at him, hoping to challenge him with my eyes just as Alysse had done when she turned in the painting and stared out at the viewer. I didn't know what to expect next, whether he might run away from me or lash out in anger, but in fact he did neither of these things, simply looked at me with a sorrowful expression on his face and let out a disappointed sigh.

'I suspected as much,' he said quietly. 'But whatever you're hoping for, it's not possible.'

'Why not?'

'Because that's not who I am,' he said.

'If you tried—'

'I don't want to try, I'm sorry. It doesn't interest me.'

'But instead you'll fuck that whore?' I shouted, feeling humiliated now, tears streaming down my face.

'Stop it, Erich.'

'Well, how else would you describe her? Taking off her clothes so you can paint her like that. And that's the girl you want to give up your life for?'

'I'm leaving now, Erich,' he said, turning away.

'Don't!' I shouted, reaching out for him. 'Please, I'm sorry.'

But it was too late. He was gone.

I chose not to follow him. Instead I turned and made my way back in the direction of home, a rage building inside me like none that I had ever known before, one that threatened to explode from inside my chest as I passed the Böttcher Tavern, where we would drink no more. Leaning against the wall, I caught my distorted reflection in the glass and that of the building behind me.

The offices of the Schutzstaffel.

I turned to look at them and there was the red-haired soldier standing on duty outside as always, looking bored as he watched the street, until his eyes landed on me. Without stopping to think, I marched across, pulled my papers from my inside pocket and demanded to speak to the Untersturmführer on duty.

'What do you want?' he asked me.

'I have information.'

'So tell me. I'm in charge.'

'Not you,' I said. 'Someone more important. I know something. Something that your superiors will want to know.'

He raised an eyebrow and laughed, as if I were just a child. 'Go home,' he said. 'Before you get yourself into trouble.'

'I know where the Jews are,' I hissed, leaning forward so he could surely see the rage in my eyes. 'They hide in the sewers like rats.'

'Go home,' he repeated.

'If you don't let me speak to the Untersturmführer,' I said, 'I will write a letter to your superiors and by then it will be too late for them to act. And you will be blamed. I will say that you sent me away.'

He took a long time to decide but, perhaps feeling the same fear of the SS officers that everyone else felt, he led me with little graciousness inside the building, my anger only increasing as I waited. Finally, I was summoned into a small, cold room, where a tired man in a grey uniform sat before me.

'You want to report something?' he asked, sounding completely uninterested.

'Jews,' I told him. 'An entire Jewish family. Four of them. Living not far from here. In the centre of Berlin itself.'

He smiled and shook his head. 'There are no Jews left here,' he told me. 'They've all been removed, you must know that. And certainly a family of four would have been apprehended by now.'

'Everyone knows that there are people in hiding,' I said. 'The ones you don't even realize are Jews, with their forged papers and counterfeit documents.'

He narrowed his eyes as he stared at me.

'And if the SS don't know who they are, then how do you?' he asked.

'Because she told me herself.'

'Who did?'

'The girl. The daughter.'

He laughed a little. 'Let me guess,' he said. 'A lover of yours? Did she jilt you for another boy and now you're trying to avenge yourself on her by inventing some story? Or did she just turn down your advances, was that it?'

'It's nothing like that,' I said, leaning forward and allowing my fury to escape me now. 'You think I'd fuck a Jew? Maybe that's what you enjoy, is it? Is that why you don't seem keen on pursuing this matter? Perhaps I shouldn't be talking to you at all, Untersturmführer. Perhaps I should be looking for your Obersturmführer instead?'

'Tell me more about this family,' he said finally, opening his notebook and licking the top of his pencil before starting to write.

'I told you, there are four of them. A man and his wife, their daughter and a young boy. He's just a child of five or six, I think. They claim to be *Mischlings*, second degree, so they've been left alone until now. But it's not true! They're fully Jewish, all four grandparents were Jews, and they live here in contravention of the Race Laws. But they're worried that they will be exposed. They have money and they have papers. They plan on travelling to France and crossing the English Channel. Then onward to America.'

'We'll visit them tomorrow,' he said. 'It won't be difficult to find out the truth.'

'Tomorrow will be too late,' I told him. 'They leave tonight.'

He looked up at me sharply. 'You know this for a fact?' he asked.

'They've pulled the wool over your eyes,' I said, hearing a certain hysteria creep into my tone now that I seemed to be convincing him. 'They stayed here even as you deported the others. They've been laughing at you as they spread their filthy Jewry before the children of the Reich and within hours they will be on their way out of the Fatherland to use their money to build an army against us.'

'Give me their names,' he said. 'And their address.'

I didn't hesitate.

A moment later he left the room and I heard the sound of soldiers assembling in the courtyard outside and realized that he was not going to return to me. Running out of the building on to the street, I saw a group of six soldiers, led by the Untersturmführer himself, pile into a jeep and watched as they drove off in the direction of

Alysse's home, a short journey of only a few minutes. I felt a moment of terror then, a sickness inside at the thought of what I'd done, but still I believed that if Alysse and her family were only sent away, then Oskar would stay in Berlin and in time he would forget her and our friendship could continue as before. Perhaps he would even miss her so much that there would be no more talk of girls ever again. Instead, there would just be the two of us.

I ran through the streets in pursuit of the jeep and, when it approached Alysse's front door, the driver pulled in as the Untersturmführer looked towards the upstairs windows, where the shades were drawn but a low light could be seen seeping through the thin fabric. Giving a signal to his Rottenführer, the young man used the butt of his rifle and his right foot to kick the door in and the SS soldiers poured inside, roaring at the top of their voices, an insult to the peaceful dignity of the night.

It took only a few moments before the family were dragged outside and lined up on the street. I could see their neighbours peeping anxiously through their curtains, no doubt fearing that the next door to be knocked down might be theirs. Two of the soldiers guarded Alysse's parents with their rifles while the rest ransacked the house, looking for anything incriminating. The little boy remained brave and silent while Alysse appeared terrified, shaking visibly in the coldness of the night. From where I stood, half hidden in the shade of a sidestreet, it gave me great pleasure to see her undone.

The Untersturmführer came out after a few minutes, brandishing train tickets in his hand. He waved them in the face of Alysse's father, who protested his innocence, but it was to no avail, as an SS lorry arrived and the back doors were pulled open, ready to transport the unfortunate group to a place from which there could be no return. I began to grow anxious now, desperate for the scene to end and for them to disappear into the night.

But before the last of the passengers – the little boy – could be loaded into the lorry, I heard the sound of someone running along

the street behind me and turned to see Oskar, charging towards the
German soldiers with a pistol in his hand as he threw his suitcase to
the side of the street. He was quick with his gun, pulling the trigger
as a first soldier fell, then pulling it again as another went down.
Alysse's mother screamed and the rest of the soldiers turned as one
in his direction, opening fire, a hail of noise and bright lights in the
darkness of the night, and it took only a moment for him to fall too.
His body collapsed close to my feet, blood pouring from his mouth
and spreading from a wound in his chest across his coat, and I
stared down at him, paralysed with fear, before Alysse screamed
his name and leaped from the lorry to run in his direction, her
younger brother following her, calling her name, as their parents
cried out for them both to come back. Oskar was still alive – just –
but with little time left. His breathing was failing, and she reached
him just before the soldiers shot again, falling across his body with
a scream, and as I stepped closer to them, the child was lifted off his
feet too and fell to the ground after his sister, the back of his head
blown away, his brain spilling like mud across the cobbled street.
Oskar and Alysse stared up at me without emotion, their bodies jolt-
ing in trauma, and within a minute their lives had drawn to a close.

They were dead. I had killed them all.

Throughout my story, I had kept my eyes focussed on the table
before me, not at Maurice. Now, however, there was nothing left to
say so I lifted my head, uncertain what expression I would find on
his face, but it was neutral.

'And after that?' he asked me, seeing that I was not going to speak
again until he did.

'After that I went home,' I told him with a shrug. 'I never saw
Alysse's parents again. I assume they were taken to the camps
and that they died there. The next day, when I returned to that
street, the bodies had been taken away and the only evidence
remaining was the blood between the cobbles and on my own

boots. And soon there was a war and I took part in it, and then the war ended and I came to England to read and to write. The rest of my life was peaceful until I won The Prize. And until I met you,' I added carefully.

'I think we should go back to the hotel,' he said, looking away.

'But don't you want to talk more? To ask me anything?'

'No,' he said, standing up and putting his coat on. 'I just want to sleep, that's all. We've talked enough. I've heard all that I need to hear.'

I nodded as I rose, feeling wounded that he was not willing to comfort or condemn me. This was my story, the story that defined my life, and yet he seemed impervious to it.

In the hotel, however, alone in my room, I became upset. I had hidden these secrets inside myself for half a century and to reveal them to anyone, let alone to one who had reawakened in me a desire that had lain dormant for decades, was so overwhelming that I knew I would not sleep. I paced in my room for a long time before crossing the corridor towards his suite, knocking cautiously on the door. When he opened it, his shirt unbuttoned, his feet bare, he seemed both surprised and irritated to find me there.

'What?' he asked. 'It's late. What do you want?'

'I thought perhaps we might talk,' I said.

'I don't think so, no.'

I pressed forward, trying to get through the door, but he held out a hand and placed it firmly against my chest.

'Please,' I said. 'I had an idea, that's all.'

'So tell me your idea.'

I hesitated. I didn't want to speak of it out here in the corridor but it was clear that he was not going to let me inside. 'You know I return to Cambridge tomorrow?' I said.

'Yes, of course. What of it?'

'It's a very good place to write.'

'So do some writing.'

81

'I thought you might like to join me there, perhaps. I daresay I could find you rooms—'

'I'm not interested in living in Cambridge,' he said. 'Don't you ever think, Erich, that perhaps you've seen me as you wanted me to be and not as who I am?'

I frowned, unwilling even to consider this as a possibility. 'You might like to read for a degree there,' I continued. 'Even if you don't have the necessary school results, I'm sure—'

'Erich, I said I don't want to live there.'

'But it's such a beautiful city. Sometimes I've thought it might be nice to buy a house,' I added, making up new ideas as I went along. 'You could have a room there,' I added, unable to look him in the eye now but staring down at the floor. 'A room of your own, of course. And as I have no children, then someday—'

'I'm tired, Erich,' he said. 'I'm going to bed.'

'Yes, of course,' I said, turning away, my voice barely audible in my distress. 'It was a foolish idea.'

I began to make my way down the corridor towards my room but his voice calling out to me made me turn around.

'What was his name?' he shouted.

'What?' I asked, confused by his question. 'What was whose name?'

'The boy. Alysse's younger brother. Do you remember his name, or was his life as meaningless to you as hers? What was his name, Erich?'

I stared at him, swallowing hard. I looked around me, at the carpet, the paintings, the lampshades, hoping for inspiration, but nothing came to mind. I turned back to him and shook my head.

'I don't remember,' I said. 'I'm not sure that I ever even knew.'

He smiled at me, shook his head, and then he was gone.

The following morning, when I came downstairs with my suitcase, I enquired after him and the receptionist told me that he had checked out an hour earlier.

He had left no message for me.

8. West Berlin

True to his ambitions, Maurice's debut novel was published the following year to both positive reviews and strong sales and, in his first interviews, he revealed that his central character, a young homosexual falling in love with his best friend in pre-war Berlin, was based on me.

'All of Ernst's actions in my novel come from stories that Erich Ackermann told me about his own life,' he repeated time and again on television, on radio and in the newspapers. 'Although I've invented some characters and amalgamated others to serve the story, the basic facts remain true. Having been a great admirer of Herr Ackermann's work since my teenage years, I was naturally shocked by some of the things he revealed to me about his past, but while no decent human being could condone his behaviour, whatever he did fifty years ago does not detract from the power of his fiction. He remains a very impressive writer.'

The first I knew of any of this was during a lecture I was giving at Cambridge on Thomas Hardy. It was one that I had given many times in the past and I was interrupted halfway through when the door swung open to reveal a cameraman and a young news reporter who stormed towards the lectern without introduction to ask the question that I had been expecting for most of my adult life:

'Professor Ackermann, do you have any reaction to claims by the novelist Maurice Swift that you wilfully sent two Jews to their deaths in the Nazi death camps in 1939 by reporting them to the SS, and also provided information that led to the murder of two other young people on the same night?'

The silence that filled the hall seemed to go on for a terribly long time. For me, it was like time itself had stood still. I looked down at my notes with a half-smile, and it was difficult not to feel the finality of the moment as I shuffled my papers and returned them to my satchel, glancing around the lecture theatre in the certain knowledge that I would never speak from that or any other dais again. Looking out at my students, I saw them staring back at me in a mixture of disbelief and confusion and my eyes settled on a girl whose hand was covering her mouth in shock. She was a mediocre student and I had recently given her a low grade for one of her essays, and I knew immediately that she would take pleasure in my downfall, revelling in the fact that she had been present to witness it. *I was there*, she would tell her friends. *I was there when they confronted the old Nazi and told him they knew all the things he'd done. I wasn't surprised. I could always tell that he was hiding something. He broke down and cried. He started screaming. It was horrible to watch.*

'In fact, it was three young people who were shot that night,' I said to the reporter, stepping off the stage and making my way towards the door without undue haste. 'Although you're correct that two were sent to the camps. So the number of deaths on my conscience is actually five.'

Events moved quickly after that. Perhaps if I had not won The Prize, the newspapers would not have taken as much interest in me but of course I had acquired some small measure of celebrity that was pure oxygen to the fire of publicity that followed. Also, it was 1989 and the last of the war criminals were still being discovered in places as far removed as South America, Australia and Africa. To add the name of a small provincial English university town to that list provided a scandal that the columnists could live off for months. As a writer, I could hardly blame them for drawing as much blood from the story as possible.

The authorities at Cambridge suspended me immediately, issuing a press statement to the effect that they had known nothing of my wartime activities and had taken me at my word that I had engaged in no criminal behaviour during the Nazi era. They summoned me to an emergency meeting but I declined the invitation, as perhaps I should have declined all invitations over the previous

year, and offered my resignation instead by letter, which they grate-
fully accepted by return of post.

Bookshops across the world removed my novels from their
shelves, although the organizers of The Prize itself refused, in the
face of staunch criticism, to rescind my award, saying that it had
been given to a book, not to an author, and that *Dread* remained a
sublime work, regardless of the monstrous actions of its creator. In
response to this a great number of writers boycotted The Prize that
year, refusing to enter their books, and only when the fuss died
down did they seek the approbation of a small glass trophy and a
sizeable cheque once again. A film adaptation of *Dread*, scheduled to
begin shooting two months later, was promptly cancelled, while
representatives from my publishing house – a company with whom
I had worked since my debut novel appeared in 1953 – contacted me
to say that in the light of recent events they felt they could no longer
offer the level of support to my writing that they had done in the
past. I was released from my contract with immediate effect, they
added, and my six novels would soon be allowed to fall out of print.
(They made no mention of my ill-advised collection of poetry,
although I can only assume that this was an oversight on their
part.) So my work was to be obliterated, my contribution to literature over half a century expunged from the record as if I had never
once put pen to paper. And I accepted all of this without rancour.
What, after all, could I possibly have said to justify myself?

It took me some time to move my belongings from my
rooms. There was a lifetime's worth of books there, not to mention
decades of correspondence and papers to organize, and to my great
dismay some five hundred students, many of whom I knew personally and with whom I had formed what I'd believed to be friendly
connections, paraded through the streets while I remained *in situ*.
They held banners with my picture in the centre, a Hitler moustache drawn above my upper lip and a red line slashed through my
face. *Nazis out!* they cried. *Nazis out!* A stone was thrown through

my window and the culprit, an undergraduate in the history department, was suspended from classes for three weeks. A petition was
delivered for his reinstatement and he acquired heroic status among
his peers, even appearing on an episode of *Newsnight* to defend his
actions. Oh, how the young people delighted in their outrage!

Most of the major newspapers and media organizations contacted me directly with requests for interviews – my agent had
stopped representing me, of course, so their invitations came by
phone to the college porter – offering ridiculous amounts of money
in exchange for putting what they termed as 'my side of the story'
in the public domain, but I declined every bid, making it clear that
I had nothing to say in my defence. I committed the acts of which I
am accused, I told them. I am guilty as charged. What more do you
want from me?

I chose not to read Maurice's novel at first but then one afternoon, as I was making my way through Heathrow Airport for the
last time, I saw it displayed in considerable numbers at the front of
a bookshop:

Two Germans
by Maurice Swift

I thought it a lazy title and, had I been in his position, might have
gone for something a little more sensational, but I picked it up
nevertheless and glanced at the endorsements on the back cover.
Naturally, both Dash Hardy and the Spanish novelist had offered
glowing praise for the book.

I did, however, eventually read it over the course of a single
afternoon. It had many flaws. For a start, it was too long. Over
three hundred and fifty pages for a story that could have been told
in half that amount. There were an extraordinary number of anach-
ronisms, place names that didn't exist at the time, and some of the
prose was unnecessarily purple. I had warned him about this in the

past. Just say what you have to say, I had told him, and then move on and say something else. Sometimes, after all, the sky is just blue.

But then I recalled something else I had told him in Copenhagen and felt rather proud that he had taken me at my word. *Everyone has secrets*, I had remarked. *There's something in all our pasts that we wouldn't want to be revealed. And that's where you'll find your story.* He must have scribbled that down in his ubiquitous notebook and, when a story began to be revealed to him, he knew exactly what to do with it. I had, quite literally, been the author of my own misfortune.

A photograph of Maurice appeared on the inside jacket and he looked a lot more adult than before. Gone were the checked shirts, blue jeans and stubble; now he wore an elegant suit with an open-necked white shirt and a pair of black horn-rimmed glasses. The great mess of dark hair had been tamed too for a more mature look. The photographer's name, I noticed, was Clémence Charbonneau, and I wondered about that. Was this the friend he had met in Paris who had photographed him nude?

It took quite some time for me to have an emotional response to my relationship with Maurice but it happened at last after I had returned to West Berlin, where I rented a small apartment at the top of a building quite near what had once been the Böttcher Tavern but was now a supermarket. It was in this flat that I had chosen to spend whatever remained of my life, close to the happy memories of my childhood. I was sorting through some paperwork one evening and happened to come across the receipts for the air and train fares that I had purchased for him over the course of our time together. Copenhagen, Rome, Madrid, Paris, New York and Amsterdam. The cities where we had talked, where I had revealed so much about myself, and where I had behaved foolishly in the hope that this manipulative boy would fall in love with me. I broke down as I threw them in the wastepaper basket, wondering whether the pain that he had inflicted, the heartless manoeuvring and theft

JOHN BOYNE

of my life story, had been worth it to him. And as I sat there weeping, I thought of Oskar, Alysse, her younger brother and the rest of her family and felt that my heart was ready to give way with grief and guilt. What right had I, I asked myself, to feel aggrieved over Maurice's actions? All he had done was take my memories and turn them into a bestseller that would be forgotten in time. How could I possibly compare his crimes to my own?

I saw him once more.

It was a few months after I'd moved back to West Berlin and by then his novel had not only been translated into German – ironically, by the same publisher who had once produced my own books – but had become an enormous success, the biggest of the season, and I saw an advertisement in a newspaper for a reading and public interview that he was due to give at the Literaturhaus. I debated whether or not to go but, on the evening itself, my feet took me there as if by their own design. I adopted a slight disguise in case anyone present might recognize me, a pair of old glasses that I had no real use for and a hat. Plus, I had recently grown a beard and moustache, and had aged considerably.

An enormous crowd had gathered for the event and I took a seat towards the back, flicking through a brochure from the bookshop advertising their new titles. There was a flurry of applause when Maurice made his way towards the platform and, to my astonishment, I recognized the man who accompanied him and took to the microphone first. It was the same disgruntled actor who had been unwilling to read my chosen excerpt from *Dread* all that time ago; he had been hired once again for this evening and must have been happier with Maurice's selection than he had been with mine for he read with great spirit, receiving a hearty round of applause from the audience when he had finished. Afterwards, as Maurice proceeded to answer questions posed by a journalist on stage, it struck me how confident he was up there, how knowledgeable in his

88

literary allusions and witty in his self-deprecating remarks. He was a natural, I realized, and would surely be a great success for the rest of his life. His writing would improve and the media would embrace him with open arms. I felt certain that his future was guaranteed.

When audience members asked about me he answered them honestly and said nothing that was either slanderous or untrue. He did not try to denigrate me and continued to maintain that while his book was a work of fiction based on fact, this did not take away from the novels that I had written over the course of my life.

'I do not believe that Erich Ackermann was an evil man,' he remarked at one point with a shrug. 'Just a misguided one. What you might call a fool in love. But a fool in love at a very dangerous time.'

I rolled my eyes at this. It sounded like something he'd said a hundred times before, a piece of bland fortune-cookie wisdom that he knew would lead the audience to nod wisely and consider him both forgiving and charmingly naïve. When the event ended he stood up, revelling in the applause, and a queue formed for his signature. I was uncertain at first whether to join it but finally took a German-language edition from the pile and took my place at the back. He barely glanced up when it was my turn, asking, 'Would you like me to put your name on this?' but then he caught my eye and what else could I do but smile at him? He had the good grace to blush as I turned the book to the title page, shook my head and said, 'Just a signature, please,' which he offered with a trembling hand, watching in some surprise as I walked away. I felt a certain victory over him at that moment, although for the life of me I don't understand why, as I had achieved nothing of consequence.

Soon, life returned to normal and the media found someone else to persecute. I had saved my money well over the years and, coupled with the royalties I had made from the sales of *Dread*, not to mention the financial compensation that had come with The Prize, I knew that I could survive comfortably for the rest of my life, which, I guessed, would only be a year or two longer at most. I could feel it slipping away from me already. My spirit was gone. I would write no more. And without writing, without teaching, there was really nothing left for me.

And then, one evening, the wall came down.

It was November 1989 and I was at home when the reports began to filter through over the radio that the German Democratic Republic had finally reopened its borders after more than forty years of closure. Within the hour the streets below my apartment window were filled with people and I had a perfect view of the crowds as they marched along, calling up to the guards standing on the watch-towers. I watched with a mixture of dread and excitement and then, just as I was about to turn away and retire to bed, I noticed a young boy of about sixteen, beautiful and dark-haired, filled with the exhilaration of youth, rising up unsteadily on the shoulders of his friends, his hands reaching out to grip the top of the wall as he pulled himself up to stand on it, his arms raised in the air in triumph now as the people cheered him on. A moment later he turned around for his first view of the East and someone there must have caught his eye for he reached down in turn, holding out his hand to help a boy from the other side, the same age as him, who had also scaled the wall in an attempt to reach the summit.

I watched closely, my face pressed against the window, waiting for their fingers to touch.

Interlude

The Swallow's Nest

Howard had gone into the village to buy peaches and Gore sat alone on the crescent terrace overlooking the Tyrrhenian Sea wearing linen trousers, a white, open-necked shirt and a pair of scarlet slippers crafted for him by Gianni Versace and handed over with great ceremony when the designer had come to stay a few months earlier. There was something faintly papal about the footwear that appealed to Gore's dual passions: history and power. He had only ever met two popes – Montini and Wojtyła – and they'd both appeared overwhelmed by a sense of their own destinies, although his grandfather had once told an amusing story about an evening he'd spent in the company of Pacelli, which had turned sour only when the burdensome subjects of Judaism and the Reich had been raised.

On the table before him was a cappuccino, a pair of binoculars, a Fabriano notebook, a Caran d'Ache pen, the galleys of his new novel and two books. The first was the latest work by Dash Hardy, which he'd read a few weeks earlier and despised for its insipid prose and the author's reluctance to describe basic anatomy. The second had been sent to him a month earlier but he hadn't got around to it yet. He supposed that he should at least have given it a cursory glance since its author, a young man whose features were not offensive to the eye, was due to arrive later that morning with Dash to spend the night at La Rondinaia.

But it was impossible to keep up with the multitude of books that arrived, unsolicited, day after day, week after week, month after month, an endless haul that had caused Ampelio, their mail carrier of many years, to write an outraged letter of complaint, citing back injuries from scaling the steps with so many packages. Fortunately,

Ampelio had recently relocated north along the Amalfi Coast towards Salerno and been replaced by a lithe, brown-legged nineteen-year-old aptly named Egidio – *young goat* – whose hare-lip offered him an erotic appeal that otherwise would have left his face beautiful but unremarkable. Egidio, who revelled in the athleticism of his youth, fairly bounded up and down those brutal steps with what could only be described as gay abandon and no further complaints had been issued, but as much as Gore welcomed the boy's daily appearances and cheerful greetings, he wished that the parcels would become a little less numerous. Over the last couple of years, he'd transported most of his own books, the ones he actually wanted to surround himself with, from Rome but they took up so much space in the villa that he sometimes felt a little claustrophobic, although Howard, peaceful Howard, never complained. Would there be no end to publishing? he wondered. Perhaps it would be a good idea if everyone just stopped writing for a couple of years and allowed readers to catch up.

Gore had known Dash for decades and although he liked him well enough he knew that he was essentially a hack with a modicum of talent who'd managed to sustain a career by taking care never to offend the middle-aged ladies and closeted homosexuals who made up the bulk of his readership. His books were efficiently written but so painfully innocuous that even President Reagan had taken one on holiday to California with him towards the end of his bewildering reign and declared it to be a masterful depiction of American steelworkers, unaware that the steelworkers in question were laying their pipes with each other in the gaps between the lines. Gore liked to think that Nancy – who had been such fun in the old days, before she sold her soul to the Republicans – knew what was really going on there but had declined to tell her beloved Ronnie for fear of destroying his innocence.

The two writers had first met at a queer club in the West Village in the 1950s. Gore had already published a few novels, pirouetting

across the scandal caused by *The City and the Pillar* with the grace
of a young Margot Fonteyn, and his reputation was more firmly
established than those of most men of his age. He trotted around
parties hand in hand with Kennedys, Astors and Rockefellers, with
Tennessee and Jimmy Dean, and invariably left some remark in his
wake for the guests to gossip over the following morning. It wasn't
uncommon for a boy to approach him at one of these gatherings,
offering his cock or his ass in exchange for an entrée into the world
of the privileged, but Gore preferred not to indulge in such base
transactions. *We can fuck, if you want,* he would tell them if they were
cute enough, *but don't expect anything more from me than an orgasm.*
Not that he liked fucking, or being fucked. He'd tried it a few times
but it wasn't really for him. He was a man of much simpler tastes.
A hand-job was pleasure enough. A little *frottage*, perhaps. And as
much as he admired the Roman emperors he'd never been interested in emulating any of their more lurid escapades.

On this particular evening, however, he'd noticed the young
man staring at him from across the room but, as he resembled
nothing more than the love-child of Charles Laughton and Margaret Rutherford, he'd done nothing to encourage his interest. Gore
had been sitting with Elizabeth and Monty, but they'd left early
when he said something that made poor Monty cry, and he'd been
thinking of going home alone when the young man – Dash – came
over and sat down at his table with a sailor, introducing himself as
the author of a debut novel due to be published that fall.

'How thrilling for you,' he'd muttered, scarcely taking the writer in
but enjoying his view of the sailor, who looked at him with the type of
smile that made it clear he had only to say the word and they could run
the Jolly Roger up the flagpole together. 'But don't tell me anything
about it, dear boy. Otherwise it will spoil the joy of reading it.'

Dash had looked crestfallen. He'd clearly wanted to recite the
entire story from beginning to end and for Gore to tell him how
wonderful it sounded. The sailor, perhaps having already spent too

long as an uninterested audience, stood up and walked towards the bar to buy three banana daiquiris and, while he was gone, Dash told Gore how much he respected his work, offering him a blow job in gratitude in the men's room, a proposal that Gore politely declined. It wasn't just that he was saving himself for the sailor later, there was also the fact that the image of this boy on his knees, his fat lips wrapped around his cock, was repulsive to him.

'But you're very kind to offer,' he added, not wishing to appear rude.

'Oh, it's my pleasure,' said Dash. 'I'd do the same for anyone.'

'And how do you know . . . what's his name, anyway? *Anchors Aweigh* over there.'

'Gene,' replied Dash, glancing towards the bar, where the boy was busy fending off the advances of a much older man who seemed keen to squeeze his buttocks. The sailor's Dixie Cup was cocked to the side of his head in a coquettish fashion, revealing neat blond curls that reminded Gore of the boy he'd loved in St Albans before the war.

'Gene,' he repeated quietly. 'Like Gene Kelly. Appropriate, I suppose. Although my own father was also named Gene and he bowed to no man in his admiration for the cunt.'

'Have you ever visited?'

'Certainly not,' said Gore with a shudder. 'And you?'

'Once,' admitted Dash. 'My mother wanted me to marry one Clara Day-Whitley, a debutante from Maryland, and in a moment of weakness, fearing for my inheritance, I agreed to do so. Only Clara insisted that we do the vile deed before she made her mind up as, in her words, she didn't want to be stuck with Floppy Joe for the rest of her life. In retrospect, I think she was a nymphomaniac. She couldn't keep her hands off me. Anyway, I agreed to her terms and we went to bed together one Saturday afternoon while her parents were at a meeting of the Rotary Club. I'm not a bad actor but it didn't take long for her to realize that she was being sold a bill of goods.'

'Your mother must have been devastated.'

'She was.'

'Did you tell her the truth subsequently?'

'Oh no, I couldn't do that. It would have brought on one of her hearts. She's still keeping an eye out for a suitable wife for me but I'm hopeful there'll be no further developments on that score.'

'And your novel?' asked Gore. 'Is it a romance?'

'Of sorts. A young man meets a girl who—'

'Yes, yes. I daresay you'll send me a copy. I promise I'll read it.'

'Really?'

'Of course. I'm moist with anticipation,' he added, writing his address on the back of a napkin and passing it across. He suspected that Dash would frame it and keep it for ever although on this point he was wrong for when Dash returned home that night – alone, for Gore had indeed left with the sailor and Dash had been happy to give the boy up to him – he copied it into his address book, before crumpling the napkin up and throwing it in the wastepaper basket like a normal human being.

When the novel arrived a few weeks later, Gore had been true to his word and, to his surprise, had rather admired it, writing to Dash to tell him so. From an unpromising beginning, a friendship of sorts had developed and they saw each other whenever they were in the same city or travelling nearby. For many years, Gore had dutifully read each of his books as they were published and, although he felt that Dash had diminished as a writer, he found that he liked him more as a person. Perhaps that was the generosity of age, he reasoned. Dash could be a fool, at times, but he was never disagreeable. He didn't have the tendency towards spite or envy that Gore had, although he'd been hurt many times over the years, always by young men who'd used him for his connections before disposing of him like yesterday's newspapers. Dash had no Howard, he'd never had a Howard, and his life would have been improved immeasurably by one. But then, as Gore knew, Dash didn't want a Howard and wouldn't have accepted one. He wanted, for want of a better word, a Howie. A kid just out of college with a pretty face, tight abs and ass cheeks that could crack a walnut. Well, he'd liked that sort of thing himself once upon a time and still did, occasionally, when the boys from the nearby villages came up to the Swallow's Nest for parties, but in truth he'd grown less and less interested in carnal pleasures with the passing of the years. Sure, if it was there for the taking and there were no complications attached, then why not? But not if he had to put any particular effort into the seduction.

The sound of voices distracted him and he noticed a small sailboat in the distance and three – no, four; there was one in the ocean – boys diving from the deck into the dark blue water. They were young, no more than fifteen, with brown bodies and energy to burn. He reached for his binoculars and put them to his eyes, watching as each one dived, swam and returned to the boat to ascend the ladder and start all over again. He recognized one of them as Alessandro, defender of mankind, the son of the woman who came twice weekly to clean La Rondinaia, and thought the second was Dante, a boy who helped out at his father's art gallery on weekends. Gore rather liked Dante. He'd once observed him fucking his girlfriend behind the church of Santa Trofimena, his buttocks moving back and forth with a machine-like efficiency as he pressed her against the wall; he'd yelped like a startled dog when he came. The other boys he didn't know and they weren't much to look at so he put the binoculars down again and finished his coffee.

They would be here soon, he knew, glancing at his watch. A part of him was looking forward to seeing his old friend again and discovering whether his latest acquisition was as handsome in the flesh as he appeared in his author photograph. The other part wished that this had all taken place the week before and was now a fading memory. The truth was, he would have preferred to spend the day reading and writing, with the promise of a few cocktails on the terrace with Howard later to sustain him through the sunshine. Easy conversation. No need to be *on*. But Dash had written to say they'd be passing through the Amalfi and hoped that it wouldn't be too much trouble if they spent the night, and Gore, who'd been in an uncommonly good mood that morning as he'd had an amusing conversation with a shirtless Egidio, had replied to say that of course they must stay, that he'd be offended if they didn't, and Dash had subsequently sent a telegram, which was quaint, to say: *THERE ON 11TH STOP CANT WAIT STOP LOVE TO HOWARD STOP*

Perhaps an hour later, having worked his way through a few dozen pages of his galleys, he watched as a car began to ascend the hill and let out a deep sigh. He had ten more minutes before they would reach the top, when they would inevitably ring the doorbell and Cassiopeia would call down to say that his guests had arrived.

He looked out into the sea again, reaching for his binoculars, but while the sailboat was still *in situ* there was no sign of the young swimmers. Perhaps they'd all drowned, he thought, realizing that he didn't care very much if they had. The bodies would wash up on to the rocks eventually, after all, and their mothers would have the time of their lives screaming through the streets, pulling their hair out and ripping their clothes as they grieved publicly for their lost heroes.

As it turned out, the boy was even better-looking in person than he was in his author photograph, but there was something about his character that made Gore immediately suspicious. He'd been beautiful himself once, of course, and knew the power that handsome boys could wield over ageing homosexuals, men who longed not only for the feel of their young skin but for the delusional sensation that they too remained *objets du désir*, despite wrinkled faces, varicose veins and hair that sprouted from ears and nose. There were boys in the village who flattered both Gore and Howard with their attentions when they discovered them sitting alone at local cafés, scanning the pages of a two-day-old *New York Times*, and he indulged them occasionally, enjoying their smiles, their white teeth and the way they reached under their T-shirts to scratch their flat stomachs, revealing a treasure trail of dark hairs that ran from navel to groin.

He never paid for a boy, he hadn't done so in years, but when he was going he would always leave a tip for the waiter and another for the youth, who would sweep the money up quickly in his brown hands and say, *Grazie, grande uomo*, before scampering back to his friends to say that fifteen minutes of conversation with the famous writer from La Rondinaia could earn you enough lire to take a girl to the movies that night and buy her a *gelato e espresso* afterwards.

From the moment he arrived on the terrace, it was obvious to Gore that the young man had put a lot of work into his appearance from the simple fact that he looked as if he'd just fallen out of bed. His dark hair was neatly cut, hanging low enough over his forehead that he was forced to brush it back time and again with his fingers. He wore an expensive white shirt, carefully crumpled, and a pair of navy shorts that reached just below the knee, revealing strong calves and pleasingly hirsute legs. A pair of espadrilles and the type of sunglasses that Marcello Mastroianni had worn in *La Dolce Vita* completed the look while a light breeze carried an appealing scent in Gore's direction, a mixture of cheap soap, shampoo, bedsheets and boyish sweat.

Dash, poor defenceless Dash, was obviously besotted, placing metaphorical palm leaves before the boy's feet as he wandered around the terrace, taking in the view. But where Jesus had approached Jerusalem weeping aloud for the suffering that awaited the city upon the destruction of the Second Temple, Gore lamented quietly, his heart grieving for the pain that this young man would inevitably cause his friend.

'It's stunning,' said Maurice, lifting a hand to his forehead to keep the sun from his eyes as he looked across the water. 'And these cliffs,' he added, leaning over and peering forwards at the steep rock face. 'To live surrounded by such beauty . . . I can scarcely imagine it.'

'The Greeks,' said Gore, walking over to join him and waving a hand in the direction of the stone, 'believed that these cliffs housed the four winds maintained as familiars by Aeolus.'

'Aeolus?' asked Maurice, turning to his host, who was momentarily caught off guard by the boy's blue eyes, which matched the colour of the water below. 'Poseidon's son?'

'No, but that's a common mistake,' replied Gore, shaking his head. 'Different Aeolus, perhaps not quite as well known. This Aeolus, *my* Aeolus, was the son of a mortal king, Hippotes. You've read *The Odyssey*?'

'Of course.'

'Recall, then, the scene where Odysseus and his crew arrive on the island of Aeolia having fled the Grotto of Polyphemus. Aeolus delivers them a west wind to speed their journey back to Ithaca but, as they approach their homeland at last, the foolish sailors open the ox-hide bag that Aeolus has given them containing all the winds of the world save the west wind. They are blown back then to their benefactor, who determines that the gods are opposed to their return. I have some nice editions of Homer in my library upstairs. I'll show you if you like.'

'I'd like that very much.'

'Maurice is a compulsive reader,' said Dash, coming over to join them, standing to the boy's right, so close to him, in fact, that Gore realized he was making a declaration of ownership. He returned to the table, irritated that his friend was so possessive of a prize that, like the work of a mediocre painter, might look good on an initial viewing but would eventually reveal itself to be holding little of substance beneath the brushstrokes.

'Well, what else is there to do?' asked Gore. 'Although I must admit there are times when I think that I should only read the work of dead writers. I'm not sure that the living have very much to say any more.'

'I can't agree with that,' said Maurice defiantly, strolling away from Dash and taking a seat opposite Gore. 'I find that it's only bitter and disappointed old men who say such things. They want to believe that literature will come to an end when they're six feet underground.'

'Charming,' said Gore, impressed by how the boy held his ground. So many others just gave in instantly, frightened of incurring his tongue. 'You've only been here a few minutes and you're already insulting me.'

'I didn't mean *you*, of course,' said Maurice, flushing a little, and Gore realized that, yes, it was possible to discomfit the boy. It didn't take very much work at all, in fact. 'It's just that, when you're a young writer, it can be hard for one to be taken seriously.'

'It's the same for old writers,' said Gore with a shrug. 'They think I've already said everything I have to say because I'm too old. If only we could all remain middle-aged for ever, then they would carve our every sentence into stone.'

'I don't want to wait that long, Gore,' said Maurice, who, Gore noted, had not been invited to use his given name but was apparently not planning to stand on ceremony.

'Come with me, Mr Swift,' said Gore, smiling, and then, perhaps aware that his own teeth did not equal the dazzling brilliance of his young companion's, stopped. He pointed towards the staircase that led into the villa proper. 'Let me show you my library. Dash, you stay down here and relax, I insist upon it. Your face is quite flushed and I'll be damned if I'm going to be calling any ambulances to collect you later.'

Upstairs, Gore led the way through the large, airy rooms into the one he had designated for his books and Maurice entered, looking around with appreciable awe as he moved towards the stacks.

'It's like a church,' he whispered.

'A cathedral,' said Gore, who took great pleasure in showing his collection to true aesthetes, and whatever else he might be, it seemed clear from the look on Maurice's face that he was a believer, a young man who felt more comfortable around books than people.

'I could live here,' said Maurice.

'I'd have to charge you rent.'

'Oh, you never know,' replied the boy, turning around and smiling at him. 'Maybe you'd just take pity on me and make me your ward.'

'We're not living in a Victorian novel,' said Gore. Was it any wonder that Dash was completely under his spell? He had an answer for everything and was willing to flirt to assert his dominance.

'You know, the last person to set foot in here was Henry Kissinger,' said Gore, recovering himself slightly as the boy turned away to scan the shelves, hands held behind his back as if he didn't want to leave finger-marks on anything. His lips moved a little as he read the names of the authors and titles under his breath. 'He visited just a few weeks ago and stayed the night. I found him in here at five o'clock in the morning, reading Polybius, *The Rise of the Roman Empire.* He'd still be here right now if his Secret Service detail hadn't insisted that it was time to go.'

The boy turned around and smiled but remained silent, his expression asking, *Are you trying to impress me with such shameless name-dropping?* Gore could name-drop all night, after all, if he had to. He'd known everyone worth knowing and still did. Even now he was almost sixty-five, people came to La Rondinaia on pilgrimages. Politicians, actors, musicians, film-makers, novelists. The Jameses and the Forsters, he called them. The former being his American visitors, the latter being his English. They all romanticized Italy and moved in circles wealthy enough that they could ignore the squalor. They loved the Amalfi Coast for its privacy and it went without saying that they all adored, and feared, Gore.

'I have something over here that might interest you,' he said, reminded now by these thoughts of a particular treasure and strolling over to a wall where two piles of books were separated by a small Picasso that took pride of place in the centre. It took him only a moment to find the one he wanted. 'It's a first edition. You've probably read it.'

'*Maurice,*' said Maurice, flipping it from front cover to back and running his finger along the lettering before opening it to the frontispiece. 'Yes, I've read it. I love Forster. It's signed and dedicated to you,' he added, a look of wonderment spreading across his face now as he looked up. 'You met him, then?'

'Several times,' replied Gore, retrieving both the book and his authority as he opened the volume at a random page, reading aloud the first lines upon which his eyes fell: '*With the crudity of youth he drew his mother apart and said that he should always respect her religious prejudices and those of the girls, but that his own conscience permitted him to attend church no longer. She said it was a great misfortune.* Mothers,' he added. 'My own mother, Nina, started off as an actress, you know. But then she forswore that career to become an alcoholic, a slut and a certifiable lunatic. I don't know why she couldn't have done both. Historically, the two careers have not proved mutually exclusive.'

'You've said that before, haven't you?' asked Maurice, smiling. 'It sounds rehearsed.'

'No,' said Gore, shocked by such a brazen remark. Who on earth did this boy think he was?

'What was he like, anyway?' asked Maurice.

'What was who like?'

'Forster.'

Gore hesitated before answering. He felt a sudden desire to anger-fuck the boy, then toss him over the cliffs into the sea below, to watch as his body bounced off the rocks and his bones smashed into a thousand pieces. 'Prissy,' he said finally, somehow managing to quell his growing temper and sense of discombobulation. 'Mannered. Officious. If the gods had descended from Mount Olympus and used a pitiless blend of blood, bone and skin to craft a creature best suited for spending its days cloistered behind the walls of King's College, Cambridge, then that creature would surely have gone by the name of Morgan. He could barely function in the real world. I daresay he started to tremble and perspire whenever he popped down to his local supermarket to buy toilet paper. Actually, it's rather hard to imagine Morgan using toilet paper, isn't it? One rather suspects that he was too prudish to engage in such a human act as excretion. *Where's Morgan? Oh, he went off to take his morning shit.* No, I can't imagine it at all. Anyway.'

He looked over at Maurice, hoping for a laugh, but the boy simply nodded, which irritated him. He'd thought all of that was rather good and deserved a little more appreciation. It was good form, after all, to laugh at the jokes of one's betters. The Queen's eldest boy, that otter-like cuckold breathlessly longing for his own ascension, had come to dinner one evening the previous year and Gore had laughed at *all* his jokes, despite the fact that the man was about as humorous as a member of the Sonderkommando. He'd barely eaten, he remembered that about him too, pushing a very good piece of fish around his plate as if he were searching for a piece of broccoli under which to hide it.

'I don't suppose your parents named you for him, did they?' he asked, returning the book to its allotted place on the shelf.

'No,' replied Maurice, shaking his head. 'No, they weren't readers. I doubt they'd ever even heard of Forster.'

'That's a Yorkshire tone to your voice, isn't it?' he asked. 'But you're trying to shake it off by doing a poor impression of an announcer from the BBC World Service.'

'I'm not trying to shake anything off,' said Maurice. 'But yes, I'm from Harrogate. Although I've spoken this way since I was a child.'

'You've wanted it that long, then?' said Gore quietly, and the question might have been a rhetorical one.

'I'm sorry?'

'It doesn't matter. I wonder what else I can show you that you might appreciate.'

He turned and walked around the library, looking for something appropriately impressive. 'What were you reading on your journey here, by the way?' he asked.

'Dash's new novel. He gave it to me when we met at Heathrow. I already had something in my bag that I'd been looking forward to but I had to set it aside.'

'How incredibly crass. Do you mean to tell me that you sat on a flight next to each other – I'm assuming you sat next to each other – and were forced to read his book while he watched you turn the pages? And then on the train from Rome too?'

'Yes,' said Maurice.

'Pathetic behaviour,' said Gore dismissively. 'It reminds me of an occasion when I agreed to meet another novelist for dinner in Cologne, a mediocre hack if I'm honest. He deliberately kept me waiting in the lobby of his hotel, possibly to assert some sort of dominance over me, and when he finally deigned to appear he was carrying a book with him, one of his own, and he claimed he'd been re-reading it on the flight. *What an ass*, I thought. Still, I suppose someone had to read the damned thing. It's not as if the general public took to it.'

He waited for Maurice to ask who the novelist had been and, when the question didn't arrive, he felt a mixture of disappointment and frustration.

'What did you think of it, anyway?' he asked. 'Dash's book, I mean.'

'It's not one of his better ones,' replied Maurice quickly. 'I still have three hundred pages to go too. I'd give up if it weren't for the fact that he'll want a full report later.'

Gore smiled and tapped his finger on the desk. Interesting, he thought. How easily the boy mocks his benefactor.

'I should have asked,' he said. 'What was the book you were intending to read?'

'*Myra Breckinridge*,' said Maurice, and Gore couldn't help himself. He burst out laughing.

'Oh, my dear boy,' he said. 'You are good at this, aren't you? I can see you're going to be a tremendous success.'

Over dinner, the discussion turned to Maurice's novel. Gore had avoided making any direct reference to it all afternoon but Howard, who had returned home in disarray, having had his wallet stolen in a café before unsuccessfully chasing the thief through the streets of Ravello, asked when it would be published.

'Oh, but it's already out,' said Dash, delighted that the conversation was turning to his protégé at last, which was far more appealing to him than the lecture on the Emperor Galba that Gore had been delivering for almost forty minutes. 'The British edition, that is. And some of the European ones. But the Americans don't publish until September. That's where you come in, Gore.'

'Me?' asked Gore, lifting a prawn from his plate and shelling it in a trio of expert movements before dipping the crustacean in Cassiopeia's excellent chilli dressing and popping it into his mouth. There were hundreds of reasons for spending the autumn of one's life on the Amalfi Coast but the quality of the seafood was near the top of that list. 'What have I got to do with anything?'

'We thought you might offer an endorsement. You don't mind our asking, do you?'

'We being . . . ?'

'Maurice and I.'

'Dash, please,' said Maurice, doing his best to look uncomfortable but proving himself an imperfect actor.

'Is that what you hoped for, Maurice?' asked Gore, turning to the boy and looking him directly in the eye. 'Did you hope that I might endorse your novel?'

'Actually, I'd prefer if you didn't,' he replied.

'Maurice!' cried Dash, appalled.

'Really?' said Gore, equally surprised by this remark. 'May I ask why?'

'Because I wouldn't want you to think that's the only reason I came here tonight. When Dash suggested you might host us for dinner, I knew I would cancel anything on my calendar in order to attend. I've been an admirer of yours for many years and the opportunity to meet you in person was one that was too good to pass up. But I wouldn't want you to think that I came here only to exploit your good nature.'

Gore couldn't help but laugh at the suggestion. Many outrageous things had been said about him over the years, after all, thousands of unkind comments from the likes of Truman, Harper, Norman, Buckley, Tricky Dick, Updike and all the rest of them, but no one had ever had the bad manners to accuse him of having a good nature. He glanced towards Howard, who was smiling too as he poured more wine.

'So how about I say that, even if you were to offer an endorsement, I would reject it,' continued Maurice.

'If your editor could hear you now, he'd put a gag across your mouth.'

'Of course, should you find the time to read my novel, I'd be very interested to know what you make of it. In a private capacity, of course. Man to man.'

Gore sipped his drink and, for once, felt stuck for words. Exactly what game was the boy playing? It was difficult to decipher. Was he serious when he said that he would turn down a quote from him if one was offered and, if so, was that an insult or a compliment? Perhaps, he thought, his name no longer held enough weight to warrant a sentence or two across the dust jacket of a debut novel. If that was the case, then it might be time to leave Italy and return to public life. Or did the boy not want the patronage of a man Gore's age, preferring the support of younger, more fashionable writers? A weight of sorrow fell upon him and, as he reached for another prawn, he changed his mind and dropped it back into the bowl with its fellows, his appetite destroyed.

'What's your novel about, anyway?' asked Howard, sitting back in his chair and looking at Maurice with an expression that suggested he would have no objection to the boy slowly removing his clothes as he answered.

'It's about Erich Ackermann,' said Dash, leaning forward enthusiastically, his face lighting up with the enthusiasm of a fat man at an all-you-can-eat buffet.

'Who's Erich Ackermann?'

'*Dread*,' said Gore. 'You've read it.'

'Have I?'

'Yes, you admired it.'

'All right.' Howard considered this for a moment. 'He wasn't the fellow we met at that festival in Jaipur, was he? With the moustache and the pipe? The one who kept bursting into song at inappropriate moments?'

'No, that was Günter Grass.'

'Oh yes. I liked him.'

Gore raised an eyebrow. He wasn't wild about Howard liking other writers, particularly eminent ones. Although he didn't much care for him liking younger writers either, those whose eminence was only imminent.

'Actually, it's not *about* Erich Ackermann,' interrupted Maurice, a note of irritation in his voice. 'Seriously, Dash, I wish you'd stop saying that. It's a novel, after all. A work of fiction. Not a biography.'

'You've written a novel that features Erich Ackermann as a character?' asked Howard.

'I suppose that's a reasonable way of putting it, yes.'

'And does he mind?'

'He hasn't said one way or the other.'

'Did you have to ask his permission?'

'No.'

'Isn't there some sort of moral conflict there then?' asked Howard.

'None whatsoever,' said Dash. 'There can be no discussion of morality when it comes to art. A writer must tell the story that captures his soul. Gore's written about Aaron Burr, after all. And Lincoln. And the Emperor Julian.'

'Yes, but they're all long dead. Ackermann is still alive, isn't he?'

'He teaches in Cambridge,' said Gore. 'Just like Morgan did back in the day.'

'Not any more,' said Maurice. 'He left. Before they could dismiss him.'

'Oh, I hadn't heard. Driven out, no doubt, by the forces of the politically correct and the righteously indignant. Poor Erich.'

'He lives in Berlin now.'

'Back where his story began.'

'Poor Erich?' repeated Dash, leaning forward on the table. 'Gore, did you just say, *Poor Erich*? Haven't you kept up with the news? Don't you know what he did?'

'I've read a few things,' replied Gore dismissively. 'Some columns in the papers, and I glanced at a typically fatuous essay that Wolfe wrote for the *New York Review of Books*. And as far as I can tell, half the world's novelists have chimed in with their opinions, which has provided each one with their intended few minutes of publicity. How competitive everyone is in expressing their outrage! As far as I can tell, Bellow is the only one who's said anything sensible on the subject.'

'Why, what did he say?' asked Maurice. 'I haven't heard.'

'That he didn't give a flying fuck what Ackermann did when he was a boy. All he was interested in was the man's books.'

'So much for solidarity,' said Dash, disgusted.

'Solidarity among whom?' asked Gore. 'Jews? Jewish writers? Old men? With whom is he supposed to share this unanimity of spirit? The fact is that we all have skeletons in our closets, histories of which we would prefer the world to remain ignorant. You should know some of the things that I did as a boy. Or that Howard did. And I daresay you were no saint either, Dash.'

'No, but I never sent a family of Jews to the gas chambers.'

'But it's a matter of perspective, surely,' said Gore calmly, picking at his food again. In debate, his appetite had returned. 'Had you, Howard or I been nineteen years old and living in Herr Hitler's Germany, where the boys gathered to march their marches and salute their salutes, filing through the streets in their handsome Hugo Boss uniforms, their hair reeking of pomade beneath striking caps, their bodies crackling like wet firewood under the weight of their exploding hormones, wouldn't we have signed up for the

Hitlerjugend too, before graduating to the Wehrmacht? I was born in West Point, for heaven's sake. I was a military brat. It's all just a circumstance of birth, isn't it? Ackermann was doing his duty by his country. Should we criticize him for that? Why, even young Maurice here might have betrayed his friends had he been alive at that time.'

'I don't believe I would have,' said Maurice, shaking his head.

'It's easy to say when the question is a hypothetical one. There are people who will sacrifice anyone and anything to get ahead, after all. They're rather easy to spot if you know the signs to watch out for.' An uncomfortable silence ensued, during which Gore looked rather pleased with himself, Howard appeared amused, Dash seemed outraged and Maurice looked entirely out of his depth. 'Of course, I'm talking about Ackermann,' added Gore eventually. 'Not you, dear boy. I'm sure you're a fellow of great integrity.'

'And have any of Ackermann's friends stepped up to defend his reputation?' asked Howard.

'No one would have the gall,' said Dash.

'What was it Woodrow Wilson said?' asked Gore. 'That loyalty means nothing unless it has at its heart the absolute principle of self-sacrifice? Something along those lines?'

'And you think other writers should sacrifice themselves for the likes of Erich Ackermann?' asked Dash. 'Would you?'

'Probably not. But then I barely know the man.'

'Well, then.'

A silence descended on the table, a mutual understanding that, were they to pursue this topic, the evening could end in an argument that no one had the stomach for. Howard opened another bottle of wine, poured a fresh drink for everyone, and the clinking of their glasses determined the end of that particular conversation.

'Can I ask how long you two have been together?' asked Howard when the silence became uncomfortable, looking back and forth between Dash and Maurice.

'Well, it's difficult to put an exact—' began Dash.

'We're not together,' said Maurice, speaking over him. 'We're friends, certainly. But that's all.'

'You're not lovers?' asked Gore.

'We're friends,' repeated Maurice.

'But you've been lovers? In the past, I mean?'

'These are such personal questions.'

'Are they? I don't see why. You're not a child and we're not gathered together at the annual convention of Stick-up-your-ass Puritans. There's nothing so peculiar about being lovers, is there? What say you, Dash?'

'As Maurice says,' replied Dash quietly, looking crestfallen, almost as if he might cry. 'We're friends. Very good friends. We care enormously for each other.'

'It doesn't matter a damn to Howard or me, you understand,' said Gore. 'So there's no particular reason for secrecy. But if you want to keep the nature of your relationship ambiguous, feel free. Although I can't help but think it's a little ridiculous. It's 1990, after all.'

'From a purely logistical point of view,' said Howard, 'we need to know whether you require separate rooms tonight. Naturally, Gore and I assumed that you'd be two gentlemen sharing.'

'If you only have one prepared,' said Dash, 'then please don't put yourself to any trouble on our behalf. I'm happy to share if—'

'Separate rooms, please,' said Maurice, looking at Howard. 'I wouldn't want to keep Dash awake with my snoring.'

'But you don't snore,' said Dash.

'Ah,' said Gore with a smile, winking at Dash, who blushed scarlet then looked up at his host, biting his lower lip.

'I'll let Cassiopeia know,' said Gore, ringing a bell and passing some instructions in Italian to the maid who appeared on the terrace above them. 'Anyway, whatever your arrangement is, I'm sure it's a very sensible one. Howard and I have always maintained separate rooms and we find it a very satisfying way to live. Dash, will you have some more wine?'

'No thank you, Gore,' said Dash.

'You look upset. Has someone said something to distress you?'

'No, I'm just tired, that's all.'

Gore softened a little. Dash was a fool and, worse, a mediocrity in his chosen profession, but there was no reason for him to be so ill-used by a child he'd taken under his wing. He had known boys like Maurice all his life. When he was young and starting to make his way in books, they'd come crawling out of the wood-work, attaching themselves to him, and then, once they made a name for themselves, dropping him without a second thought. At first, their Machiavellian ways had proved hurtful. Then, for some time, it had simply been annoying. But soon enough he mastered the rules of the game and used the boys purely for sex, giving them nothing in return, throwing them out before they had an oppor-tunity to ask for favours. If only Dash could be so shrewd. Time to cheer him up a little, thought Gore.

'By the way,' he said, 'I meant to tell you that I've read your new novel.'

'You have?' asked Dash, looking up hopefully.

'Yes. It's your best in many years, if you don't mind me saying so. I thought I might write a little notice about it for the *New Yorker*, if that's all right with you. Something to recommend it to readers.'

'That would be very kind of you,' said Dash. 'Every little helps, as you know.'

'Maurice was telling me earlier that he was reading it on the plane,' said Gore.

'Yes, I must admit I was flattered when he plucked it out of his bag as we took our seats.'

Gore, lifting his wine glass, set it down and looked from Maurice to Dash and back to Maurice again.

'You brought the novel with you?' asked Gore.

'Of course, I posted him a copy upon publication,' continued Dash. 'But I know how busy he is and didn't expect him to find the time to read it.'

'I thought you said that Dash gave it to you at the airport,' said Gore, looking at the boy.

'You must have misunderstood,' said Maurice. 'I said that there were many copies of it in the airport bookshop.'

'Is that what you said?' asked Gore. 'I remember differently.'

'It's a fine piece of work, Dash,' said Maurice, turning to his bene-factor. 'Very moving and insightful on the ways of the flesh. I hope to be able to write as well as you one day.'

Dash looked around the table proudly, beaming from ear to ear, while Maurice reached for his wine glass and drained it in one go. Gore enjoyed the look on the boy's face at that moment, although it was almost impossible to interpret exactly what he was thinking. Why, he thought, he could write a thousand words on that expression alone.

He discovered Dash walking the grounds early the following morn-ing, when Howard and Maurice were still asleep. Gore usually took a walk at this time of day, immediately following his bath, the morning air clearing his mind of the fog that lingered from the night before. In recent times his dreams had become disturbing and his sleep more fretful, a condition he put down to looming old age. He would be sixty-five this year. Pensionable. Neither of his parents had made it past seventy-four and the idea that he had less than a decade to live was alarming to him. There were still so many books to write and, although he feigned indifference to the current publishing world, so many that he wanted to read.

Sometimes he wondered who would go first, he or Howard. Wasn't there something in *Wuthering Heights* about Heathcliff want-ing Cathy to die before him so she wouldn't have to go through the trauma of a life spent alone? Or was it the other way around? He couldn't remember. It had been so long since he'd read the novel. But the line was in there somewhere. Do I want Howard to die before me? he asked himself now; and *no* came the unequivocal answer. *Let me go first*, he muttered, appealing to the gods. Let him deal with the loneliness. In ancient times, a sacrifice would have been offered for such petitions. An animal slaughtered and its vital organs burnt upon an altar while the priest wore a mask to prevent himself from witnessing evil rising in the smoke. For a brief moment, he considered how easy it would be to set out a dais at La Rondinaia and how he could procure a young lamb from one of the village boys, but then shook his head, laughing at the absurdity of the notion. Howard would have him committed if he came out to discover him dressed like a monk and chanting incantations on the terrace.

He spotted Dash strolling where the garden met the cliff-face, cutting a ridiculous figure in a garish Hawaiian shirt and shorts that revealed pale, hairless legs. Gore's first instinct was to walk back towards the villa, where he could breakfast in solitude, but his friend's dejected gait and unhappy expression persuaded him to walk in his direction.

'Mio amico,' he said, raising a hand in greeting, and Dash smiled back, nodding gloomily. He looked tired and Gore suspected that he hadn't slept well. Cassiopeia had put Dash and Maurice in adjoining rooms, only a thin wall separating the beds from each other, and it was possible that he had heard the young man rising in the night as he went about the business of ambition.

'Hello, Gore,' said Dash. 'It's a beautiful morning, isn't it?'

Gore didn't reply for he hated talking about the weather and despised people who did so. But his step fell in time with Dash and they walked in silence at first, looking at the wild flowers as they made their way in the direction of the olive groves and the vineyard.

'You're lucky to live in so beautiful a place,' said Dash eventually.

'I am,' admitted Gore. 'I don't believe I could ever leave.'

'Don't you miss America?'

'Not particularly. I've had enough of America to last me ten

JOHN BOYNE

lifetimes. It's not the country it was. Occasionally I even find myself missing Nixon and, when things have reached that point, it's time to wave goodbye.'

Dash smiled. 'Who do you see?' he asked. 'From the past, I mean?'

'Everyone. Sometimes when I'm awake, sometimes when I'm asleep. I was sure that I could sense Nina here last month, even though she's been dead more than ten years.' He paused, reached down for a stone and threw it casually into the greenery. 'Jackie comes when she's in Italy, which is good of her. She and Lee visited together last year, in fact. We got drunk and took turns seeing who could make the most vulgar comments about George Bush.'

'Who won?'

'The Princess Radziwill, of course. She may be a terrible actress but she knows more dirty jokes than a sailor and her delivery is always pitch-perfect.'

Dash said nothing as Gore cocked his head back a little, closing his eyes and breathing the scent of the flowers deep into his lungs.

'You're working on something new, I suppose?' Dash asked after a while, and Gore nodded.

'A compendium of my essays,' he told him.

'*All* your essays?'

'Well, a lot of them, anyway. It'll be a big book.'

'Will you come home to promote it?'

'My dear Dash, I *am* home.'

'You know what I mean.'

'I expect so,' said Gore. 'I may even stay for a month or two. Catch up with whoever's still alive and terrified of running into me.' In the olden days, of course, he would have been invited to stay in the White House when he was visiting Washington but there was precious little chance of that now. He'd slept in the Lincoln Bedroom dozens of times when Jack and Jackie were in charge. Never under Lyndon, who'd frozen him out because he didn't like the idea of a queer sullying the bedsheets. Twice under Tricky Dick,

116

including a night where they'd got drunk on whisky and ended up making midnight raids on the kitchen, like a pair of teenage boys, leading Pat to come down and give them a thoroughly enjoyable scolding. Ford had never liked him, Carter had never understood him and Reagan had never approved of him. Bush, he assumed, had never even heard of him. So that was that, he was certain, until a cultured Democrat, if such a thing still existed, got elected again. 'Shall we sit?' he asked, indicating a bench that stood beneath the shade of an olive tree, facing in the direction of the coastline.

'What plants are these?' asked Dash, pointing to a cluster of bright pink five-leaved flowers with serrated edges that resembled the hem of a debutante's ballgown.

'Yes, they're pretty, aren't they?' said Gore. 'But you'd have to check with Howard. He's the gardener. Are you in love with the boy, Dash? Is that what this is all about?'

His companion didn't seem surprised by the question or by how suddenly it had been asked. He swallowed and looked down at the ground, where an elongated family of ants were scuttling past in single file, and nodded.

'It's ridiculous, I know,' he said. 'I'm fifty-eight years old, after all.'

'And what is he?'

'Twenty-four.'

'Is he a bugger? It's hard to tell. He was so enigmatic on the subject over dinner last night.'

'I think Maurice is whatever he needs to be, whenever he needs to be it. He's an operator, that's for sure. And I don't much like him, Gore, if I'm honest. Sometimes I think I might hate him. He's rude and unkind, utterly self-centred, and treats me like a dog. But I can't seem to break away from him. When we're together, I'm in torment, but when we're apart he's all that I can think about. I wonder who he's with and what he's doing and whether he's thinking of me at all. It wasn't like that when we met, of course. I had the upper hand then. I'm . . . well, I am what I am.'

'A successful writer,' said Gore, placing a hand on his friend's arm. 'And a good one too. A rare dyad.'

'A competent one,' said Dash, offering a half-smile. 'Let's not pretend otherwise. I can write, yes, but I won't be remembered. Not like you. My books lack whatever alchemy is needed to ensure immortality. You'll be read when we're both worm food, Gore. I won't.'

Gore said nothing. This was an accurate representation of the future, as far as he was concerned, and he had no wish to patronize his friend by pretending otherwise.

'When I first met him,' continued Dash, 'it was as if every nerve in my body became alert to his presence. I couldn't take my eyes off him and when I approached him—'

'Where was this?' asked Gore.

'In the Prado.' He laughed and shook his head. 'I know, it's the stuff of clichés. Like something out of a terrible Hollywood film.'

'There's no other sort, as far as I can tell, these days,' said Gore. 'What room was he in?'

'What?'

'Maurice. When you discovered him. Do you remember what room he was in? What he was looking at?'

'The El Grecos. He was wearing white trousers and a navy shirt, the colour of which matched his shoes. He wore no socks and his cologne contained a scent of lavender. He was carrying a rather nice shoulder bag, leather and cream, and a copy of that morning's *El País*, featuring a large photograph of Felipe González on the front page, pointing a finger at Francisco Ordóñez.'

'Oh, my dear Dash,' said Gore, shaking his head sadly. 'You do have it bad, don't you?'

'Of course, he was with Erich at the time.'

'With him in what sense?'

'It's hard to know, although I'm reasonably certain that nothing physical happened between them. He was simply using him the same way he's been using me. Poor Erich was in love with him too, of course.'

'You chastised me last night for using the phrase *Poor Erich.*'

Dash shrugged. 'Perhaps I'm feeling rather better disposed towards him today. He probably went through the same level of torment that I've been going through over the last couple of years.'

'He doesn't let you touch him, does he?' asked Gore, and Dash shook his head. 'And nor does he touch you?'

Dash said nothing, simply staring into the distance, watching the spin and roll of the early morning waves.

'I don't quite see it,' said Gore when it became clear that Dash wasn't going to reply. 'He's good-looking, yes. He has an undeniable sex appeal and he's aware of the power of his beauty. Too aware, some might say. But so do most boys his age. What's so special about him? What is it that you and Erich see in him that I'm missing?'

'I don't know,' admitted Dash. 'But whatever it is, I'm enslaved to it. As was Erich, I'm certain. I was so incredibly jealous when I first encountered them together. I assumed that Maurice was just some trick that Ackermann had picked up on his travels. But I quickly realized that their relationship was more complicated than I'd initially understood it to be. I wanted to break them up from the moment we met and, once I put it into Maurice's head that he'd gained everything he could from mentor number one, it wasn't difficult to persuade him to move on to mentor number two. Someone with an "in" on the New York literary scene. Which Erich never really had, even after *Dread.*'

'And, what? He just dropped Ackermann?'

'Like a red-hot coal. Erich was devastated. Maurice didn't tell me much, he can be rather discreet when he wants to be, but it wasn't long before the poor man's life fell apart.'

'But surely that was due to the revelations in Maurice's book?'

'I think he could have fought his way through them if he'd wanted to,' said Dash. 'But I suspect he didn't have the energy for the battle, not without the boy by his side.'

'And since then?'

'Well, Maurice's novel has been a tremendous success. He's much in demand, the hot young star of London literary circles, while I'm nothing more than the desperate old fag whose best work is behind him, trotting around after a young boy with his tongue hanging out, humiliating himself more and more at every turn. There are times that I wish he was dead or that I was dead or that we both were dead. Yesterday, while we were driving up the road to your house, I gave serious thought to tipping us both over the edge into the sea. But I couldn't do it, of course.'

Gore reached over and took Dash's hand in a gesture of friend-ship, squeezing it tightly.

'And what happens next?' he asked. 'When you leave today, I mean?'

'I don't know,' said Dash. 'He's going back to London, he's already working on his next novel. I offered to accompany him but he said he'd prefer if I didn't. He told me he'd catch up with me the next time he was in New York. *Catch up with me!* I suppose I'll just go home and wait for him. There's nothing else I can do.'

'Will you start work on a new book?'

'I'll try. It's hard to imagine being able to focus on a novel when I feel so overwhelmed by desire.'

'You know he won't come, though, don't you?'

'Yes.'

'You know that when he says goodbye today, it will most likely be for ever?'

'I know.'

He sighed and watched as a bird landed on one of the flowers, investigating its stamen for a few moments before looking up, its beak quivering slightly.

Movement on the terrace caught Gore's eye. Two men, walking towards the breakfast table.

'They're up,' said Gore. 'Should we go back?'

'I suppose so.'

They rose and started to walk towards the villa.

'Did you ever wish you had a wife?' asked Dash. 'Did you ever wish that you could just have lived a normal life instead of suffering the endless pain that men like us undergo, falling for beautiful boys who will never stay with us, no matter what we do for them?'

'No,' said Gore, shaking his head. 'No, I've never wished that for a moment. The very idea seems hellish to me.'

Ahead, Maurice was leaning over the railing, watching them approach, and, Gore thought, enjoying how Howard was staring at him from behind. He was shirtless, his muscles glistening in the sunlight, the definition of his abdomen startling and his hair, still wet from the shower, brushed away from his forehead.

'That line from *Villette*,' said Dash quietly. 'How does it go? *Where is the use of caring for him so very much? He is full of faults.*'

'Funny,' said Gore, laughing a little. 'I was thinking about *Wuthering Heights* earlier, just before we met. You know you've gone off the deep end when you start obsessing about the Brontës.'

The bedroom door was ajar and he pushed it open wordlessly, watching as the boy lifted the shirt he'd worn the night before from a chair and folded it carefully before placing it in his suitcase.

'Gore,' said Maurice, looking up and smiling. 'How long have you been standing there?'

'Not long,' replied Gore, stepping inside and closing the door behind him. 'You don't mind if I come in, do you?' he added, his tone making it clear that he didn't much care whether the boy minded or not.

'Not at all. I was just finishing packing.'

'You slept well?' he asked, sitting down heavily in a wicker arm-chair by the window and crossing his legs.

'Very well, thank you.'

'Greta Garbo slept in that bed once, back when we lived in Rome,' said Gore, glancing around the room as if he were checking the inventory. The paintings were still hanging on the walls. The *objets d'art* seemed to be still in place. 'So did Bettino Craxi. Nelson Rockefeller. Princess Margaret. Here in Ravello, it's played host to Paul Simon, Edmund White. Paul and Joanne. The list goes on. It makes one wonder, doesn't it?'

'Makes one wonder what?' asked Maurice.

'How *you*,' said Gore, pointing a finger at the boy, 'ended up sleeping in it. A Yorkshire lad, barely in his twenties, with not much to show for his life so far.'

'Well, except a fairly successful novel.'

'Yes, but I'm not sure that means very much any more.'

Maurice rolled his eyes and Gore felt a stab of irritation. He was a giant and would not be dismissed by a boy who had barely started to shave. 'You're not going to tell me that literature is over, are you?' Maurice said. 'We've argued that point already.'

'I wasn't going to say anything of the sort,' replied Gore, trying to control his annoyance. 'You must remember that I published *Williwaw* when I was nineteen. And I was only your age when *The City and the Pillar* appeared, provoking a scandal. E. P. Dutton told me that I'd never be forgiven for it and for years the *New York Times* blacklisted me and wouldn't review any of my books. I had to go to work in Hollywood to earn my living on account of their puritanism. And believe me, you don't know what it's like to roll around in the shit until you find yourself driving in and out of a studio gate every day.'

'I have no interest in film,' said Maurice carelessly. 'I only want to write novels.'

'So, no, literature is far from over,' continued Gore, ignoring the interruption. 'What you're doing to Dash, you know. It's deeply unkind.'

'I don't know what you're talking about.'

'Of course you do. Don't play the fool.'

'And have you always been kind, Gore? Because from what I've read about you, I suspect that you've hurt many people along the way.'

'That's probably true. But I don't believe I've ever deliberately set out to ruin a man. No, I don't believe I've ever done that.'

Maurice said nothing, but returned to his packing.

'But you haven't answered my question,' said Gore.

'What question was that?'

'How a young man like you ended up sleeping in a bed like that.'

'Howard told me to use it. He said it was more comfortable than the one he was giving Dash.'

Gore smiled. 'Some might say that your mentor should have been assigned the better room.'

Maurice frowned. 'I'm not sure I'd describe Dash as my mentor.'

'No? How would you describe him then?'

'I told you last night. A friend. Someone I admire. He's a good writer, is Dash.'

'*He's a good writer, is Dash,*' repeated Gore, mimicking the sudden appearance of the boy's accent. 'Be careful, Maurice. Your roots are showing.'

'Yes, and that's all he'll ever be. Let's not pretend he's Proust.'

'No, he's not Proust,' admitted Gore. 'But he's shown a generosity of spirit towards you for which you should feel grateful.'

'And I do,' said Maurice. 'Have I done something to make you think otherwise?'

'The way you look at him. The contempt with which you treat him. How you keep him dangling on a string, desperate for some affectionate word from you. I assume you're finished with him now and are ready to move on to pastures new?'

Maurice shrugged. 'I think so,' he said. 'My life has become rather busy of late. And Dash can be . . . How shall I put this? Very needy. It becomes exhausting after a while.'

'I can only imagine. I have to hand it to you: you know what you want out of life and you're determined to get it. Perhaps I wasn't so very different to you when I was your age. Although I was better-looking, of course.'

Maurice smiled. 'I've seen the pictures,' he said. 'And yes, you were.'

'So, is this it?' asked Gore. 'Being a writer. This is all you've ever wanted? There's nothing else?' Maurice hesitated, and Gore noticed him biting his lip. Was there a weakness in there somewhere, a chink in the boy's armour? 'There is something, isn't there?' he said. 'There's something more that you want? I took you for utterly single-minded, but no. Tell me, I'm intrigued.'

'You'll laugh,' said Maurice.

'I won't.'

'It will seem ridiculous.'

'Probably. But everything seems ridiculous to me these days.'

'I'd like a child,' said Maurice.

'A child?'

'Yes, a child.'

Gore sat back in his chair, his eyes opening wide. 'A *child*?' he repeated.

'God, is it so unusual?'

Gore stared at the boy, uncertain what to make of this declaration. 'I thought I could see right through you,' he said finally. 'But I must admit I hadn't expected that. What on earth do you want a child for? What good is a squealing infant to anyone? They demand instant attention. A puppy, I could understand. But a child? Really?'

Maurice shook his head and smiled. 'You wouldn't understand,' he said. 'You've obviously never wanted one.'

'I don't even like passing them in the street. Children are banned here at La Rondinaia.'

'Well, there you are. You met me for the first time twenty-four hours ago, Gore. Don't presume to understand me. You don't.'

'All right. But you know what they say in Italy, yes? *Quando dio vuole castigarci, ci manda quello che desideriamo.*'

'Which means?'

'When the gods wish to punish us, they answer our prayers.'

A long silence ensued, one that neither man seemed keen to break. Gore could scarcely remember any of his writer colleagues over the years talking about children. Not even the women. *Especially* not the women.

'Well,' he said finally, unwilling to leave the room while he was still one game down. 'You know, I stayed up late last night.'

'Oh yes?'

'Yes, I decided to read your novel.'

Maurice sat down on the bed now and ran a hand across his chin, looking a little apprehensive. 'All right,' he said. 'And what did you think of it?'

Gore glanced up towards the ceiling for a few moments as he considered his answer. 'You write well,' he said. 'You're very good on place. The dialogue rings true, even though it must have been difficult for you to recreate it from such a distance of time and geography. I struggled with that too on *Burr* and *Lincoln*, but you work through it successfully. Perhaps you're a little too fond of alliteration and you've clearly never met a noun that you didn't think would look better all dressed up in an adjective. But there's a strong erotic element to the book that works very well. The moment where Erich and his friend go to the lake and Oskar strips off, it's rather arousing on a purely physical level.'

'I wanted to write Oskar Gött as shameless about these things.'

'I didn't read him as shameless so much as proud. But also a little naïve. It wouldn't have crossed his mind that Erich wanted to touch him. I liked when they both woke up on the bank afterwards, tumescent, and were uncertain how to explore the moment. Yes, it's a good book, I really can't offer any major criticisms. I'm not surprised it's doing so well for you.'

'Thank you,' said Maurice, looking relieved. 'It means a lot to hear you say that.'

'Why?'

'I'm sorry?'

'Why does it mean a lot?'

Maurice shrugged, as if the answer was so obvious it was hardly worth pointing out. 'Well, because you're you, of course. And I'm only me.'

'And what does it mean for me to be me and for you to be you? What is it that you think separates us, other than forty years?'

'You're a significant figure in twentieth-century literature. You'll be remembered.'

'Will I?'

'Yes, I think so. I'm certain of it.'

Gore smiled. 'Dash said something similar to me earlier,' he said. 'Although to be honest, I couldn't give a fuck whether I am or not.'

Maurice smiled too and shook his head. His teeth were gleaming white. 'I don't believe that for a moment,' he said.

'*Sic transit gloria mundi*,' said Gore.

'*All glory is fleeting*. Erich used the same line with me once. When we were in Rome.'

Gore's smile faded a little now. He hadn't expected the boy to know what the words meant. Nor did he enjoy repeating the lines of others. He needed to be first, always first.

'Last night,' he said.

'What of it?'

'It must have been three or four o'clock. I'd finished reading and switched my light off. And then the strangest thing happened.'

Maurice looked at him, his expression controlled. 'And what was that?' he asked.

'Very quietly, the door to my bedroom opened and a figure stepped inside, dressed only in a red bathrobe. He closed the door behind him and walked across to the window before turning around and looking down on me. I opened my eyes and wondered whether I was lost in the midst of a dream. I've had such dreams in the past, you know. Of boys I've known, boys I've never known and boys I've wanted to know. Anyway, the moonlight was entering the room in such a way that the figure was only half illuminated but when he removed his robe, letting it fall to the floor, he was naked underneath, his body a work of art. Michelangelo might have sculpted it and failed to capture its beauty. The fierce definition of the pectoral muscles. The stomach so lean. The impressive member that lay between the boy's legs, apparently ready to offer pleasure if given a signal of consent.'

'And what did you do?' asked Maurice.

'I turned over,' said Gore. 'Not to invite the figure into my bed, you understand. But to make it clear that I had no interest in him.'

'Perhaps you'll live to regret saying no,' said Maurice, standing up and gathering the remainder of his belongings, not bothering to fold them now, simply tossing them carelessly into his case. 'One day it might feel like a lost opportunity.'

'Don't get me wrong,' admitted Gore. 'I'm not made of stone, so I considered it. But I resisted because I'm not a fool. I feel rather pleased with myself this morning that I said no. Something tells me that, had I lifted the covers and invited the figure in, my life would have taken an unhappy turn afterwards.'

'Maybe you ate some rotten cheese before you went to bed,' said Maurice.

'We didn't have any cheese.'

'Then perhaps you're just losing your mind.'

'Oh, I've been doing that for years. But not long enough not to recognize when I'm being played.'

'You think I've been playing you?'

'I think you came here hoping to. And have been disappointed to find that I'm not such an easy mark. Erich Ackermann was one thing, a pussycat I imagine. And Dash, what is he? A tomcat. Slinking around the neighbourhood, hoping for a little night-luck. But I'm a different beast entirely, aren't I? I'm a lion. I belong in the jungle. And so, I suspect, do you. This is why things could never work between us.'

Maurice said nothing but walked to the window and stared out at the view. The sea was calm but, from somewhere beneath the cliffs, the playful sounds of young swimmers could be heard. When he turned around again, his face was cold.

'You're probably just having sex dreams because you're not getting any,' he said. 'It's not as if anyone in their right mind would want to fuck Howard, after all.'

'My dear boy, that's not how things are between us,' said Gore, momentarily thrown off guard. 'Don't imagine you understand what goes on between Howard and me because you don't. What exists between us runs far deeper than sex.'

'I'm glad to hear it,' said Maurice. 'I mean, the image of two fat old men writhing around on top of each other, tugging at each other's limp old cocks, would rather make me want to throw up.'

'Dash might be a fool,' said Gore, rising from his chair now and making his way towards the door, shocked to realize that he was more susceptible to insults than he had imagined. Better men than Maurice had abused him over the decades and he'd never given a tuppenny damn before. 'And Ackermann might have been a fool too, for all I know. But I'm not. So do me the courtesy of remembering that when you reconstruct the events of last night in whatever medium you choose, portraying yourself as the innocent victim of an old man's lecherous advances.'

Maurice said nothing, simply stared at him as if he'd grown tired of this entire conversation.

'I've known a lot of whores in my life,' added Gore, running his hand along the red bathrobe that hung on the bedroom door before stepping outside into the corridor. 'Both men and women. And in general, I've always found them to be good company, with a highly evolved sense of honour. A whore will never cheat you, they have too much integrity for that. But you, Mr Swift, you give the profession a bad name.' He shuddered as he glanced around the room, unwilling to look the boy in the eye for fear of what he might see there, disinterest being the worst horror. 'I'll be out on the terrace in a few minutes to wave you both off. I'm looking forward to say-ing goodbye.'

'So?' asked Howard when they were alone later, sipping cocktails on the terrace, enjoying the eternally rewarding view of the sea. The sailboat and the boys were back – none of them had drowned after all – and this time they had brought some girls with them. They were screaming in delight and desire as they dived from the deck into the water and scrambled up the ladder to do it all over again, pulling up their ill-fitting trunks as they went, a glimpse of white backside occasionally visible against their tanned skin. 'What did you make of him? Handsome, yes?'

'Oh yes,' agreed Gore.

'And Dash is crazy about him.'

'Besotted.'

'Do you think he'll make it?'

'As a writer?' He thought about it and closed his eyes for a moment, trying to imagine a literary world of the future, one that he would no longer be a part of. 'I don't doubt it for a moment,' he said. 'The boy will be an extraordinary success.'

'Good for him,' said Howard.

'One thing,' said Gore. 'The bed in the guest room. The one that Maurice slept in last night. We've had it for so many years. I think it might be time we got rid of it, don't you? Invested in something new?'

PART II

THE TRIBESMAN

'When a thing has been said and said well, have no scruple. Take it and copy it.'

– Anatole France

1. September

It was the early autumn of 2000 and we were marking our fifth wedding anniversary by going out to dinner. We'd only recently arrived in Norwich and were still unfamiliar with the city but you'd done a little research and reserved a table at a restaurant in Tombland that, you told me, had received a positive review in a local newspaper. You looked very handsome that night, I remember, wearing a dark blue jacket with a crisp white shirt underneath, the two top buttons open to reveal a glimpse of your chest. You'd spent the afternoon at the gym and your face had a glow that reminded me of why I'd always found you so irresistible.

I had only been to East Anglia once, when I interviewed for the job, but you had been three times, first to give a talk to the creative-writing students at the university where I would now be working and, later, to take part in a couple of literary festivals.

'Milk-fed calf's intestines with the mother's milk inside,' you said, taking great delight in reading out a rather distasteful item from the menu.

'They don't go out of their way to make it sound appetizing, do they?' I said.

'Oh, I don't know. Could be worth a try.'

'I think I'll have the sea bream,' I said.

'Coward.'

A candle flickered on the table between us and, after we ordered our meals and the wine arrived, you unexpectedly mentioned that you loved me. I could see the flame reflecting in your iris and your eyes appeared so moist that, for a moment, I thought you were going to shed a tear. I'd only ever seen you cry once, after our fourth miscarriage, when we started to realize that things were never going to work out for us on that front.

Of course, you wanted children very badly. You were clear about that from the start and it was something that made you extremely attractive to me. I did too, although perhaps not with the same intensity of feeling. I suppose I'd always assumed that I'd have them one day and so it had been simply a question of when, not if. Only when I began to understand that it was unlikely to happen did I begin to feel cheated. The miscarriages became increasingly traumatic to me then, four lives mercilessly evicted without warning from what my gynaecologist referred to as my inhospitable womb.

'Are you excited about the job?' you asked me after our main courses had been brought, devoured and taken away again and we'd decided to order another bottle of wine.

'I'm a little nervous,' I admitted.

'Of what?'

'Of the students. That they might consider me a fraud.'

'Why on earth would you think that?'

'Because I've only published one novel.'

'Which is one more than all of them combined.'

'I know, but still. It's important to me that they don't feel they've wasted their time and money, that if they'd only come a year or two earlier they would have been taught by someone with more experience.'

'I'm sure they'll be thrilled to have you. You're famous, Edith, after all.'

'I'm hardly famous,' I said dismissively, although it was true, I was a little bit famous because my debut had been such an unexpected success, both critically and commercially. It had even been adapted for television. But I had never taught on a creative-writing course before, nor had I been a student on one, and I wasn't entirely sure how to go about it. I'd only applied for the job because it had been three years since the publication of *Fear* and, even though I was making good progress on my second book, it wasn't coming together quite as quickly as I'd hoped. I thought a stint in academia, where I would be involved in writing every day but not glued to my computer from morning till night, might help me. And you had been very positive about the idea, putting up no objections to our relocating from London for a year. We could sublet the flat, you said. With the rents in Norwich being cheaper, we might even make some money out of the deal.

'They might be arrogant,' I continued, returning to my concerns about the students. 'Particularly the boys.'

'Now you're just being sexist.'

'No, I'm being realistic. I'm only thirty-one. Chances are that some will be close in age to me. They might feel resentful.'

'I think you're worrying over nothing,' you said, dismissing my anxieties with a wave of your hand. 'You have to go in on day one with confidence, that's all. Accept that you've achieved more than they have and that they're there to learn from you. Ignore any condescension.'

'Maybe you could take the class instead of me?' I asked with a smile, knowing as the words emerged from my mouth that it had been the wrong thing to say, for you frowned as you took a long drink of your wine. When you returned the glass to the table, your lips held a faint purple stain that, for some reason, put me in mind of a priest I had known as a child whose lips always had the same tint. He used to come to my school to talk about the importance of keeping ourselves pure for our future husbands and had a particular obsession with a red-haired friend of mine who, he claimed, had the devil lurking inside her.

'They wouldn't want me,' you said. 'They want rising stars, not has-beens.'

'They'd be lucky to have you,' I said.

You threw me a look, one that said *Please don't patronize me*, and I changed the subject immediately. Christmas was still three months away but we discussed where we might spend the day, with your family or mine, settling on yours. And then we talked about my sister, Rebecca, who had recently gone through a messy divorce. There were two children involved, my nephews Damien and Edward, and this only complicated matters as Rebecca was behaving appallingly towards their father, Robert, making it difficult for him to see the boys and then complaining that he didn't spend enough time with them. I'd always liked my brother-in-law and wondered why it had taken him so long to leave my sister, who had spent a lifetime bullying people, including me, but I was obliged to take her side. I confided in you, however, that Robert had phoned me the previous evening and asked whether we might meet to talk.

'To talk about what?' you asked.

'I'm not sure,' I said. 'He said that he'd prefer not to discuss it over the phone and asked whether he could call over to the flat next week. I told him that we weren't there any more, that we'd be up here in Norwich for the next eight months, and he hummed and hawed a bit and said that he could always drive up if I had an afternoon free.'

'I hope you told him no,' you said.

'Well, I didn't know what to say,' I replied. 'It was all so unexpected and he just stayed silent on the phone, waiting for an answer.'

'So you told him yes?'

'I think I did.'

'You *think* you did?'

'All right, I did.'

'Oh, for God's sake, Edith! If Rebecca finds out you've been talking to him, she'll show up here shouting bloody murder and before we know it she won't let us see the boys either.'

'Why should she find out?' I asked.

'Because people always do. It's impossible to keep secrets within a family. Anyway, he's hardly driving all the way to Norwich for a friendly catch-up, is he?'

'I don't know why he's driving here,' I protested. 'Like I told you, he didn't go into details over the phone.'

'Well, it will only lead to trouble, I promise you that. He'll want you to get involved with the custody hearing.'

'Oh, I couldn't possibly do that.'

'Of course you couldn't! But he'll ask you to. He'll want you to talk about all the things your sister has done over the years, about the verbal abuse, about the time she hit him—'

'Christ, do you think so?' I asked, for it had been just over a year since I had run into Robert in a supermarket and seen the black eye discolouring his face and, although he denied it, I knew who had given it to him. She used to hit me too when we were children, even when we were teenagers. Vicious, uncontrollable violence that would burst out of her like lava from a volcano whenever she thought our parents were favouring me over her. She only stopped when I started punching back.

'Well, I'll worry about it when it happens,' I said with a shrug.

We grew silent again and I tried to build my resolve to ask you the question that had been preying on my mind ever since I'd accepted the position at UEA.

'And what about you?' I asked finally. 'Have you decided what you'd like to do while we're here?'

'To do?' you said. 'In what sense?'

'Well, to fill your days,' I replied. 'Are you going to do some writing?'

'What's the point? Publishers aren't exactly beating a path to my door, are they?'

'You could start something new?' I suggested.

'Why would I do that?'

'Because you're a brilliant novelist,' I said, and you looked at me with such a wounded expression that for a moment I thought you were going to stand up and walk out. 'I'm sorry,' I said. 'I never know what to say when this subject comes up. I hate to hear you sounding so defeated.'

The truth was that I hated how unhappy you became whenever we discussed your stalled career and, although you would have grown angry had you known, I pitied you for it too. But more than anything, it just *annoyed* me. I wished you would simply accept that things hadn't turned out as you'd hoped and work to improve them. For God's sake, you were only thirty-four years old! Most writers are just starting their careers at that age! But things had come so easy to you at the start, hadn't they? You were only twenty-four when you published your first novel and probably hadn't been mature enough to cope with the success that *Two Germans* brought your way. And I think even you would agree that you rushed your second, *The Treehouse*, which is why it had been such a disaster. Your third book was turned down because it really wasn't good enough and the three that followed were rejected because by then you were simply throwing ideas at the wall and hoping that one would stick. Which was when you said that you were done with writing for ever. That you'd only ever had one good idea and even that hadn't been yours, it had been someone else's story that you'd simply transcribed, receiving praise not for the quality of the book itself but for how you'd exposed a man with a treacherous past.

And yet when I read the books that followed, I could see why they had been met with failure or rejection, for they were utterly devoid of authenticity. And – the worst crime of all – they were bor-ing. But then, you always said that you struggled when it came to thinking up good ideas, didn't you? That if someone gave you a story, you could write it better than anyone else, but that you needed that basic idea to begin with.

'You shouldn't forget that you love writing,' I said quietly, hoping that you wouldn't overreact to my words.

'I don't,' you replied, pouring another glass of wine for yourself but ignoring my glass, which was almost empty. 'I hate it.'

'That's not true.'

'I think I would know.'

'You hate what writing has done to you, that's all. How it's let you down. But the craft itself, I know you still love it. I *know* you do. From the first day we met you were obsessed with the idea that the world should see you as a writer.'

'What rubbish,' you said.

'I remember you even told me that you thought you might only publish four or five books in your lifetime so the world would take you more seriously.'

'I never said anything of the sort,' you said, shaking your head. 'What kind of narcissistic *knob* would say something like that?'

'I remember it distinctly,' I said, refilling my own glass now. 'I can even remember where we were when you said it.'

'Honestly, Edith, if that's how you see me, then I don't know why you married me at all.'

'Well, if you're not going to write,' I said, ignoring this remark, 'then what are you going to do? You can't just sit around the flat all day staring at the four walls.'

'I'll figure something out,' you said. 'Someone needs to do the shopping and the laundry and so on.'

A shadow fell across the table and I looked up to see a boy standing there. He was young, in his early twenties, with floppy blond hair. His skin was pale but his cheeks had a slight redness to them. If Eton College had a brochure, which they probably did, he could easily be the cover star.

'I'm sorry to interrupt you,' he said, looking from me to you and back to me again. 'It's Edith Camberley, isn't it?'

'Yes,' I said, surprised that he knew who I was. I had never once been publicly recognized.

'I'm sorry to interrupt you,' he repeated, toying with a silver ring on the middle finger of his right hand. 'My name's Garrett Colby. I'm one of your students. Or I will be, anyway, from next week.'

'Oh,' I said, feeling strangely excited. 'How nice to meet you!'

'I saw you but wasn't sure whether to come over or not. I'm sorry to interrupt you.'

'You've said that three times now,' you remarked, and I threw you a look but you deflected it with a smile, reaching for one of the mint chocolates that had come with the coffees and popping it into your mouth, masticating noisily.

'It should be an interesting year ahead,' I said.

'I must admit I'm quite nervous,' he replied.

'What are you working on?' I asked him. 'A novel?'

'Short stories,' he said. 'I've been writing stories since I was a boy.'

'But you're still a boy,' you told him. 'You look about twelve.'

'I'm twenty-two,' he replied.

'You don't even look like you shave.'

Poor Garrett blushed even deeper and I felt sorry for him. I tried to kick you under the table but succeeded only in banging my toe on the leg of your chair.

'Just ignore him,' I said. 'My husband is being ridiculous.'

'What kind of stories do you write?' you asked.

'They're mostly about animals,' he said.

'Animals?'

'Yes. I've been working on first-person stories narrated by . . . well, animals.'

'What sort of animals?' I asked.

'There's one narrated by a giraffe,' he replied. 'And another by a gorilla. I published one in *Granta* last year that was narrated by a pelican.'

'Of course, strictly speaking, a pelican is a bird, not an animal,' you said.

'That's true,' said Garrett. 'But I let birds in. Is there a collective noun for animals and birds?'

'Banimals,' you said. 'Birdimals. Animirds.'

'They sound fascinating,' I said, although, to be honest, I thought it all sounded a little strange.

'So, you're a children's writer?' you asked, looking at the boy. 'Or hoping to be?'

'No,' said Garrett, taking a step back, and I could see, for some reason, that he felt insulted by the remark. 'No, they're very definitely for adults.'

'Then why don't you write about people?' you asked. 'Actual human beings. Aren't you interested in them?'

'I am, yes, but it's the relationship between people and animals that interests me most,' he replied. 'It's hard to explain. You'd probably have to read one, to be honest.'

'Fortunately, that will be my wife's job,' you said. 'Not mine.'

Garrett looked a little upset now, as if he regretted having approached us in the first place, and glanced back towards his own table, where another young man was seated, staring over at us with an anxious expression on his face.

'And who's that?' I asked, trying to lighten the mood. 'Another student?'

'Yes,' he replied. 'Well, no. I mean yes, he's a student but not on the creative-writing course. He's studying medicine.'

'Veterinary medicine?' you asked.

'No, regular medicine. We met a few weeks ago. We both arrived in Norwich early to settle in. We're in the same halls.'

'Is he your boyfriend?' you asked, and I stared at you, wondering why you were trying to embarrass him, but there didn't seem to be anything unkind in the tone that you'd used.

'Sort of,' said Garrett, growing a little more confident now. 'We're not sure yet. Anyway, I didn't mean to interrupt you.'

'You've said.'

'I just wanted to say hello.'

'I'm glad you did,' I said. 'I'll look forward to seeing you on Wednesday.'

He smiled and nodded. The expression on his face as he walked away was one of humiliation crossed with disappointment. I turned to remonstrate with you but before I could open my mouth he'd returned.

'I'm sorry to interrupt you,' he said.

'Oh, for God's sake,' you said, looking away in irritation.

'It's just' – and now he was looking at you, not me – 'didn't you used to be a writer too?'

I felt a sudden spasm in the pit of my stomach, like someone had just pushed me from a great height and I was tumbling down, unable to grab hold of anything to prevent me from falling.

'What do you mean *used to be*?' you asked.

'It's just that when I knew Miss Camberley was going to be the course tutor—'

'Please call me Edith,' I said.

'I read her novel. Or re-read it, I should say. And then I looked up some interviews with her and they mentioned your name. It's Maurice Swift, isn't it?'

'That's right,' you said.

'I think I read your novel too.'

'Which one?'

'*Two Germans*.'

'You *think* you read it?'

'When I was in school, I mean. I think I borrowed it from the library.'

You smiled a little. 'But you're not sure?' you asked. 'It might have been something else? It might have been *Murder on the Orient Express*, for example? Or *War and Peace*?'

'I'm fairly certain it was *Two Germans*. It's just that I can't really remember what it was about, that's all.'

'Well, it was about two Germans. The clue is in the title, you see.'

'Yes, of course. I suppose what I mean is that I can't remember the plot.'

'Well, never mind,' you said. 'There wasn't much of one, anyway.'

'And are you working on a second book?'

'My husband's second novel was published in 1991,' I said.

'Oh, I'm sorry,' said Garrett. 'I must have missed it. So you're working on your third, then?'

You breathed in deeply through your nose and then exhaled. For a few moments, I felt as if the entire restaurant had turned to dust. 'I'm afraid I never talk about work in progress,' you said. 'And my wife and I are celebrating our wedding anniversary so perhaps you would be so kind as to stop apologizing for interrupting us and just fuck off.'

I looked down at the table. I couldn't apologize to the boy because to do so would have been to take his side over yours. But I felt badly for him. He gave a slight laugh, as if the whole thing had been a terrific joke, but walked away without another word, returning to his table and his maybe-boyfriend.

'Did you have to?' I asked, looking across at you. 'I haven't even taught my first class yet and already you've alienated one of my students.'

'Arrogant cunt,' you said, waving a hand in the direction of the waiter for the bill, and I knew, even as you said it, that you were being deliberately vague as to whom you were referring, Garrett or me.

You see, Maurice, you might not have been very good at coming up with ideas for your books but no one could ever have denied that you had a way with words.

2. October

Three weeks into term, I was reminded of an incident that took place during our first year together. The catalyst for the memory was a short story submitted to workshop by one of my weaker students detailing an unpleasant encounter between two old friends, many years after their estrangement. The story itself was not very good and received a negative reception in class. Garrett, the boy you tried to humiliate during our anniversary dinner, was particularly harsh, which disappointed me for I had hoped that his shyness might mask a degree of empathy, but in fact it was simply a cover for the brutal ambition that would reveal itself as the year went on.

But the student's story is neither here nor there. It simply recalled to me the time, a few months after we started dating, when I accompanied you to a literary festival in Wales. It hadn't taken long for me to become infatuated with you and the opportunity to present myself in public as your girlfriend boosted my hopes that ours would not be a casual relationship but something more long term. I'd been to literary festivals before, of course, but always as a reader and had never found myself in the secret rooms where writers and publishers gathered in advance of their events. As I was sketching out ideas for my first novel at the time and wondering whether I would ever find myself part of this world, the experience was an exciting one.

There was still some time before your event was due to begin and, as we sat with a glass of wine, I noticed how you kept glancing towards the entrance from where, every few minutes, another writer would appear. You offered waves to some, ignored others, and a few came over to say hello, but then I noticed your eyes open wide and your face fall as you leaned forward, reaching for the programme that sat on the table between us and flicking through it for the schedule of the day's events.

'Fuck,' you said, as your finger stopped on a listing.

'What is it?' I asked.

'Nothing.'

'It can't be nothing. You look like you've seen a ghost.'

It was obvious that something was wrong. I looked around and noticed an elderly man staring in our direction, an expression on his face that I'd never witnessed before. It seemed to combine humiliation, regret and acceptance all at once. He came towards us slowly, walking with the aid of a stick.

'Maurice,' he said in a strong New York accent when he reached our table. 'It is you, isn't it?'

'Hello, Dash,' you replied, standing up to shake his hand. 'It's been a long time.'

'Just over five years. You haven't changed much. A little older, of course, but still as handsome as ever.'

'Thank you,' you said, smiling, and as it became obvious that he was not going to walk away, you invited him to sit down, which he did, pushing me a little to the side as he took the seat opposite you. You both sat silently for a moment, simply staring at each other, and as things began to grow awkward I introduced myself and he shook my hand, offering his name too. Of course, I recognized it. I hadn't actually read any of his books, although I'd always meant to as he'd been publishing for decades and had a good reputation.

'Did you two read together somewhere?' I asked, looking from one to the other. 'Is that how you know each other?'

'Oh no,' said Dash. 'Maurice would never share a stage with some-one as long in the tooth as me. No, we met many years ago when he was still trying to get his foot on the ladder. Seville, wasn't it?'

'Madrid,' you said.

'That's right, Madrid. Erich Ackermann was receiving an award of some sort, I think—'

'It wasn't an award,' you told him. 'It was just a lunch.'

'My goodness, your memory!' he said, bringing his hands together, and I noticed thick liver spots on both that discoloured the skin. 'You remember it as if it were only yesterday. Can you remember what we ate too?'

You smiled at this but said nothing.

'Anyway,' he continued, 'Maurice and I met that afternoon and became firm friends. For a time, anyway. He lived in my apartment in New York for . . . how long was it, a year? Eighteen months?'

'Less than that,' you replied. 'Ten months at most.'

'Well, all right. We won't quibble over minor details. Interesting days, as I recall. We went everywhere together, we were quite the odd couple.'

147

'Not exactly a couple,' you said, interrupting him.

'I introduced him to everyone who was worth knowing. We dined with Mrs Astor, spent a weekend with Edmund on Fire Island, travelled to the Amalfi Coast to spend a night with Gore and Howard. We even went to Jets games together, didn't we?'

'But you hate sport!' I said, turning to you in surprise.

'But *I* love it,' said Dash. 'And Maurice was very . . . what's the word I'm looking for? *Obliging*. A most obliging boy indeed. Up to a point, anyway.' He paused for a moment and gave a deep sigh. 'But then his novel was published and he was far too busy to bother with me any more!'

'That wasn't it,' you said coldly. 'I was travelling a lot and—'

'As I say, you were very busy. Have you ever read Erich Ackermann, my dear?'

I shook my head. 'I don't read books by fascists,' I said.

'Why ever not? There's not much left to read if you ignore them. Writers are all fascists. We like to control the discourse and crush anyone who dares to disagree with us.'

'Are you here for an event?' you asked, before I could engage with this observation.

'Yes, I have a new novel out. Didn't you know?'

'No, what's the title?'

'*The Codicil of Agnès Fontaine.*'

'Sorry, I haven't heard of it.'

'It's been widely reviewed.'

You shrugged your shoulders. 'Well, I'll make sure to pick up a copy at the festival bookshop and you can sign it for me.'

'I remember the first time I signed a book for you,' he said, leaning forward. 'It was very early in the morning in New York and you were staying in a hotel with Erich, doing whatever it is you did for him in those days. Do you remember?'

'No,' you said.

'Well, I do. I read your second book, by the way,' continued Dash. 'What was it called again? *The Garden Shed?*'

'*The Treehouse.*'

'Not quite as good as *Two Germans*, was it? I wonder what poor old Erich made of it.'

'Well, he was dead by the time it came out, so I doubt he made anything of it.'

'Of course he was,' said the American. 'He died alone in Berlin, didn't he? I read somewhere that he'd been dead a week before anyone discovered the body. One of his neighbours complained about the smell. Such a sad end to an illustrious career.'

'I thought you didn't rate him?'

'Whatever gave you that idea?'

'The hundreds of criticisms you made of his work when we knew each other.'

'Oh no,' he said, looking appalled by the accusation. 'No, I admired Erich greatly. His novels will be remembered, I think. And the scandal will fade away. The poems will last too.'

'He always said they were ill advised.'

'He was wrong about that. But then he was wrong about a lot of things, wasn't he?'

Before you could reply, a young volunteer came over and said that she was there to escort Dash to his event. He stood up carefully, taking a long time to adjust his body to the vertical and to grip his stick just so, and then looked down at us and smiled.

'Well, I might see you later, Maurice,' he said.

'Unlikely,' you replied. 'After my talk, we're catching the next train back to London.'

'Probably for the best,' he replied, before waving a hand in the air as he turned his back on us. 'Goodbye, my boy. I daresay we won't meet again.'

I watched him as he walked away and felt torn between laughter and confusion.

'Cantankerous old swine,' you muttered. 'He was in love with me once.'

'Really?' I asked.

'It does happen.'

'Well I, of all people, know that,' I said, smiling at you. 'You let him down easily, I hope?'

'It's all so long ago, I can barely remember. Anyway, what time is it? Let's take a walk around the site. I wouldn't mind having a look in the bookshop.'

I nodded, following you as you stepped outside. Dash Hardy died shortly afterwards, didn't he? I remember reading about it in the newspaper over breakfast one morning and feeling shocked that someone who had sat with me so recently could have hanged himself in his Manhattan apartment. You read the article too but said nothing about it, although you were rather quiet throughout the day, as I recall.

One month in, and Norwich was proving a positive experience. My initial fears about teaching creative writing had dissipated as the students seemed both respectful and hard-working. Only one, a Polish girl named Maja, gave me reason for concern. Due to visa difficulties, she'd arrived late on campus, missing the first two weeks of class, and it seemed that she was struggling to fit in. She was working on a novel that had the most bizarre premise – Adolf Hitler solving crimes in post-First World War Germany – and any critical comments made of her work left her in a state of fury. At the same time, she was making little attempt to engage with the work of her classmates, and so I took her aside, asking whether I could help in some way, but she seemed offended by my question and I quickly backed off. I confided in you and your first instinct was to ask me how her English was.

'Her English is perfect,' I told you. 'There's no issue there at all.'

'I only ask because, if she's struggling with the language, then maybe she feels she can't contribute as much as the others.'

'No, it's not that,' I said. 'I'm not sure what it is, if I'm honest. She just seems to hate everyone, me included. I don't know why.'

I wanted to discuss this further with you, to seek your advice, because I suspected that there was trouble brewing with Maja, but you were reading a novel that had been shortlisted the previous autumn for The Prize and I could tell that you were growing increasingly enraged by it. It was a long novel, more than five hundred pages, and I knew that the author, Douglas Sherman, had published his first book the same year that you'd published *Two Germans*. I remember you telling me how you'd enjoyed touring together in the early days, two handsome young novelists with assured futures, the literary world falling over itself to embrace you both. But since then, Douglas had published four more novels, each one better received than the previous one, and his stature had grown considerably while you, of course, were flailing.

'I don't know why you keep reading that,' I said. 'It's masochistic behaviour.'

'Because I never *don't* finish a novel once I've started it,' you replied. 'It's a rule of mine.'

'Not me,' I said, collapsing on to the sofa and glancing towards the pile of class scripts sitting on the coffee table but making no effort to reach out for one. 'Life's too short. As far as I'm concerned, a writer gets one hundred pages and, if they can't keep my attention during that time, I move on.'

'Ridiculous,' you said.

'Don't call me ridiculous.'

'I wasn't calling you ridiculous. I was calling that policy ridiculous. You can't say you've read a novel unless you've read it cover to cover. Yes, perhaps you'll be bored at the start but what if it gets better and suddenly everything that went before falls into place?'

'Whatever,' I said. 'But I still think it's a mistake, considering your history.'

'You make it sound like we were lovers.'

'Particularly when you're feeling so—'

'When I'm feeling so what?' you asked, putting the book aside

151

and staring at me. You parted your legs a little and gripped the sides of the armchair and an image of Lincoln on the Mall came into my mind.

'When you're feeling so lost,' I said.

'What makes you think I feel lost?'

'Don't let's do this,' I said, looking past you and through the front window, where a black-and-white cat had climbed on to the mantel and was staring in at me. He raised a paw and pressed it against the glass and, for one surreal moment, I thought he was beckoning me to him, like one of those *maneki-nekos* that sit in the windows of Chinese restaurants.

'Do let's,' you said, enunciating each word. 'Go on, Edith, tell me why you think I feel lost.'

'Because you're not writing.'

'We've been over this.'

'Which is why I said that we should talk about something else.'

You remained silent for a long time, eventually conceding with a sigh. 'Perhaps you're right. Sorry, Edith. I shouldn't be such a prick. None of this is your fault.'

'You don't have to apologize,' I replied.

'I do, actually. Here we are in this nice flat. You're the one working, earning the money and writing at the same time, and I sit here doing nothing but complaining. I'll try to be better, I promise.'

'Well,' I said, with a smile. 'That would be nice. You could start by painting the bedroom. The colour in there gives me a headache.'

'All right.'

'And fixing the railing on the staircase up to the flat would be helpful. Have you noticed how shaky it is?'

'Or I could read those scripts,' you suggested, nodding at the pile on the coffee table. 'And write up some notes for you?'

'Why would I want you to do that?' I asked.

'So you don't have to read them yourself. I assume they're all rubbish.'

'They're not, actually. And they're my students' work. They're relying on me to come to class prepared. I have to read them; otherwise how could I possibly advise them?'

'It was just a suggestion,' you said. 'How is your book coming along, anyway? Are you getting much done?'

'I think it's going quite well,' I said.

'How far along are you now?'

'Close to the end of this draft.'

'And how many more lie ahead?'

'One? Maybe two at most?'

'And then I'll get to read it?'

'Not till it's published, sorry.'

You scowled. I knew you didn't like that I refused to share my work with you in advance, but I had explained why many times. I respected your opinion, of course I did, but I loved you too and I didn't want a novel to come between us. If you thought it was awful, after all, you might not tell me. And if you thought it was good, then I might find your praise insincere.

'So how long?' you asked. 'Before you turn it in, I mean?'

'Four or five months, I'd say.'

'Well, I won't push you on it,' you said, standing up and coming over, raising my chin with your index finger and kissing me gently on the lips but holding the kiss for a long time, so long that I felt the need to pull away before you suffocated me.

A few days later, during class, there was a tap on the door, and when it opened I was surprised to see my brother-in-law Robert standing there with an apologetic smile on his face. The students turned to look at him, displeased by the interruption, and for some reason I found myself blushing.

'Sorry, Edith,' he said. 'Am I disturbing you?'

'Well, we're in the middle of class.'

'Could I just have a quick word?'

I stepped out into the corridor, feeling a little flustered as I closed the door behind me. 'What's wrong?' I asked. 'Is it Rebecca? The boys?'

'No, no,' he said quickly. 'No, it's nothing like that. Everyone's fine. I just needed to speak to you, that's all.'

I stared at him, feeling a mixture of pity and irritation. 'Well, I can't right now,' I told him, nodding back in the direction of the workshop. 'We've only just started.'

'That's all right, I can wait.'

I nodded and gave him directions to the graduate students' bar, saying that I'd meet him there at five, and later, when I arrived, I was glad to see that he'd chosen a table in the corner where we could talk quietly.

'So, how are you, anyway?' I asked.

'Miserable. And you?'

'Tolerable.'

'And Maurice?'

'He's fine. He's been incredibly supportive of me coming here. I couldn't have done this without his help, to be honest.'

'That doesn't surprise me,' said Robert. 'I've always envied you the—'

'The what?' I asked, uncertain how that sentence was going to end.

'Well, the love that you share. It's obvious to everyone how good you are together.'

I felt incredibly touched by this remark and, to my surprise, felt tears form behind my eyes.

'I assume you're here to talk about Rebecca,' I said, looking up again at last.

'Yes. Have you talked to her lately?'

'Not much,' I admitted. 'I went over to see her shortly before we left for Norwich but I haven't heard from her since then.'

'So you've met Arjan, then?'

'Well, he was there,' I said. 'So, yes.'

'What did you think?'

I glanced across the room to the tables where my students were drinking and laughing and, as much as I loved Robert, I longed to be in their company, talking about writing, rather than sitting here, caught up in a family drama.

'He seems friendly enough,' I said. 'It does feel a bit soon for her to be shacked up with someone else, of course, but he was quite pleasant, I thought. I'm sorry, I know you probably want me to say something else but—'

'Actually, no,' he said, interrupting me.

'No?'

'No, he's living with my two boys so of course I'd prefer if he was a good guy. I've met him myself, you know. I wanted to hate him but couldn't. Rebecca will grow bored of him in time, though.'

'I think so too,' I said. 'Look, do you want me to be honest? Arjan is . . . well, he's fit, isn't he? And young. But he's too nice. Either she'll get tired of him or he'll get sick of her bullying and walk away. I suspect that beneath the kind façade there's a strong backbone, and anyone who gets caught up with my sister would need one of those.'

'You don't think that I have a backbone?'

'That's not what I said.'

'It's what you implied.'

I put my glass down and reached out to take his hand. As I did so, I noticed my angry Polish student Maja glancing over at me. She knew that Robert wasn't my husband, of course, and perhaps she was wondering why I was touching him.

'I'm not your enemy, Robert,' I said quietly.

'No, I know. I'm sorry.'

'So look, why don't you tell me why you came to see me?'

'To ask a favour.'

'All right.'

'I want you to talk to Rebecca for me.'

I closed my eyes for a moment. I'd hoped that wasn't what he was going to say. 'Do I have to?' I asked.

'I need you to. She won't take my calls any more.'

'Well, what do you want me to say to her?'

'You could start by asking her why she won't take my calls any more.'

'And after that?'

'I hadn't thought that far ahead.'

'Oh great,' I said. 'Thanks.'

'I think we need an intermediary of some sort.'

'Perhaps. But do you really think I'm the best person for the job? She hates me.'

'She doesn't hate you.'

'Oh, come on.'

'She may not be your biggest fan, but—'

'She told me that she thought my novel was shit. I believe her actual phrase was *a work of blush-making vulgarity*. The words are emblazoned on my memory.'

'She's jealous of your success, that's all.'

'Good, I'm glad.'

'You should take it as a compliment.'

'Well, I don't.'

'Edith, please. She won't let me see the boys.'

'Well, that's not fair,' I admitted. 'But shouldn't you just speak to a solicitor? Wouldn't that be easier? Find out what your rights are?'

'I don't want to go down that road just yet,' he said. 'The moment we start getting legal is the moment that things get completely out of hand. I want to appeal to her better nature.'

'Ah, you see, that's where you're making your mistake.'

'I just think if someone could tell her how important it is to me to be a good father, how important it is for me to be a positive influence on the boys, then she might behave a bit more—'

'Like a human being?'

'Yes, I suppose so.'

I sighed. It was obvious that Rebecca was treating Robert appallingly. I was going to say as much but that's when the door to the grad bar opened and you walked in.

You glanced around, your gaze settling on the students, and you scanned the group, expecting to see me among their number. Only when you looked around the rest of the room did you notice the two of us together and you raised an eyebrow in surprise before walking over.

'Robert,' you said, throwing an arm around him. 'This is a surprise.'

'Yes, I called in on Edith's class unexpectedly. Things have been a bit rotten at home, as you know. I thought I could do with a little advice.'

You nodded and asked what we were drinking before making your way to the bar. I could sense in the way you carried yourself that you weren't happy, and I immediately felt uncomfortable, unable now to concentrate on what Robert was saying. I looked in your direction but you had your back to me. Our eyes met in the mirror behind the bar, however, and there was something in your expression that made me feel guilty, as if I'd let you down in some way.

I wasn't quite sure what I'd done wrong but I knew that, whatever it was, you would hold it against me for a while yet.

3. November

It wasn't my idea to invite you to talk to the students and, if I'm honest, I assumed that you'd refuse anyway. No, this particular notion had been dreamed up by Maja, who approached me after class one day, claiming not only to be a great fan of *Two Germans* but even more of *The Treehouse*, which I thought a peculiar statement. I promised to put it to you but warned her that you were unlikely to say yes. To my surprise, however, you agreed immediately.

A date was set and I spent that morning reading the stories that had been submitted for workshop later in the week and feeling a strange anxiety at the pit of my stomach that I found hard to understand. You came to my office around three thirty, the first time you'd been there, and spent your time examining the books that had been left behind on the shelves by the writer whose maternity leave I was covering. You took a few out and made disparaging comments about their authors.

'Is that a new shirt?' I asked as we made our way towards the classroom shortly before your talk was due to begin. 'And new jeans? Have you bought all new clothes for today?'

'Don't be ridiculous,' you said, and I looked away from you because you were blushing and seeing people embarrassed has always made me embarrassed too. They *were* new clothes, of course. I couldn't decide whether the fact that you were making such an effort for a group of aspiring writers was endearing or pathetic. Did you want to impress them that badly?

When we walked in, I noticed how the students – *my* students – looked at you with more reverence than they'd ever shown towards me. I don't think I'm being paranoid, Maurice, when I say that it was as if they believed that, finally, a *real* writer had come to speak to them, simply because you happened to have a penis. Even the girls, who all liked to pretend that they were such staunch feminists, looked at you with more respect than they ever did me. *Especially* the girls, actually.

I began by introducing you, mentioning the names of both your published novels, and made some predictable joke about how easy it had been to persuade you to visit as we were sleeping together. Without any preamble, you reached for a copy of *The Treehouse* – you always favoured it over *Two Germans* – and read from a section of the book near the centre, where a young boy collapses through the floorboards of the titular building and hangs there for most of the afternoon until a passing farmer arrives to save him. When you were finished, they applauded ecstatically and I could see from the expression on your face how much their approval meant to you.

'I'm not going to ask Maurice any questions,' I said when they quietened down. 'I already know everything there is to know about him.'

'Not quite everything,' you said, to laughter.

'So, I'll leave it to all of you instead.'

Maja started the questioning, as I knew she would. She had spent the entire reading staring at you, as if you were the Second Coming of Christ, and it was obvious from the expression on her face that she found you highly attractive. I'd like to say that she was undressing you with her eyes but it would probably be more truthful to say that she was stripping you naked and falling to her knees to fellate you. I can't recall what she asked but I remember you took her question as simply a starting point for a monologue about the current state of the literary world, which, in your view, was appalling. I tuned out, thinking about where we might go for dinner afterwards. And yes, I allowed my eyes to rest on one of the boys, Nicholas Bray, who was very young but very cute and who I'd fancied from the start.

Several more questions were asked before Garrett Colby raised his hand and you turned to him with a look that said you recognized him from somewhere but couldn't quite remember where.

'I wondered whether you could tell us what you're working on at the moment,' he asked, and you shook your head.

'No, I don't think so,' you told him. 'As I told you before, Garrett, I prefer not to talk about work in progress. Just in case.'

'Just in case what?'

'Just in case someone steals my idea.'

'But an idea is just an idea,' he countered. 'You could outline *The Great Gatsby* for us all right now and it's not as if any of us could just sit down and write it.'

'No,' you agreed. 'But still, I'd prefer not to.'

'Of course, this leads us to a bigger question, doesn't it?' said Garrett.

'Does it?'

'Yes. The concept of literary ownership itself, or even literary theft. Of whether our stories belong to us at all.'

'I don't quite see what you're getting at,' you said, but I could see where he was going and wondered how he had the nerve. Looking back, it was pretty rude of him to treat a visiting writer like this, let alone one who had achieved the success that you'd achieved.

'Well, take *Two Germans*,' continued Garrett. 'It wasn't really your idea, was it? You were simply telling Erich Ackermann's story and presenting it as a work of fiction.'

'But it *is* a work of fiction,' you insisted. 'Not everything in that book is exactly as Erich detailed it to me. I took what he told me about his own life, embellished some details, ignored a few others. There were several things he told me about Oskar Gött, for example, that might have influenced the reader's opinion of that character, but I chose not to write about them as I had a very particular idea of how I wanted to present the relationship between the two boys.'

'What sort of things?' he asked.

'I'd rather not go into all that,' you said. 'Once I start down that road I become obliged to talk about every aspect of the story and to separate Erich's personal history from my own creation. Ultimately, it's a novel and you should treat it as such. Don't expect facts in fiction. That's not what novels are about.'

'Then what *are* they about?' asked handsome Nicholas, piping up now.

'I've often wondered that myself,' you said with a smile. 'I don't really know, if I'm honest with you. I only know that I enjoy reading them. And writing them.'

'So you *are* working on something new, then?' asked Garrett, persistent little Garrett.

'I said so, didn't I?'

'No, you said that you never talk about work in progress.'

'Exactly.'

'But there *is* a work in progress, then? It's just that it's been such a long time since *The Treehouse*.'

Sitting next to me, I could feel you growing uncomfortable in your chair, and you took a long time to answer.

'You're the one writing the children's book about the talking animals, aren't you?' you asked eventually.

'It's not a children's book,' replied Garrett. 'The whole thing's an allegory. It's not the fact that the animals speak that matters, it's what they have to say. Like in *Animal Farm*.'

'You're comparing your work to Orwell's?' you asked, laughing now.

'No, of course not,' said Garrett, growing a little more flustered. 'That's not what I meant.'

'It's what you implied,' interrupted Maja.

Garrett rolled his eyes and delivered a loud sigh. The two students had clashed several times in workshop and Maja seemed to take pleasure in bringing him down to earth.

'Look, some novels take a long time to write,' you said, getting back to the original question. 'When it's ready, it will be ready. Until then I don't have a lot more to say on the subject other than I hope to publish it within the next . . .' You paused for a moment and stared up towards the ceiling. 'Within the next two years.'

I turned to look at you and tried to keep the surprise off my face. But I was delighted that you were thinking in these terms at last. Perhaps Norwich, I decided, was having a positive effect on both of us.

There were a few more questions and then we all retired for a drink to the grad bar, where you ordered pizzas for the students and made sure to spend a little time with each group, as if you were doing them a tremendous favour by granting them your wisdom.

'Have you read any of it?' asked Nicholas, my crush, coming over to where I stood by the window and handing me a glass of white wine.

'Any of what?' I asked.

'Your husband's new novel.'

I shook my head and took a moment to appreciate his good looks. He was about eight years younger than me – twenty-three – with short dark hair that looked impossibly clean and a boyish face. I imagined that when he was a child he would have been a *Just William* sort, always getting into mischief but confident that no one could possibly stay angry with him for very long.

'No,' I said, deciding not to say that I had only learned of the existence of a new novel at the same time as the rest of them had. 'No, he doesn't let me read anything while he's working on it.'

'Does he think you're going to steal it too?'

I laughed and shook my head. 'I doubt it,' I said, feeling that I had to make up for my unfaithful thoughts by defending you. 'Although that's not such a bad idea. He's a much better writer than I am.'

'Do you really think that?' he asked.

'Yes, of course,' I said, and I think I did believe it at the time. But maybe that was just because you'd already been published when we met and so I'd looked up to you ever since. 'Why, don't you?'

'No, not at all,' said Nicholas, looking me directly in the eye. 'Quite honestly, I think you're in a different league. Or you will be someday.'

Despite the tension that seemed to be developing between us during those weeks, my work, at least, was going well. I was getting closer to the end of a draft of my novel and felt sure that I'd have something presentable by late spring. The occasional email from my agent and editor kept my spirits up, although I still refused to tell them anything of the story, preferring for them to respond to it in its finished state rather than having any preconceptions about it. They seemed content with this and my days were filled with teaching, reading and writing. I could get used to this, I thought, wondering whether a more permanent position might open up at the university soon that would allow me to stay on for a few more years. I liked the idea of writing a third novel, a much shorter one, in an intense period of creativity.

UEA was holding its autumn literary festival during November, a series of curated interviews in one of the theatres on a Tuesday night, and although you generally avoided such events you suggested that we go together to hear Leona Alwin be interviewed by the novelist Henry Sutton. A few years earlier, Leona had been sent a proof copy of *Fear* and had been kind enough to read it, offering a line of support that was used on the jacket, something that had impressed you, for you'd always been an admirer of her books.

In the late afternoon, I came home to change and, as I made my way up the staircase to our flat, the handrail shook in my hand and I stumbled, tripping forwards, preventing an injury only by throwing my hands out to cushion my fall.

'Jesus Christ,' I muttered as I stood up and, when I opened the front door, you emerged from the spare room that I used as my study.

'What was that noise?' you asked.

'I fell over,' I said. 'I thought you said that you were going to fix that handrail? One of us is going to break something if we're not careful.'

'Sorry. I forgot,' you said, helping me inside while I rubbed my bruised shin. 'Are you all right? You didn't hurt yourself, did you?'

I shook my head as I brushed myself down. 'I'm fine,' I said. 'What were you doing in there, anyway?'

'In where?'

'In my study?'

'*Your* study?' you asked, raising an eyebrow. I could hear the petulance in my voice and tried to control it as I didn't want to ruin the evening ahead. But it *was* my study and we'd always referred to it as such. On the rare occasions when you used your laptop you always did so at the kitchen table.

'*The* study, then,' I said.

'Nothing,' you told me, stepping past me into the kitchen and turning on the kettle. 'I was looking for a pen, that's all. Anyway, I thought the plan was to meet on campus later?'

'I needed a shower,' I said. 'I've been running around like a lunatic all day. I won't be long and we can walk in together.'

Before going towards the bedroom to undress, however, something made me go into the other room to look around. Glancing towards my desk, I could see a few pens lying there, and when I placed my hand on top of the desktop computer, ignoring the part of my brain that told me to leave well alone, it was warm. My first thought was that you had been using it to access pornography. Had I disturbed you in the act? I moved the mouse to wake it from sleep and checked the search history but there was nothing incriminating there, only searches that I'd made myself over the previous few days. Perhaps it had simply been the sun, I thought. After all, due to the positioning of the house, the study could become oppressively warm during the afternoon.

The reading and interview went very well. Leona Alwin combined erudition with a wonderful sense of humour, talking about her work and the work of others with real insight. You seemed dazzled by her and, as the lights came up, you turned to me with the sort of enthusiasm that I hadn't seen on your face in a long time.

'Isn't she terrific?' you said, and I nodded in agreement as you took my hand. We walked across the courtyard towards the reception being held in the registry building. Once inside, we sipped champagne, waiting for an opportunity to introduce ourselves to the guest of honour. Out of the blue you reached forward to kiss me and it wasn't just a peck, it was a real kiss, our lips parted and as your tongue entered my mouth I felt a warmth spreading through my body that reminded me how I had never wanted a man as much as I continued to want you. When you pulled away, you had a mischievous expression on your face. You leaned in and I thought you were going to kiss me again but no, you simply whispered in my ear:

'Let's go somewhere and fuck.'

My eyes opened wide in surprise and I put a hand to my mouth to stop myself from laughing aloud, but the idea, the spontaneity of it, aroused me instantly. I looked around at the increasingly busy room. 'We can't,' I said. 'We'd be caught.'

'So what?' you said, taking me by the hand and leading me down a corridor, where we tried a few doors, all of which were locked. I glanced back in case we were being followed but no one was going to leave the main party while Leona was still holding court. We turned the corner into a dead end with just two office doors, one on either side. I tried one and you tried the other but neither would open.

'Out of luck,' you said.

I looked at you, grabbed your arm, and smiled.

'What?' you asked.

I stepped back into the corner and you raised an eyebrow. I didn't know what I was doing, it was terribly risky because there were about a hundred people gathered at the end of the hallway, but I knew that I had to have you right then or I would go mad.

'Here?' you asked.

'Here,' I said, and you came towards me and pressed me against the wall, reaching under my dress to pull my underwear down as you unzipped your trousers. It was only a matter of seconds before you were inside me and, as we fucked, we looked into each other's eyes and your hand wrapped itself lightly around my throat, your thumb pressing hard against my carotid artery. When we came, we came together. It was intense and sexy and when we were done we stared at each other, our lust somehow amplified now rather than quenched. A few moments later, we tidied our clothing and returned to the party, giggling like teenagers.

The first person we met as we walked through the doors was Leona Alwin herself and, although I would have liked to go to the bathroom to clean up before talking to her, there was no way we could just ignore her. I introduced myself, embarrassed by what I was sure was the smell of sex that enveloped us, but she didn't appear to notice it. Instead she seemed overjoyed to meet me.

'Oh, of course,' she said enthusiastically. 'You wrote that wonderful novel!'

'You're very kind,' I said. 'And very generous. Your endorsement was really helpful.'

'I'm sure it did very little,' she said, waving my gratitude away. 'Good work will always out, that's what I believe. It was one of the finest debuts I'd read in years.'

'It's really admirable that someone of your stature is so interested in the work of new writers,' I said.

'Well, I try to keep up,' she replied. 'I can't bear ageing novelists who refuse to bother with the young. Most of them seem to think that they're the only ones worth reading, you see, and that literature as we know it will come to an end when they publish their final book. Well, the men do, certainly. Can you imagine a seventy-five-year-old white Englishman with twenty novels under his belt reading a debut by a twenty-eight-year-old black girl of Caribbean descent? It would never happen. They'd much rather tell the world that they're re-reading all of Henry James in chronological order and finding him a little smug.' She turned to you then, Maurice, and I knew by the way you were standing that you were waiting for her to recognize you.

'Lovely to see you again, Leona,' you said, reaching forward, and, I think, surprising her by kissing her on both cheeks. 'That was a wonderful talk.'

'Thank you,' she said. 'Mr . . . ?'

'It's Maurice,' you told her then, rearing back a little, and the expression on your face changed as quickly as it had when I had stood at the end of the corridor and invited you to fuck me. 'Maurice Swift.'

'Well, it's nice to meet you too, Mr Swift. Are you Edith's

boyfriend? Oh no, her husband. I can see your wedding rings. How long have you been married? You must be very proud of her!'

You stared at her and said nothing for a few moments. I could see the horror of what was about to happen but couldn't think of any way to prevent it.

'We met at the Edinburgh Festival a few years ago,' you said.

'Oh, I'm so sorry,' said Leona, touching your arm and looking quite embarrassed. 'You're a writer too, then? I didn't realize.'

'I'm Maurice Swift,' you repeated, your tone making it clear that you could not have been more astonished if she'd said that she'd never heard of William Shakespeare.

'My husband wrote *Two Germans*,' I said, but it was obvious from the look on her face that she'd never heard of it.

'Well, that's wonderful,' she said. 'Congratulations. And how is it doing for you?'

'It was published eleven years ago,' you said.

'Oh, of course it was. I remember now.' She wasn't very good at lying. 'You must forgive me, Mr Swift. I'm as old as the hills. There are days when I can barely even remember the titles of my own books.'

'No, that's not true,' you said coldly. 'I heard you in there. You're completely on the ball. You've just never heard of me or my books, that's all. It's fine, I don't care. There's no particular reason why you should have.'

Leona smiled awkwardly and turned back to me, asking me how my next book was coming along, and I offered a few platitudes, but the conversation was ruined. I wanted to leave, to deal with whatever mood you would be in now and just get past it. I suspect Leona wanted to get out of there too for she quickly moved on to someone else and we were left alone again, the rush of our recent sex vanished now, instead replaced by the humiliation that had been rained down on you.

'Shall we go?' you asked, and I nodded, draining my glass and rushing to catch up with you as you led the way out of the door.

Do you remember what happened when we got home, Maurice? You'll say that I'm exaggerating but I remember it clearly. We barely spoke in the taxi but once we were in the front door and up the stairs you pulled me to you and started kissing me again. But there was none of the romance of earlier; instead you spun me around, pulling my underwear down roughly, and before I could make any protest you were inside me again. I cried out but you forced your way deeper into my body, and I held myself up, telling myself that this was what I wanted, this kind of passion, this kind of impulsiveness, even though it seemed as if the desire we'd felt earlier had been replaced now by cruelty and spite. As if you weren't fucking me at all, but punishing me.

'Twice in one night,' you said when you were finished, smiling at me. 'Who said romance is dead?'

I turned around to face you, trying to smile, desperately wanting to look as if I'd enjoyed it so that I could convince myself that I had. And then my legs seemed to give way beneath me and I slid down to the floor, where I stayed for a few minutes while you went into the kitchen to pour yourself a beer.

4. December

When my mother broke her arm slipping on some ice, we decided to go to my family after all, instead of yours, for Christmas and I got the impression that you were relieved about that. Although I knew that your parents had never particularly liked me – your mother blamed our miscarriages on my writing, telling you time and again that you should not 'let' me work, while your father refused to accept that I was English, insisting that my skin colour meant I was an immigrant, regardless of the fact that I was born in Hackney – I was willing to put up with their outdated gender stereotypes and casual racism if it meant not having to be around my sister. But eventually my conscience got the better of me and I knew that I couldn't leave my mother to cater for herself, Rebecca and the boys without some help, particularly when I had barely seen her since September.

The smell of pigeon peas, plantain, cush cush and candied yams that drifted through the air brought me instantly back to my childhood. My parents had arrived in England from the Caribbean in the early 1960s and, when we were kids, the whole family returned there once every couple of years to see the relatives they'd left behind. I felt out of place there, though, more at home in England, which was the only home I'd ever known, despite the fact that the children in school, and even some of the teachers, had no hesitation in using racial epithets against me.

We went into the living room with glasses of wine and I made my way over to the shelf by Mum's reading chair, where she kept her library books, and as I scanned the titles I was surprised to see a copy of *The City and the Pillar* by Gore Vidal.

'Look,' I said, holding up the cover, and you glanced over and smiled.

'I wouldn't have thought that was your sort of thing, Amoya,' you said, turning to my mother. 'All that boy-on-boy action.'

'Well, I didn't realize that it would be so full of sex when I borrowed it,' she replied. 'But I'm rather enjoying all the rudeness. Now that Henry's gone, reading about sex is the closest I ever get to it. Speaking of which, you know that Rebecca is bringing Arjan with her, yes?'

'I didn't know it for a fact,' I replied. 'But I guessed she would. Have you met him yet?'

'I have,' she replied cautiously, for she loved Robert just as much as I did and didn't want to appear disloyal. 'It's very difficult to know what to say, isn't it? None of this is his fault, after all, and he does seem like a very nice man.'

'Where's he from?' you asked, for you hadn't come with me the day I'd visited him and Rebecca and had shown scant interest in him in the meantime. 'India or somewhere?'

'Eastern Europe, I think. Latvia or Estonia. One of those places.'

'And what does he do?'

'He's an actor. Or trying to be. He's younger than Rebecca, though, which should come as no surprise. And very good-looking.'

'Well, if you're going to cheat on your husband and then leave him,' you said, 'I suppose there's no point doing it for someone old and ugly.'

Afterwards, we all tried to blame the argument on what Mum delicately referred to as Arjan's not quite perfect grasp of English, but of course there was much more to it than that.

Rebecca, Arjan and the boys arrived laden with Christmas presents. Too many, I thought, as if she was trying to prove something through her generosity. Damien and Edward both had new phones, which seemed ridiculous, considering they were only nine and seven years old, and she had bought me one of my favourite perfumes but had forgotten to remove the Heathrow duty-free sticker from beneath the box.

'If I'm honest,' said my sister, sitting back in the armchair with a glass of champagne, 'I would have preferred to stay at home this year instead of coming here.'

'Well, you could still go back,' I told her. 'The roads will be quiet at this time of day and we could always do you up a doggy-bag.'

'My schedule has been simply crazy,' she continued, ignoring me. 'Two weeks ago, I was actually in three different countries over three different days. Absolutely exhausting.'

'Which countries?' I asked. 'England, Scotland and Wales?'

'No,' she snapped. 'England, France and Italy, if you really want to know.'

'I'm not sure England counts, dear,' said Mum. 'I mean, you do live here, after all.'

'Of course it counts. It's a country, isn't it?'

'So, tell us a little about yourself, Arjan,' you said, turning to him, and I could see that you were uncertain whether to be on his side yet or not. He was ten years younger than my sister, who had only recently turned thirty-eight, and very handsome with a muscular frame and beautiful skin. Of course, that also made him six years younger than you.

'What would you like to know?' he asked politely.

'You want to be an actor, is that right?'

'Oh no,' said Arjan, shaking his head.

'That's what we were told.'

'I don't *want* to be an actor,' he said. 'I *am* an actor.'

'Right,' you said. 'Of course.'

'I've been acting all my adult life.'

'And are you in something at the moment?'

'Not right now, no.'

'Resting, I suppose,' you said, nodding your head. 'I hear a lot of actors do that. Well, it's not as if you have to wait on tables, is it? Not with the money Rebecca earns.'

'Actually, I don't take any money from Rebecca,' he replied with a certain dignity. 'I get enough work to pay my way.'

'Arjan has just been cast in a major new television series,' said Rebecca. 'He's going to play a serial rapist who dismembers his victims afterwards and dines on their internal organs. So who knows where that will lead?'

'Wouldn't you prefer to work in film or the theatre?' you asked, an edge coming into your tone now.

'I'm happy to take whatever work comes my way,' said Arjan, taking no obvious offence from your condescension. 'Maybe I'll get some film work in the future but that doesn't happen for everyone. As long as I get to keep acting, I don't mind.'

'Yes, but I'm sure you didn't grow up hoping to be a serial rapist. It's not exactly Shakespeare, is it?'

'Anthony Hopkins played something like that in *The Silence of the Lambs*, didn't he?' I asked. 'And he won an Oscar for it. What was he called again?'

'Hannibal Lecter,' said Mum. 'Hannibal the Cannibal.'

'I couldn't sleep after watching that,' said Rebecca with a shudder.

'Actually, I played Laertes for six months once,' said Arjan.

'Really?' you replied, raising an eyebrow as if you didn't believe him. 'In whose Hamlet?'

Arjan frowned, clearly confused by the question. 'Shakespeare's,' he said.

'No, I meant who played Hamlet?' you said with a derisive sigh, and when he named the actor you shook your head and claimed that you'd never heard of him, even though I knew you had. We'd watched him in a mini-series not so long before and both thought he was rather good.

'I've done some other classical theatre too,' said Arjan. 'I played Perkin Warbeck at the Royal Exchange, Manchester, and Bonario in *Volpone* at the Edinburgh Festival. And last year I played McCann in *The Birthday Party*, although I didn't get great reviews for that.'

'Oh yes?' you asked, smirking. 'Why was that?'

'The critics said I was too young for the part. It's meant for a much older man. Someone your age, I think.'

I was taking a drink of my wine when he said this and almost snorted it out when I saw the expression on your face.

'Well, I'm not an actor,' you said, after a lengthy pause. 'I prefer to create the words, not just stand on a stage and parrot them like a . . . like a . . .' You struggled to finish the simile.

'Like a parrot?' suggested Rebecca, delighted by how her lover had scored such an easy victory over you.

'Actually, I read your novel,' continued Arjan, and it seemed that he'd built up his confidence now. We both looked up to see which one of us he was talking to.

'Thank you,' I said. 'You didn't have to.'

'I didn't read it because I was meeting you today. I'd already read it before I met Rebecca. Maybe two years ago? I liked it very much.'

'What did you like about it exactly?' you asked, and I turned to

172

look at you, surprised by the question. Were you trying to catch him out in a lie, was that it?

'I liked the story,' he replied. 'I liked the characters. And I liked the way it was written.'

'Could you be a little more specific?' you asked, and I felt my stomach sink, certain that, having given such a bland response, the chances were that he couldn't be. 'You see, it's always helpful for a writer to know which passages particularly impressed a reader. We're such bad judges of our own work.'

He looked at you silently for a few moments and I could see that he knew you were trying to take him down a peg or two. You held each other's gaze before he turned back to me, placing his wine glass down on the table.

'The moment where the girl takes her uncle's car,' he said. 'And she's been drinking and crashes into a ditch. The doors, they were . . .' He thought about it. 'What's the word? They couldn't open the doors because they were squashed between two trees, yes?'

'Yes,' I said.

'I liked the tension in that scene. And when she climbed into the back seat to escape. I did something like that myself once. Took my uncle's car, I mean, without him knowing. And I was in a crash. The girl I was with, a girl I liked very much, she was badly injured. And she never forgave me.'

'What happened to her?' I asked.

'The windscreen smashed and hundreds of slivers of glass went into her face. She needed a lot of surgery.'

'And did it work?' I asked. 'The surgery, I mean?'

'Yes, but there were still some scars. Anyway, I liked this passage very much. You write about fear very well.'

'Well, that is the title of the novel, after all,' you muttered irritably. '*Fear*.'

'Yes, but the novel isn't really about that, is it?' continued Arjan.

'In fact, I think the novel has very little to do with fear. In my view, it's about bravery.'

'You're very perceptive,' I said. 'Not everyone recognizes that.'

'I wouldn't be too flattered,' said Rebecca. 'As an actor, Arjan is obviously very interested in literature, so he reads a lot.'

'Something tells me that when you were in school, you were the boy who always came to class well prepared,' you commented, and I threw you a look, annoyed by your peevishness.

'I suppose I was,' admitted Arjan, refusing to rise to your bait. 'I wanted to pass my exams and to—'

'Yes, yes,' you said, dismissing him now with a wave of your hand.

'Rebecca tells me that you used to be a writer too,' said Arjan, and I winced at his choice of words.

'I beg your pardon?' you said.

'She says that you wrote a novel once,' he replied.

'I've written two actually,' you told him, and *Six*, I thought.

'There must be some competition between you then?' he asked, looking back and forth between us, and I shook my head.

'Oh no,' I said. 'Nothing like that. My husband has been publishing much longer than I have and is highly respected. I'm pretty new to it all.'

'And yet your book was such a success,' he said.

'Yes,' I admitted, for once wanting to accept the compliment. 'Yes, it was.'

'It's your use of the past tense that bothers me,' you said.

'I don't understand this?' said Arjan, narrowing his eyes.

'You mentioned that I *used* to be a writer. I didn't *used to be* anything. I *am*.'

'Just like I'm an actor,' said Arjan. 'Perhaps you're resting too. I hear a lot of writers do that. Anyway, I look forward to reading your next book. Eventually, I mean. If it finds a publisher.'

Before you could respond to this, Mum came in and clapped her hands to tell us that dinner was ready. I don't think I'd ever been so happy to see anyone in my entire life.

Later, I found you brooding in the hallway, staring at some old family photographs. I felt a rush of anxiety that you were angry with me but this eased when you smiled, leaned forward and kissed me.

'How about next year we don't go to your family or mine for Christmas?' you suggested. 'We could go away on holiday instead. Somewhere hot. Just the two of us.'

'Sounds good to me,' I said. 'How are you doing, anyway?'

'Fine,' you said. 'Why do you ask?'

'You were very quiet during dinner.'

'I was eating.'

I hesitated for a moment, uncertain whether I should bring this up or not. 'You know Arjan wasn't trying to be rude to you,' I said at last. 'He was probably just—'

'I don't give a fuck about Arjan,' you said. 'There's something sort of tragic about him, don't you think?'

'No, not really,' I said.

'You don't think he's a bit deluded?'

'In what sense?'

'His dreams of making it big in Hollywood.'

I said nothing for a moment, wondering whether you actually believed this or had simply decided to spin his remarks to fit your own design. 'Actually, I thought he seemed quite realistic about his future,' I replied finally.

'You fancy him, don't you?'

I rolled my eyes. 'Please tell me you're joking,' I said, hating where this conversation seemed to be leading.

You stared at me for the longest time and then broke into a wide smile. 'Of course I'm joking,' you said. 'Lighten up, Edith! It's Christmas!'

I pulled away from you but, before I could say anything, the

175

doorbell rang and I heard Mum call out to me from the living room, asking me to answer it.

'Excuse me,' I said, trying to move around you, but you were pressing me against the wall. 'Maurice, you're in my way,' I said, raising my voice a little, and now you stepped a little to the side, just enough to let me pass, and I walked towards the front door and opened it. Standing outside, the light from the overhead bulb shining down on him as it snowed, was Robert. He was wearing a grey overcoat that looked brand new and the sort of scarf that could only have been a present from his mother. He'd had a haircut too. The style was a little too youthful; it would have looked good on someone ten years younger but, on him, it seemed a little desperate.

'Hello, Edith,' he said. 'Happy Christmas.'

'Robert,' I said, standing back a little, surprised to see him there. 'Nobody mentioned that you . . . Is Rebecca expecting you?'

'I may have forgotten to tell her that I would be stopping by.'

'Right.' I stood there, staring at him, uncertain what I should do next, which was when you appeared behind me.

'Hello, Robert,' you said.

'Maurice.'

'You look cold, mate.'

'Well, I'm freezing my bollocks off, actually. Can I come in?'

'I'm not sure,' I replied. 'Do you think it's a good idea?'

'Of course you can,' you said, opening the door wider. 'You're still family. Come in.'

I stepped aside as he walked into the hallway, taking off his coat and scarf before reaching forward to give me an awkward kiss on my cheek. His cold lips made me shiver a little. 'You haven't been drinking, have you?' I asked. 'You're not here to cause any trouble?'

'I'm perfectly sober,' he said. 'I had lunch with my mother and didn't touch a drop of alcohol as I wanted to drive over to see the boys.'

'They're just in there,' you told him, pointing towards the living room.

'They're quite tired,' I said. 'They've been playing all day and practically ate their body weights over dinner.'

'Robert,' said a voice from behind me, and I turned around to see my sister standing there, her face a mask of annoyance. 'What the fuck are you doing here?'

'Happy Christmas,' he repeated, stepping forward to kiss her too, but she backed away and held her hands in the air as if to keep a careful distance from him.

'Don't *happy Christmas* me,' she said. 'I asked you a question. What the fuck are you doing here?'

'Full of the season of goodwill, I see.'

'Robert, I—'

'I wanted to spend a little time with my sons,' he said with a sigh. 'Is that a criminal offence?'

'No, but we already spoke about this. They're yours all day on the twenty-seventh.'

'But it's not the same thing, is it?' he said. 'I missed out on seeing them opening their presents this morning. That's the first time I haven't been there for that.'

'Well, I was there. And so was Arjan. So everything was fine. They didn't need you. They didn't even mention you, actually.'

'Rebecca, that's just cruel,' I said, and she turned on me now, pointing her finger in the air and telling me to keep my nose out. She was a little drunk and her tone brought me back to our shared childhood, when she would turn on me without any warning and the scene could rapidly descend into violence. The memory frightened me.

'I just want to see my children,' said Robert quietly. 'Can I go in? Please?'

'No, you cannot,' she said. 'If you go in there now, you'll only get them all excited again when I was planning on putting them to bed soon. It would be best if you just left.'

'But Rebecca, he's come all this way,' I protested. 'Surely a few minutes wouldn't—'

'Oh, here we go,' she said, rolling her eyes. 'You always take his side, don't you?'

'I'm not taking anyone's side,' I said. 'But it's Christmas Day, after all.'

'See?' she said, turning to Arjan, who had joined us in the hallway but was standing back a little, looking uncertain what his role, if any, in this conversation should be. 'This is what I have to put up with. No one ever supports me.'

'I'm honestly not looking for an argument,' said Robert calmly. 'Hello, Arjan, how are you?'

'I'm well, thank you,' replied Arjan. 'And you?'

'Never better,' he said. 'I had a slight head cold earlier in the week but it seems to have—'

'Can we *please* stop with the small talk?' asked Rebecca, raising her voice now.

'You want to take a little cold and flu medicine,' you said. 'This time of year, if you catch something it can lay you out for days.'

'I have some Nurofen, if that would help,' said Arjan.

'Thanks, Arjan,' said Robert. 'But I think I'll be all right for now.'

'Well, I can give you a couple to take with you if—'

'*Arjan!*' roared Rebecca, and I jumped a little. 'Can you . . .' She stopped talking, closed her eyes and breathed in deeply through her nose. It was the kind of thing I imagined a therapist might have told her to do in moments of stress.

'It's only right that I see my children,' said Robert. 'Even Edith thinks so.'

'I asked you to leave Edith out of this,' you said, stepping forward and putting your arm around my shoulders.

'I know,' he said. 'Sorry. But look, shall I just go in, Rebecca, and say hello? There's no point in us all standing out here in the hallway.'

Before she could reply, Damien, the eldest of my two nephews, came out into the hallway and gave a whoop of delight when he saw his father standing there, running towards him and throwing his arms around his legs. A moment later, Edward appeared, following suit, and the two boys immediately started telling him about the various presents they'd received, taking him by an arm each and dragging him into the living room to show him their toys.

'Sorry,' said Robert as he passed Rebecca, failing to keep the note of triumph out of his voice. 'I promise I won't stay long. An hour, tops.'

'I am *not* having this,' said Rebecca as soon as he had disappeared inside and closed the door behind him. 'If he thinks he can just show up here whenever he likes and—'

'Perhaps if you organized proper visiting times for him,' I said. 'From what I understand, you're being terribly difficult.'

'Oh, shut up, Edith. You don't know what you're talking about.'

'But you're addressing all of us, Rebecca,' you said. 'So it's not unreasonable that your sister should offer an opinion.'

'You're on his side too, then, are you?' she asked. 'What a surprise! Look, it's over between us and I don't want him hanging around all the time, is that so difficult to understand? The boys belong to me and—'

'Oh, for God's sake,' I said, throwing my hands in the air. 'The boys don't belong to anyone! And if they did, they would belong to both of you!'

'They belong to *me*,' she insisted, 'and they need to be left alone to adjust to the new reality of their lives.'

I couldn't take any more of this nonsense and followed Robert into the living room and slowly, one by one, you, Rebecca and Arjan followed too. Robert was true to his word, staying only an hour, and had it not been for the boys' tears when he finally left, it would have been a perfectly pleasant visit.

It was only later that night as I was falling asleep that a line from the argument popped into my head. Something that you had said to Robert.

I asked you to leave Edith out of this.

When did you ask him this, Maurice? Because it wasn't while we were standing there. Did you call him after he came to see me at UEA? Or did you take a train to London and not tell me anything about it? And what else were you doing during those months that I knew nothing about? All things considered, you'll forgive me if I sound a little suspicious.

5. January

The new term got off to an exciting start with two pieces of news, one a cause for celebration, the other a source of scandal.

The former was the announcement by Garrett Colby that he'd secured a publishing deal over Christmas for his debut collection of short stories, *The Voices of Animals*. He told us as we settled down for our first workshop, during which he himself was due to be critiqued, and the reactions of the other students ranged from delight to envy to disbelief to a sort of carefully controlled fury.

I weighed up whether or not to tell you but decided that I should. You would find out eventually and wonder why I hadn't mentioned it myself. But I waited until a couple of days later, when we were having dinner and you seemed to be in a good mood. That evening, I'd come home and been a little frustrated to find you working in my study again. You pointed out that it overlooked the garden rather than the street and that you needed peace in order to write and, besides, I was on campus throughout most of the day, so what did it matter?

'You're in very good spirits,' I remarked as we ate. 'Your work must be going well.'

'Very well,' you said cheerfully. 'You know that moment when you realize you've got a firm grasp on your book and know exactly where it's going?'

'Sort of.'

'That's how I'm feeling right now. Writing a novel is a war and I think I'm winning at last.'

'I'm really glad to hear that,' I replied. 'So are you going to give me some clue as to what it's about?'

'Afraid not,' you said, shaking your head and grinning like a mischievous child. 'You don't mind, do you?'

'I'm hardly in a position to,' I said. 'It's not as if I've been willing to tell you about mine.'

'Exactly,' you said. 'You must be getting close to a final draft, anyway?'

'Another six weeks or so. And you?'

'Around the same.'

'What?' I asked, staring at you in astonishment. 'But you've only been working on it since November.'

'I know, but it's just coming together a lot more quickly than I imagined. These things can happen. Anthony Burgess wrote *A Clockwork Orange* in about three weeks, you know. Faulkner wrote *As I Lay Dying* in six.'

'Well, that's wonderful,' I said, unsure whether it was or not. I couldn't even conceive of writing a novel in so short a time, but I was aware that you'd often worked in sustained periods of creative intensity.

'Actually, I have some news too,' I said carefully, praying that my announcement wouldn't destroy your positive mood.

'Oh yes?' you asked. 'What's that?'

'You remember Garrett Colby?'

'The children's writer with the talking animals?'

'He's not a children's writer,' I said with a sigh. 'You've been told this before. Many times. They're adult stories.'

'With talking animals.'

'Murakami has lots of talking animals in his books,' I said. 'As does Bulgakov. And Philip Pullman.'

'Yes, but you can't compare that little twat to any of them,' you said.

'Don't call him that. It's not nice.'

'You don't like him any more than I do.'

'I know, but still.'

'Fine,' you said, laughing a little. 'I'll be nice. What about him, anyway? Has he had a breakthrough of some sort? Decided that his novel needs some trees that can dance the tango or a few lamp posts that can juggle while singing show tunes?'

'No. Actually, he's sold them.'

'What do you mean, sold them? Sold what?'

'Sold the stories. As a collection.'

You put down your cutlery and looked at me with an incredulous expression on your face. 'You don't mean to an actual publisher?'

'Yes,' I said.

'Jesus Christ.' You stared across the room, refusing to meet my eye, and I could see that you were allowing yourself a few moments to digest this information and decide how to react to it. 'Who bought them?' you asked when you finally looked back.

'You won't believe this,' I said. 'But it was Rufus.'

You didn't even blink. 'Not my Rufus?' you asked.

'Yes, I suppose so,' I replied. 'If that's how we think of him.'

I had only met Rufus Shawcross twice, and briefly on both occasions. The first time was only a few weeks after I'd started dating you and I was waiting in the lobby of your publishing house while you met with him in his office upstairs. Afterwards, you came down together and I could tell by the expression on your face that things hadn't gone well, but you couldn't avoid introducing me. I liked him immediately. He was exactly my idea of what an editor should look like: button-down shirt, thick-rimmed glasses, floppy hair, boyishly handsome, looking like he needed to shave about once every second month. The second time was several years later, after you'd had all those novels rejected and effectively been dropped. We'd run into him in a health-food store on Glasshouse Street and the whole thing had been terribly awkward. You'd pretended to be friendly but everything you said was clearly intended as an insult and he seemed upset by your rudeness. For my part, I was simply embarrassed. I knew the poor man had taken no pleasure in turning down your novels, but he'd had no choice. After all, they weren't any good.

'He must have lost his mind,' you said, trying to sound chipper, but I could tell that it was taking every fibre of your being to stop yourself flinging our bowls at the wall and watching the food slowly trace a furious, misunderstood path down the paintwork.

'He's actually quite good,' I said.

'Rufus?'

'No, Garrett.'

'Oh, don't be ridiculous.'

'Maurice, you haven't even read him,' I pointed out. 'You don't know.'

'I didn't go down on the *Titanic* either but I know that it wouldn't have been a pleasant experience,' you said, shaking your head. 'Fucking Rufus. Did you hear what he got? The advance, I mean.'

'No,' I said. 'He didn't mention it.'

'It probably wasn't very much.'

It was, actually. He'd been offered one hundred thousand pounds for the story collection and a novel to follow. But I chose not to tell you that.

'Well, good luck to him, I suppose,' you said, after a lengthy pause filled with a barely concealed frenzy of anger.

I sighed. A pleasant evening together had disintegrated yet again. I wasn't sorry that I'd brought it up but I wanted to let it go now. Looking back, I wonder if I wanted to hurt you by telling you Garrett's news. You had hurt me, after all. You had hurt me *physically*. Perhaps I wanted revenge. For even if you'd played it cool and pretended that whatever happened with my students held little meaning to you, I knew that you would brood over it for weeks.

'Something else happened today,' I said after a prolonged silence, ready to tell you the second piece of news. 'One of my students got thrown off the course.'

'Really?' you said, sitting up straight now. 'Who?'

'Do you remember Maja Drazkowski?'

You frowned. 'Which one is she?'

'When you came to talk to the students, she was the one who looked like she'd rather fuck you than listen to you speak.'

'You'll have to narrow it down.'

'Oh, shut up,' I said, laughing.

'Yes, I remember her,' you admitted. 'What happened? Why did she get cut?'

'Plagiarism,' I replied.

'You're kidding!'

'No.'

'Who did she plagiarize?'

'No one I'd ever heard of, to be honest. A story that had been published in the *New Yorker* three or four years ago.'

You stood up, gathering the bowls and plates, and began carrying them over to the sink to rinse them off before putting them in the dishwasher. When I rose to help, you placed a hand on my shoulder and told me to stay where I was, that I'd had a busy day and should relax.

'How was she caught out?' you asked.

'The tutor who was marking my group recognized it. Apparently, he's quite a fan of the *New Yorker* and keeps all his back issues. She was called in this morning, presented with the evidence, and the stupid girl said it was nothing more than a coincidence.'

'A five-thousand-word coincidence?' you asked, laughing.

'Well, exactly. That was never going to fly. Anyway, she gave up that defence quickly enough. Within a couple of minutes the tears were flowing and she was telling us how she felt she didn't belong on the course, that she couldn't compete with the others. *I could have written something, of course,* she told us, *but it wouldn't have been good enough and I refuse to give in sub-standard work. I just refuse.*'

'But she's happy to give in someone else's work?' you said.

'That's what I said! And then she just started crying again. Anyway, the whole thing went on for an hour and became rather tedious, and when we reached the point where she started telling us how her uncle used to make her sit on his lap when she was a little girl and she wondered whether this was what led to such behaviour on her part—'

'Oh, for God's sake.'

'I know. We told her that our only concern was her academic work and that she had lost our trust.'

'So you kicked her out?'

'Well, we told her that we would be referring the matter to the dean of students, but that she couldn't attend any more classes until the situation was resolved. Then she threw a fit and told us that she wanted to drop out, effective immediately, that I was the worst teacher in the world and that if she'd written *Fear*, she would have eaten it page by page rather than let anyone read it. *Aren't you embarrassed by it?* she asked me. *All that clichéd writing, the one-dimensional characters, the trite resolution. I'd be mortified if I'd written it.* And I couldn't help myself. I said that maybe she would one day, since she had such little scruple about stealing other people's stories.'

'Ha!'

'Yes, that shut her up. She flounced out then and later this afternoon I got an email from my department head saying she'd formally resigned from the course and I was to inform the other students.'

'Well, it sounds like she got what she deserved,' you said. 'Plagiarism is the greatest crime any writer can commit. But you shouldn't blame yourself for any of this.'

'Blame myself?' I asked, turning to you as you loaded the dishwasher. 'Why on earth would I blame myself?'

'You shouldn't,' you replied. 'That's what I'm saying. It's not your fault.'

'No, I get that,' I said. 'But if I *were* to blame myself, in error, I mean, what would I be blaming myself for?'

'I don't know,' you said. 'Perhaps she felt you were putting her under too much pressure? Or felt that she couldn't write in the environment that you'd created? She'd be an idiot to think any of that, of course. Which is why I'm saying don't blame yourself.'

'But I don't,' I said in frustration. 'At least I didn't until you suggested that I shouldn't.'

'Good,' you said, coming over and kissing me on the forehead. 'Then we're in agreement. Now, I think I'm going to take a walk, if you don't mind. That stew was a little heavy, don't you think? And I need to think about tomorrow's work. I'm reaching a crucial stage in my novel and need to arrange my thoughts clearly in my head.'

And before I could say anything, or offer to accompany you, you'd taken your coat from the hook and were gone.

Blame myself? I thought. *Why the fuck would I blame myself?*

Three days later, I was shopping in Market Place when it started to rain and I took shelter in the Sir Garnet pub. I don't usually sit in bars on my own in the middle of the afternoon but I had the new Anne Tyler in my bag and thought I might just settle down with a glass of wine and relax for a while. I'd finished my drink, the rain had stopped, and I was trying to decide whether I should order another or leave when a familiar face walked past the window, noticed me sitting inside and waved. I waved back and a moment later the door opened and in he came.

It was my crush. Nicholas Bray.

'Hello, Edith,' he said, smiling at me, and I liked the dimples that appeared in his cheeks. 'Is this how you spend your afternoons when you're not teaching? Drinking alone?'

'Not usually, no,' I replied, not wanting him to think that I was some sort of lonely alcoholic in my spare time. 'I was shopping, you see, and the rain—'

'I was kidding,' he said, sitting down opposite me before standing

186

up again. 'Oh, sorry. I suppose I should ask whether you want company before assuming that you do.'

'Please,' I said, indicating the seat. 'I was thinking of having a second, actually. You're welcome to join me if you like.'

He went to the bar and ordered a pint for himself and another wine for me, and when he sat down we clinked glasses and he told me off for not looking him in the eye as I did so. 'In some countries,' he said, 'you can be barred from pubs for such behaviour.'

He was wearing a tattered denim shirt that was open halfway down his chest and a white T-shirt underneath. His sleeves were rolled up and, for the first time, I noticed that he had a tattoo on the underside of his right arm. Two letters: EB.

'My aunt's initials,' he told me when I asked what they signified. 'She brought me up after my parents died.'

'What happened to them?' I asked, for I didn't know that he'd been orphaned.

'A car crash,' he said with a shrug. 'It's okay, I was only three at the time. I don't really remember them. Anyway, my aunt – my dad's sister – took me in. She's a social worker. She doesn't have any kids of her own. She took care of me.'

We talked a little about his work then, about how it was coming along, and soon enough it was my turn to go to the bar and order a round. I brought back some peanuts as I was worried that I would get drunk too soon and switched to lager so I wouldn't find myself drinking an entire bottle of wine on my own.

Soon, our defences were down and I asked him to fill me in on the class gossip.

'What sort of gossip?' he asked.

'Well, who's sleeping with who, and so on.'

'I don't think there's been too much of that,' he said, narrowing his eyes a little as he considered it. 'You've probably noticed that there isn't a lot of sexual tension in workshop.'

'Yes, that's been very disappointing,' I said, flirting shamelessly with him now, enjoying the freedom just to look at his beautiful face. 'When I was a student we spent half our time in each other's beds. I hoped there'd be a few broken hearts at least, followed by classroom recriminations and walk-outs.'

'There's still six months to go,' he replied. 'We could surprise you yet. Anyway, the one girl that all the boys fancy is completely unattainable.'

I thought about it, running through each of the female students in my mind, uncertain who he might be referring to.

'Who's that?' I asked, and he simply smiled and took a long drink from his pint, keeping his eyes fixed on mine.

'Oh, please,' I said, blushing a little but utterly delighted. 'I doubt anyone is thinking of me in those terms. I'm old enough to be . . . well, a big sister to most of the boys in the class. What about you? Have you been seeing anyone?'

He shrugged, then shook his head. 'No one special,' he said. 'No one from our workshop, anyway. I guess I've been focussing on my work.'

'Fair enough,' I said.

'Can I ask how long you and your husband have been together?' he said.

'We got married five and a bit years ago,' I told him. 'And we were dating for a few years before that.'

'He's incredibly handsome,' said Nicholas, and I nodded.

'He is,' I said. 'Why did you say that? You don't fancy him, do you?'

'No,' he replied. 'I'm straight. But I mean he's just obviously very good-looking.'

'I couldn't agree more,' I said, waving towards the barman for another round.

'I think Garrett fancies him,' he said.

'Really?' I said, surprised. 'He and Maurice have met a few times and there always seems to be some sort of mutual loathing going on there.'

'He's only acting that way because he wants to get into his pants. You know he's driving us all crazy right now? Telling us that we aren't to think of him any differently now that he's going to be a published writer.'

'And do you?' I ask.

'No. I thought he was a cock before and I think he's a cock now. Just a soon-to-be-published cock, that's all.'

I laughed but didn't disagree. A part of me knew that it was wrong to be spending so much time drinking alone with one of my students but, if I'm honest, I didn't care. I was enjoying the sense of freedom he offered me, the feeling of being twenty-three again and dreaming of a writing career. The more we drank, the more attractive he grew and when he leaned back in his chair at one point to produce a dramatic yawn, his T-shirt rode up, displaying a lower belly that was covered in fine, dark hairs. Just looking at them made me imagine what he might look like if he stripped that T-shirt off.

Perhaps he guessed. Perhaps, after our first couple of drinks, he'd wondered whether our afternoon might end with us going to bed together. After all, I'd alluded to such things already. Because when we finished our next drinks, he asked me whether I wanted another or whether I might like to go somewhere else.

'Like where?' I asked him.

'Like my place,' he said, without an ounce of self-consciousness. 'I only live a few minutes away.'

I shrugged. I didn't want him to think that I was in any way shocked. 'To fuck, you mean?' I asked him.

'Sure,' he said. 'If you want to.'

'Tell me it hasn't always been your fantasy to fuck your teacher.'

'You wouldn't think that if you'd seen the teachers I had in school.'

'Why don't we just . . . walk down the street and get a little air?' I said, standing up, and soon enough we were outside, feeling the disorienting effect of sunshine on our eyes when we were both a little drunk. We strolled around St Peter's Street and on to Goat Lane but didn't speak the entire time. The anticipation was making me incredibly aroused and I had no clear idea what I was going to do next, whether I would in fact go to bed with him or whether I might turn around on his doorstep, place a hand against his chest and say something like *You're very sweet, Nicholas, but there's no way this could end well for either of us.* It felt as if I were watching myself from above, like I was a character in a film about to make a bad choice that would inevitably lead to catastrophe, but when he finally stopped outside a door and put a key in the lock, I felt an extraordinary longing to follow him inside and let him do anything he wanted to me.

He turned around, saw the expression on my face, and offered a half-smile.

'That's a no, isn't it?' he said.

'Sorry,' I said. 'Wrong time, and all that.'

He shrugged. I could tell that he wasn't going to beg. He did, however, lean forward and kiss me and I kissed him right back and, I don't mind telling you, Maurice, that boy knew how to kiss.

'I'd better go,' I said, turning around, and as I walked back down the street I knew he was watching me and that felt good.

When I got back to the flat, stumbling on that bloody handrail again, which you *still* hadn't fixed, I had a long shower and later, when we were sitting on the sofa together watching a movie, I found that I was barely thinking about the events of the afternoon at all. Come Wednesday, there was no awkwardness between Nicholas and me and he seemed so untroubled by the whole thing that I began to wonder whether I had simply imagined the flirtation and the kiss.

6. February

In early February, the department head, George Canter, dropped into my office to discuss some student issues and while he was there I took the opportunity to ask him whether I might be able to stay at UEA for a few more years.

'Of course we'd be delighted to have you, Edith,' said George. 'And if a job should come up, then we could certainly discuss it. Although for legal reasons, we might have to advertise it formally. But even if we did, I think it would take a strong candidate to defeat you. Particularly since you're already *in situ*, so to speak. Just so I know,' he added, 'when are you hoping to publish your second novel?'

'I plan on delivering it by April,' I said. 'And all going well, I hope that it'll be out by next spring.'

'Well, that will certainly help too,' he said. 'It looks good for the faculty to be actively publishing. The students need to see that we're *doing* as well as teaching.'

There was a knock on the door and you poked your head in. This was only the second time you'd visited my office since our arrival in Norwich and you looked ridiculously cheerful as you glanced from me to George and back again.

'Not interrupting, am I?' you asked, stepping inside. 'Hello, George, how's things?'

'Maurice,' he said, standing up and shaking your hand furiously. 'No, we were just finishing up. I was telling Edith that, even if she does have to apply for the job, I think I could say, without prejudice, that her application will be favourably received.'

I saw the expression on your face harden as you digested this piece of information. Of course, I hadn't yet spoken to you about staying on at UEA and had no idea how you might feel about it. But you didn't pursue the conversation and, when George finally let go of your hand, you leaned down to kiss me on the cheek with a 'Hello, gorgeous' that was completely out of character for you.

'Hello yourself,' I said. 'What brings you here?'

'Some good news,' you replied.

'Perhaps I should leave you both to it,' said George, edging towards the door.

'No, stay,' I said, for in that moment I felt as if I didn't want to be left alone with you, when you might ask me what we had been discussing before you arrived. 'There were a couple of other things I wanted to talk to you about.'

'All right,' he replied, sitting down again, and I could see that you looked as irritated by his continued presence as he was made uncomfortable by it.

'So what's the good news?' I asked, looking in your direction and trying to ease whatever tension lay between us.

'It's about my novel,' you said.

'You haven't finished it!'

'No, not quite. But I wanted to be certain that I was on the right track so I sent the opening few chapters to someone in the industry.'

'Who?' I asked.

'Peter Wills-Bouche,' you replied.

'The agent?' said George, looking up, clearly impressed. Everyone knew who Peter Wills-Bouche was. To be represented by him was to be considered part of literature's elite, whether you were a Nobel Prize-winner – he represented three – or a debut writer.

'I'm glad you sent it, Maurice,' I said. 'He's exactly the sort of agent you deserve. But I imagine it will be a while before you hear back from him so let's not get too excited just yet.'

'But that's the thing,' you replied. 'He phoned this morning, just after I got back from the gym. He wants to meet me.'

'You mean he's read it already?'

'He said that he took it home with him last night, only intending to read a few pages, but ended up showing up two hours late for his daughter-in-law's birthday party because he couldn't put it down.'

'You're kidding!' I said, opening my eyes wide in a mixture of astonishment and delight.

'He said that these were the best opening chapters of any novel that he'd read in the last ten years.'

'But Maurice, that's wonderful,' I said, jumping up to embrace you, feeling genuinely thrilled on your behalf. 'I'm so proud of you.'

'Thank you,' you replied, grinning from ear to ear.

'Yes, well done, you,' said George, standing up and shaking your hand again. 'You must be thrilled.'

'I knew that one day you'd find your way back,' I said. 'I've always believed in you, you know that, don't you?'

'I do, Edith,' you said, and the warmth in your expression made me recall the happiest times of our years together. 'And I appreciate it, I really do. You've been the one person who's always believed in me. Even when I haven't always believed in myself.'

I smiled. When you shone your light on me, it was still impossible not to feel the wonderful glow. 'So presumably he's going to take you on, then?'

'Well, I assume so, yes, but let's not count our chickens just yet. That's why I called in here. I'm taking the train up to London in about an hour to meet with him. He said he'd like to meet today, before I show it to anyone else. I'll know more after that.'

'Gosh, he is keen!' I said.

'Seems like it.'

'Maybe we'll even end up publishing our books around the same time,' I said. 'That would be fun, wouldn't it?'

'Oh God, let's not,' you said, rolling your eyes. 'No, we should wait to see what's happening with my book first and then you can have a word with your publisher to ensure that our dates don't clash. Makes more sense that way, don't you think?'

'Well,' I replied, feeling my heart sink a little. I'd been working on my novel for three years, after all, and didn't want to delay its publication for any reason. Also, I didn't see why your work should suddenly take priority over mine. 'I'm not sure, but we can always—'

'I'd better go,' you said, glancing at your watch. 'I don't want to miss my train. I just wanted to see the expression on your face when I told you!'

'Maybe we should be asking *you* to apply for a job here,' said George, and I glared at him in disappointment. 'It's a real asset to the university when we have up-and-coming writers in our faculty.'

You laughed and shook your head. 'I don't think I quite fit that description, do you?' you said. 'I'm a little more established than that.'

When I returned home that evening, I found a letter waiting on the mat that infuriated me. I read it carefully several times then forced myself to wait until the first rush of temper had passed before picking up the phone to call Rebecca.

'I got your letter,' I said without any preamble when she answered, trying to control the anger in my voice. 'Or rather, your solicitor's letter.'

'Oh good,' she said. 'The sooner we get the ball rolling on this, the better. I was very lucky to get an early hearing. Some couple reconciled so an appointment opened up. Don't you think these people should stop being so fickle? Anyway, their loss is my gain. I assume you'll be able to make it?'

I held the phone away from my face for a moment and stared at it furiously, as if the handset were somehow responsible for my sister's insufferable behaviour.

'You don't actually think I'm going to do this, do you?' I asked.

There was a long pause. I wondered whether she was truly surprised by my response or simply pretending to be. 'Of course I do,' she said. 'Why wouldn't you?'

'Let me just read out what your solicitor wrote,' I said to her. '*It is our contention that Robert Gelwood lacks the essential skills needed to be a father to the miners, Damien and Edward Gelwood. As you have been a witness to his erratic behaviour since the birth of both children, we are requesting that you testify to his fragile state of mind, his unpredictable temperament and his lack of parental responsibility. We further hope that*

194

you will support our position that the children be placed in the sole custody of their mother, Rebecca Camberley-Gelwood.'

'It's such legalese, isn't it?' said Rebecca, giggling a little. 'Even you could write better than that.'

'It's not the wording that I object to,' I said. 'Although, by the way, you might want to tell your solicitor that *minors* is spelled with an *o*. As far as I know, Damien and Edward aren't being sent a few miles underground every day to dig for coal.'

'Oh, don't be so pedantic, you know what he meant. Is that all that's bothering you?'

'No, it's the fact that I don't believe for a moment that Robert is an unfit father.'

'Of course he isn't,' she agreed. 'Actually, he's a very good father.'

'Then why on earth . . . ?' I paused and pinched the top of my nose to control my annoyance. 'Seriously, Rebecca, if you think that, then why are you going to court to say otherwise? And why do you want my help?'

'Because he won't let me take the children,' she said.

'Take them where?'

'To America.'

'Why are you going to America? Do you mean on holiday?'

She gave an exasperated laugh, as if she couldn't quite believe that she had to explain something so obvious to me. 'No, we're moving there.'

'Who's moving there? And why? And since when?'

'Oh my God, Edith. So many questions! It's like having a conversation with Miss Marple. Arjan, the boys and I are all moving there for his television show. To Los Angeles – can you believe it?'

'Well, that's good news for him, I suppose,' I said. 'But what about the boys? What about their schooling?'

'They do have schools in America, as far as I understand.'

'Yes, with metal detectors on every doorway to hold back the shooters.'

'Oh, don't exaggerate.'

'And what about their friends?'

'They'll make new friends.'

'Why didn't you tell me about any of this before?'

'Sorry, I thought I had. Well, I told Mum, so I assumed she'd pass it on.'

'Actually, no. This is the first I'm hearing of any of it. What did Mum say?'

'She was very upset. She started going on about how much she was going to miss the boys growing up and blah, blah, blah. I told her, *Mum, there are such things as aeroplanes! You can come and visit whenever you want!* Although don't get me wrong, Edith. I don't literally mean whenever she wants. We'll probably be quite busy with a new social circle so please don't think that either of you can just show up unannounced.'

'I can't believe you didn't tell me personally. I'm going to miss the boys too. So will Maurice. You know how fond he is of the children.'

'Well, you don't have to worry too much. It's not for a couple of months yet and there are so many things to be sorted out this end before we even think of booking flights. But, you see, Robert is being a complete pain about the whole thing. He's refusing to let the boys go and, since we currently have joint custody, I'm not allowed to leave the country with them without his permission.'

'That's perfectly reasonable,' I said. 'What father would want to be separated from his sons?'

'He's so bloody selfish,' said Rebecca. 'He always has been. If you ever have children, I hope you'll think twice before putting Maurice's name on the birth certificate. It gives men all these rights that you could otherwise keep from them and, let's face it, when have they ever put us first on anything? Not that that's really something you'll need to worry about. You're career, career, career all the way, aren't you? We're so different in that respect. I've always had such a deep maternal streak.'

I almost laughed. Not just at the insensitive nature of her remarks – she knew about the miscarriages, after all, or at least about some of them – but at her assumption that our marriage would end in failure, just as hers had.

'Look,' I said. 'You can't expect me to testify that he's a bad father when he's not. I won't do it.'

'Why not? I don't think it's unreasonable for a person to offer her first loyalty to her sister.'

'I think, in this situation, my first loyalty should be to the boys. And whether I think they should be separated from a loving and selfless father. What's their view on this, anyway? I presume they don't want to leave Robert behind?'

'Oh no, they're up in arms,' she told me. 'They don't want to leave England. But that's neither here nor there. I'm not going to be dictated to by a nine-year-old and a six-year-old.'

'Edward is seven,' I pointed out.

'Oh, shut up, Edith,' she said. 'Look, all I need is for you to sit down opposite a judge and say that Robert has a terrible temper, that he's called the boys a few beastly names and that he's threatened to hit me on occasion, that sort of thing.'

'I'm not going to do that!' I cried.

'It won't take more than an hour or so. Then you can get back to your book or your students, or whatever it is you do to fill your days.'

'Rebecca, I'm not going to lie in court. Especially about something so important. For one thing, it's perjury. I could go to jail.'

'Lots of people have written books in jail. Look at Jeffrey Archer.'

'I'm not sure Jeffrey Archer is someone on whose career I want to model my own.'

'Don't be such a snob. He's sold millions of books all over the world, which is more than you've ever done. Anyway, you're not going to go to jail, you're just being melodramatic. Just stick to your story and no one will be able to prove that you're lying. If you don't help me on this, then there's a good chance that custody arrangements will remain exactly as they are and we won't be able to leave. And this is Arjan's big chance, after all.'

'Can't he just go on his own?'

'Oh no,' she said. 'No, I wouldn't allow that. Our relationship would never survive such a distance. He'd probably meet someone else over there. Hollywood is full of bimbos, all with their eyes on the main prize.'

'I'm sorry, Rebecca,' I said, trying to adopt as firm a voice as I possibly could. 'But I'm not going to do it. I'm not going to perjure myself, I'm not going to lie about Robert and I'm not going to put my nephews' futures in jeopardy. Sorry, but no.'

'I can't believe how selfish you're being,' she said after a lengthy pause.

'Try,' I said.

'Edith, you're the only one I can ask. It's too much to ask of a friend and, besides, I don't really have any friends. They all seem to have slipped away over the years, for some reason. Jealousy, I expect. Women have always been jealous of me. Well, you should know that better than anyone. No, it has to be you. A family member.'

'The answer's no,' I repeated. 'And I'm sorry, but I have to go now.'

'But—'

'Sorry, Rebecca. Let's talk soon.'

And I hung up, waiting expectantly for the phone to ring again. But, to my relief, it stayed silent. I wondered whether I should call Robert and tell him what she'd asked me to do but decided against it, wishing that I could be left out of the whole thing entirely. Looking back now, that's one of my biggest regrets. If I'd simply phoned him up and recounted this conversation, even agreed to sign a statement to this effect for his solicitor, everything in his life might have turned out differently.

Although it wouldn't have made any great difference to mine, I suppose.

★

When you returned from London the following evening, you were almost hysterical with happiness. You phoned me from Thorpe Station to ask where I was and I told you that I was on campus, in the grad bar, where one of my students was celebrating her birthday. I expected you to ask me to leave and meet you in town for a drink but, to my surprise, you said that you'd jump in a taxi and meet me there.

You arrived around twenty minutes later, striding towards our group as if you owned the place, and when I stood up you wrapped your arms around me, kissing me passionately, and I immediately felt embarrassed by such a public display of emotion.

'So how did it go?' I asked, dragging you away from the group so we could talk in private.

'Brilliantly.'

'He likes it, then? He wants to represent you?'

'He had the contract all ready for my signature when I arrived.'

'That's wonderful, Maurice.'

'He claimed that he'd always been an admirer of my fiction, particularly *The Treehouse*.'

'Ha,' I said. 'I bet that pleased you.'

'Well, yes,' you replied, frowning a little, and I realized immediately that I'd said the wrong thing. 'It did, as it happens. It's always been a far subtler work than *Two Germans*. We had a long conversation about my career to date and he feels that this is the right novel to relaunch me. He wants me to say that I've been working on it for seven years, just to increase the sense of the book's importance.'

'But you've barely been working on it seven months,' I said.

'I know, but look, I'll say whatever needs to be said. It's the novel that matters. Getting it out there. Bringing readers to me. To it, I mean.'

'The truth matters too, though, surely?' I said.

'Oh, come on, Edith,' you replied, rolling your eyes. 'It's only a little white lie. It hardly matters. He's putting it out to auction in a couple of weeks' time. He thinks it's going to be the most sought-after novel of the year.'

'Jesus, Maurice,' I said. 'What the hell have you written?'

You shrugged, as if the act of writing something that was provoking such interest was rather simple, really. 'Just a novel. That's all.'

'It sounds like it's more than *just a novel*,' I said. 'It sounds like it's something very special.'

'Well, I hope so, yes.'

'And did he talk advances?'

'He did. He thinks it'll be high. He even said . . .' You paused and shook your head. 'Well, no, I don't want to jinx it.'

'Go on, tell me.'

'It's silly, it doesn't matter.'

I punched you playfully on the arm. 'Tell me,' I insisted.

'He said he'd put his house on it that I'll win The Prize next year.'

My eyes opened wide. 'Are you kidding me?'

'That's what he said. But look, there's no point thinking about things like that right now. Awards are neither here nor there. You know things like that don't matter to me in the slightest.'

Which was a *total* lie, of course, because you'd read every book ever shortlisted for The Prize throughout its history. You were practically its unofficial historian. Even making it on to the longlist had been your life's ambition and, the previous year, when Douglas Sherman had come close to winning, you'd almost lost your mind in bitterness and envy.

'In a way, it would be like the completion of a circle, wouldn't it?' I said, thinking about this. 'If you were to win, I mean?'

'How so?'

'Well, Erich Ackermann won for *Dread*. And that's where things started for you. With Erich's story.'

'Poor Erich would roll in his grave if my name got added to his on the honour roll,' you said, but I could see that you were pleased by the idea. 'Oh, Garrett,' you said, leaning forward and raising your voice so the students were forced to pause in their conversations and look our way. 'I haven't seen you since you got your deal, have I? Edith told me all about it. Congratulations, you must be thrilled.'

'Thank you,' said Garrett, smiling happily as he brushed the hair out of his eyes. 'I didn't expect to be published so young. I never really saw myself as a prodigy.'

'I'm sure you didn't,' you said. 'I don't think anyone would have predicted that you'd ever find a publisher. But they do say there's a boom in children's writing at the moment, don't they? And that's where the money is too, from what I understand.'

'It's not a . . .' began Garrett, and I could see that he was doing all he could to stop himself from roaring this at the top of his voice. I knew you were just taking the piss out of him and I had to bite my lip to stop myself laughing.

'Yes, we know it's not a children's book,' shouted Nicholas, throwing his arms in the air in frustration. 'Jesus, Garrett, why don't you just get that printed on cards and hand them out to people every time the subject comes up?'

'It's vital that we get children reading,' you continued. 'Then when the little monsters grow up they'll read books by Edith and me and some of your colleagues here. We actually owe people like you, Garrett, a debt of gratitude.'

'And what about you, Maurice?' asked Garrett, who was never one to back down from a fight. 'Will you be joining me on the festival circuit, or is that all a thing of the past for you?'

'I don't really do children's festivals,' you said.

'You don't really do adult festivals either any more, do you?' he asked. 'It's been so long since *Two Germans*. I know there was that other little book after that – what was it called again? *The Cubbyhole*? Something like that? – but as far as I understand, that's best left unmentioned.'

'Actually, my husband has just sold his latest novel,' I said, stretching the truth a little, but it seemed clear that this was only a matter of weeks, if not days, away.

'Really?' said Garrett, his face falling a little. 'An actual novel or just an idea?'

'An actual novel,' you replied, smiling. 'Full of sentences and paragraphs and chapters.'

'Well, good for you,' he replied. 'Are you going to tell us what it's about or is it a state secret?'

'I thought I'd go for something really original,' you said. 'Animals that *can't* talk. Like in real life, you know? No, I'm just kidding, Garrett. Don't look so annoyed. If you don't mind, I won't tell you the story right now. You can read it when it comes out, if you like. I'll make sure to get my publisher to send you a copy. But let's not talk about all this right now. It's someone's birthday, yes? Shouldn't we be celebrating?'

And we did celebrate. And when we got back to our apartment, we celebrated again, just the two of us. A celebration that was only slightly marred when you asked what George had been talking about the previous morning when he'd said about my applying for a job and I was forced to tell you that I'd been thinking of staying on at UEA. But you said no, that it was important that we get back to London when your book came out, as it was important that you be in the heart of things.

'I'm sure you'll find another teaching job there,' you said. 'From what I understand, you might have found your true calling in the classroom.'

'Thanks,' I said, although for the life of me I didn't know what I was thanking you for.

7. March

When I woke that Tuesday morning, how could I have known that everything I had worked for since I was a girl, every dream and ambition that had found its way into my heart, would be stolen from me by nightfall?

It seems ironic in retrospect but I remember opening my eyes to the sun pouring through the curtains and feeling an overwhelming sense of well-being. A few days earlier, I'd finished my novel and was finally ready to show it to my editor. Unlike when I completed *Fear*, which you'd encouraged me to submit to agents despite my doubts about its merits, I felt a measured confidence in this one and had even decided on a title, *The Tribesman*. I knew it still needed some work but, I felt, not an enormous amount. It would certainly be ready by the end of the academic year, which had been my original plan when we'd arrived in Norwich.

It had already been an exciting week. Two days earlier, Peter Wills-Bouche had sold your manuscript for an astonishing four hundred thousand pounds to one of the most prestigious publishers in London and it was currently on submission with five American publishers. To my surprise, you'd been quieter than usual over recent days, less ebullient than I might have been in your position, and I worried that your distance sprang from anxiety or a sense of anticlimax.

I could hear you in the shower as I climbed out of bed, opening a window on to the bright, clear morning and reaching my head outside for a moment to breathe in the air. As I did so, however, I felt an unexpected convulsion in my stomach, and it was all that I could do to run to the kitchen sink before I threw up. I kept my head over the porcelain for a minute or two until the retching came to an end. Feeling shaky, I sat down at the kitchen table, placing a hand against my forehead. My skin was slick with perspiration and, a moment later, I touched my stomach and then felt the tenderness of my breasts. I knew the symptoms only too well; I'd been pregnant four times already, after all. And now I was pregnant for a fifth.

A rush of conflicted thoughts shot through my head simultaneously. How would this affect the publication of both our books? No, I'm being disingenuous. I wondered how it would affect the publication of *my* book. Would I carry the baby to term or lose it like I had lost the others? Where would we live? I liked Norwich and wanted to stay at the university but even if I could convince you that we were better off there than in London there was no way we could stay in a small flat with a broken staircase. The idea of trying to get a pram up and down the stairs several times a day was ridiculous. I'd kill both myself and the child. We'd have to find somewhere else.

I said nothing to you about any of this when you emerged, fully dressed, slipping past me wordlessly as I made my way towards the bathroom.

'Edith?' you said, perhaps surprised by my silence. 'Are you all right?'

'Fine,' I replied, not turning around. I guessed my face was still pale and sweaty. 'Just desperate for the loo, that's all.'

When I was showered and dressed, you were already gone, a note left on the pillow saying that you'd be out for the day and would see me that evening. No mention of where you were going, but I assumed it was the library in the centre of town. You'd been spending a lot of time there recently as you worked on your rewrites. I didn't give it much thought as I made my way to the pharmacy at the end of the road, where I bought a pregnancy test then took it back home.

The line turned blue. The line had always turned blue for me. I was incredibly fertile, we both were, but my inhospitable womb, as my gynaecologist described it, was still the enemy.

'Please let her live,' I said quietly, uncertain whether I was addressing God, my womb or the universe itself. 'Let me keep this one.'

And somehow, I felt absolutely certain at that moment that the child would survive and that we would be a family.

Later, when the doorbell rang, I was both surprised and annoyed to see Rebecca standing outside. It was the first time that she'd visited me in Norwich and, naturally, she hadn't bothered to call in advance to say that she was coming.

'I'm not actually visiting you,' she said as she sat down, pushing the students' scripts off the seat and on to the floor as if they were worthless things.

'It feels like you are,' I said. 'I mean, you're here, after all.'

'No, I'm only passing through. I had a meeting in King's Lynn this morning and, as I was driving through Norwich on my way home, I thought I'd stop by to tell you what a terrible sister you are.'

'Marvellous,' I said, feeling my heart sink and wishing that we had one of those video cameras at the front door so I could see who was outside before admitting them. 'Would you like a coffee before you list all the reasons or are you happy just to get started?'

'No, I would not like a coffee,' said Rebecca. 'And if I did, I would go to a coffee shop.'

'Well, there's one at the end of the road,' I said.

'I'd go there because you'd probably poison me.' She sat back and looked me up and down as if she were trying to figure something out in her head. 'I don't know what I ever did to you,' she said.

'Really?' I asked, already fed up with this conversation. 'Not a single idea? When you look back to our childhood, there's nothing there that rings any bells?'

'I was such a kind and loving sister. Always attentive to your needs.'

'Don't be ridiculous. You were horrible to me from the day I was born.'

'What rubbish. Your problem, Edith, if you don't mind me saying so, is that you've always thought you were superior to other people. Morally superior, I mean.'

'Not to all people, no,' I said. 'Just to you.'

'You see? I come here to visit and all you can do is—'

'You've already made it clear that you *didn't* come to visit. Look, I'm assuming this has something to do with Robert.'

'In a way. You should have backed me up, Edith, it's that simple. So when the shit hits the fan, remember: all of this is your fault.'

'What are you talking about?'

'Just that it would have been a lot easier for everyone if you had done as I asked. And, you know, Robert could have come to the States to see the boys whenever he wanted. Now, that won't be so easy. You see, you've actually hurt Damien and Edward more than me. It's they who'll suffer.'

'So you're still going ahead with the move to Los Angeles?'

'Of course I am. Why wouldn't I?'

'And Robert's allowing that?'

She smiled, as if it were clear that she knew something that I didn't know and was desperate for me to ask, but I was determined not to.

'Look,' she continued, 'despite the fact that you've been such a terrible sister to me, I want you to know that you're welcome to visit us whenever you want. I won't hold your actions against you.'

'That's very forgiving of you,' I said.

'I know. And if you want to say goodbye to the boys, then you should probably make plans to do so. We'll be leaving in the next few weeks.'

'But how is this even happening?' I asked. 'The last time we talked you said that Robert was refusing to let you leave the country. What's changed?'

'Nothing's changed. He's still putting up as many barriers as he can.'

'So you're just going to leave anyway? You'll probably be breaking all sorts of laws if you do, and then he'll hire a lawyer, you'll be dragged back, thrown in jail and he'll be given full custody. Surely you don't want that?'

She smiled and shook her head. 'Oh, he'll need a lawyer all right. But not for the reason you think. Robert,' she added, leaning forward with a triumphant smile on her face, 'is about to receive a very nasty shock.'

'What sort of a shock?'

'A visit from the police.'

'Why will the police be calling on Robert?' I asked. 'What's he done?'

'Kiddie porn,' she said, clapping her hands quickly like a child. 'On his computer.'

I stared at her. 'No,' I said, feeling sick all over again. 'No, I don't believe it. Not in a million years. Not Robert.'

'Not Robert, no. But on Robert's home computer.'

'How do you know?'

'Because I put it there.'

I couldn't speak. I felt my head begin to grow a little dizzy.

'I have a key to his flat,' she continued, ecstatic now. She'd obviously been dying to tell someone. 'I need it to let the children in when they're staying with him. So I went over one afternoon while he was at work and downloaded hundreds of images. You'd be surprised how easy it is to find them. Then I put them in a file called HOUSEHOLD ACCOUNTS and planted that in a folder on his desktop called OLD WORK. I doubt he ever even looks in there.'

'Rebecca—'

'And this morning, I made an anonymous call to Crimestoppers. I pretended that I'd been on a date with him and that he'd brought me back to his place, which is where I saw the images as he shut down his computer. I didn't give my name or number, just said that I was disgusted by the whole thing and someone should look into it. Well, of course they took *his* name and address, and I imagine they'll be following up very soon.'

'What the fuck is wrong with you?' I asked, when I found my voice again.

'What do you mean?'

'That's . . . I've never heard of anything so . . .' I was so flabbergasted by the depths to which she had sunk that I could scarcely find the words.

'Oh, get off your high horse,' she said, waving a hand in the air to dismiss me. 'It means that everything will be all right for me and Arjan.'

'Why are you telling me this?' I asked, shell-shocked.

'Because you asked.'

'You don't think I'll let you get away with it, do you?'

'But of course you will,' she said, smiling. 'What are you going to do, tell the police what I've said? First, it's your word against mine. And second, even if they did believe you, which they won't, and even if they prosecuted me, which they wouldn't, it would reflect poorly on you and Mum and the boys—'

'And their father going to jail for possession of child pornography won't affect them?'

'They'll be far away. In Hollywood!'

'This is fucking insane,' I said.

'Yes, well, as I said, if you want to say your goodbyes—'

'I'll go to the police myself,' I insisted. 'I'll swear in a court of law—'

'No, you won't,' she said, standing up.

'I will.'

'We shall see. You have a new novel coming out soon, don't you? Are you sure you want your name linked with a child-pornography scandal? Anyway, I should go, Edith. I still have to drive all the way home. You have my number so, if you want to say goodbye, you can get in touch. Otherwise, perhaps I'll see you in LA one day? I know the boys would be thrilled if you could visit. You and Maurice, I mean. He was always better with them than you were.'

And with that she simply laughed, took one more look around the room as if the entire set-up was even worse than she'd expected, and left.

A few moments later, the phone rang. And my world really fell apart.

You came home shortly after six o'clock. I'd been sitting on the sofa in the living room for a long time, simply staring into space, although I'd thrown up once again, this time in the hallway by the telephone stand, a mess that I hadn't even bothered to clean up. All the love and respect that I'd ever felt for you had completely disappeared over the previous few hours and now all I could do was figure out how to leave you and where I would go.

You knew me well enough to realize that something was wrong when you came through the door and, even if you hadn't, the pile of vomit would have alerted you to the fact.

'What the hell's gone on here?' you asked.

'I've been sick,' I said.

'I can see that. You might have cleaned it up, Edith. It's ghastly. And it stinks out there.'

'You clean it up,' I said, and the tone in my voice, so hostile and aggressive, probably surprised both of us in equal parts. You stared at me but said nothing and I could see that you were wondering which of your lies I'd discovered.

'Obviously something's wrong,' you said, making your way towards the fridge, taking out a bottle of beer and flipping the lid off, finishing a good third of it in one draught.

'You could say that,' I said quietly.

'Well, are you going to tell me what it is?'

'First things first,' I replied. 'Our marriage is over, Maurice, and I'm leaving you. Today. This evening. Actually, no,' I said, wondering why this hadn't occurred to me earlier. 'You'll be the one leaving. I want you to pack your things and get out within the hour. And I'm going to start divorce proceedings against you tomorrow morning.'

You said nothing for a moment, then simply nodded and sat down in the armchair by the window.

'All right, then,' you said, trying to sound nonchalant, but there was a tone in your voice that I hadn't heard before. 'If that's what you want, I won't stand in your way. Any particular reason why, though? I mean, we've been married for five years and when I left here this morning everything seemed fine between us. So it would be nice to know what I'm supposed to have done wrong in the meantime. Did I leave the toilet seat up again?'

'I received a phone call this afternoon,' I said, turning to look at you, watching as you tried so hard to keep your expression neutral.

'A phone call from whom?' you asked.

'From Peter.'

'I love phone calls from Peter,' you replied with a smile. 'They always contain good news. Have I sold some more foreign rights? Or perhaps a film deal is in the offing.'

'That wasn't what he called about. He asked me to pass a message on to you. Apparently, he'd been trying to get hold of you on your mobile all afternoon but it was switched off.'

'Ah, that's because I was in Maja's apartment,' you said.

'I'm sorry?' I replied, uncertain that I'd heard you correctly. 'Maja?'

'Yes, Maja Drazkowski. Your former student. You remember her, right? Pretty little thing? Not a big fan of yours! Thinks you're a bit of a bitch, to be honest, but I've told her that she'd like you more if she got to know you. We've been having a thing for a few months now, ever since she dropped out of the course, actually. I wouldn't have told you, but I don't suppose it matters any more, since you've decided to leave me anyway.'

I shook my head and laughed. Surprisingly, I found that I didn't care very much. In a day filled with surprises, the fact that you'd been cheating on me with a plagiarist was the least of my problems.

'So are you going to tell me what Peter wanted or leave me to guess?' you asked, and I turned to you, certain that you could guess.

'He said that your publisher called and they're wondering whether you might give the title of your novel another thought. Turns out they don't like it very much. They want something a little more commercial.'

'Really? I thought it was rather good.'

'I thought so too when I came up with it,' I said, raising my voice now. '*The Tribesman.*'

'Sweetheart, it's just a title,' you said, smiling, and I knew you were rattled, for you'd never once, in all the years of our acquaintance, called me *sweetheart* or *darling* or *honey* or *baby* or any of those other bullshit words that I've always hated so much.

'It's more than just a title,' I said. 'It's the whole fucking book! You've stolen it from me!'

'Oh, please,' you replied with a laugh. 'I haven't stolen anything. Don't be so melodramatic.'

'Jesus, Maurice, I looked on your computer! I found the file. And the emails to and from Peter. I found *my* novel there. *My* novel!'

'But do novels really belong to any of us?' you asked, looking up towards the ceiling as if we were engaged in a profound philosophical discussion. 'Other than to readers, I mean? It's an interesting question, don't you think?'

'That's what you've been doing here all year,' I said, standing up and starting to pace the floor as the depth of your betrayal hit me. 'While I've been at work, you've been sitting in that office, transcribing my book, word for word. And the drafts! You even managed to get some of them on there! I have to compliment you, Maurice. You've been pretty good at covering your tracks.'

You opened your mouth to protest but I knew that you couldn't be bothered to deny it. You'd been caught out. It was easier to change tack.

'I needed it,' you said quietly, unable to look me in the eye. 'I'm sorry, Edith, but I had no story. You know that. I've never had a story of my own. I'm just no good at them.'

'That doesn't mean you can steal *mine*!' I shouted.

'Look,' you cried, standing up and coming towards me, frightening me a little as you took me by the arms and I pulled free. 'No one has to know. Just give me this, Edith, that's all I ask. If you love me, if you truly love me, then just give me this. The novel is wonderful, by the way. Everything that Peter has said about it is true. It really is a masterpiece and you're a terrific writer. I've got a real shot at

The Prize with it. I'll certainly be shortlisted, I don't think there's any doubt about that.'

I stared at you, bewildered, wondering whether you'd lost your mind completely. 'But then it's *my* masterpiece,' I cried. 'And it will be *my* shortlisting!'

'Does it matter whose name is on it? We're married, aren't we? We're a team. In it for the long haul. What difference does it make to you if I put my name on this one and you start another? I'm better known than you are, after all, and this is my way back into the publishing world. I'll write something else myself afterwards, I promise.'

'Are you fucking kidding me?' I roared. 'You actually think I'm going to just *give* you my novel? After all the work I've put into it?'

'Why not?' you asked, looking confused. 'Is it really that much to ask?'

'Because it would be a complete lie!'

'I think you're being terribly selfish,' you said, and I started to laugh, my laughter quickly becoming a little hysterical. I felt as if this couldn't possibly be happening. I looked at you, you smiled, and I couldn't help it, at that moment I remembered how attractive I'd always found you, and for a moment I wondered how it would feel to fuck you right there and then, knowing everything about you that I knew now. But of course I didn't, I turned around instead and left the room, making my way towards the bedroom, where I was going to start packing for you. Before I could get in there, you'd caught up with me at the top of the stairs and had spun me around. The stink of vomit on the floor was overwhelming.

'What are you going to do?' you asked, and I could see how pale your face had gone now. The terror you felt that I was going to expose you as a liar.

'First, I'm going to throw you out,' I said. 'Then I'm going to phone my agent and tell her what you've done. After that, I'm going to phone *your* agent and tell him what you've done. How you've lied to him, made a complete fool of him in the industry. I can't imagine that he'll be very happy, can you? It might delay the press release by a few days. Oh, and then I should probably call your publisher too—'

'You can't!'

'Of course I can! Do you actually believe you can get away with saying that you wrote it? You might have created a few drafts on your computer, Maurice, but I have dozens of notebooks, all dated, all filled with notes. You never looked for them, did you? I have so much proof that the novel is mine that it will take about five minutes to show you up for the plagiarist you are. It's no wonder that you're fucking Maja Drazkowski, you probably gave her the idea of stealing someone else's story from the *New Yorker*.'

'That's true, I did,' you said with a mocking laugh. 'I didn't think she'd have the guts to go through with it, though. Although I didn't say the *New Yorker*. I told her to pick a much more obscure magazine. Something from some mid-Western university press with about five readers. She slipped up badly there. I mean, the *New Yorker*. What an amateur.'

'Christ,' I said, shaking my head. 'You're psychotic.'

'Not really. I just need to be a writer, that's all. It's all I've ever needed to be. That and a father. And it's not as if you've been much use to me on that score, is it?'

'Don't bring that up,' I said quickly, feeling a twinge inside myself at what I knew that you didn't. 'That's got nothing to do with any of this.'

'It's got everything to do with it,' you said. 'You can't give me a child so surely you can make up for that by giving me a book. I need it, don't you see that? Without a writing career, what am I, after all? Please, Edith,' you said, your tone changing slightly now, becoming less aggressive and more beseeching. 'If you tell anyone, you'll ruin me. There'll be no coming back from it. My reputation will be completely destroyed.'

'Just like Erich Ackermann's was,' I said.

'Erich Ackermann was a Nazi!' you shouted, losing your temper now. 'You said so yourself. You can't compare me to him.'

'The truth is,' I said, looking you directly in the eyes, 'you're not a writer at all, Maurice. You're desperate to be but you don't have the talent. You never did have. That's why you've always attached yourself to people more successful than yourself, pretended to be their friend and then dropped them when they were no longer of any use to you. You must have thought that all your Christmases had come at once when my career started to take off.'

'Shut up,' you snapped, your face contorting in anger now.

'But the thing is, I *am* a writer,' I continued. 'And that book you've been passing off to the world belongs to *me*. I'm everything that you're not. You're just a hack. You stole Ackermann's life, you stole my words. On their worst day, any one of my students has more ability than you.'

'You'd better stop talking,' you said, your chin trembling in fury.

'I want you out, Maurice,' I said, feeling strong now, stronger than I'd felt since the night you raped me. 'I want you out right now, do you understand? Unless you want to be here when I start making my phone calls.'

I turned away from you and you pulled me back, spinning me round. As you did so, I felt my ankle twist beneath me at the top of the stairs. I reached out for the railing, that broken railing I'd asked you to fix on so many occasions, but my hand didn't connect with it. The whole thing felt as if I were moving in slow motion. As if I were watching myself from above while I stared at you, aware that I was about to fall. All I needed was for you to reach out and grab me and I would be safe. I said your name.

'Maurice.'

I stood there for what felt like an eternity, unable to fall, unable to recover, and that was when I saw the clear resolution on your face. You knew exactly what you had to do to save yourself.

You reached out and, with a gentle, almost loving, tap, pushed me.

8. Now

I've lost track of how long I've been here. The concept of time loses whatever credibility it had when you're locked in a coma. It's been more than a few weeks, though, of that I'm sure. Perhaps a month or two? I'm in no pain, which is good, but nor am I alert to a particular lack of pain. The best I can do is describe it as having a consciousness but no body, no movement or expression. I'm an anthology of thoughts and memories trapped within a static shell. I can see everything around me and yet my eyes refuse to open. I can hear every sound but can't make myself heard. I'm alone and yet I'm frequently surrounded by people.

There are nurses, of course. They wash me every morning using soft sponges and tepid water. They move my arms and legs, bending them carefully at the elbows and knees, to ensure that my muscles don't atrophy. They rotate my wrists and ankles, trim my fingernails, apply moisturizers to my skin. They empty bags filled with my excreta and replace them, so I can void again. And yet they seem to forget that I was once alive, that I'm *still* alive, holding conversations over my inert form that go something like this:

Nurse 1: You know who she is, don't you?

Nurse 2: No, who?

Nurse 1: She's a writer. She wrote that television programme, *Fury*, that won all them awards a couple of years back.

Nurse 2: Oh, I never saw that. I read the book and thought it was a bit pretentious.

Nurse 1: I didn't read it. I always say that if a book's any good, sooner or later it'll find its way on to the box. I don't have any time to read these days, anyway.

Nurse 2: Well, you haven't missed much.

Nurse 1: I used to read a lot when I was younger.

Or this:

Nurse 1: You've seen her husband, I suppose?

Nurse 2: Lord, yes. If I was ten years younger and twenty pounds lighter!

Nurse 1: The poor man is inconsolable. He must have really loved her.

Nurse 2: I don't see it. I mean, she's not bad-looking but he's in a different stratosphere. And, you know, there's the colour thing too.

Nurse 1: (*laughing*) You can't say that!

Nurse 2: Oh, I don't mean anything by it. I'm not racist or anything. I'm just saying. My cousin Jimmy married a black girl and she ran off on him in the end. Took the children too. The poor bloke never got over it. You have to be careful, that's all.

Or sometimes:

Nurse 1: How long more will they keep her on this, do you think?

Nurse 2: Your guess is as good as mine. It's down to the family in the end, isn't it?

There are doctors too. They stand over me and check their charts, telling each other where they went for dinner the night before. I'm privy to their most intimate conversations and all I can do is lie here while the machines by my bed breathe for me. Sometimes I sing songs in my head, whole albums even, challenging myself to remember every word of the lyrics.

You visited a lot in the early days and were very good at playing the grieving husband. Sometimes, when we were alone, you would sit next to me, take my hand and speak in a quiet voice that, strangely, I found very relaxing.

'The university keeps calling me,' you said. 'They've been very solicitous. They're desperate to help in some way but, of course, there's nothing they can do. At one point, I considered asking whether they might like me to take over your classes for you, but I thought they might think that a bit odd.'

Another time, you worked through the page proofs of *The Tribes-man* while sitting at my bedside and told me whenever you were changing one of my sentences for one of your own. I must admit that your corrections were, for the most part, good ones.

I overheard a conversation between you and Nurse 2 one evening when she said that she really admired how well you were holding it together. Not everyone does, she told you. Some people go to pieces, others cause trouble for the hospital, as if the doctors aren't trying hard enough. You told her that you had no choice, that you were sure that I could hear every word you said and that if I knew how much you loved me, I'd wake up. You said that you hadn't told me that enough before the accident – your word, not mine – and that that was one of your biggest regrets. Then you started sobbing, she hugged you and I heard myself screaming, literally screaming like a banshee, inside my head. Only the room, of course, was in silence.

Once, you placed a hand on my stomach, quite gently, and told me I'd been pregnant but that the child hadn't survived the fall. I knew that, you didn't have to say it. She would have lived too, had you pulled me back rather than pushing me. I can sense her spirit sometimes, but we haven't made any connection. Not yet, anyway. Soon, perhaps.

A few nights ago, you arrived with someone else. The room was a dark blur then and I couldn't identify who it was. Eventually, I realized it was a young woman. She leaned over me and whispered in a familiar European accent.

'Don't wake up, Edith,' she said. 'Don't ever wake up. Things are just perfect here without you.'

It didn't take me long to figure out that it was Maja Drazkowski. Are you a couple now? I imagine you must keep it very quiet, as you'd lose all sympathy if anyone discovered that you were fucking one of my students while I was stuck in hospital, showing no sign whatsoever of recovering. She's a strange choice for you but I imagine you'll get rid of her once the novel takes off and you're back in literary circulation. There are much more significant catches out there lying in wait for you. I almost feel sorry for Maja. Almost.

But, of course, you're not the only one who visits. Mum comes up from London every few days and tries to be strong but ends up in tears. She tells me over and over how much she loves me and recounts happy stories from when I was a child. I want to tell her that I love her too. She brings a friend occasionally, who puts an arm around her and says things like:

She looks well, all things considered, doesn't she?

and

Shall we stop off for a bite to eat on the way home? I could murder a cod and chips.

Life goes on, I suppose.

Rebecca came only once. She started by smoothing down the bedsheets and clearing up whatever detritus had been left behind on the bedside table. I don't know why she bothered.

'Hello, Edith,' she said, in a normal tone of voice, as if we'd just run into each other on the street unexpectedly. 'I brought some grapes. Shall I just leave them over here?'

Why on earth she brought grapes is a mystery to me. I wanted to scream, *I'm in a coma, you stupid fucking bitch*, and I did scream it, in my head, anyway. She sat down and looked around the room, keeping her hands firmly in her lap. I don't think she wanted to touch any of the surfaces in case she came down with MRSA.

'Shall I catch you up on the gossip?' she asked.

No, I thought.

'Arjan's arrived in LA and started shooting. He's loving it. It's obvious that the show is going to be an enormous hit. I've advised him that he should only commit to two seasons because, after that, film companies are going to want to cast him in movies. And if he's stuck in a long-term contract with a TV show, then that'll mess things up for us. That happened to the actor who played Magnum. What's his name? I can't remember.'

Tom Selleck, I thought.

'Oh, it'll come to me. Anyway, it happened to him—'

Tom Selleck, I re-thought.

'He was offered the part of Indiana Jones but he couldn't do it because he was locked into his contract and so Kevin Costner got it instead.'

Harrison Ford, I shouted.

'And I don't want that to happen to Arjan. Anyway, the boys and I are going over next Thursday – can you believe it? Me! In Hollywood! I suppose you thought that you'd be the one to end up there because of your novels, but no, it's me! I'll write, of course, but I can't see myself coming back here any time soon. I think England will seem so drab once I'm over there.'

And Robert? What about Robert? I wondered.

'I'm going to let you in on a little secret,' she said, leaning in and lowering her voice. 'It's very hard being without Arjan for even a few days. Sexually, I mean. Honestly, Edith, I've never known anything like it. And nor have you, I promise you that. He's young, of course, and men that age can go all night. With Robert, it was always one quick fumble and lights off. I actually thought that was normal – well, it probably *is* normal, but it's not the way things are with Arjan. I wish you were well enough to come and visit us when we move. You'd be green with envy!'

And then, just before she left, she came over and kissed me on the forehead and something damp fell on my nose. A tear? It must have been.

'Try to wake up, Edith,' she said. 'We all miss you.' And for a moment, I genuinely thought that she meant it.

Soon after this, Robert visited too. There was some commotion about this because he arrived while you, Maurice, were on the ward, and you didn't want to let him in. The door to my room was open and I could hear the two of you arguing in the corridor.

'Look, she's my sister-in-law,' Robert was saying. 'And we've always got on well, you know that. I just want to sit with her for a little while, that's all.'

'I know,' you said, and I could tell from your voice that, although you were uncertain whether to allow this or not, you were leaning towards no. 'But the thing is, she can't hear you anyway, so there's really no point. And I don't think you should be here while all these other things are going on in your life. Honestly, Robert, I think Edith would be very disappointed if she knew what you've been accused of.'

'She'd have no reason to be,' he said. 'I've done nothing wrong.'

'Kiddie porn is hardly nothing wrong.'

'I swear to you I don't know how it got there.'

'But that's what they all say, isn't it? That a virus got downloaded or someone hacked into their computer. I've heard it all before.'

'But in my case, it's true! I've never . . . I've never been even remotely interested in things like that. Not for a moment.'

'Actually, Robert,' you said, 'if I'm completely honest with you, I don't give a fuck. Do whatever you want, it makes sod all difference to me.'

'I'm just trying to explain—'

'But you're explaining to the wrong person. It's not me you have to convince, it's the judge. When's the trial, anyway?'

There was a long pause and then Robert spoke again, so quietly that I struggled to hear him. 'Not for months,' he said. 'About seven months from now.'

'That's a lot to have hanging over your head in the meantime.'

'I've lost my job too. And as I'm not allowed access to the inter-net, it's practically impossible for me to find another one. And even if I could, how could I convince any employer to take me on in my current situation?'

'I understand,' you said, and I could tell that you were shrugging your shoulders or looking at your watch, hoping he'd just go away. 'It's not really my problem, though, is it?'

'Edith would believe me,' said Robert.

'I doubt it,' you said. 'She could be very mistrusting, actually.'

'How so?' he asked, and you pulled back. It was as if you were saying that for an invisible audience – me – but knew better than to pursue it.

'I just want to spend some time with her,' said Robert plaintively. 'To talk to her about the boys.'

'Have you seen them?'

'No, I'm not allowed. At least not on my own. I have a supervised visit the day before they leave for the States, but that's it. Thirty minutes. They were interviewed too, you know. By some sort of specialist. To find out whether I'd ever . . . you know . . .'

'Jesus,' you said, sounding disgusted. 'For what it's worth, I wouldn't believe that of you for even a moment. I've seen you with them. I know how much you love them. If you need me to say so, I will.'

'Thank you,' said Robert, and I could hear him crying now. 'That's very good of you, Maurice. Because I'd never . . . not in a million years . . .'

I tried so hard to wake up then. I really tried. I wanted to drag myself out of bed and tell Robert the truth, to tell him how Rebecca had set him up. I couldn't believe that he hadn't figured it out for himself, but it was such a monstrous thing for anyone to do that he probably couldn't even imagine it. Nor could you. But then you never did have any imagination.

'I'm sorry,' you told him, steering him away from my room. 'But look, until this whole mess is cleared up, I'd prefer if you didn't visit again.'

And that was that. I haven't seen or heard from him since.

There was another visitor, an unexpected one, and he arrived quite late one evening, long past the time when visitors are usually admitted. I expect he simply came up in the lift – assuming I'm not on the ground floor, which I might be – and waited until the nurses' station was empty before wandering in.

Nicholas sat by my bed for more than an hour, reading sections from *The Go-Between* in a quiet voice. I'd told him once that this was my favourite novel and he'd remembered, which was sweet of him. Whenever he took a break from reading he held my hand. He told me that I'd helped him enormously with his work and he hoped that I would recover. He said that the afternoon we'd spent together remained very special to him, that he'd never spoken about it with anyone including, he pointed out, me.

Still, it touched me that he visited. None of the other students did. I wonder what they were doing, what they were writing, who they were reading. I wonder whether any more of them have secured agents or publishers. I won't be there to read my name in their acknowledgements, will I, Maurice? I bet you take a few of them under your wing, though. That would be just like you. You'll identify which ones are the most likely to make it and attach yourself to them as a mentor. And they'll love you for it.

Which brings me to my last visitor, my agent, Adele. She came to see me and cried a little before talking.

'You were such a wonderful writer,' she told me. 'I think you would have been magnificent if you'd had the chance to live longer. I knew when I first read *Fear* that I'd found someone special, the kind of young novelist that every agent hopes to find. I only wish we'd received something more from you. You told me that you were writing in Norwich—'

I was, Adele.

'You said you'd been working on a novel for the last two years—'

I was, Adele.

'But it seems that you weren't being honest with me, were you, dear? You could have told me the truth. That you were blocked. Frightened about being unable to repeat the success of *Fear*. Maurice told me everything. How you'd been struggling and felt that a year being around creative young people might help you. But it only made you worse.'

And you believed him, Adele?

'I hope you don't mind, dear, but we went through your laptop, looking for something, anything that might be salvageable. But there was nothing. Just notes for stories and all the old drafts of *Fear*. And a blank Word document titled NOVEL 2. I opened that file with such hope and when I saw that it was empty, that's when Maurice told me the truth. He was very upset about it, poor man. But at least we have one novel from you, and I'm going to make sure that it stays in print for as long as possible. And, my dear, I don't know if you can hear me or not, but I think you'd be pleased to know that Maurice himself is about to have a great success. I read a proof copy of *The Tribesman* last week and it's simply magnificent. Easily the best novel I've read since . . . well, since yours, in fact. It actually has a little of you in there, I think he must have picked up on some of your style, which is a lovely epitaph.'

If it sounds like me, it's because I wrote the fucking thing!

'He's dedicated it to you as well, did you know that? The first words you see after the title page: *To my darling wife, Edith. Without you, this novel would never have existed.* Isn't that lovely? I know I'm not his agent – Peter Wills-Bouche is so lucky to have him on his list – but I'm going to do everything I can to see that the book is a success. It will be his success, of course, but at least it will be a testament to you. For ever.'

Things feel very different today, and I'm not sure why. There have been more nurses coming in and out, and a lot more doctors. Mum was in again earlier, crying, and this time when she left she kept telling me over and over how much she loved me and how she always would. There was a lot of talk between unfamiliar voices, and various checklists were being attended to.

And now you've arrived. You're standing over me, looking down, holding my hand. I can see you, Maurice. Handsome as ever. More handsome, perhaps. Almost everyone else is leaving and now there's just you and one doctor left and he's asking whether you'd like a moment alone with me and you say yes.

What is it, Maurice? What do you want to tell me? That you're sorry? That you love me? That if you could go back in time, none of this would ever have happened?

You lean down and whisper in my ear:

I'm going to be the greatest novelist of my generation.

That's it? That's what you wanted to say, you fucking idiot? Jesus Christ! Did you ever love me, even for a moment? You must have, once, because when we met you were the famous one and I had barely started out. There was nothing in it for you then. You *must* have loved me once. You *must* have.

You're calling the doctor back in now and nodding at him. But why? He hasn't asked you anything. I can't see him, he's disappeared to the left of the bed, where the machines are. Where everything becomes too blurry for me to focus.

I can hear switches being turned and the wheezing of an artificial breather as it starts to slow down, and that's when I realize. You're turning me off, aren't you, Maurice? You're turning me off. You're killing me. To protect yourself and, more importantly, to protect your novel. My novel. Your novel.

I see you.

You're reaching down and taking my

           that thing   at the end of my arm

     holding it now

        your fingers

      ginfers

nifris

I can't see you any more

there's no light

no sound

no more words.

Interlude

The Threatened Animal

Although the phone call brought unwelcome news, it could not have arrived at a more opportune moment.

Maurice was seated behind his desk on the seventh floor of an office building next to Union Square Park, while Henrietta James, a twenty-eight-year-old writer who had tried and failed to seduce him at the *New Yorker* Christmas party the previous December, sat opposite, incandescent with rage.

Henrietta, who went by the name Henry Etta James in print, had first come to Maurice's attention a little over a year before, when his then assistant, Jarrod Swanson, had turned down one of her short stories. He was well aware that submissions to *Storī* went through a less than rigorous screening process before they landed on his desk, but so many unsolicited manuscripts arrived each month that he simply didn't have the time to read them all personally, even if he wanted to, which he didn't. But this led to a singular problem: since most of the magazine's interns, those who did the bulk of the reading, were graduates of creative-writing programmes, each one was single-minded in pursuit of his or her own publishing deal. They attended literary salons and book launches, and mixed with editors, agents and publicists, identifying their competition through a shared network of covetous hostility. In recent years, several writers who'd been discovered through the pages of *Storī* had seen their debuts signed up by publishing houses while a couple had even gone on to win prestigious awards, building the reputation of the quarterly magazine considerably. The pie, however, was only so big, and the interns knew that. When a manuscript arrived from someone whose talent they envied or feared, there was always the risk of their rejecting it in order to damage their rival's chances of claiming a slice. Which meant that the stories that found their way to Maurice were not always the very best ones. But there was little he could do about that.

Occasionally, he wandered into the Trash Can – which was what he called the room in which they kept a copy of every story that had ever been submitted to the magazine – and had a look through the rejection pile, casting his eye over a few pieces there, and that was how he had discovered Henrietta's story. A little investigative work on his part revealed that Jarrod and Henrietta had been classmates at the New School, where they'd enjoyed an ill-fated romance, and he had turned down her work as revenge for her decision to break up with him on his birthday. Maurice had published the story, which had gone on to feature in that year's *Best American Short Stories* anthology, and Jarrod, as far as he knew, was now working in a Foot Locker on East 86th Street.

Henrietta's debut novel, *I Am Dissatisfied with My Boyfriend, My Body and My Career*, was due to be published by FSG later that year and was already being touted as a significant work, '*Bridget Jones* meets *A Clockwork Orange*'. A few weeks earlier, she had submitted a new story directly to Maurice, who had passed on it, a rebuff that precipitated her unscheduled appearance in his office that morning, just when he'd been hoping to relax while watching Rafael Nadal play Andy Murray in the Wimbledon semi-final.

'Sorry to burst in unannounced,' she said, charging in and hurling a large carpet bag that even Mary Poppins would have rejected as being unwieldy to the floor, where it landed with a considerable thump. She peeled herself from her coat, scarf and gloves, a curious combination, considering it was July and, outside, New York was melting. The room filled with an unmistakably stale scent of musty body odour. Henrietta, Maurice knew, only bathed on Saturdays, in order to help preserve the planet's natural resources and today, unfortunately, was a Friday. 'But I think we need to talk, don't you?'

'How lovely to see you,' he lied, moving his laptop a little to the left so he could keep an eye on the match – Murray had won the first set, but Nadal was leading comfortably in the second – while listening to whatever she was here to complain about. 'Just passing, were you?'

'No, I came deliberately, and the journey was horrendous.' Despite growing up in Milwaukee, Henrietta modelled her speech on Merchant Ivory period films starring Emma Thompson or Helena Bonham-Carter. 'First, I stood in some frightful dog poo on the pavement and had to return home to change my shoes, which was a terrible bore. Then, while travelling on the 4 train, I was forced to switch carriages as a woman nearby was, quite literally, going into labour and her screams were giving me one of my headaches. Upon changing, I found myself seated next to an Indian gentleman who proposed marriage on the basis of what he called my childbearing hips.'

'That's nice,' said Maurice. 'Did you accept?'

'Of course not.'

'And how did he take it?'

'No one likes rejection, Maurice. But we'll get back to that in a minute. Anyway, he seemed to get over it quickly enough. By 28th Street, he had proposed to a young African-American man who did not take his advances with good grace and, by 23rd, to a border collie, who seemed much more interested.'

'Excellent.'

'I hate coming into the city. I really do.'

'Then you should have stayed at home.'

'No, it was important that we confront this situation face to face.'

'And what situation is that?' he asked.

'Don't play silly beggars, Maurice. You know exactly why I'm here.'

'I assume you've brought something new for me to read?'

'Ha! As if I would. After the way I've been treated by your magazine? Not a cat's chance in hell!' She leaned forward and rearranged the letter opener, stapler and hole-punch on Maurice's desk so they were perfectly aligned. 'I don't give my work to people who despise me.'

'I don't despise you, Henrietta,' replied Maurice. 'Why on earth would you think such a thing?'

'Well, you don't respect me, that's for sure.'

She reached into her carpet bag and shuffled around for a bit in it before removing a sheet of A4 paper folded into eighths. '*Dear Henrietta*,' she read aloud as she unravelled it. '*Thank you so much for allowing me to read your latest story—*'

'If I may,' he interrupted.

'*THANK YOU SO MUCH FOR ALLOWING ME TO READ YOUR LATEST STORY*,' she repeated, raising her voice now, '*a wonderfully quirky fable that illustrates just why FSG were so keen to sign you up! Unfortunately, space in Storī is rather limited at the moment and I don't think I'll be able to publish it, although I daresay I'll regret that when the New Yorker snaps it up! Keep sending me your stuff, though, I can't get enough of your particular brand of whimsy. Much love, Maurice Swift. Editor-in-chief.*'

'You're upset,' said Maurice.

'Upset? Why would I be upset? It's only "stuff", after all. It's not as if I pour my very lifeblood into every sentence, paragraph and chapter. *Stuff!* Fuck you, Maurice. Fuck you and the horse you rode in on.'

'That might have been an unfortunate choice of word,' he admitted.

'You think? I never would have imagined that you would treat me with such contempt. You've let me down, Maurice, you really have.'

'Well, I wouldn't take it personally,' he replied. 'I've done that to quite a few people over the years. There's an army of them out there, both living and dead, who don't look at me with any particular benevolence.'

'Anyway,' she continued with a sigh, looking around the office, which was filled with books, manuscripts and multiple back issues of *Storī*. Several shelves were taken up with various foreign-language editions of *Two Germans*, *The Treehouse*, *The Tribesman*, *The Breach* and *The Broken Ones*. 'I wouldn't normally do this, but since we have so much history together I thought I'd come in and offer you a second chance.'

'A second chance?' he asked, raising an eyebrow. 'At what exactly?'

'At publishing my story,' she replied, rolling her eyes. 'Because if you don't want it, I'll take it across the street and find someone who does.'

Maurice tried not to laugh. *Across the street?* Did she think she was a character in a David Mamet play? There was nothing across the street except a vintage-clothes store, a coffee shop that reeked of marijuana and an elderly homeless man who sang the chorus of 'American Pie' whenever anyone handed him money. If she wanted to take it across to any of them, then she was perfectly welcome.

'Of course, I hate to pass up such an opportunity,' said Maurice. 'But I read the story several times and I just didn't think it was the right fit for our upcoming issues. I don't like turning people down but—'

'And I don't like being shitted upon from a great height!' shouted Henrietta. 'Particularly by someone I respect and admire.'

He frowned. Weren't *respect* and *admire* essentially the same thing? She'd made similar blunders in the story he'd rejected. The opening line, for example, had gone:

Every evening as he took the train home from work, Jasper Martin began to feel both anxious and apprehensive.

The same thing. And there was another on page four:

Lauren glanced up towards the light, which was flickering and quivering, and wondered whether she should put off hanging herself until the connections were secure.

The same thing.

'I don't think I've shitted on you, Henrietta,' said Maurice. 'Not from any height, great or small. I just didn't feel the story was right for us, that's all. And I'm sorry, but I don't think I can be persuaded otherwise.'

'What was wrong with it?'

'There was nothing wrong with it, *per se*,' replied Maurice, glancing back towards the screen, where Nadal was celebrating taking the second set. 'I suppose I just didn't feel that it had your usual *je ne sais quoi*.'

'And what is *that* supposed to mean?'

'It's French.'

'I *know* it's French. And I know what it *means*. I'm asking what you mean by it.'

'Do you want the truth?'

'Of course I do.'

'It's just that, usually, when I ask writers whether they want the truth, they say that they do but actually they want anything but. They want me to lavish praise on them and tell them to dust off their dinner jackets for the Nobel Prize ceremony.'

'I don't own a dinner jacket,' said Henrietta, narrowing her eyes. 'Now, are you going to—'

'I just thought the story was a little boring, that's all,' he said. 'It didn't seem to go anywhere. There were some interesting moments, of course, and your writing is as strong as ever, but the overall effect was—'

'You're just insulting me now,' she said.

'I don't believe I am. I certainly don't mean to.'

'Two can play that game. I read the last issue of *Storī* cover to cover and, if you ask me, it was entirely pedestrian and utterly unexciting.'

Which is the same thing, thought Maurice.

'It's like you don't want to take risks or chances.'

'And now you're insulting *me*,' he replied.

'I'm not insulting you. I'm insulting the magazine.'

'A magazine that I founded.'

'Why don't you just admit that my story was too challenging for you and your readers? That you didn't fully understand it?'

'If I didn't understand it, then how would I know it was too challenging?'

'Don't play games with me.'

'I'm not. But your interpretation of why I said no to the story is simply incorrect. I understood it perfectly well, I'm not an idiot. I can read, even the big words. Look, it's not a bad story, it's just not your best, that's all. And you wouldn't thank me if I published something that went on to be criticized by others, particularly with your novel coming out soon. You need to keep your reputation as high as possible during these next few months. It's critical. Believe me, I know what I'm talking about here. I'm not new to this industry and I know how easily one can turn from being flavour of the month to a sour taste in some publisher's mouth. I've seen it. I've *been* it.'

'I just feel hurt, that's all,' she said after a lengthy pause, softening her tone a little. 'It's been a very stressful time for me recently. Did you know that my grandmother died in January?'

'No,' said Maurice, who didn't particularly care. 'I'm sorry to hear that.'

'She was only ninety-eight.'

'Well, that is quite a good age.'

'And then my dog was run over in the street by some idiot on a motorbike. And then I got cancer—'

'What?' he asked, leaning forward. This was new.

'Well, I *thought* I had cancer,' she said, correcting herself. 'There was a mole. On my shoulder. One that hadn't been there before. Anyway, my doctor said that he was worried about it so he sent a sample to the lab and it came back clear. But, you know, for a few days there I was convinced that I had cancer.'

'But you didn't.'

'No, but that's hardly the point. I might have done.'

Maurice tapped his pen against the desk. This was one of the reasons he preferred working from home for the most part, only visiting the office once or twice a week. Bloody writers. He'd spent so many years desperate to be among their number but there were times when he truly despised them.

'So your rejection really hit me hard,' she said.

'Well, if you can beat cancer, then surely you can get over a rejection from *Storī*,' he said, and she was just opening her mouth to reply when his phone rang. He rarely answered calls, preferring to let them pile up before deciding which ones to return later in the day, but he picked it up quickly now, glad of the distraction, glancing at the screen first.

School, it said.

'Sorry,' he said, holding his index finger in the air to silence Henrietta before she could start barking at him again. 'It's my son's school. I should take this.'

She threw her hands up as if she couldn't quite believe that he was prioritizing his son over her and he stepped outside, marching past the interns and into the stairwell beyond where there was an occasional chance of privacy.

'Maurice Swift,' he said.

'Mr Swift,' said the voice at the other end, who sounded simultaneously bored by her job and thrilled by the momentary drama of calls such as this. 'This is Alisha Macklin from St Joseph's.'

'Oh yes?' said Maurice, already feeling the first rush of irritation build inside him. He didn't much care for Daniel's school and felt a certain anxiety every morning when he dropped the boy off at a place that might be riddled with child molesters or gun-wielding psychopaths. It was like living in some dystopian society or a Young Adult novel. He still couldn't believe there was an airport scanner on the door that each of the children had to pass through before being admitted to classes. 'What's he done this time?'

'First, let me say there's nothing to worry about,' replied Alisha. 'Your son is perfectly fine. But we think you should make your way to the school as soon as possible.'

'Why, what's happened?'

'There's been an incident.'

He didn't ask anything else, just hung up and pressed the button on the lift. The school was only a ten-minute walk away, but the sun was shining so he took it leisurely. One of the interns could deal with Henrietta. That's what I pay them for, after all, he thought, ignoring the fact that he didn't actually pay them anything. They worked for free but with the unassailable conviction that a couple of months spent on a desk at *Storī* would add a solid detail to their résumés. Ultimately, he knew, they were using him to get ahead. And who was he to argue with that?

Daniel, as it turned out, had slapped one of the girls in his class.

'We've been experiencing problems between Daniel and Jupiter for some time,' said Mrs Lane, the forty-something school principal, who, with her bouffant dyed-blonde hair and sensible sweater, gave off an air of mild desperation. A photograph in a silver frame was turned towards her on her desk and Maurice longed to see the picture it held, a human or a pet. He bet the latter.

'Jupiter?' he said, trying not to laugh. 'I'm sorry, did you say Jupiter?'

'Yes, Jupiter Dell,' said Mrs Lane.

'And she's a little girl? Or a boy, perhaps?'

'She's a little girl, Mr Swift.' The principal's face relaxed a little, and she shrugged. 'Between you and me, her parents are rather hippy-dippy types, if you know what I mean.' She looked around and, despite the fact that they were alone, leaned forward and lowered her voice. 'She has a younger brother named Mercury.'

'He'll have an easy time of it in school. Maybe you should bring the parents in to chastise them for forcing their children to grow up with such ridiculous names.'

'Actually, the Dells were in here just before you,' replied Mrs Lane. 'Naturally, we had to call them first. Jupiter is very upset.'

'Perhaps you could tell me exactly what happened,' said Maurice, feeling the same level of anxiety in this room as he had thirty years before when he'd been dragged to the principal's office, along with his best friend at the time, Henry Rowe, two fifteen-year-old boys trembling in anticipation of what was to come. This memory, one that he had tried to block from his mind for decades, made him feel nauseous.

'Miss Willow, Daniel's teacher—'

'I know who Miss Willow is,' said Maurice.

'Yes. Well, she'd already noticed an unusual dynamic between Daniel and Jupiter and had brought it to my attention.'

'An unusual dynamic?' he repeated, wondering whether these were terms drilled into teachers and school principals to avoid any potentially slanderous, and thereby litigious, remarks.

'Jupiter has . . . I suppose we can just call it a crush on your son.'

'But he's only seven,' said Maurice with a bewildered smile.

'The children don't recognize it as a crush, of course, but it happens all the time. One child forms a strong attachment to another and the object of their affections doesn't reciprocate the emotion. In this particular case, Jupiter had started bringing little treats into school for your son. A ladybird that she was keeping alive in a matchbox, for example. A book that she particularly enjoyed. She even made him a sandwich one day and brought in a strawberry cupcake to follow.'

'I wish someone would do that for me,' said Maurice. 'And what does Daniel do? When she gives him these things?'

'What all boys that age will do, I suppose,' she replied with a shrug. 'He takes the gifts and eats the food but once he gets what he wants from her he goes right back to playing with his friends and then she's left upset by his rejection. In that respect, perhaps there's not a lot of difference between boys and men.'

Maurice raised an eyebrow, surprised by the comment, which seemed based on some unfortunate personal experience instead of a professional evaluation of the situation. He thought about challenging her on it but became distracted by an abacus placed on the windowsill behind her desk. It was fairly basic, ten rows of multi-coloured beads supported by a wooden frame and stand. He hadn't seen one in a long time but, like Proust's madeleine, it brought back a wave of memories that he knew had the power to overwhelm him if he did not remain steady. Dr Webster's abacus, of course, had been much more elaborate, monochrome but constructed from maple wood, the beads polished ivory. It had been passed down in the Webster family since before the Great War, he had been told, and the inscription on the base – *A. F. P. Webster, 1897* – had always made him wonder whether the original recipient had gone on to make a success of his life or had forfeited it in the trenches.

Looking at this cheaper version now, Maurice felt an urge to pick it up and hear the click of the beads as he slid them along the wires, but he resisted, uncertain whether he would find himself throwing it to the ground and smashing it underfoot, actions that would surely provoke an even stronger reaction than that to one child slapping another in the playground. Mrs Lane noticed him staring and turned to see what he was looking at, misinterpreting his interest in the abacus as an observance of the children playing outside.

'They are being supervised, you know,' she said.

'I'm sorry?'

'The children. They're being supervised. There's always at least two teachers in attendance during playtime.'

'No, I wasn't . . .' he began, but shook his head, not bothering to continue the sentence.

'Anyway,' she said, her voice loud, sharp and hectoring now. 'This morning, between classes, Jupiter went over to Daniel while he was talking with some of the other boys, threw her arms around him and kissed him. On the lips. I suppose she'd seen someone do that on television or in a movie and—'

'She *kissed* him?'

'Yes. Only for a moment. The poor boy was mortified, particularly as the other boys immediately started to laugh at him, and that's when he did it. When he slapped her, I mean.'

'Jesus.'

'Indeed.'

'And was she badly hurt?'

'Well, no. I don't think the attack was particularly brutal. There was a red mark on her cheek afterwards, of course, but I think she was more shocked than anything else. Not to mention humiliated.'

'I suppose you're going to tell me now that her parents are planning on suing me. Or you. Or the school.'

'Oh no,' she said, shaking her head. 'Quite the opposite, in fact. They made a point of saying that they believe America has become far too litigious a society and that they have no intention of going down that road.'

'Thank God for that.'

'Yes, I echo your sentiments there. The last thing St Joseph's needs is a costly lawsuit. The attendant publicity alone could be ruinous. No, what they want is for Daniel and Jupiter to attend a couple's counselling session together.'

'You're kidding me, right?'

'No, not at all.'

'They're seven. And they're not a couple.'

'It's a figure of speech, Mr Swift. A forum where they can air their grievances aloud. Jupiter's parents like to talk, you see. They talk *a lot*. They never stop talking, if you follow my meaning.'

'And what if I say no?' asked Maurice. 'What if I say that I don't like the idea of my son seeing a shrink at such a young age?'

'Well, that would be entirely up to you, of course,' said Mrs Lane, picking up a fountain pen from her desk and removing the cap before tapping the nib against a piece of blotting paper in what Maurice took to be a nervous gesture. 'But my advice would be to go ahead with the session, if only to appease them. I can't imagine it would do any harm and it might do a lot of good. After that, I expect the entire matter will be put to bed.'

'Fine,' said Maurice, who had no particular opinion on psycho-therapy one way or the other but was happy to do what was necessary if it meant that he could leave her office soon. 'One session?'

'One session, yes. It might be useful for Daniel, anyway,' she added, and Maurice could tell that she was choosing her words carefully now because her speech pattern had slowed down and she wasn't looking him in the eye. 'One wonders, after all, where he picked up such behaviour.'

'Like you said,' said Maurice. 'From TV. Or a movie. Although I don't allow him a lot of screen time and he never really wants any. We're readers in our family.'

'That's good. Yes, Miss Willow says that Daniel loves books. And that he's a very good writer too.'

'He has a terrific imagination,' said Maurice. 'I don't know where he gets it from.'

'Well, you, most likely,' she replied. 'You're a writer, aren't you?'

He didn't reply.

Discomfited, she hesitated, replacing the cap on her fountain pen and returning it to a stand with holes for a dozen more, almost all of which were empty. 'There's nothing going on at home that you'd like to discuss with me?'

Maurice smiled. It was obvious what she was getting at. 'I don't hit him, if that's what you're getting at,' he said. 'I've never laid a finger on the boy.'

'I wasn't suggesting that you had. And Daniel hasn't witnessed any violence against women, I suppose?'

'I'm a widower, Mrs Lane,' said Maurice. 'I thought you knew that.'

'I do. But am I correct in thinking that Daniel's mother died many years ago?'

'No, that's not correct.'

'It's not?' she said, frowning. 'But in your file, it says that—'

'My late wife wasn't Daniel's mother,' he explained. 'Daniel was conceived through a surrogate after Edith died. I wanted a child but didn't want to share my life with a woman and, as my career began to take off around the same time, I did what I had to do in order to become a father.'

'I see,' said Mrs Lane, looking as if she wanted to extract every juicy detail that could be offered but was uncertain whether she could ask or not. 'That was very selfless of you, Mr Swift.'

'No it wasn't,' he replied, shaking his head. 'Had I gone to an orphanage in China or India and rescued a baby from a life of poverty, then that would have been selfless. But I didn't do that. I paid a woman a lot of money to carry a baby for me and hand him over the moment he was born, then disappear from our lives. It was an entirely selfish act in some ways but one that I was happy to commit.'

Mrs Lane's mouth opened and closed like a fish's.

'So, going back to your original question, I presume you were asking whether I have girlfriends over to stay and, if I do, whether I smack them around. Perhaps you're wondering whether it's a sexual fetish on my part and Daniel has had the misfortune of walking into my bedroom in the middle of the night to find some woman naked on my bed and me fucking her from behind while she's tied up? No, would be the answer to all such queries. I don't have girlfriends and I don't expose my son to anything like that. That part of my life has been over since before we came to New York. My writing and my son are all that I need.'

'That must be . . .' Mrs Lane searched for the right word. 'You must have loved your wife very much,' she said. 'To swear off all other women after her death. Particularly when you're so . . . so . . .'

'So what?' he asked, smiling a little.

'Well you're a . . . you're not an unattractive man, Mr Swift. Obviously, I don't mean anything by that. I'm a happily married woman.'

'You've gone quite red,' he said.

'It's the heat.'

Maurice smiled again.

'But don't you get lonely?' she asked, leaning forward.

'No. Why, do you?'

Mrs Lane's expression changed suddenly and her cheeks flushed even more. 'I mean . . . no,' she said. 'I have . . . there's so much to keep me occupied, what with . . . And Mr Lane has his business and—'

'People seem to think that a life is worthless unless it's shared with someone,' said Maurice with a sigh. 'But why must that be the case? I've been married, I know what the experience is like, and while there were certainly times when it was pleasurable there were just as many times when I wished that I was alone, not answerable to anyone, not needing to account for my every movement throughout the day. When Edith died, I promised myself that I would never get involved with anyone again. I don't much like women, if I'm honest. But don't get me wrong, I'm not some tragic misogynist. I don't much like men either. I'm an equal-opportunities hater, so to speak. And as for sex, well, it never really interested me, not even when I was young. I could never quite see the point of it, if I'm honest. And, you'll forgive me for sounding immodest, but I know that I'm good-looking. Throughout my life, both men and women have made their interest in me obvious. But I can't control any of that. It was simply the way I was born. Ultimately, it means nothing. I could have a heart of stone for all they know. I could be a psychopath or a sociopath. Not all monsters look like the Elephant Man, and not everyone who looks like the Elephant Man is a monster. So I don't really think about sex that often, although, strangely enough, it's very present in my work. Have you read any of my novels, Mrs Lane?'

The principal stared at him, barely registering that he had asked her a question, and swallowed hard, looking down at the notebook before her and smoothing its pages with trembling hands.

'I read your most recent one,' she said. 'When I realized who Daniel's father was I went to Barnes &—'

'*The Broken Ones.*'

'Yes.'

'Well, that novel doesn't have very much sex in it at all,' admitted Maurice. 'But then, if you've read it, you know that. Anyway,' he smiled, slapping his hands down on his knees so loudly that he made her jump, 'I shouldn't keep talking about myself like this. It sounds as if it's me who needs the services of a counsellor and not my son.'

Mrs Lane said nothing, and he took pleasure from seeing how uncomfortable he had made her. It was reassuring to know that he still had this sort of power over people.

'So is that everything?' he asked, standing up. 'Or was there something else you wanted to discuss with me?'

'No,' said Mrs Lane, remaining seated. 'No, that was it. You may leave.'

'Thank you,' he said, laughing a little at the manner of his dismissal.

'I'll email you details of a psychologist that the school recommends,' she said as he turned away. 'And you and Mr and Mrs Dell can liaise on that. I think you'll find them very accommodating. Believe me, if Daniel had to hit a girl, then Jupiter was probably the best one to hit.'

When he opened the door he smiled when he saw a small, seven-year-old boy sitting on a chair outside, his legs swinging in the air, his hands pressed together as if in prayer.

'Am I in trouble?' asked Daniel, looking up. Not for the first time, it struck Maurice how beautiful he was.

A fresh collection of manuscripts had arrived at home from the *Storī* office and Maurice piled them up on the coffee table. There looked to be about twenty in total, the usual amount selected for his evaluation, whittled down by the interns from the three hundred or so that arrived unsolicited every month. Having got past those merciless gatekeepers, each one should, in theory, have something to recommend it and, as he was judicious in his reading, it typically took him the best part of a week to get through them, pulling out the wittiest and most perceptive dialogue, the most ingenious plot lines and arresting images, and entering each one into a file on his computer. He'd pick four or five to publish too, of course, but send letters to the rejected authors, signed by a fictitious employee, apologizing that, due to time constraints and the pressures of writing a new novel, Mr Swift had not personally had an opportunity to read their submission – it was important that he should make this clear in case of any future problems – but that the editorial team at *Storī* had considered their work and decided it was not quite right for them at this time. Generally, he assumed, the writers would be so pleased to have received even an acknowledgement of their writing that their disappointment would be salved and they would set the piece aside for ever, believing that it just wasn't good enough.

The pile arrived four times a year and there was often very little in it worth stealing, but once in a while he came across a moment of brilliance that justified his decision to set up the magazine in the first place. His fourth novel, for example, *The Breach*, had been constructed around two different ideas that he'd discovered in stories by an American and a Chinese-American writer. Combining them into one, and using a central character that he created himself as the link between the pair, he'd managed to build a novel that had been highly praised upon publication and sold even more copies than *The Tribesman*, which of course was always going to do well after it was shortlisted for The Prize. His most recent book, *The Broken Ones*, published three years earlier, in 2008, had found its origin in a story written by a nineteen-year-old Viennese student that recounted a couple's visit to Paris on the eve of their twentieth wedding anniversary, where an unexpected infidelity took place in a restaurant. (He had changed the setting to Israel, the wedding anniversary to a birthday, the restaurant to a museum, and when combined with a comic character he purloined from the work of a young British writer, the book had once again been a commercial and critical hit.) He'd been putting off starting a new book for a while now as he hadn't found the right idea yet, and had been rather looking forward to receiving this group of submissions, hoping that there might be something in there that would be worth appropriating as his own.

The sound of a door opening to his left made him turn around, and he watched as Daniel walked towards him. The boy was wearing his favourite *Spider-Man* pyjamas and carrying a furry animal of no obvious species. He smelled of the lavender bubble-bath that he'd been splashing around in only an hour before and he was carrying his blue Ventolin inhaler. His asthma had been particularly aggressive lately and he'd had to spend ten minutes sitting quietly when they got home, taking puff after puff, before the congestion in his lungs cleared.

'Feeling better?' asked Maurice as the boy jumped up on to the sofa next to him, leaning over to bury his body into his father's side. Maurice held him close, kissing him on the top of his head, breathing in his scent.

'If I say sorry to Jupiter tomorrow, will I still have to go to see the doctor?' asked Daniel, sounding a little less anxious about that particular ordeal than he had when they'd arrived home. There had been tears then and a declaration that he shouldn't have to be kissed if he didn't want to be, a sentiment that Maurice thought was actually rather fair.

'I think so,' said Maurice. 'Otherwise this could all end up in a big drama that neither of us needs. I'm sure the doctor will be very nice, anyway.'

'Will she use a needle?' he asked.

'What do you mean?'

'The doctor. Will she use a needle when she sees me? I don't like needles.'

Maurice shook his head. 'She's not that type of doctor,' he said. 'There'll be nothing like that. All you'll do is talk to her, that's all. And then it will be over.'

Daniel frowned, his expression suggesting that he couldn't believe you could attend a doctor with no pain being involved, just conversation.

'I didn't like it when she kissed me,' said the boy.

'I never really cared for it much either,' said Maurice. 'But you can't go around committing random acts of violence when people do things you don't like. You should have just told her not to do it again.'

'Everyone was laughing at me,' whispered Daniel.

Maurice hugged him again and looked down at the perfect feet and toes emerging from the ends of his son's pyjamas. He had always expected to feel unadulterated love for a child, if he ever had one, but things hadn't quite worked out that way. He was terribly fond of Daniel, certainly, but the boy irritated him as often as he pleased him. He was always *there*, was the problem. Hanging around. Needing food, toys or new clothes. Saying that it was time to go to school or to be picked up again. It was endless harassment. Maurice did his best to keep an even temper with the boy – he was just a child, after all, and he recognized that – but still, he looked forward to the day that he turned eighteen and was heading off to college. He might get his life back then.

The idea of using a surrogate had come to him on the night that he'd been shortlisted for The Prize, which, to his immense disappointment, he'd lost out on to an old rival, Douglas Sherman. He'd been thinking about what to do with the sudden influx of royalties and made an appointment with a solicitor later that same week in order to get the ball rolling. Six months later, a young Italian girl working as a chambermaid in a Central London hotel was pregnant with his child and there had been no trouble whatsoever

during the pregnancy or the birth. Although the legal agreement had been tight, he had naturally worried that the woman
might have second thoughts once the baby was born, but no, she
had kept to her part of the bargain and disappeared from his life the
moment he took Daniel home from the hospital.

It hadn't been easy at first, of course. He had no experience of
babies and had to rely on books for most of his knowledge. But
Daniel had not been a difficult infant, sleeping through the night
almost from the start and apparently happy to lie in his crib, reaching up for the toys that swung from a mobile above him, as long as
Maurice was in his sight-lines, which he always was, since he
worked from home in those early years, only spending more time
at the *Storī* office after Daniel started kindergarten. They'd travelled
to international literary festivals together, where other writers
seemed charmed by the image of this handsome novelist, hugely
successful at a young age, going everywhere with a small boy in
tow. It helped that Daniel liked books too, as he was content to sit
reading while his father offered himself up for endless interviews
or took part in public events.

'Why did you slap her, anyway?' he asked now, and the boy
shrugged.

'I told you. Because she kissed me.'

'No, I know that,' said Maurice. 'I mean, why was that your reaction? Violence. Striking out. When have you ever seen people
behave in that way? No one has ever hit you, have they?'

The boy paused for a few moments, and Maurice wondered
whether he was trying to decide whether or not to tell the truth.

'Sometimes in school,' he said eventually, letting out a deep sigh
as he looked down at the floor.

'A teacher?'

'No,' said Daniel, shaking his head.

'Who then?'

'No one.'

'Come on,' urged Maurice. 'Tell me.'

'Just some of the boys in my class.'

'Which boys?'

'I don't want to say.'

Maurice frowned. He didn't want to push him, but if Daniel was being bullied, then he wanted to get to the bottom of it.

'Please, Daniel. You can tell me. Maybe I can make it stop.'

'James,' said Daniel, after a lengthy pause during which he snuffled a few times and looked as if he might start to cry. 'And William.'

'But I thought you got along with them? You sit beside James in class, don't you?'

'Yes, but he doesn't like me.'

'Why not?'

'He says I'm a freak.'

Fuck him, the little fucking shit, thought Maurice. But, 'You're not a freak,' he said.

'He says I am.'

'Then he's an idiot.'

'It's because I don't like playing with them,' he continued.

'Why not?' asked Maurice.

'Because every time they play someone always ends up going to the nurse's office with blood pouring from their nose. And they say I never speak either. They say I'm scared.'

'And is that why they hit you?'

'I don't know,' he replied with a shrug. 'They say it's just a game.'

'Well, it seems like a stupid game to me,' said Maurice, and Daniel looked up at him now, wounded by the irritation in his father's voice. 'Just stay away from them from now on, all right?' he continued. 'You're only seven years old, after all. I don't want you acting like you're in *Fight Club*.'

'What's *Fight Club*?'

'It doesn't matter. Just don't let your friends hit you, and don't you hit anyone either. Especially not the girls. We got lucky this time, there's no lawsuit, but remember, this is America. People here will sue you just for looking at them the wrong way in the street and, if they find out that we have a little money, then they'll try to find a way to take it off us.'

'Are we rich?' asked Daniel.

'We're comfortable. You don't have to worry, put it that way. But we're nowhere near as rich as most people who live in this city. So we have to hold on to what's ours and not let anyone steal it from us. Okay?'

The boy nodded. 'Okay,' he said. 'Stealing is bad.'

Maurice smiled. 'Stealing is *very* bad,' he agreed. 'Only really bad people take things that don't belong to them. Now, it's time for bed, don't you think?'

Henry Rowe had been new to the school that year. His family were originally from Belfast, Catholics who lived on the junction where the Falls Road met Iveagh Drive, but his mother, sister and he had relocated to Harrogate in 1980 to escape the Troubles. Even though he'd heard reports on the news of the bombing campaign in England and was vaguely aware of the hunger strikes taking place in the H-Block of the Maze Prison, Maurice had almost no interest in what was taking place on the island next to his own and, at fourteen, the concept of death, such a distant and other-worldly idea, bored him. Politics, he believed, was for other people and while he longed to be set free from the daily tedium of his home life, he had scant interest in the causes that his peers wore, quite literally, like badges of honour on their school uniforms. Only when the rumour went around that Henry Rowe's father had been murdered by the IRA for betraying them was Maurice's interest piqued. That would make a good idea for a story, he thought: *a teenage boy, forced to relocate to a strange country, gradually begins to understand his father's criminal past.* He might have been out of step with his classmates when it came to their political concerns but Maurice already knew exactly what he wanted to do with his life, which was more than most of them could claim.

'A writer?' his dad had said when he first told him his plans. 'You've more chance of winning the World Cup for England. You have to come from London if you want to write books. Have a fancy education and all that.'

'Not every writer comes from London,' said Maurice, rolling his eyes at the parochial nature of his father's worldview. He'd never read a book in his life, as far as he knew, and barely worked his way through the local newspaper once a week. 'D. H. Lawrence's dad worked at Brinsley Colliery. Isherwood came from Derbyshire. William Golding's from Cornwall.'

'That D. H. Lawrence only wrote filth,' replied his father. 'Naked men wrestling with each other and posh pieces having it off with the gamekeeper. Queer stuff, if you ask me. Written for poofters with fancy ideas. I'll not have any of it in the house.'

'You'll be a plumber, like your dad,' said his mother. 'That's good honest work, that is.'

'I'll not,' said Maurice, and meant it.

He was popular in school, of course, because despite being a bookworm, he was good-looking, which somehow made the other boys want to be his friend, even if they didn't quite understand why. The teachers liked him too – he was one of the students with whom they tried to ingratiate themselves – and he'd only found himself in trouble once, when it was discovered that he'd plagiarized a history essay from a book he borrowed from the local library, an offence that resulted in a week's suspension. There were boys who wanted to know him better, to get closer to him, but he was essentially a loner and kept others at a distance. Until Henry arrived, that is.

Even now, thirty years later, he could still remember the moment when the boy walked through the classroom door for the first time, a few steps behind the headmaster, Dr Webster, to be introduced to his new classmates. He was tall and lean with brown hair that both fell into his eyes and stood up above his head. When he opened his mouth to tell the class his name and what had brought him to Harrogate, the room broke into uncontrollable laughter at his strong Northern Irish accent and Henry's face had betrayed a mixture of anger, humiliation and confusion at how they mocked him. He looked around the room, disconcerted by this unruly and vaguely threatening group of strangers with whom he would be spending his days, until his eyes met Maurice's, the only boy who wasn't laughing. Maurice tilted his head a little, a sort of greeting, and Henry stared back, his tongue peeping out from between his lips, unable to look away.

They formed an alliance of sorts, spending time in each other's houses after school and at weekends, and it was while they were in Maurice's room one Saturday afternoon, listening to a Kate Bush cassette and discussing how much they both despised the school football captain, that Henry tried to kiss him. Kate was singing about Kashka from Baghdad, who lived in sin with another man, when he turned to his friend and pressed his lips against his own, his hand reaching up to press itself flat against the other boy's shirt. Maurice had been expecting something of this sort to happen but was surprised that there had been no lead-up to the moment. He'd never been kissed before, had never made a pass at any girl or boy, nor had he ever felt any particular desire to do so. It was something he'd wondered about from time to time, this curious lack of interest in sex. In moments of experimentation, he'd looked at pornographic magazines but had found himself entirely unaroused by the tragic expressions on the girls' faces as they spread their legs or pressed their breasts out towards the camera. In the school showers, after games, he'd surreptitiously examined the naked bodies of his classmates and felt no particular desire for them either. When he masturbated, it was solely for the pleasure of touching himself, for the trembling ecstasy of the orgasm, but it seemed unnecessary to him to share the experience with anyone else and he did not see the faces of others in his fantasies, only his own.

Now, however, with Henry pushing him back against the bed, he felt willing to investigate the moment a little in order to examine what effect an intimacy such as this might have on him. He could write about it afterwards, he thought, in a story. Most writers wrote about sex, didn't they? Even those, like Forster, for whom carnality in their private lives seemed unimportant. One of his favourite writers, Aldous Huxley, had said that experience is not what happens to a man, it is what a man does with what happens to him, and this was surely an experience, the body of another fifteen-year-old-boy lying above his own, his tongue in his mouth, his unfamiliar erection pressing against his thigh through the fabric of his clothes.

'What can I do?' asked Henry, pulling away for a moment, his face red, his entire body pulsating with desire as he looked down at his friend with such longing in his eyes that Maurice began to realize just how much power he already had. 'What will you let me do?'

'Tell me about Belfast,' he replied, and Henry pushed himself up on his elbows, frowning, uncertain that he'd heard him right.

'What?' he asked, running his hand down Maurice's shirt and releasing it from his trousers, tentatively opening a couple of buttons, his palm against the boy's navel and firmly muscled stomach.

'Belfast,' he repeated. 'What was it like over there?'

Henry shook his head and leaned down to kiss him again, but Maurice pushed him away, sitting up on the bed and re-buttoning his shirt. 'Tell me,' he said. 'Tell me the stories. I'm interested. I want to know.'

And Henry, confused and disappointed, his body crackling with hormones, sat up and stared at the carpet, trembling in bewilderment. 'What do you want to know?' he asked.

'Anything,' said Maurice. 'Did you ever see anyone get shot?'

Henry nodded. 'Once,' he said. 'Outside a petrol station in Ardoyne.'

'Tell me about it,' whispered Maurice. 'Tell me everything you saw and everything you heard and then I'll let you do some more.'

And, of course, he did.

They were in Maurice's house when it happened next, watching television, his parents having gone to Cardiff to visit a dying relative. Maurice was enjoying the tension as they sat together on the sofa and only when Henry reached across and took his hand did he feel a little unsettled at being the focus of so much obvious desire. *Why don't I feel the same way?* he asked himself. *Why don't I feel it for anyone? Could there be a story there?*

'You're so fuckin' gorgeous,' said Henry, leaning forward, and Maurice not only permitted himself to be kissed again but he kissed back, his tongue exploring his friend's mouth, a new sensation that was neither unpleasant nor arousing. Soon, they were upstairs, lying on his bed, and again Henry asked what he was allowed to do. Sensing that he needed to allow the burning boy more freedom than last time, he shrugged and said, *Anything you like*, and Henry, with an expression that suggested he couldn't quite believe his luck, unzipped Maurice's trousers and took his cock into his mouth. Maurice closed his eyes and enjoyed the feeling but his mind wasn't fully engaged with it. Would Henry tell him another story when he was finished or was this all a waste of time?

He came, and Henry looked up at him, smiling in delight, and Maurice smiled back, only mildly embarrassed. He could only imagine how ridiculous they looked.

'My turn,' said Henry, unbuckling his belt and pulling his trousers down.

Maurice looked at him and then stared at the boy's cock, feeling no particular repulsion at the idea of sucking him but no great desire to do so either. He reached down and touched his penis tentatively, running his index finger along the shaft as Henry closed his eyes and groaned in pleasure.

'Another story first,' he said. 'Then I'll do it.'

And so it went on, week after week for almost two months, the two boys finding opportunities to be alone together when Henry could indulge his desires and Maurice could hear tales of the boy's life before coming to England. His father, he revealed, had not been shot by the IRA as the boys in school believed. In fact, he'd died of nothing more imaginative than a heart attack, although he had, the boy claimed, been a member of the organization for many years and men in balaclavas had shown up at the funeral, acting as pallbearers as they carried the tricolour-adorned coffin to the grave. He talked about what it was like to hear shootings in the night, how a teenage boy from down the street had been kneecapped for an unexplained crime of which he had sworn his innocence, how a mother had gone missing after a visit to a local church, how a family had gone into hiding after becoming informers. It wasn't to Maurice's taste, most of it, but he wrote it all down and found a way to turn the boy's disconnected memories into a coherent narrative. It seemed that all he had to do was continue to give Henry orgasms and his story would eventually be completed. It seemed like a worthwhile trade to him.

They made their mistake when Henry's lust overcame him in school one lunchtime and, as Maurice was coming to the end of his story anyway, he decided to indulge him by taking him to a cluster of trees in the corner of the school, a shaded area that the other pupils usually avoided, and stood against a tree, his trousers around his ankles as the Irish boy fucked him from behind. Their minds were on separate things – sex and stories – which explained why they didn't hear one of their teachers approach.

The headmaster, Dr Webster, was informed, but he waited until the end of the day before summoning the boys to his office, where he told them that they could be expelled for what they had done, that their deeds were so shameful they should be sent to a young offenders' institution, but that he was willing to take pity on their youth, promising not to tell their parents if they agreed to end their friendship immediately and stay away from each other in future. Readily, they agreed, but it was then that the headmaster explained that there could be no forgiveness without punishment and that if they wanted to leave his office with their souls washed clean then they would have to do as he said. He walked towards the cabinet by his desk where he kept a two-foot-long cane and removed it, running his finger along the side of the oak with obvious pleasure.

'Trousers down,' he told them. 'Bend over the desk.'

The boys obeyed and, as he beat them, Maurice counted the number of the strokes by working his eyes along the lines of the abacus propped up on the headmaster's windowsill. There were ten rows and he counted them all off, and then half again, before it was over.

'Now,' said Dr Webster, his eyes alert as the boys turned around. 'Let me see what you filthy little bastards do to each other anyway. First you,' he said, nodding towards Maurice. 'And then you,' he said to Henry.

There were no more stories after that. Henry kept his distance, humiliated and frightened by the events of that day, and whenever Maurice approached him he turned on his heels and fled. Only when Maurice knocked on his door one night and demanded to be heard did the boy let him in.

'I don't want to any more,' said Henry, unable to look him in the eye.

'But my story isn't finished,' complained Maurice.

'What story?'

'Just . . . let's go upstairs. To your room. You can do whatever you want to me. Just tell me more about Belfast. Tell me what you saw, what you heard, what you—'

But Henry shook his head and pushed him back on to the street, looking around as if he feared that Dr Webster would be out there somewhere, watching them. Maurice tried several more times, but to no avail, and the piece remained unfinished.

What a waste of time, he thought, unable to find a way to complete it to his satisfaction and leaving it unfinished in a drawer. *I won't make that mistake again.*

After they left the psychologist's office, Maurice and Daniel decided to go for ice-cream. It had taken them almost fifteen minutes to break free of the Dells, who had been suggesting playdates and trips to the zoo together, despite the fact that Daniel clearly disliked their daughter and Jupiter, feigning victimhood, had already turned her attentions to another boy.

Maurice was glad the ordeal was behind them. The doctor had been young, no more than twenty-eight or twenty-nine, with that good-looking Brooklyn hipster vibe that had recently begun to grate on him. There was an effortlessness to the way the boy dressed, to his unkempt hair and white teeth, that made Maurice feel of lesser importance, and when both of Jupiter's parents had fallen over themselves to laugh at his jokes he felt, for the first time in his life, as if he was not the most attractive person in the room. He wasn't entirely uncomfortable with this idea – he knew that he'd always be good-looking and people would always be drawn to him – but still, he wasn't sure he was ready to give up his throne just yet. And certainly not to some clown in a J. Crew T-shirt, a sweater vest and vintage brogues.

Strolling past Barnes & Noble on East 17th Street now, close to where the *Storī* offices were located, Maurice glanced in the window and saw a display of *Beyond the River* by Garrett Colby, and his heart gave him a kick of resentment in his chest. It was the film tie-in edition, for Garrett's third book had not only been adapted by a famous Danish theatre director making his first foray into cinema, but the film had gone on to win several Academy Awards at the most recent ceremony, including an acting prize for a young man with whom Garrett was now in a heavily publicized romance.

'I used to know that guy,' Maurice said, looking down at his son, who was kicking his heels on the pavement, wishing they could move on to the ice-cream portion of the afternoon. 'Years ago. Back in England. He wrote stories about talking animals.'

Daniel looked up, interested now, for talking animals were a particular favourite of his, particularly if they had some prehistoric element to them. 'Were they good?' he asked.

'They weren't bad,' admitted Maurice.

'Can we go in and get them?'

'They weren't children's books,' said Maurice, shaking his head. 'But maybe you'll get to read them when you're older.'

'Can I get something else then?' asked Daniel, and Maurice nodded. He never denied the boy a book and considered it rude to leave a bookshop without making a purchase. And so they stepped inside, the soft music and smell of new hardcovers giving Maurice that instant hit of belonging he'd felt all his life whenever he walked into such places. Daniel immediately made his way towards the children's section – this was their local bookshop and he knew its every nook and cranny intimately – and Maurice watched him for a moment before picking up Garrett's book from the table and reading the author biography.

'Mr Colby is one of the most exciting young writers at work today,' it concluded, and Maurice rolled his eyes, recognizing the third-person biography that had clearly been written by the author himself. *Supercilious little shit*, he thought.

He returned it to the table, then picked up a novel by another writer, Jonas Ramsfjeld, before placing it on top of Garrett's. He'd read his novel *Spiegeltent* some years before and admired it and the two writers had read together at a festival in Listowel once and got along quite well, which had surprised Maurice, as he tended not to like other writers very much. Ramsfjeld was gay and handsome and, after spending an evening together, drinking in the hotel bar, Maurice had expected him to make a pass at him, but it had never happened. When he'd gone to bed that night, he'd almost regretted it. Now, it crossed his mind to wonder how many students from Edith's class had gone on to secure publishing deals in the ten years since her death.

He made his way towards the New Fiction section, where he recognized books by people he knew, people with whom he'd read at festivals, people he'd reviewed both well and badly for various publications. And then, just as he was about to take down a new edition of Maude Avery's *Like to the Lark*, which had been re-published in a hardback series of her novels, each with a jacket designed by Tracey Emin, he noticed a familiar face staring out from the non-fiction titles, the younger version of a man he had once known very well.

It was a biography of Dash Hardy, the first, as far as he knew, that had been written about the American writer. The author's name was unfamiliar to him. And the book itself was almost six hundred pages long, which suggested that it was an exhaustive account of the writer's life. Did Dash merit such a work? he wondered. Gore did, certainly. And Erich, probably. But Dash? Hadn't he turned into something of a second-tier writer by the end?

He took the book down and moved directly to the index at the back, running his finger down the names. To be included ran the risk of something negative being said but to be ignored would be wounding. But no, there he was, *Maurice Swift, 131, 284*. Just two entries and not spread across multiple pages. He flicked to the first, where the author mentioned Maurice's initial encounter with Dash in the Prado all those years ago and how a friendship had struck up between them.

Hardy was a crucial factor in Swift finding a publisher for his debut novel [it said]. *He took the young writer under his wing, as he had done for one or two boys of his type before, accommodating him in New York for two years and introducing him to publishers on the scene. That novel,* Two Germans, *was a huge success, although it precipitated the public disgrace of the novelist Erich Ackermann, with whom Dash had also been acquainted, in a manner that left a sour taste in the mouths of some readers.*

Well, that was true enough, he reasoned. Nothing libellous there, although in fact he had only lived with Dash for nine months, so there was an error there. And what did 'one or two boys of his type' mean?

He flicked to the index for the other entry and then to page 284, where, despite quickly scanning the page, he could find no mention of his name. He turned back to page 283 and then forward to page 285, but no, there was nothing there either, and he frowned, wondering whether another mistake had been made. But just to be certain, he began to read page 284 in its entirety and came across this line, which appeared in an interview with Edmund White:

Dash told me a story about a young writer he met in Europe to whom he had taken a particular shine. The boy was beautiful, of course, and Dash was always a sucker for a pretty face. He did everything for him, introduced him around town, helped him find a publisher and an agent, and the moment success came his way, the boy just dropped him like a hot potato. He'd done it before, from what I'd heard. The boy was an arch-manipulator and impossibly calculating. An operator of the first order. I remember meeting him myself at some reading and he told me that he would be staying with his editor on a trip to the UK soon. 'Why don't you just get a hotel?' I asked him, and he shook his head and said no, that he thought if he became friendly with the editor and the editor's family then there was no chance that he'd ever be dropped. I thought it such a cynical move but I suppose there was something in it. It was my belief that the boy knew he was essentially talentless, nothing more than a good-looking hack, and that only charm and sycophancy could keep him in the game. It did, too, for a time.

Maurice slammed the book shut, causing some of the other shoppers to turn and look in his direction. He hadn't been named, of course, so it was unlikely that he could sue, but the page reference in the index confused him. Of course, he realized, after a moment. His name must have been originally part of the Edmund White quote, and indexed, but then the lawyers must have taken it out before publication, forgetting to remove the reference at the back. He was almost amused by their stupidity. But was it worth pursuing? He couldn't decide. He would have to acknowledge that the description was one that fitted him and he wasn't sure he wanted to do that.

A moment later, Daniel returned with a brightly coloured paperback and Maurice took it, along with the Dash biography and the Maude Avery novel, to the till before walking hand in hand with him towards Union Square Park, where they sat on a bench, eating ice-creams.

'When you're older,' said Maurice, 'and you think back on this morning, don't blame me too much for it, all right? It was only an hour of your life, and it's saved us both a lot of grief. I'm proud of you for going along with it.'

'Blame you for what?' asked Daniel, who had seemed to rather enjoy telling a stranger all the details of his day-to-day pedagogical life and the sexual harassment that he'd suffered from a girl whose attentions he had never encouraged.

'Blame me for anything,' replied Maurice. 'There's a good chance that, when you're a teenager and complaining about how I've ruined your life, you'll bring this up and say that it all started here.'

Daniel shrugged; he wasn't interested. His breath caught a little and he reached into his bag for his inhaler, taking a quick puff. Maurice sat quietly, his sunglasses resting on his nose, watching the people go by. One of his own interns marched past, oblivious to his presence on the bench, while reading something on his phone. He was carrying a luxurious brown saddle bag over his shoulder and Maurice wondered how the boy could afford it – it was an expensive brand – but then recalled that his mother was on the board of the New York Ballet and so, presumably, he came from money.

And then, to his dismay, he noticed Henrietta James walking in his direction, still covered in multiple layers of clothing, as if she were about to embark for the Arctic, and before he could tell the boy that it was time to go she'd spotted him too and was waving manically at him, as if trying to generate her own electricity with her arms.

'Hello, you,' she said, grinning like the cat who'd got the cream.

'Henrietta,' he said, standing up to kiss her on both cheeks. 'How nice to see you!'

'And who's this?' she asked, looking down at Daniel, who barely glanced up from his ice-cream.

'This is my son,' said Maurice. 'Daniel.'

'How charming!' she said. 'I'll join you for a few minutes, if you don't mind,' she added, not waiting for an answer as she sat down. 'I need to rest. It's been a horrendous day. My publisher emailed me the proposed jacket for *I Am Dissatisfied with My Boyfriend, My Body and My Career* and it was so awful that I came all the way downtown to tell her exactly what I thought of it. I might not have been as polite as I could have been and we left things on a rather sour note. Lashings of apologies to make later, I daresay.'

'Well, I'm sure you'll figure it out,' said Maurice.

'What an adorable little boy,' she said, smiling a little as she reached a hand out to ruffle Daniel's hair, but when he looked up and narrowed his eyes, emitting a low growling sound from the back of his throat like a threatened animal, she changed her mind and made a hasty retreat.

'Is he staying with you for the summer?' she asked, and now it was Maurice's turn to frown, uncertain what she meant, before realizing that she probably assumed he was divorced.

'No, he lives with me,' said Maurice.

'Oh. And your . . . partner? Your . . . ?'

'My wife died some years ago,' he said, a non-sequitur, of course, since Edith had borne no relationship to Daniel, but he had no intention of getting into the intricacies of his life with an author he barely knew and didn't much like.

'Maurice, I'm so sorry,' she replied, lowering her voice. 'I had no idea.'

'And now you do.'

'It's a bit like *Kramer vs Kramer*, isn't it?' she said.

'How so?'

'You know, when Meryl Streep walks out on Dustin Hoffman and

262

he doesn't know how to cope at first with the little boy. He can barely even cook dinner. But then they form a connection that's been missing since he was born and, when Meryl comes back, Dustin doesn't want to give the child up and they have the most frightful rows.'

Maurice stared at her, wondering how someone so stupid could have publishers begging for her work. 'As I said, my wife died,' he said quietly. 'So I don't think she's going to show up demanding custodial rights any time soon.'

'No, I suppose not,' said Henrietta, who didn't look entirely convinced that this would be the case. 'Oh, by the way, I meant to tell you. I sold that story.'

'Which story?'

'The one you rejected.'

'I didn't reject it, Henrietta,' he said with a sigh. 'I simply passed on it for now as I didn't think it was a good fit for our next issue.'

'That sounds a lot like semantics to me, which is unworthy of you. You hated it. Just be honest and tell the truth.'

The same thing, thought Maurice.

'All right, fine,' he said, throwing his hands in the air. 'You're right. I hated it.'

Henrietta sat back in her chair in shock, as if he'd just pulled a gun on her or told her that he'd impregnated her mother. 'That's a little rude, isn't it?' she asked.

'Well, you're so insistent on the point that it seems easier to agree with you than anything else.'

'So you didn't hate it, then?'

'I don't know,' he said, smiling a little. 'What do you think?'

She stared at him, looking as if she was torn between annoyance and laughter, but finally gave in to the latter, slapping his knee sharply.

'You shouldn't hit people,' said Daniel, sitting up straight.

'I beg your pardon?' she said.

'Don't hit people!' he insisted, and Henrietta looked from father to son in bewilderment.

'She didn't mean anything by it,' said Maurice, looking at the boy. 'But he's right, Henrietta, you shouldn't hit people. It's not nice. How would you like it if I hit you?'

The smile faded from her face now. There was nothing in his tone to suggest that he was joking. She waited for him to smile and to say that he was only teasing her and, when he didn't, when his face remained as still as a block of stone, she shuddered a little and placed both hands on the table, pushing herself into an upright position as if she were morbidly obese and needed assistance.

'I'd better go,' she said.

'Actually,' said Maurice, reaching into his bag and removing a small camera that he always kept there, 'before you do, could you do me a favour? I don't have many pictures of Daniel and me together. Would you take one for me?'

Henrietta seemed slightly bored by the request but took the camera as Maurice put an arm around his son, who was still focussed entirely on eating his ice-cream. Just as she asked them to smile, Maurice tapped the boy on the head lightly so his nose dipped into the tip of the cone, covering it with vanilla, and both father and son burst out laughing.

'Thanks,' he said when Henrietta handed the camera back, and she kissed him briefly on the cheek before continuing on her way.

'I didn't like her,' said Daniel when she had gone, and Maurice shrugged.

'I don't like her very much either,' he said. 'What do you want to do now, anyway? We could go to see a movie, if you like?'

'Let's just go home,' said Daniel, shaking his head. 'I want to read my new book.'

'I was hoping you'd say that,' said Maurice, standing up and taking his son by the hand as they left the park behind. 'I have twenty short stories waiting for me and I'd better make a start on them if I'm going to figure out what my next novel will be about.'

PART III

OTHER PEOPLE'S STORIES

'Drunkenness is temporary suicide.'

– Bertrand Russell

1. The Crown, Brewer Street

Although I never exchanged so much as a hello with any of them, I recognized most of the drinkers in the Crown by sight and, over the years, assigned each one a name. Sitting at the end of the bar, endlessly playing games on his iPad, was Spencer Tracy, so called because of an uncanny resemblance he held to the actor. At a table by the window sat Professor Plum, a tall, elderly man in a purple turtleneck who drank pints of cider and worked his way through a succession of newspapers, shaking his head and muttering obscenities under his breath. Mrs Thatcher sat at the table closest to the toilets and appeared to have a bladder condition because she was in and out of the Ladies every twenty minutes. True, she didn't look anything like the former prime minister, but her name was Maggie – I'd heard the barman call her that – and somehow that transformed itself into Mrs T in my head. She nursed her drinks and generally kept herself to herself although occasionally she showed up with a bespectacled, balding man – Denis, to me – and smooched with him shamelessly. It was a repulsive thing to witness.

There were others, of course, a few regulars and plenty of passing trade. Occasional stagehands from the nearby theatres and a small crew of four or five from a local bookshop. Once in a while I saw a young boy, probably a student, nursing a pint for about two hours while reading one of the Great Works of Literature. I'd seen him make his way through *Anna Karenina*, *Moby-Dick*, *Crime and Punishment*. Cheap paperback editions, usually. A few months earlier, I'd watched as he turned the opening pages of *A Sentimental Education*, reading from a Penguin Classic for which I'd written the introduction, and he flipped past those six or seven pages without reading a word. I felt offended at first – that introduction had been one of the last things I'd published – but then remembered that I never read introductions either, so I could hardly blame him for ignoring it.

I wondered if any of the patrons of the Crown noticed me too and, if they did, whether they wondered who I was or what had brought me there. I'd had a fantasy for a long time that one of them might ask and I had my answer ready for such a moment, eleven simple words that summed up my past, present and what I believed would be my future:

I used to be a writer but now I'm a drunk.

It might seem embarrassing to make such an admission but there was just no getting around the facts. I didn't consider myself an alcoholic, although a doctor would probably have disputed this. If I was, however, then I was a *functioning* alcoholic, which is surely the best kind to be. When I first returned to London four years ago and checked in to the hotel I was staying at until I found a more permanent residence, I couldn't think of any constructive way to spend the afternoon and so wandered down to the bar, where I got completely pissed, and somehow, I seemed to have stayed that way ever since.

It helped, of course, that I had money. Over the years I'd earned a decent amount from book advances, royalties, speaking engagements and commissioned articles, and when I sold *Storī*, the magazine I'd set up in New York, it was at the height of its influence. The seven-figure sum that came my way from a liberal media corporation was a wonderful surprise in a world that seemed to value literature less and less. A few months later, exhausted by hotel living, I purchased a comfortable home within walking distance of Hyde Park and planned to live there until the world came to its senses and re-discovered me.

I longed to write a new novel, of course, to get back in the game, but the old problem that had plagued my life since my teenage years reared its head once again. I changed city, social groups and daily routine in the vain hope that this might produce a good idea, but none came. My creative abilities remained in abeyance. I wrote a book that even I could tell was hopeless and it was rejected by my publisher during a highly unpleasant face-to-face encounter, where I may have behaved in a manner ill suited to a man of my accomplishments. Before marching out in a fit of pique, however, I declared that I'd been dropped before and had stormed back with *The Tribesman*, so all he was doing was replicating Rufus Shawcross's mistake of twenty years earlier, an imitation that he would surely come to regret one day. I started another book soon after but was only a hundred pages in when I came to realize that it was more of a narcoleptic than a novel and quickly abandoned it. For a time, I feared that I was finished. The greatest writer of his generation, stalled for lack of an original thought. Really, I should have had more self-belief. If I'd learned nothing else since leaving Yorkshire at the end of the 1980s, it was that, like the proverbial cat, I had a habit of landing on my feet.

I developed a routine and stuck to it religiously. Rising every day at around nine o'clock, I made my way towards Bayswater Road, where I entered Hyde Park and walked at a good pace in the direction of Kensington Palace, keeping a wary eye out for one of the lesser Royals, then strolled back towards the Serpentine, around to Speakers' Corner and finally home again. It was good exercise, ninety minutes or so, and on a fine day it filled my lungs and almost made me feel glad to be alive. I shaved and showered and made sure to dress well as, although I'm perfectly happy to be a drunk, I prefer not to look like a tramp. One never knows, after all, who one might run in to. And then I packed my laptop and the book that I was reading and left for the afternoon.

My week followed a simple but fixed pattern. Although I drank every day, I didn't like the idea of being considered a 'regular' – indeed, during my first year I stopped frequenting two pubs, replacing them with others, on account of the growing over-familiarity of the staff – and so I had seven bars, one for each day of the week, which meant that my visits to each one were rare enough that I didn't end up on first-name terms with anyone but frequent enough that I felt comfortable there. I chose the West End because I knew that part of London to be so busy with tourists and shoppers that I would never be anything more than another face in the crowd. Also, from where I lived, it was an easy Tube ride into Piccadilly Circus before a quick stroll to that day's sanctuary.

From the start, I visited the Crown on Brewer Street every Monday. It stands on land once held by the Hickford Rooms, a concert venue where Mozart played the piano at the age of nine. I always preferred the seat in the corner for, although I had no particular reason to believe it so, I liked to think that was where the young Wolfgang sat to perform the minuets and allegros that he composed as a child while his audience listened in astonishment to his precocity and his father, Leopold, watched from the corner, counting his money.

The Crown, in its peaceful way, had become a good friend to me. The staff behind the bar came and went and were far more interested in engaging with strangers through their smartphones than in conversing with an actual human being, which suited me perfectly. I suspected that none of them remembered me from one Monday to the next and, even if they did, that my presence meant nothing to them. I didn't bother them and they didn't bother me. The proof of this, surely, was that they never recalled from one week to the next what I drank, which pleased me. The single phrase that would have driven me from any pub for ever would have been 'The usual, sir?'

While my daily routine never changed, nor did the subtleties that lay at the heart of each drinking schedule. I've never been much of a wine drinker, preferring the grain to the grape, and so, beginning at precisely eight minutes past two, I drank four pints of lager and two double whiskies. That usually took about three hours and then, shortly after five o'clock, I enjoyed three more pints, followed by a single malt. At seven, I had a Baileys with three ice cubes and, by seven thirty, I was done for the day, at which point I made my way back towards Piccadilly Circus and took the Tube home, where I ordered some food, ate a little of it, and went to bed. Occasionally, I would suffer from bad dreams but more often than not I slept the sleep of the innocent.

What did I do while I was drinking? I started by opening my laptop and reading through the news sites, followed by the literary pages, keeping up with every book review and author interview that I could find, searching for clues that might answer that most tedious but prolific of questions, *Where do you get your ideas?* I had bookmarked the culture section of all the major newspapers and made it my business to study every trend, every bestseller and every word of wisdom that was sent my way, trying to understand the secrets of others. And then, when I'd soaked it all up, I read for a while, devoting myself exclusively to contemporary fiction. I visited a bookshop once every few weeks to stock up, and even though the 'New Titles' section infuriated me because I had nothing to offer it, there was no question in my mind that I would reclaim my place there soon.

I'd devoted myself exclusively to young writers since my first arrival in New York, when I set up *Storī* and was attending parties three or four times a week, making sure to be familiar with the work of my peers in order to be part of the conversation. I had an opinion on them all and I was happy to share those opinions freely, delighted when I could cause an occasional controversy with a well-judged put-down, which I would innocently claim had been taken out of context when I next encountered the writer in question.

'It's the media, darling,' I would say, leaning in towards my opponent's ear. 'You know what it's like. You can't say a word without it being misinterpreted.'

And I was generally believed too, for I knew them and they knew me and, anyway, we were all at it. We drank together, had countless spats, made up, pretended to take pleasure in each other's successes and to commiserate over each other's failures. What mattered was that *I* mattered, that I was taken seriously.

Now, however, sitting in the pub and tired of reading, there would be nothing left for me to do but open a Word document on my laptop and stare at its accusatory blankness while I got drunker and drunker. But to my frustration, not once did my fingers ever touch the keyboard other than to write the words 'Chapter One' at the top of the page. The simplest phrase of all, but the most intimidating.

It was on a Monday afternoon in the Crown on the last day of April – coincidentally, my birthday – that I read Theo Field's letter and saw an opportunity to forsake this rather humdrum existence and return to the one that suited me best. My afternoon was passing in its usual manner and I was enjoying my third pint while staring at an empty screen when I remembered an envelope that had arrived from my literary agent's office that morning, an all too rare offering those days. I'd thrown it into my bag as I left the house but reached for it now, tearing it open, and I was immediately impressed by the quality of the stationery that the writer had used, not to mention the fact that he'd gone to the trouble of writing instead of sending an email. Old-fashioned, yes, but something I appreciated.

Dear Mr Swift [it began],

Forgive this unsolicited letter but I write to you as a great fan of your novels. I remember reading *Two Germans* when I was a boy and it sparked an interest in the war that remains with me to this day. I don't believe that a novel set during those years has ever moved me quite as much as yours did. *The Tribesman*, *The Breach* and *The Broken Ones* are among my favourite works of contemporary literature but I'm a particular fan of *The Treehouse*, which, for me, is an underrated classic. I'm currently a student at the University of London, where I'm in my final year of study in the English department, and I hope to make your work the subject of my final thesis, although I have ambitions towards ultimately developing that thesis into a book. For me, you are the finest British writer of your generation. If you'll forgive the flattery, the range of your work is so extraordinary that somehow it seems astonishing to me that it could all have come from the same mind. That's your genius, I think. Surprising the reader with each new novel.

I wondered whether I might meet you at some point and learn a little more about your work and your life, in order to better inform my thesis. It's important to me that I write something honest and singular, as my ultimate ambition is to be a literary biographer and this will be my first effort to forge a path towards that career. My father, an editor at Random House, has been very encouraging in this respect. (I'm not a fiction writer, you'll be pleased to know, and have no ambitions whatsoever in that direction!) Anyway, I assume that you're working on a new novel and have very little free time but I would appreciate if you could spare a little for me one day. It would mean an awful lot.

Yours sincerely,

Theo Field

After reading the letter I reached for my pint and noticed that my hand was trembling a little, so I returned the glass to the table and closed my eyes for a moment while breathing slowly and carefully through my nose, using a technique that I'd been taught which often helped at moments like this. I could sense Daniel near me at that moment, could almost feel his hand in mine, his voice whispering in my ear in that accusatory way he developed towards the end. He was telling me to throw the letter away and leave the boy alone, that he was just an innocent student trying to get a start in the world, and I knew that I needed to step away if I were to block him out. And so I made my way into the Gents, where I stood before the sink, my eyes shut, my hands pressed against the cool white porcelain, and waited a minute or two before throwing water on my face and staring at my reflection in the mirror, uncertain whether I even recognized myself any more.

I rarely bothered looking in mirrors at home but there, in that narrow bathroom with its dull neon light flickering, I could see how altered my appearance had become in recent years. All my life I had been handsome. I took no particular pride in the fact, but a fact it was nevertheless, and one that I'd been aware of since the age of thirteen or fourteen. Both women and men had been attracted to me since I was very young and I understood the power that I held over them, a power that had always been very easy to exploit. Several had fallen in love with me. One had married me.

I had long since come to understand, however, that I was different from other men in that I had no particular desire for the bodies of others and that whatever instinct guided people towards the bedroom was somehow lost on me. Whether or not this has been a blessing or a curse is hard to know but I suspect it's the former. I've seen so many people's lives destroyed by failed love affairs or unrequited passions that I've always felt rather fortunate to remain essentially disinterested. Why would anyone want to be part of such calamitous drama, after all? It had been years since I'd enjoyed a romantic encounter or even desired one. During my time in New York, there had been plenty of people who'd expressed an interest, but I'd taken none of them up on their offers.

Staring at my reflection now, however, I wondered whether I would ever have the opportunity to turn someone's advances down again. My hair was turning grey and my blue eyes, which had once shone so bright, had grown dull. Worst of all, however, was my skin, which appeared grey and was tinged with red capillaries, probably from the excess of alcohol. I glanced down at my hands, which had spent so much of their lives typing away at a keyboard before me. My recollection of them was as smooth collaborators with just the hint of a blue vein running from the wrist to the middle finger, but now, the skin was tight and my fingers appeared bony, the nails pockmarked, with large semicircles spreading outwards from the cuticles, like slowly exploding planets. I was growing old, it was clear, and not gracefully.

There was only so long that I could stay and observe the ruins and eventually I turned my attention away, washed my hands and made my way back outside to my seat, re-reading Theo Field's letter, several times in fact. Outside the flattery and the oleaginous remarks, there remained the central idea that he wanted to write about me. Only a thesis, yes, but he mentioned that he had ambitions towards literary biography and, indeed, towards publishing a book. And that delicious morsel he had thrown in, mentioning that his father worked at Random House! Of course, the naïf had wanted to impress me with his credentials, and it had worked, for I could surely use his family connections to my advantage in due course. A critical study would undoubtedly revive my drooping reputation and perhaps there would be something in the boy and his questions that would reignite my creative spark. And then a novel. The path back to glory was so wonderfully simple.

After Daniel's death, there had, quite naturally, been an outpouring of sympathy towards me within the publishing industry, but it hadn't provoked quite the interest in my work that I had hoped. It was something that my editor had the gall to bring up when he rejected the book I wrote immediately after the accident.

'Considering everything that you've been through, Maurice,' he told me that day as we sat in his office, 'there's nothing I'd like more than to publish a new novel by you. And certainly, from a publicity standpoint – well, I hope you don't take this the wrong way but there is an enormous amount of goodwill out there towards you and the media would fall over itself to interview you. But it has to be with the right book and this . . . well, I hate to say it but this just isn't it. It's well written, of course, but the story . . .'

I could feel the fury building inside me as I recalled that afternoon, the suppression of my pitiless ambition, and returned to Theo's letter one final time, smiling to myself as I read it.

I opened my laptop and began to type, taking great care with my reply. Indeed, it could be said that I worked harder on this one sentence than I had on anything in years, both in terms of the words that I used and the words that I didn't.

Dear Theo [I wrote],
    I would be happy to meet you on Tuesday 8 May at 3 p.m. in the Queen's Head, Denman Street.
    Yours,
    Maurice Swift

As I went to bed that night, I tried not to think about my aspiring biographer or my lost son, but they both lingered in my thoughts, two sides of a single coin that could be thrown in the air and land on either side, and I found my emotions torn between excitement and grief, that terrible agony within my soul that lingered regardless of whether I was awake or asleep, sober or drunk, writing or not writing. And thinking of Daniel, I asked myself whether he would approve of what I was about to do but insisted to myself that he would, despite his irritating and adolescent belief in moral absolutes. For he had loved me and I had been a good if imperfect father, almost to the end. What else would he want for me than that I be happy? Otherwise, what had it all been for?

2. The Queen's Head, Denman Street

The Queen's Head has always been my favourite of my weekly pubs. I like the dark wood panelling, the ornate chandelier, the mirrors that have reflected the lives of its patrons for so long. It was the perfect place for Theo and me to have our first encounter and, eight days after receiving his letter and having received a positive reply to my own, I sat within its walls, eagerly anticipating the start of the next stage of my writing life.

    I left home early that day, wanting to steady myself with a couple of drinks before he arrived. I'd spent much of the last week thinking about the book I would soon begin and felt a sense of excitement that I'd only experienced twice before in my life. The first was on that afternoon in Rome many years earlier when that fool, Erich Ackermann, had begun to tell me the story of his one-sided love affair with the unfortunate Oskar Gött. I knew that there was a story there, if only I could figure out how to drag it from his terrified memory. Ultimately, it hadn't proved that difficult. All I had to do was smile, stretch back in my seat a few times so he could catch a glimpse of my flat, muscular stomach, and the ridiculous old queer was putty in my hands. Not my finest moment, I know, but it hardly compares in malevolence to the things that he had done.

The second occasion was on that rainy afternoon in Norwich when, out of sheer boredom, I switched on Edith's computer and opened the file marked 'BOOK 2' and began to read the document contained within, sensing immediately that she'd written something extraordinary. It was a novel worthy of me, I knew, not of her. She didn't care for glory or immortality, which is just as well, as neither was to be her destiny. I remember the horror I felt when she suggested that we stay in Norwich after the publication of her second novel rather than returning to London and re-entering the literary world there. It seemed bizarre to me that she would even suggest such a thing. A strange woman, in retrospect. Still, one shouldn't speak ill of the dead, I suppose. She had many fine qualities, but ambition wasn't one of them.

Nothing since then, not even the novels I'd cobbled together from rejected work at *Storī*, had sparked my interest in the same way until the arrival of Theo Field's letter. All I needed was for him to write about me, to finish his thesis, publish his book, and I would have breathing room for a few more years until I found a story to tell.

He arrived at three o'clock precisely and I wondered whether he'd been pacing up and down the street outside anxiously until his watch struck the hour, not wanting to arrive too early. I'd had these sorts of encounters with young aspirants before, each of whom had their eye on the main chance and didn't want to say or do anything that might destroy their opportunity.

As soon as I saw him, however – and it was obvious that it was him by his age and the manner in which he looked around the bar before locating me – it was I who felt disconcerted for, to my surprise and alarm, he bore a striking resemblance to Daniel. The same thick blond hair, although his was quite clearly dyed, and the same frameless glasses. Pale skin that looked as if it would bruise easily. Good-looking, certainly. Yes, he was seven or eight years older than my son had been when he died but it was as if I were looking at the boy that Daniel might have become if he hadn't been such a meddler. As he made his way over to my table, it was all that I could do to drag myself back to the present moment and away from a past that I preferred not to think about.

'Mr Swift,' he said, standing before me and extending a hand. 'I'm Theo. Theo Field.'

I stood up and greeted him uneasily. He wore a ring on the fourth finger of his right hand, a thin silver band, an affectation that my son had taken to as well during the last months of his life. He'd bought it at a street market and, although I thought it looked ridiculous on a boy of his age, I took it as a sign of his incipient development from child to teenager and would never have mocked his first attempt at individuality. After all, I prided myself on being an indulgent father.

'Theo,' I said, trying to collect my thoughts. 'Of course. It's nice to meet you. And please, there's no need for such formality. Call me Maurice.'

'Thank you,' he replied, sitting down. 'It's very generous of you to make the time for me. I really appreciate it.'

He ordered the same as me, a pint of lager, and I made my way across the room, where, as I waited for the drinks to be poured, I had an opportunity to collect my thoughts. It was stupid, I told myself, to feel so unsettled. After all, his was a standard look among boys his age and, if he put me in mind of my dead son, then perhaps that would help to build a connection between us. Maybe, at the right moment, I would even tell him.

'Cheers,' I said, as I sat back down and we clinked glasses.

'I can't believe I'm sitting having a beer with Maurice Swift,' he replied, shaking his head and smiling.

'I'm just surprised that someone as young as you even knows who I am,' I said. 'Or that you'd recognize me. I've kept a fairly low profile in recent years.'

'Of course I'd recognize you,' he replied. 'I'm a reader. A voracious reader. I always have been.'

'Very few people are.'

'Very few people are interested in art,' he replied, triggering a memory in me, an almost forgotten conversation from many years before. I had said something like that to Erich once, hadn't I? Or he had said it to me. The past had begun to grow a little muddled with age and it wasn't always easy to separate the voices across the years.

'That's true,' I told him, drawing the years back. 'But the lack of an audience should never be a deterrent to the artist.'

'Books have been my passion since I was a kid. My father's uncle used to write a little and my dad has always worked in publishing. I suppose it must be in the blood somewhere.'

'Yes, you mentioned him in your letter,' I said. 'Random House, was it? He's an editor there?'

'That's right.'

'Fiction or non-fiction?'

'Fiction.'

I smiled. *Perfect.*

'That's probably why I wanted to study English at university. I discovered your books when I was only thirteen or fourteen and they made a huge impression on me.'

'That's quite young to read my work,' I said.

'Well, I grew out of children's books very early,' he replied. 'I was reading Dickens at ten. The orphan books, mostly.'

'Any particular reason?' I asked.

'No, I had a very happy childhood. I just enjoyed books about children on their own in the world. I still do.'

'All right,' I said. 'And are you enjoying your course?'

'Very much,' he replied enthusiastically. 'I like exploring the lives of writers. Trying to make connections between their work and what was going on in the world at the time. Sometimes there's very little but more often than not there's an enormous amount, whether or not they intend there to be. It's one of the things that's always fascinated me about your novels.'

'How so?' I asked.

'Well, you're not present at all in *Two Germans* but then, of course, that's pretty much based on Erich Ackermann and—'

'Only partly,' I said, the old wound reopening a little. I hated it when people looked at my debut in such basic terms. I had written it, after all. Every word on every page was mine. 'I simply took what he told me and—'

'No, I know that,' he replied, interrupting me. 'But it takes a lot of skill to take a person's story and build something from it. What I mean is that there's nothing in there that reflects your life at all, only his. There is in *The Treehouse*, I think, but not in *The Tribesman*. Or either of the subsequent novels.'

'I'd agree with that,' I said, impressed by how perceptive he was. After all, *The Treehouse* was the only novel I'd published that was essentially mine so it made sense that he could see something of the personal in there.

'And then, with *The Breach* and *The Broken Ones*—'

'You're writing a thesis?' I asked, interrupting him. 'On me? Is that right?'

'That's the plan,' he said, nodding.

'I've been working on it for a while now. Analysing each of the novels and trying to build connections between them.'

'I'm flattered,' I said. 'I didn't think I'd be on the curriculum at universities quite yet.'

'Well, you're not,' he said, a little sharply, I thought. 'It's an area of private study.'

'Oh,' I replied, amused by my own egotism. 'I don't suppose any-one of my generation is yet.'

'One or two,' he said.

I paused and took a long drink of my beer. 'Oh yes?' I asked. 'Who?'

He named a few people, most of whom weren't that much older or younger than me. Douglas Sherman, who had beaten me to The Prize on the year that *The Tribesman* was shortlisted, was men-tioned and I felt a slight kick at the pit of my stomach.

'I know her,' I said, when he mentioned one novelist I particularly despised for making a terrific career over the last decade or so, writ-ing some really interesting novels. 'Or I knew her, at least.'

'Really?' he said, his eyes opening wide.

'Yes, we've read together many times. On the festival circuit, you know.' Not true. We had read together only once but for some rea-son I felt an inexplicable desire to impress the boy.

'What's she like?'

'Oh, she's awful,' I said, inventing a story on the spot about how she had been rude to some young volunteers at a festival and left one boy, barely out of short pants, in tears after he brought her red wine instead of white.

'How disappointing,' said Theo. 'I used to really like her work.'

'Well, you still can,' I pointed out, uncertain why I felt such a need to denigrate a writer who had never said or done anything unkind to me. 'Just because she's not a very nice person doesn't neg-ate the value of her books.'

'Maybe,' he said, pulling a face. 'But when I hear stories like that they just make me never want to read the person again. You shouldn't meet your heroes, should you? Not that I've met her, but you know what I mean. They'll always let you down.'

'I hope I won't,' I said. 'And student life suits you?'

'It does for now,' he said, nodding as he drank his beer. 'I like studying. I like the discussions we have. And I get on pretty well with the others on my course.'

'Do they all want to be writers?' I asked.

'Some do,' he told me. 'Some are just filling in a few years until they can figure out what to do with their lives.'

'And you?' I asked. 'I know you said that you don't want to be a novelist, but I suppose I'm a little sceptical.'

'I really don't,' he said. 'I never have. I love fiction but I don't have the sort of brain that could create my own. I mean, I can *write* pretty well, I think. But only essays and things like that. Non-fiction. I could never write a short story or a novel. I wouldn't be able to think up a plot, you know? It's just not a gift that I've been given.'

'Well, there are ways around that, of course,' I said quietly, looking around as the girl behind the bar dropped a glass and it smashed on the floor, leading to the inevitable jeers and rounds of applause from those seated nearby.

'I mean, it would be great to be a writer,' he continued, ignoring my comment, and I was surprised that he hadn't looked towards the bar too. I always thought it was a Pavlovian response to turn one's head at a loud noise, but no, he seemed more interested in our conversation than in what was going on around him. 'But if you've got no imagination, then there's no point even trying, is there? And, quite honestly, I've never had much of an imagination.'

'Many modern novels are plotless,' I told him, not entirely sure as I said this that it was actually the case. 'In fact, I was in a bookshop recently where I saw a shelf-talker that referred to "Plotless Fiction".'

'That sort of thing doesn't interest me,' he said.

'You don't like experimentation?'

'I suppose I feel that those books don't age very well,' he said, considering it. 'What feels quirky or unusual today can often seem ridiculous, even embarrassing, a few years later. Endless streams of consciousness. Pages and pages of nonsense designed to fool people into thinking you're some sort of genius because you don't put words in their proper order or spell them correctly. It's just not for me. I don't mind admitting that I like traditional novel-writing. You know, with a plot. And characters. And good writing.'

'But biography is where you hope to make your career?'

'It is,' he replied, grinning. He had a nice smile. Perfectly even white teeth. I imagined there were many girls, and boys, who would like to kiss him.

'What age are you, anyway?' I asked.

'Twenty,' he said, and then, without asking whether I wanted another, he stood up, went to the bar, purchased two more pints and brought them back to the table. I finished my first quickly and started on the second. It tasted wonderful. My body was waking up as the alcohol entered my bloodstream, a glorious sense of well-being that always kicks in around then.

'When I was about your age,' I told him, leaning forward, nearer to him, and no matter how close I got I noticed that he didn't pull back, 'there were only two things that I wanted out of life. First, to be a published novelist and, second, to be a father. And, of course, I had to leave home if it was ever going to happen. My parents had no interest in books at all. There was no encouragement there, nothing to excite my imagination.'

'And where did you go?' he asked, pulling a notebook from his bag and starting to scribble down some notes. *So, you've begun*, I thought, smiling to myself. *Well, so have I.*

'Germany,' I said. 'Berlin, to be precise. Well, it was still called West Berlin at the time. This was before the wall came down, of course. I got a job as a waiter at the Savoy Hotel on the Fasanen-straße. And when I wasn't working, I was writing.'

'Is that where you wrote *Two Germans*?' he asked.

'Some of it,' I said. 'It's certainly where the novel had its genesis.'

'It's such an interesting book.'

'Thank you.'

'The love story is heartbreaking. Did someone break your heart when you were that age? Is that where the story came from?'

'No one has ever broken my heart,' I said, shaking my head. 'No one ever could. You must remember, this is what a writer does. Uses his or her imagination. Tries to understand how it feels to be alive in a moment that never existed with a person who never lived, saying words that were never spoken aloud.'

'Well, you did it with such empathy,' he said. 'The funny thing is, and maybe this is wrong of me, but it always left me feeling a little sorry for Erich Ackermann.'

'Really?' I asked. 'Why so?'

'Because he was just a boy,' he replied. 'And in love for the first time. Not to mention in love with a guy, which only complicated matters. Particularly back then. And no one knew at that time what the Nazis would become. That's what makes the book so interesting, though. Trying to decide whether he was evil or just young and confused.'

I nodded and tried not to look too bored. I'd spent so much of my life talking about *Two Germans* that I was justifiably tired of it. It didn't even seem like something that had come from my pen any more. After publication, it had taken on its own life so quickly. I remained proud of the book, of course, but it seemed to exist at a certain distance from me these days. I barely recognized myself in it any more, even though it had given me the life I'd always wanted.

'Although there must be a part of you that wonders whether he deserved what you did to him,' he said. It took a few moments for the line to hit me as I had been barely listening while he yapped on and on. Instead I had just been staring at him, taking that familiar but not quite recognizable face in. True, he didn't have the cheekbones that Daniel had, his face was a little too full for that kind of definition, but other than that the resemblance between my son and this boy was uncanny.

'What was that?' I asked, snapping back to the moment, unsure whether I'd heard him right. He couldn't possibly have said something so impertinent, could he?

'I asked whether you'd like another drink? It's just such a pleasure to sit here and talk with you.'

'It's my round,' I said, standing up and telling myself not to invent things. After all, I had never been able to before, so this was hardly the time to start. I made my way to the bar, where I ordered two more pints and focussed my gaze on the girl behind the counter as she poured them. 'You missed a bit,' I told her when she placed the drinks on the counter before me.

'I'm sorry?'

'In the corner there,' I said, pointing to a space behind her where a thick and sharp chunk of glass lay on its side, broken side up. 'From when you let the glass fall earlier.'

'Oh, thanks,' she said, turning to look at it as I paid for the beers and returned to the table. Theo had disappeared while I'd been away and I looked around, catching his shadow through the window to where he stood outside, smoking a cigarette. I watched him for a few moments, then reached forward and ran my finger around the rim of his empty pint several times before lifting that same finger to my lips and sucking on it slowly. I closed my eyes and when I opened them again I had a sense that I was being watched. I was right, for the girl behind the bar was staring at me with an expression of disgust on her face. She turned away when I caught her eye and busied herself with sweeping up the broken glass. I didn't care. I knew what she thought, that I was either trying to seduce the boy or already had, but it didn't matter to me. Not in the slightest. I had a job to do and I would do it.

He came back a few moments later and we clinked glasses once again.

'I'm enjoying our conversation,' I told him.

'I am too,' he said.

'I hope it won't be our last.'

He smiled. He seemed so happy, so innocent. So like my dead son that it was all I could do not to take him in my arms and hold him tight, to beg for his forgiveness.

'I hope so too,' he said.

3. The Coach and Horses, Greek Street

It was just over a week before I saw Theo again. After leaving the Queen's Head that afternoon, we exchanged numbers and I planned on texting him by the weekend at the latest, but, due to an unfortunate accident that took place as I was leaving my Thursday pub, I had to wait a little longer to get in touch.

Brooding over the events of earlier in the week, I felt as if Daniel's ghost were standing behind me at every minute of the day, whispering in my ear in that accusatory way of his. He was on my mind more than he had been in recent times and I was uncertain whether this had something to do with Theo's appearance in my life or my plans for rebuilding my career. And so, as I stepped out on to the street a few days later, perhaps I wasn't paying as close attention to my surroundings as I should have been and I stumbled, losing my footing, and fell heavily to the ground, where my face crashed into the pavement with such force that I was momentarily stunned. When I managed to gather myself together, I sat upright and could feel something wet running down my face. When I put my hand to my forehead, it came away bloody and, when I spat, a tooth fell from my mouth. I looked up at the people who were walking quickly past me, rushing to the Tube at the end of a day's work, and each one was doing their best to ignore me. It was only when a policewoman approached me that my real humiliation began.

'Now, what's happened here, sir?' she asked, crouching down to my level as if I were a lost child. She looked almost like a child herself; she couldn't have been more than twenty-three years old and wore a gentle expression on her face that probably belied her seriousness.

'I fell,' I told her, my words slurring a little from a mixture of inebriation and shock. It embarrassed me to sound so pathetic.

'I can see that,' she said. 'Had a little too much to drink today, have we?'

I narrowed my eyes at her. If there is one thing I've always despised, it's when people – figures of authority, generally – speak in the first-person plural, as if whatever mishap has occurred has somehow been a shared concern.

'*We* haven't been doing anything together,' I said. '*We* have only just met. And no, *I* haven't been drinking, if that's what you're asking.'

'I think we have, sir,' she replied, smiling at me. 'We smell like a brewery, don't we? We smell as if we've been dunked into a keg of beer, head first!'

'Oh, fuck off,' I muttered, but I suppose she was accustomed to such abuse for she didn't so much as flutter an eyelid. Instead she stood up, then took my arm in hers as she attempted to pull me to my feet.

'That's a nasty cut we've got there, isn't it?' she said, reaching for the walkie-talkie by her hip and muttering some strange, indecipherable commands into it, a series of numbers followed by our location. 'We'll need to get that looked at, won't we?'

I could see the pedestrians watching us now, each one silently judging me. They thought I was nothing more than a tragic old alcoholic, drunk in the middle of the day. A hopeless middle-aged man who needed the assistance of a policewoman young enough to be his daughter to get himself home.

'I was shortlisted for The Prize once, you know!' I shouted at the top of my voice. 'Which is more than any of you fuckers have ever done.'

'Of course you were, sir,' said the policewoman, obviously having no clue what I was talking about. 'I won a prize too when I was a girl. Came first in the hundred-metres dash at school. But we don't need to broadcast it to all and sundry, now, do we? Let's keep our manners about us and not cause any fuss.'

Before I could speak again, I heard the siren of an approaching ambulance and looked down the street to where the traffic was parting to let it through, at which point I glanced back at my benefactress in annoyance.

'That better not be for me,' I said.

'It is, sir,' she said. 'We can't let ourselves walk around London with blood pouring down our faces, can we? It might scare the horses! We gave ourselves a nasty bang.'

'Oh, you stupid bitch,' I replied quietly, with a sigh.

'Now now, sir,' she said, squeezing my arm a little now. 'There's no need for any unpleasantness, is there? We're just doing our jobs.'

'Can you stop talking like that, please?' I said. 'You're making my brain hurt.'

'We'll tell the ambulance men that, shall we?' she replied. 'Best to be honest with them about everything. We've cut our forehead and our brain is hurting. What's our name, sir? Can we remember?'

'Of course I can fucking remember,' I said. 'I'm not a complete imbecile. It's Maurice Swift.'

'And do we have a home to go to tonight?'

I stared at her in bewilderment. She surely didn't think that I was homeless? I looked down at my clothes and, true, I might have looked a little ragged that day, and the blood pouring down my face probably didn't help, but still. This was a degradation that was almost intolerable.

'Of course I have a home,' I said. 'I live near Hyde Park. I'm not some sort of vagrant, you know.'

'Oh, very nice, I'm sure. Can I call someone for you there? Is your wife at home?'

'My wife is dead.'

'A son or daughter perhaps?'

'Only a son. But he's dead too.'

'Oh dear,' she said, looking a little uncomfortable at last. Still, I thought about it. If I did need someone, if I needed help at some point in the future, who would I call? My parents were long dead and I hadn't spoken to my siblings in decades. My son was gone. I had no friends. My publisher and I were no longer on speaking terms. For a moment, I thought of handing her my phone, where one of the only numbers listed was Theo's, but I had enough sense not to do that.

'I'm fine,' I said. 'I don't need anyone. I just want to go home.'

'Well then, we shouldn't be drinking in the middle of the day, sir, should we?' she said as the ambulance pulled up alongside us. 'It's not a good idea at all.'

'It's an excellent idea, actually,' I told her. 'You should try it some-time. Believe me, it will cure almost every ailment you have.'

'But it leaves us with a bloody face and a missing tooth,' she said, releasing my arm at last as a burly man of about sixty emerged from the ambulance, before giving him a quick rundown of my condition.

'We've been drinking,' was her first comment. She lowered her voice as if she didn't want anyone to hear and, before I knew it, I had been thrown into the back of the ambulance and was being whisked off to St Peter's, where my forehead was stitched and my mouth was cleaned. I think I fell asleep on a trolley and when I woke I felt utterly disoriented and my head ached. No one seemed to be taking any responsibility for my well-being so I dragged myself to my feet and made for the exit, hailed a taxi and went home.

My point being that I didn't want Theo to see me like that so put off contacting him, waiting instead until early the following week, when the wound was less discoloured, to get in touch again.

*

Across the eight days until we met again, I felt an unexpected longing for Theo's company, one that I hadn't anticipated when I began this project. Finally, after hours of deliberating over the wording, I texted some nonsense about having meetings in town on Wednesday morning, that I would probably be in the Coach and Horses around three o'clock and, if he was interested in joining me, I'd be happy to buy him a drink and answer more of his questions then. To my delight, the message had barely left my phone when he replied with a quick 'See you there!' and a smiley face, followed by an image of two beer glasses clinking against each other. It was all that I could do not to sit down and weep in gratitude.

I had said three o'clock because I wanted an hour to myself first to settle my nerves. I sat at the small table in the corner, watching as Londoners walked by the window and, as I had done so often in my professional life, tried to invent stories for them, wondering if they had some quality that could help to populate a novel for me, but failing every time. Finally, a sense of relief. The door opened. He was here. My boy.

'You made it,' I said, standing up and awkwardly embracing him. He extended his hand just as I opened my arms and when he put it down, the whole thing became too complicated and embarrassing to pursue. I ordered two pints and brought them over as he took his coat off. I could already tell that he was distracted. He looked tired and had that strange habit Daniel had suffered from when he was anxious of tapping the tip of his index finger against his thumb rapidly, like a woodpecker attacking an oak tree. It was an unusual gesture, one that my son had never seemed conscious of, and here was this boy doing the same thing.

'Of course,' he replied, smiling now, his expression lightening a little as we began to drink. 'I wouldn't have missed it.' He leaned forward, peering at my forehead. 'What happened to your head?'

'A slight accident,' I told him, waving his concerns away. 'I woke in the night to use the bathroom and walked straight into my bedroom door.'

'Ouch.'

'Indeed. It needed seven stitches. But I was a brave little soldier. And how was your week?'

'Good,' he said. 'And you? Did you get much work done? On your book, I mean.'

'Which book?'

'The book you're writing.'

'Oh,' I said. Of course, he assumed that I was working on a new novel. Why wouldn't I be, after all? I always had been, since I was not very much older than him, and it had been some years now since my last publication. It would seem strange if there weren't something in progress.

'How's it coming along, anyway?' he asked. 'Are you close to the end?'

I smiled and tried to think how best to answer this. Before Daniel died, I had been engaged on a new book, but I had all but abandoned it since then. My working title was *Other People's Stories*, but I hadn't been able to look at it since my son's death. It was still there, of course, sitting on my computer desktop like an unexploded bomb, but I couldn't bring myself to open it. The truth was, I was nervous of returning to a manuscript that had effectively cost my son his life.

'I hope so,' I told him finally. 'It's hard to know. These things can go either way.'

'Can you tell me anything about it?'

'I'd rather not,' I said, shaking my head.

'Fair enough. I suppose it's difficult to talk about a work in progress. You never know who might steal your ideas.'

'It's not that,' I said, anxious for him to believe that I trusted him. 'It's just—'

'I'm kidding,' he said, looking a little abashed. 'It's not as if anyone could just take someone else's story and write it themselves, is it? These things need to form in a writer's mind over time. After all, a novel is about a lot more than just plot, right?'

'Right,' I said, wondering how many of my peers would argue with that notion. 'So, what you're saying is that if someone *did* do that, they'd have to be . . . what? Actually, what *are* you saying?'

'Well, they'd have to be really talented,' he said. 'But also a complete psychopath.'

I laughed. 'Well, yes. But, of course, those two things aren't mutually exclusive.'

'Can you at least tell me when you think it might be published?'

'I don't know,' I said, wishing he would change the subject, for I didn't want to talk about any of this. 'Late next year, perhaps. Or early the following one.'

'Well, I'll look forward to reading it whenever it's ready,' he said, before making his way up to the bar and ordering some more drinks. When he came back, he reached into his bag and removed a Ventolin, put it to his mouth and took a quick breath. I stared at him in horror. My head began to grow slightly dizzy, as if the earth had shifted a heartbeat quicker on its usual rotation but I had been left a few paces behind.

'You have asthma,' I said quietly, more a statement than a question, but he looked across at me and nodded.

'Yes,' he replied. 'It's not too bad, though. The inhaler gets me through.'

'My son had asthma,' I said. 'He suffered from it quite badly.'

He nodded and inhaled again, before returning the familiar blue device to his satchel. 'Some people get it worse than others. Mine has always been manageable.'

'It's how he died.'

Theo sat back in the chair and stared at me. 'Christ,' he said. 'I'm so sorry. I didn't realize.'

'There's no reason why you should have.'

'Do you mind if I ask what happened?'

I looked away. There was no harm in telling him the truth. Up to a point, at least.

'It was hay-fever season,' I told him. 'And, of course, his asthma was always much worse at that time of year. He was in our apartment, doing some homework on my computer.' And now time to massage the details. 'I wasn't there. I'd gone out to pick up some take-away. It seems that he had a particularly bad bronchospasm attack and couldn't reach his inhaler in time. He collapsed on the floor. By the time I got back, he was gone.'

'That's awful,' said Theo. 'How old was he?'

'Thirteen.'

I looked down at the table, scratching my nails into the woodwork. I could sense him again, a small hand gripping my shoulder, an arm wrapped around my throat. He pressed against my windpipe and I tried to push back but he was too strong for me and when I looked up, he was sitting opposite me in Theo's place, watching me, an expression on his face that broke through my chest and clutched at my heart, squeezing it, cutting off the blood from pumping around my body.

'It was your own fault,' I whispered.

'What?'

I blinked a few times, felt an immediate release from my delusion and shook my head. Daniel was gone; Theo had returned.

'Nothing,' I replied. I noticed the cigarette packet on the table and frowned. 'You know, if you have asthma, you really shouldn't be smoking.'

'I'm trying to give up.'

'Well, try harder,' I said forcefully.

'And did Daniel—'

'That's enough about him,' I snapped, more heatedly than I had intended. 'Let's talk about something else.'

'All right, sorry,' he said. A long pause ensued. The tension that descended on us was almost unbearable but, finally, he spoke again.

'Actually, before I forget,' he said. 'I was talking to a friend of mine the other day – she runs the literary society at UCL – and I told her that you were giving me some help on my thesis. She wondered whether you might come in some day to talk to the writing students?'

I sat back in my chair, lifted my pint and took a long draught from it. It had been a long time since I'd spoken to any students about writing or, for that matter, spoken to *anyone* about writing. I wasn't sure if it was something I would feel comfortable doing any more.

'No pressure, of course,' he said quickly, when I didn't answer immediately. 'I'm sure you're busy with your work and—'

'I don't think so,' I said. 'I prefer only to do such things when there's a new book out.'

'Of course, I understand.'

'Maybe when the next novel is published.'

'Whenever works. It's entirely up to you.'

I nodded and drank some more. A roomful of students intimidated me more now than it would have in the past. And, of course, they would probably want me to speak in the middle of the day, which would be a problem, as it was important that I was in one of my pubs every day by eight minutes past two.

'I'll let you know,' I said.

'Thanks,' he replied, and he looked down at his pint, staring at it for a few moments before lifting it to his lips.

'How's the thesis coming along, anyway?' I asked eventually. 'I hope our meetings are proving helpful to you.'

'They are,' he said. 'But it's important to me that I create a work of scholarship and not just a lazy trawl through your catalogue.'

'Of course.'

'Which means that I might have to be critical as well as

complimentary. I hope you can understand that. I just don't want you to read it one day and feel that I've been duplicitous.'

'I wouldn't expect anything less,' I said. 'I daresay not every word I've written over the years has been perfect, after all.'

'I've been doing some work on *Two Germans*, you see,' he continued. 'Reading back over old reviews and some of the subsequent commentary. I suppose you're aware of the criticisms of the book.'

'Vaguely,' I said. 'Which, in particular?'

'Well, there are those who feel that you took advantage of Erich Ackermann. Seduced his story from him as a way to build your own career.'

I nodded. I'd heard that one before, of course, many times, and had a stock answer. 'Erich's actions were his own to account for,' I said. 'For whatever reason, he chose me as his confidant and never once suggested that our conversations were supposed to remain private. I was free to use them in any way I chose. You must remember that when Erich and I originally met I knew nothing about what had happened during the war. I had never even heard the name of Oskar Gött. I simply made the man's acquaintance and one thing, as they say, led to another. It wasn't a set-up. I can hardly be blamed if he revealed things to me that, later on, he came to regret saying.'

His trusty notebook was out again and he was scribbling away.

'So you felt no guilt about what happened to him?' he asked.

'Not particularly, no,' I said, frowning. 'Why, do you think I should have?'

'There are those who say that you deliberately targeted Ackermann. And that if it hadn't been that story, then it would have been another. That he was doomed from the moment he met you. Is that unfair?'

'Totally unfair,' I said, feeling a little unsettled by the accusatory tone he was taking. 'He was a grown man, after all. He could have walked away from me at any time but he chose not to. The fact was, Erich Ackermann was in love with me.'

He stopped writing for a moment and looked up.

'He told you this?' he asked.

'Not in so many words, no,' I admitted. 'But it was obvious. He wasn't very good at hiding it. The poor man had tied himself up in emotional knots over so many decades, cutting off any potential romantic attachments, that when the dam broke, so to speak, he was absolutely incapable of dealing with the subsequent psychological trauma. But I never led him on, if that's what you're suggesting.'

'All right,' he said.

'You don't sound convinced.'

He smiled and shook his head. 'Sorry, Maurice,' he said. 'I'm just trying to get to the heart of the story, that's all.'

He took off his jacket now, revealing a T-shirt featuring a band that my son Daniel had loved. I stared at the familiar faces that had once adorned a poster in my son's room.

'You like them?' I asked, pointing down at the image.

He glanced down and nodded. 'Yes,' he said. 'Why, do you?'

'Not really,' I said. 'I'm a little too old for bands like that. But my son did.'

He said nothing for a few moments. 'How intimate can I be with my questions?' he asked at last.

'You can ask me anything you like. I don't mind.'

'All right. Do you have a girlfriend?'

'No,' I said, surprised that he should be interested in my personal instead of my professional life.

'Are you gay?'

'No. Why, have I done something to give you the impression that I am?'

'It doesn't matter to me one way or the other, you understand,' he said. 'I'm just trying to understand you better as a person so I can more clearly contextualize your work.'

'Well, I suppose if I'm anything, I'm straight,' I said. 'Although I don't feel an enormous pull in any direction these days. I never really did, if I'm honest. I was never a terribly sexual person, not even when I was your age. Perhaps I'm missing a certain hormone, I don't know, but it was just something that was never very important to me. Are you driven by sex, Theo?'

He blushed a little and I felt pleased to be able to discombobulate him, for he had been too in control of today's meeting for my liking.

'Well, I mean I like it,' he said. 'When I can get it, that is.'

'And do *you* have a girlfriend?'

'No.'

'A boyfriend?'

'No.'

'All right.' I smiled at him, wondering whether he was going to give me anything else, but it seemed that he was determined to stick to his role as interlocutor.

'Anyway,' I said finally, 'I'm pretty certain that that part of my life is behind me. Can I just say,' I added after a moment, not wanting to scare him away, 'just so there's no confusion, I haven't invited you here in order to seduce you, if that's what you're thinking.'

'What?' he said, looking at me now with an expression of such surprise on his face that I realized he hadn't been thinking anything of the sort.

'Sorry,' I said. 'Perhaps I'm misreading things. I was worried that you thought I was agreeing to these meetings for some unsavoury reason. That I've only taken an interest in you because I want to form a romantic attachment. I just want to reassure you that nothing could be further from the truth.'

'I honestly hadn't even considered it,' he said. 'Not for a moment.'

'Right,' I said. 'How embarrassing. For me, I mean.'

'I mean, if you *are* interested in me in that way—'

'I'm genuinely not. It's the furthest thing from my mind, I promise you. I was simply concerned that's what you thought and wanted to set your mind at rest. I can see that all I've achieved is the opposite. Let's talk about something else. I think I've made rather a fool of myself.'

'It's okay.'

He looked as if he wanted the ground to open up beneath him and I cursed my own stupidity. Was I going to lose him now? I couldn't risk anything like that. He needed to finish his thesis and it needed to become a book. For that to happen, I needed to focus. I decided it was time to give him something. A small morsel to stimulate his appetite.

'Actually,' I said at last, 'if you don't mind, I'd like to confide something in you.'

'Really?' he asked, looking up hopefully.

'Yes. Something for your thesis. Something I've never really talked about before.'

He turned another page in his notebook, his pen hovering over the paper. His eagerness was endearing.

'I want to be honest with you, you see,' I continued. 'And I agree with you that it's important that your thesis is a work of true integrity. Especially if it's to become the basis of a full book. You're still planning on that, I hope?'

'Well, yes. But that's a long way—'

'Good. I want to tell you something about Dash Hardy.'

'The American writer?'

'Yes.'

'I think I read somewhere that he was a mentor to you, is that right? When you were starting out, I mean.'

'I'm not quite sure that I'd describe him in those terms,' I replied, 'although *he* probably would have. But, to be fair, yes, he was very generous towards me. Have you read any of his books, Theo?'

'No, I've never got around to them,' he replied, shaking his head. 'Are they worth reading?'

'Not really,' I said. 'I mean, one or two maybe. But there are so many books out there in the world that I wouldn't bother if I were you. You won't find anything particularly interesting in them. Not today. They're very much of their time. I met Dash many years ago, not long after I met Erich Ackermann, as it happens. Our paths crossed in the Prado in Madrid and, like Erich, he was entranced by me. They were both homosexuals, of course, but very different types. Where Erich was content just to stare at me across the dining tables of Europe, fantasizing about a relationship that would never come to fruition, Dash came straight out and told me what he wanted on the day that we met. He wasn't looking for romance, he said, he didn't want a lifelong companion or someone to show up on his arm at parties. He just wanted to fuck me. Really, I admired his forthrightness. And so I let him. The very night that we met, in fact, but never again after that. I drifted towards him after I parted from Erich because he had a higher profile in the States but, in retrospect, I think I may have treated him unkindly. You see, when we met, he just desired me, so the sex was probably not that interesting, but after that he fell in love, desperately in love, and the moment he did I made sure to deny him everything he wanted. I would barely let him put his arms around me and certainly never let him in my bed again. The poor man went around in a state of such abject misery that one day, having grown tired of him following me around like a bewildered puppy, I announced that I'd grown bored of him and didn't want to see him ever again. It was just after we'd spent an evening at Gore Vidal's house on the Amalfi Coast, in fact. I broke the bad news to him while we were driving back down the mountain. Actually, I waited until we got close to the bottom in case he drove us over a cliff. Gore wasn't my biggest fan, I should say. He felt that I was just using Dash to get a good American publisher and that, once I had what I wanted, I would walk away.'

'And was he right?'

I shrugged. 'He wasn't entirely wrong. But that was Gore. You couldn't make a fool of him. Only a fool, in fact, would have tried.'

'And you did all this consciously?'

'Yes. What can I say? I was ambitious. I still am.'

He hesitated for a moment. 'That's quite an admission,' he said.

'It is,' I said, feigning surprise. 'Oh, I'm not sure it amounts to very much. Although, are you aware that Dash committed suicide?'

'No.'

'Well, he did. Years later, mind you, but not long after he'd run into me again at the Hay Festival. The poor man looked as depressed as ever, and I suppose seeing me again after all that time re-lit the flames that he'd tried so hard to extinguish and he decided to end it all. He contacted me after our brief encounter, you see, and begged me to come back to him. He said that he'd never stopped loving me and that he would do anything if I would simply return. I just laughed, told him I wasn't even slightly interested. I was seeing Edith at the time, anyway, the woman who would become my wife. I told him I could scarcely imagine anything more tedious than returning to a life with him in New York and he shouldn't bother me again. Later that evening, he hanged himself in the apartment we'd once shared in Manhattan. I suppose, in some ways, I have his death on my conscience.'

'I see,' said Theo, thinking about this. I could see his eyes moving back and forth as he wondered how best to use this in his thesis. He waited a long time before speaking again and I determined not to break the silence. 'Well, you can't blame yourself for what he chose to do,' he said eventually, a certain hesitation in his tone. 'I'm sure you didn't intentionally hurt him.'

'Are you?' I asked, smiling.

'Well, you didn't, did you?'

I was still smiling. It was decent of him to think that. Time to pull back a little. I didn't want to make myself out to be too much of a monster. 'Of course not,' I said. 'I was young, that's all. And we all take a little help where we can get it when we're that age. But still, if I could go back in time, perhaps I would have acted a little more kindly towards him.'

'Towards all of us,' said Daniel, who had returned to the table now and was once again sitting in Theo's place. He stared at me before attempting to take a deep breath and failing badly, the sound of congested lungs pouring from his mouth like a cry from a banshee.

'Are you all right?' asked Theo. It took only a blink of my eyes for reality to return.

'I'm fine,' I said, stepping away from the table carefully. 'I just need the bathroom, that's all. I'll be back in a moment.'

When I returned, he was still scribbling in his notepad and I ordered some more drinks, placing them on the table, but didn't speak until he'd finished writing.

'You don't have to if you don't want to,' he said at last, looking up at me, 'but if you'd like to talk about your son, then I'd be happy to listen. I don't know if you have anyone in particular who you can discuss him with.'

'Thank you,' I said, surprised that he was even interested in a dead child. I had expected that he'd want some information about Dash and whether I treated anyone else with such heartlessness. 'And perhaps I will at some point. I so rarely do, you see. But not today, I think. I'd need to compose my thoughts. Tomorrow, maybe? I don't know what you're doing around two o'clock?'

4. The Lamb and Flag, Rose Street

'You know, Charles Dickens used to drink here,' I said the following afternoon as we sat in the window of the Lamb and Flag pub on Rose Street, the rain pouring down outside on another wet London day. 'And out there,' I added, pointing to the alleyway beyond, 'is where the Poet Laureate John Dryden was almost beaten to death by thugs in the service of the Earl of Rochester.'

'What had he done to deserve that?' asked Theo, looking out on to the street as if some of the blood might still be visible on the cobblestones. He had arrived wearing a shirt and tie rather than his usual T-shirt and hoodie and looked very smart; when I asked him why such formality, he told me that he'd had a meeting that morning with his thesis adviser and liked to dress more professionally whenever they met, which I thought a rather quaint tradition. I couldn't remember my son ever wearing a tie in his life, though, so I asked Theo to take it off, which he did without complaint, unbuttoning the top of his shirt as he did so, which set me more at ease. Daniel had always preferred open-necked shirts.

'It's hard to know,' I told him with a shrug. 'They'd been friends once, of course. Dryden dedicated one of his plays to Rochester, who had something of a hand in the writing of it, and maybe the Earl felt he didn't get enough credit for his work. *Marriage à la Mode*, if memory serves. But then you know writers. They can be merciless in how they use each other to get to the top. I'm surprised more of them don't kill each other, to be honest.'

'You say "them",' said Theo with a half-smile. 'Not "us"?'

'All right, us,' I replied, correcting myself. 'I'm surprised more of *us* don't kill each other. For such an artistic field, there's an awful lot of people who desperately want to beat someone else and be seen as the very best. Succeeding on one's own terms just isn't enough.'

'Whenever a friend succeeds,' said Theo, 'a little something in me dies. That was Truman Capote, wasn't it?'

'No, that was Gore,' I said, recalling the plaintive eyes that had looked up at me from beneath the sheets in the early hours of the morning at the Swallow's Nest, La Rondinaia, when I had stood before him and removed my robe, preparing to make my greatest conquest yet. But he had simply shaken his head, perhaps in regret that he was longer capable of playing the game, and rolled over on his side, falling back asleep. It had been disappointing, of course, and not a little humiliating, but I'd rather admired him for his resolve.

'And you've heard the old proverb about ambition, haven't you?'

He shook his head.

'That it's like setting a ladder to the sky. A pointless waste of energy. Anyway, where did we leave things yesterday? I was planning on telling you something about Daniel, wasn't I?'

Something had shifted in my relationship with Theo since the previous afternoon. Although I had been using him all along and was prepared to continue with my plan until I had achieved my goal, I had begun to feel that it might be helpful to me to unburden myself of some of my regrets along the way. Perhaps it would dismiss Daniel's ghost from shadowing me. Somehow, I felt a kindred spirit in this young naïf and I felt that he might actually understand why I had done some of the things I'd done. And that he might forgive me. But in order to do that, I needed to be honest with him. Obviously, there was only so far I could go without giving myself away entirely, but I wondered whether I could minimize some of my crimes and still command his respect.

'Only if you want to,' he said, notebook on the table, pen at the ready. 'I don't want to pry.'

'I don't mind,' I replied. 'I never have much opportunity to talk about him, despite the fact that he's on my mind almost constantly. But before I do, I suppose I should go back a little further. To my wife.'

He flicked through his notes. 'Edith Camberley,' he said, nodding. 'Actually, I read her novel a few weeks ago. *Fury*. It was very good.'

'It was,' I agreed.

'She died quite young, didn't she?'

'Sadly, yes. We were living in Norwich at the time. She fell down a staircase. I'd been intending to repair the handrail since we'd moved in but, somehow, I'd never quite got around to it. Too busy working on my novel. She ended up in a coma for several months and eventually the decision was made to turn off the life support.'

'You made that decision?'

'I did, yes.'

'That must have been very difficult.'

'Of course,' I said. 'She was my wife.'

'And you loved her.'

'I wouldn't have married her if I hadn't loved her.'

'She was black, wasn't she?' asked Theo, and I frowned, surprised by the question.

'Is that relevant in some way?' I asked. 'To your thesis, I mean?'

'Only that it must have been difficult back then. To be in a mixed-race relationship.'

'Not especially, no,' I said, shrugging my shoulders. 'It wasn't the 1950s, you know, it was the 1990s. That might seem a long time ago to someone your age but, really, it's just the blink of an eye. And the circles we moved in would have been the least likely to hold any racist attitudes. Yes, once in a while someone might have given us a sideways glance on the street, and from time to time some uneducated prick might have made an offensive comment as we passed. But it was nothing compared to what previous generations went through.'

'Can I ask, when her novel became such a success, did you feel any sort of . . . What's the word . . . ?'

'Envy?' I suggested, trying to keep the smile off my face. 'A deep and embittered sense of resentment?'

'I suppose.'

'Not in the slightest,' I said. 'Edith was a brilliant writer. She might have been one of the greats, had she lived. I was pleased for her.'

'Still, for a time she must have taken some of the spotlight away from you.'

'I've never been much interested in that,' I lied. 'And, as I said, I loved her. What kind of man would it make me if I had begrudged her her success?'

He said nothing but scribbled a lot of things down in his notepad. Whenever he went to the bar, to the bathroom or outside for a smoke, he always took his notepad with him. Young Mr Field was diligent in that respect.

'Your son must have missed her,' he remarked eventually, looking up again.

I shook my head. 'No, Edith wasn't Daniel's mother. I conceived him with an Italian chambermaid who worked in a London hotel.'

'I'm sorry?'

'It was a business transaction. Nothing more, nothing less. She wanted money and I wanted a child. The arrangement was mutually beneficial.'

'Isn't that . . . ?' He hesitated for a moment and gave a half-laugh. 'Isn't that illegal?'

'Probably,' I said. 'Why, are you going to report me to the police? I assure you, there are worse things that you could tell them.'

'No, I just—'

'The law is ridiculous on this point. Why shouldn't a girl be allowed to sell nine months of her life if she wants to? And why shouldn't I be able to buy them? We were both entirely happy with the choices we made and, ultimately, it was no one else's business. I can't even remember her name, to be honest, if I ever knew it. I expect she's gone on to live a happy life and never thinks about her first baby.'

'She probably does,' he said, and I was surprised that he would contradict me, but perhaps he was right. Wherever she was, there was a good chance that she thought of him a hundred times a day. I know I did.

'Anyway, it was just Daniel and me all those years,' I continued. 'We were a pair, you see. Rarely apart. He didn't even have his own bedroom until he was three years old because he didn't want to be separated from me. He never asked about a mother; the absence of a female presence in his life didn't seem to be an issue for him. We were in New York then, of course. Daniel lived there all his life. You're aware of *Storī*?'

'Of course.'

'Well, I set that up when we first moved to Manhattan and then I edited it for several years. Before my son started school, he used to come into the office with me every day and sit in the corner at his own desk, colouring, reading or playing with his toys. I think people thought it was rather sweet, a father and a little boy so attached to each other, but it rather annoyed me when they did. I wasn't doing it for appearances' sake. We just enjoyed each other's company.'

'What was he like?' asked Theo. 'Personality-wise, I mean.'

'He was quiet,' I said, and I felt a deep pain at the pit of my stomach, remembering his good qualities, of which he had many. 'Bookish, like me. Shy. Very loving. Very warm. A good cook for such a young boy. It's something that he might have pursued as a career, had he been given a chance. He was interested in photography too and had started talking about taking dance classes, which I encouraged, as I thought he was rather too introverted.'

'Did he have many friends?'

I shook my head again. 'Not many. At least, not many that I knew of.'

'How old was he when he died?'

'Thirteen.'

'Too young to have a girlfriend, I suppose.'

I smiled regretfully. Daniel had never introduced me to a girl, nor had he ever spoken about girls he liked, but I knew that he was beginning to get interested because he'd grown very self-conscious around an attractive young woman who was interning at *Storī*, and once, when she engaged him in a conversation about a movie she'd just seen, he'd turned bright red, startlingly so, and I'd felt embarrassed for him, being unable to control his emotions like that. I thought it rather sad that the boy had surely died with his innocence intact.

'Yes,' I said. 'He kept that part of his life very quiet from me. I mean, he was thirteen years old, and boys that age don't like to discuss such things with their fathers, do they?'

'I certainly didn't. Do you have a picture of him? Of Daniel?'

'Not with me,' I said.

'So Edith and he weren't related,' he said quietly, more to himself than to me. He glanced out of the window for a moment, tapped his finger against his chin, then turned back, scribbled something down and turned his page.

'There was something else I wanted to ask you about your wife,' he said.

'Feel free.'

'I hope you won't take it the wrong way. It might seem rather . . . audacious on my part.'

'I'm intrigued now.'

He nodded but took a long time to speak. I decided to do nothing to hurry him along. I was rather enjoying his discomfort.

'As I mentioned,' he said eventually, 'I read *Fury* recently.'

'And I'm glad you did. It's actually rather hard to find a copy these days. It's been out of print for years.'

'I tracked it down in the British Library. It wasn't very difficult.'

I took a sip from my pint but avoided his eye.

'There were a few stylistic points in it that intrigued me.'

'Oh yes?' I said.

'She was very fond of the ellipsis, wasn't she? Too fond, I would suggest. And she had a habit of introducing new characters by describing their eyes. I was surprised that an editor didn't ask her to watch out for that. She does it with almost every character.'

'That's true,' I agreed. 'It was a habit she fell back on time and again. We all have these little quirks, I suppose.'

'Also, there was her fondness for giving characters alliterative names. Charles Chorley, for example. Elsie Engels. It's very noticeable. It actually becomes a little annoying at one point.'

'Did you think so?' I asked, for I'd always rather enjoyed this conceit of Edith's. 'Well? What of it? Dickens did it all the time too. John Jarndyce in *Bleak House*. Tommy Traddles in *David Copperfield*. Nicholas Nickleby.'

He rummaged through his notes again, this time pulling a separate folder from his bag and running his finger down the page. 'It's just that I noticed you do the same thing in *The Tribesman*,' he said.

'Six out of the eleven main characters are introduced with descriptions of their eyes, while the protagonist's name is—'

'William Walters, yes, I remember.'

'And the woman he loves is—'

'Sara Salt.'

Theo gave a half-shrug and looked me in the eye. 'Can I ask you a direct question?'

'You can.'

'Did Edith have anything to do with *The Tribesman*?' he asked.

I smiled at him, rather impressed. Maybe the boy wasn't quite as much a fool as I'd thought. 'Now why would you ask that,' I queried, 'instead of asking whether I had anything to do with *Fury*? Wouldn't that be the more obvious conclusion, considering my previous successes?'

'Because none of these traits is visible in either *Two Germans* or *The Treehouse*. Not a single time. But you do it compulsively in *The Tribesman*. Which, of course, was published the year after your wife died.'

I glanced around to ensure that we couldn't be overheard, but there was no one seated at any of the tables nearby. I could deny it, of course. Indeed, my first instinct was to deny it. But as I looked at him, the resemblance between my biographer and my son seemed so striking that I believed I might be able to make him understand what Daniel never had.

'You're very perceptive,' I said. 'Are we off the record now?'

'I'm not a journalist.'

'No, but are we off the record?'

He stared at me, then put the top back on his pen and placed it on his closed notebook. 'Go ahead,' he said.

'The thing is,' I said, feeling a delicious rush of excitement at what I was about to say, 'I didn't actually write *The Tribesman*. Edith did.'

He stared at me for a long time, then burst out laughing. 'Now you're just making fun of me,' he said.

'No, I'm being entirely serious,' I replied with a shrug, my expression completely neutral. 'Oh, she didn't write *every* word in the book, don't get me wrong. A lot of it is mine. In fact, I had to rewrite some sections substantially. The traits you've already listed were just some of her flaws as a writer and I was, shall we say, a more experienced hand.'

'I don't . . .' He shook his head, looking at me as if I had started speaking in a foreign language. 'I'm sorry, Maurice, I don't quite understand what you're telling me here.'

'It's quite simple. I'm saying that the original manuscript of the novel was written by Edith. Then Edith fell down the stairs and I took what she had written, worked pretty hard on it, I have to say, and turned it into a Maurice Swift novel. As a sort of . . . homage to her.'

'But you've never mentioned this before,' he said.

'Haven't I?'

'No. I've read every interview you gave regarding that book and you never said a word about your wife's contribution.'

'I suppose it didn't seem that important at the time. It's a bit like what happened with Erich, in a way. He told me a story and I adapted it for my own use. Edith had a novel, she died, and I adapted it for my own use too. There's not a great deal of difference between the two scenarios. It was a perfectly legitimate endeavour.'

As I heard myself say these words aloud, they didn't sound as terrible to me as I had expected. In fact, my explanation sounded rather reasonable.

'And you don't think there's something dishonest about that?' asked Theo.

'Not in the slightest,' I said, feigning innocence. 'Why, do you?'

A scene from a novel flashed through my mind. The moment at the end of *Howards End* when Dolly, the silly girl, reveals that the house had been left to Margaret Schlegel in Ruth's will but Henry had thrown the offending note in the fire. *I didn't do wrong, did I?* he asks in all innocence.

311

And Margaret, who has been through so much, shakes her head and says, *You didn't, darling. Nothing has been done wrong.*

Theo, however, was no Margaret Schlegel.

'I do, to be honest.'

'Oh, then I think you're just being a little uptight. Look, Edith was dead. Or she was in a coma, anyway. And a manuscript existed. It was obvious that it was going to be a major success if it was knocked into shape. So, of course, I used what she'd left behind. I owed that to her. If you'd been in my position, wouldn't you have done the same thing? Out of love?'

'No!' he said, leaning forward, and the look of astonishment on his face rather frightened me. Had I underestimated how seriously he would take this? 'It wouldn't even have occurred to me!'

'Hm,' I said, considering this. 'Then perhaps I do have an imagination after all.'

'Maurice, I don't know how—'

'Look, I did what I did and I stand by it, all right? What else should I have done? Publish it posthumously under her name? What good would that have done? There would have been no writer to publicize it. No one to read from it at the festivals. The book probably would have died a death. No, it made far more sense to claim it as my own and accept the garlands that came in its wake. If anything, it was a tribute to Edith that it was so well received.'

'Fuck me,' said Theo quietly, shaking his head and burying himself in his pint for a few minutes. From time to time he scribbled a few notes on the pad which I couldn't make out from where I was sitting, and I didn't enquire as to what they were. I waited until he was ready, sitting quietly, enjoying my drink, until he finally looked up at me, and I smiled at him.

'Another drink?' I asked.

While I was standing at the bar, I felt a curious mixture of relief and anxiety. I had told the truth, or a version of it, anyway, and had done so in such a way that I'd made it clear I didn't believe it was anything to get too worked up over. Theo might have been surprised by what I'd said, but it wasn't as if he could hold me to account for it. Edith's original manuscript had long since been shredded and, if he chose to write about this in his thesis, I could either deny it or stand by every word and say that yes, my late wife had been working on a vague idea, or we had been working on it together, but it was in its very early stages when she died. And I had simply continued with the book.

The barmaid poured the drinks and I happened to glance over to the other side of the pub and a familiar face – two familiar faces, in fact – caught my eye. I turned away quickly, hoping they hadn't spotted me, but perhaps my sudden movement alerted them for they looked in my direction and recognized me immediately. An awkward moment followed before they raised their hands in greeting and I nodded in return, attempting a smile, before carrying the drinks back to our table. I wanted to sit down and see whether things felt different between Theo and me now, but there was simply no way around it. I wouldn't be able to concentrate until I'd gone over.

'Will you excuse me for a moment, Daniel?' I asked him. 'I just spotted a couple of old friends in the corner and I should probably go over and say hello.'

'Of course,' he said. 'And it's Theo.'

'What?'

He shook his head and reached into the pocket of his coat for his phone as I walked across the room, hoping that I looked reasonably healthy and not too much like the tragic old drunk I had turned into.

'Hello, Garrett. Hello, Rufus,' I said, shaking their hands in turn. Garrett Colby, my late wife's former student, and Rufus Shawcross, my erstwhile editor. The man who'd dropped me after the failure of *The Treehouse* and come to regret that when I was shortlisted for The Prize with *The Tribesman* a few years later.

'Hello, Maurice,' said Rufus, standing up and shaking my hand as if we were close friends. 'It's been such a long time! How are you keeping these days?'

'Very well, thank you,' I said.

'You know Garrett Colby, don't you?' he asked, turning to his companion.

'We were friends back in my UEA days,' said Garrett, not standing but offering his hand too. 'Hello, Maurice, it's nice to see you again.'

'Well, we were acquainted,' I said, correcting him. ' "Friends" might be pushing it a little. I almost didn't recognize you. What happened to all that lovely blond hair of yours? It used to be rather a signature piece, didn't it? Drove all the boys crazy, as I recall.'

'I got older,' he said with a shrug. 'And it fell out. Are you growing a beard? I didn't realize they were back in vogue for men on the wrong side of fifty.'

'No, I just haven't shaved in a few days,' I said.

'Actually, we're celebrating,' said Rufus, and I noticed now that they had a bottle of champagne standing between them in a silver ice bucket. That wasn't something you saw in the Lamb and Flag very often. 'You've heard the wonderful news, I presume?'

'No. Has Mr Trump died?'

'Even better. The shortlist for The Prize came out this morning and Garrett is on it.'

'Garrett who?' I asked.

'Garrett,' repeated Rufus, looking a little baffled by my question. 'This Garrett.'

'Oh, right,' I said, turning back to the buffoon next to him, who was grinning like the cat that got the cream. Of course, I knew only too well that he'd made the shortlist. It had made me scream aloud in my flat earlier that day when the news was revealed. I had thrown four dinner plates, two cups and a vase at the wall and they had all smashed into pieces that I would have to clear up later. 'I didn't even know that you were still writing.'

'Apparently, I am.'

'Well, congratulations you.'

'Thanks, but it's not really all that important,' he said with the insouciant air of a man who was beside himself with happiness but didn't want to make it too obvious in case he came across as gauche. 'Prizes are rather ridiculous, don't you think? Writers of my generation make such a fuss about them. It's an unedifying sight. I mean, you ask someone how their book is doing and they reply by telling you that it didn't make this shortlist or that longlist and it just makes one roll one's eyes in despair.'

'So you won't be going on the night then?' I asked. 'You'll be making a stand, on principle?'

'Oh, well, I have to go,' he said, colouring slightly. 'I mean, I owe it to Rufus and to everyone at the publishing house who's put so much work into my book. But whether I win or not is neither here nor there. I'll just get drunk and enjoy the silliness of it all. I daresay it will make for a good scene in a later novel.'

'Of course you're going to win,' said Rufus, reaching across and gripping Garrett by his pathetic little biceps, around which a small child could have comfortably wrapped his thumb and middle finger. 'It's your year. It has to be.'

'Do you really think so?' he asked hopefully.

'I'm sure of it. The reviews for Garrett's book have been extraordinary,' he added, turning to me. 'Have you read them?'

'I was neither aware of the reviews nor of the book,' I lied. 'But I'm delighted to hear it's gone down so well. Edith would be proud of you.'

'We'll be adding your name to the list of all those great writers whose names have been associated with The Prize,' he said, turning back to Garrett. 'Including, of course, our friend Maurice here.'

'Well, that was all a long time ago,' I said.

'Oh, that's right, you were shortlisted once, weren't you?' said Garrett. 'I'd completely forgotten that. When was it? Sometime back in the nineties?'

'Who can recall? My memory isn't what it was. I am, as you say, on the wrong side of fifty.'

'Well, if you will spend your afternoons in a pub, you can expect a little diminishment of your powers.'

'You're in a pub too,' I pointed out. 'And look at you! Enjoying your fifteen minutes of fame.'

'Yes, but I'm celebrating. I've been shortlisted.'

I smiled and felt an unexpected rush of affection for the boy, who'd always been able to give as good as he got. I'd rather missed his cuntish behaviour.

'Who's that you're with over there, anyway?' he continued, looking back towards my table. 'He looks like something you'd pick up at King's Cross Station in the men's toilets on a Thursday night.'

'That's my son, actually,' I said, the words out of my mouth before I could even consider the wisdom of the lie. I glanced at Rufus, whose expression hadn't changed, and I assumed that he knew nothing about what had happened to Daniel. Or perhaps he did and thought that I had two sons.

'Oh right, sorry,' said Garrett, who at least had the good grace to look embarrassed at his faux-pas. 'My mistake.'

'No, it's fine,' I said. 'Anyway, I daresay you're more familiar with that type of fellow than I am. Thursday night, you say? Why Thursday night? Is that a particularly good time to catch some rough trade?'

'I said sorry. It was just a joke.'

'A hilarious one,' I muttered.

'And are you working on anything at the moment, Maurice?' asked Rufus, who was blushing scarlet for some inexplicable reason, and I turned back to him with a shrug.

'Oh, I'm sure you're not that interested,' I said. 'You were never a great fan of my work, after all.'

'Well, I did publish *Two Germans*,' he said, pushing his glasses up his nose and looking a little wounded by that remark. 'So, to be fair, I was the first person to spot your talent.'

'Erich Ackermann was the first person to spot my talent,' I pointed out.

'And look what happened to him,' said Garrett.

'But you're right. You did publish me. Twice, in fact. Before you dropped me.'

'In retrospect, that whole situation was handled rather badly,' Rufus replied, looking down at the floor. 'I was fairly new to the game myself and I listened to the bean counters upstairs when I should have followed my gut. I always knew that you were the real deal.'

'It would have been nice to have heard that at the time,' I said. 'It was quite a blow when you showed me the door. It led to some pretty dark years.'

No one said anything for a few moments. I'd only been at their table a few minutes but had already managed to insult them both and make them each feel like shit, so I was beginning to feel that my work there was done. Suddenly I longed for the days before I'd met Theo, when I was just a solo drinker and rarely spoke to anyone. Life was simpler then.

'Anyway,' I said at last, placing a hand on both their shoulders simultaneously and squeezing them just enough to leave a bruise, 'I've probably taken up enough of your time. It was nice to see you both. And congratulations again, Garrett, on your longlisting.'

'Shortlisting,' he said, but the word was thrown at my back for I'd already walked away and was heading back to our table.

'Sorry about that,' I said as I sat down, and Theo shook his head as if to say, *No problem*, while he put his phone away. 'A couple of old friends. You probably know one of them. Garrett Colby?'

'The writer?'

'Yes.'

'I've heard of him. I've never read him.'

'You're better off. He's an idiot. And his work is infantile. His first book had something to do with talking animals, if I recall correctly.'

'Like *Animal Farm*.'

'Yes, just without the wit, the politics, the style or the genius.'

Theo laughed and took a long drink from his pint. He still seemed distracted by the revelation I had made but I was determined not to talk about that any more. I didn't want to make a bigger issue of it than it needed to be.

'Anyway,' I said. 'Where were we?'

'You were telling me about *The Tribesman* and how you—'

'No, we've covered that. Something else.'

He raised an eyebrow. 'All right,' he said. 'Well, you were going to talk to me about Daniel, but instead we—'

My good humour melted away instantly. 'Yes, that's right,' I said. 'Well, what else would you like to know?'

'Anything you want to tell me. Was he a writer?'

'No. A good reader but not a writer.'

'Did he see much of the world?'

'Some. A little of Europe, with me, when we travelled to festivals. But not enough.'

'And when he died—'

'I don't want to talk about the day itself, if you don't mind,' I said.

'Of course. That's fine.'

'Another time, maybe,' I said, looking away. 'It's not an afternoon that I like to revisit.'

'Time for a smoke then, if you don't mind,' he said, standing up, and I nodded as he made his way out of the door, glancing at Garrett and Rufus as he went. I put the beermats on top of our pints and made my way into the toilet, where I pressed one hand against the wall as I pissed. When I went back outside I ordered more drinks and sat waiting for him. Upon his return, he sat down, brushed the hair out of his eyes, and the smell of nicotine from his jacket made me sit back a little. I've never liked the smell of cigarettes. I had caught Daniel with them once and we'd had a rare argument when I'd pointed out how damaging it could be to him, given his asthma.

'By the way,' he said, finishing his pint and starting on the next one. 'I have some good news.'

'Oh yes?' I asked. 'What's that?'

'I got a commission to write a couple of book reviews for *Time Out*. I sent them a sample of my work and they offered me two novels for next month's issues. If they're happy with what I produce, then there's a good chance I'll get some more.'

'That's excellent news,' I said, pleased for him. 'Congratulations.'

'Thanks, yeah. I'm really happy about it. It doesn't pay much but it gets my name into print.'

'And what have they asked you to review?'

He named a couple of authors and their new books and I nodded. 'They're good writers,' I said. 'I like both their work.'

'So do I,' he said. 'That's what worries me.'

'Why?' I asked.

'Well, it would be much better if I got some bad novels to review. Preferably bad novels by famous writers. Then I could, you know, write some killer reviews. Really take them down.'

'Make a name for yourself, you mean.'

'Exactly.'

'I suppose there's nothing to stop you doing that, anyway,' I said. 'You don't owe them anything.'

'Problem is, if they get good reviews everywhere else and I write a negative one, I might just be seen as someone who didn't fully understand the work.'

'Or as someone with an independent mind.'

'Perhaps. Anyway, I'm going to start reading the first one later tonight. Hopefully it will be terrible.'

'Fingers crossed,' I said.

I looked up as a shadow fell across our table and was alarmed to see Rufus and Garrett standing there, dreading the idea that they might want to join us.

'Just wanted to say goodbye,' said Rufus, setting my mind at rest.

'We're meeting some people for drinks at the Charlotte Street Hotel. To celebrate Garrett's shortlisting. You're welcome to join us if you like.'

'Oh Lord, no,' I said, shaking my head. 'I can scarcely think of anything I'd enjoy less.'

He reared back in surprise, as if I'd just made an unkind remark about his mother. He pushed his glasses up his nose again – really, he ought to get them tightened – and turned to Theo, and, in a heartbeat, the smile vanished from my face when I remembered my earlier lie.

'Rufus Shawcross,' he said, extending a hand. 'I published your father's first two novels.'

Theo stared at the hand for a moment, then shook it. 'I'm sorry?' he asked, frowning.

'You're . . . Danny, is that right?'

Theo looked at me for a moment, but I was lost for words. There was simply nothing I could say that would not make me look ridiculous.

'Daniel,' said Theo, turning back to Rufus. 'No one ever calls me Danny. At least not since I was a little boy.'

'Daniel, then,' he said. 'You have a very talented father. We need him to write another book, it's been far too long. Well, it was nice to meet you, anyway. Goodbye, Maurice.'

'Goodbye,' I said, watching the pair of them as they walked away and dreading the moment I would have to turn back to Theo.

'I'm sorry about that,' I said. 'I don't know what made him say such a thing. He mustn't know . . . he must have just assumed . . .'

'It's fine,' he replied. 'When you didn't say anything, I thought it was easier just to go with it. I wasn't sure what you wanted me to do.'

'I don't think I knew myself,' I said. 'But thank you, anyway. It made an awkward moment almost bearable.'

'He seemed like a bit of a twat, anyway,' said Theo.

'No,' I replied quietly, shaking my head. 'No, he's a very decent man, really. I shouldn't have spoken to him in the way that I did.'

At home that night, I tried to put the events of the afternoon behind me, uncertain why I had passed Theo off as my son. The more I thought about it, however, the more I felt that I hadn't lied, at least not intentionally. When Garrett had made his vulgar assertion, I had simply said what had felt real to me in the moment.

My routine had become completely destroyed since I'd met this boy and, unusually for me, I'd picked up a bottle of whisky on my way home and sat alone in my living room, drinking glass after glass. I wanted that sensation of release, of complete surrender to the alcohol. I wanted to fall into bed and have the empty dreams that I used to enjoy. I wanted to escape my life. But drinking alone at home held little appeal and I only managed a third of the bottle before I put it away and stumbled to my bedroom.

The days ahead would be peaceful, at least. Theo had essays to write, two novels to read and the *Time Out* reviews to draft and, having spent two consecutive afternoons together, I knew that I couldn't ask him to join me on Friday too, even though I longed for his company now. I'd suggested the following Monday but he'd said no, that it was his father's birthday, and before I could suggest Tuesday, he'd said the following Friday, which was just over a week away. I wasn't sure that I could be without him until then, but I could hardly fall on my knees and beg him to reconsider so I had simply smiled, said that sounded good and that I would text him with a place at some point next week, even though I already knew where, because Fridays meant the Dog and Duck on Bateman Street.

I struggled to sleep that night and, shortly after midnight, returned to my whisky, this time managing to finish the bottle. It sat in my stomach, burning me from the inside out, and I stumbled several times as I made my way back to bed. When I finally fell asleep, I dreamed of Edith. She was standing in the bar of the Charlotte Street Hotel, surrounded by dead writers, drinking champagne. William Golding was sitting in a corner with Anthony Trollope, smoking a pipe. John McGahern was trying to catch the barman's attention while Kingsley Amis emerged from the Gents, buttoning up his trousers. They were all offering congratulations. Something wonderful had happened to her and she was proud and excited. I looked around in search of myself among the party, but I was nowhere to be seen.

'Has anyone seen Maurice?' asked Edith, looking directly at me but failing to recognize me. 'He should be here with me. Has anyone seen my husband? I wouldn't be here if it wasn't for him.'

5. The Dog and Duck, Bateman Street

It was the first time that Theo was already waiting for me in the pub when I arrived.

'Your bruise has healed,' he said, nodding at my forehead.

'It has, yes,' I said. Although I'd been drinking steadily every afternoon and evening since our last encounter the previous Thursday, returning to my daily routine with a mixture of relief and dismay that he wasn't there to join me, I had made sure to be extra careful when leaving each pub to make my way home. I couldn't risk another accident. 'And how was your week?'

'Good,' he said. 'I read the first of those books that I agreed to review.'

'And?'

'Unfortunately, it was really good,' he said.

'Oh, well. Can't be helped.'

'I know. But I've started the second one and, so far, it's a bit slow. So things are looking up.'

'Excellent. You might find something to criticize there.'

'Hopefully, yes.'

I smiled at him, but he didn't smile back. I wondered whether he'd spent our time apart thinking about what I'd told him the previous week concerning Edith's novel and how poorly I'd treated Dash.

'Are you all right?' I asked. 'You seem a little quiet.'

'I'm fine,' he said, shaking his head but still failing to smile. I didn't care for the fact that he seemed to be growing less deferential to me and more like an irritated friend. 'How's your work going?'

'What work?' I asked.

'Your novel.'

'Oh, you know,' I said with a shrug. 'Good days and bad days.'

'Which are there more of?'

'The latter,' I said. 'Definitely the latter.'

He nodded and seemed as if he wanted to ask me something else but was nervous of how it might come out.

'What?' I said, not wanting to sit there all afternoon with an awkward silence hanging over us. 'Just spit it out, whatever it is.'

'I don't want to sound rude.'

'I don't much care if you do.'

'It's just . . . well, I've been thinking of how we meet. Of where we meet. Of what we do together.'

'You make it sound like we're having an affair behind our wives' backs.'

'I mean how we always meet in pubs,' he said. 'And how we drink all afternoon.'

'But what else would one do in a pub?'

'It's just that you seem to spend a lot of time in places like this, that's all.'

'Oh, I see.'

'And I wondered when you get your writing done? Surely you don't go home and work in the evening after six or seven pints?'

'If you didn't want to meet in a pub,' I said, ignoring his question,

'then you didn't have to. You could always have suggested somewhere else.'

'It's not that.'

'Then what's the problem?'

'Can I be really honest with you?'

I sighed. 'Oh, for God's sake, stop pissing about, Daniel,' I said.

'Theo.'

'What?'

'It doesn't matter,' he said. 'It's just . . . I was doing some more
online research this week.'

'Why do online research when I'm right here with you? You can
ask me anything you want. I've been incredibly honest with you so
far, wouldn't you agree?'

'I was looking at old photos,' he continued. 'From when you
were younger. I even found one of you and Erich Ackermann
together.'

'Really?' I said, surprised, for at first I couldn't recall us ever having our picture taken.

'Yes, you're sitting outside a bar, having a drink, and your arm is
around his shoulders. You're looking into the camera. He's looking
at you.'

I threw my mind back almost thirty years and had a vague recollection of us sitting in Montmartre while a young waitress took our
photo. Had Erich held on to that for years afterwards, I wondered,
and it had somehow found its way into a newspaper obituary or a
critical work? How utterly tragic, I thought.

'Yes? And? What of it?'

'Well, you must know. You were very handsome.'

'I suppose I was.'

'I don't mean to be rude.'

'If anything, that was a compliment.'

'It's just that you don't look like that any more,' he said.

'Well, of course I don't,' I said, growing irritated by his

obfuscation. 'It's been over twenty-five years since *Two Germans* was published. I'm hardly going to look the same as I did when I was little more than a boy.'

'And I was thinking about a neighbour of mine,' he said.

'A what?' I asked. 'A neighbour, did you say? Well, what about him?'

'He drank himself to death.'

I sighed. I could see where this was going now. 'Did he indeed?' I said quietly.

'It wasn't his fault. He was an alcoholic. But in those last years, his skin looked just like yours. Very grey, I mean. And he had the same dark bags under his eyes that you have and red lines across his cheeks and nose. I was just a kid, but he always frightened me when he came too close.'

'You're really making me feel very good about myself,' I said.

'I'm not trying to upset you.'

'And yet I feel upset.'

'I just wondered whether, you know, you might have a problem. And, if so, whether you should do something about it.'

I sat back in the chair and found myself, quite unexpectedly, laughing. I was aware that I was coming across as a little hysterical so it was no great surprise when he began to look at me nervously and shift uncomfortably in his seat.

'Oh, Theo,' I said, reaching across and patting his hand a few times. 'Bless you. But of *course* I have a problem. Do you think that's news to me? I drink a minimum of seven pints of beer, two double whiskies, a single malt and a glass of Baileys every day, seven days a week. Does that seem like the actions of a rational, uncompli- cated, sober man to you?'

'No, but . . .' He frowned. 'I mean, if you know you have a prob- lem, then why don't you look for help?'

'Because I don't want any.'

'Everybody needs some—'

'Hold on,' I said. 'I'm not trying to be funny, but let me get another drink first. I feel like I'm going to need it. And I'm sure you need a cigarette if you're going to keep impersonating the Archbishop of Canterbury on the first day of Lent.'

I stood up and he looked annoyed that I was interrupting this particular conversation to return to the bar and, a moment later, he marched past me towards the door, his cigarette pack and lighter in hand, his notepad sticking reliably out of his pocket. I watched him go and couldn't help but laugh. There was something adorably guileless about the poor boy, I thought. He'd always been like that, of course, ever since he was a child. He'd believed in the tooth fairy a lot longer than other children.

'I'll take a whisky too,' I told the barman when he took my usual order and when it arrived I knocked it back in one go, leaving the empty glass on the counter as I carried the beers to the table.

'We've talked about Dash, about Edith and about *The Tribesman*,' said Theo, when he returned. 'And I think I've got everything I need on them. Since his name has come up, perhaps we should finally talk about Erich.'

'There's nothing I'd enjoy more,' I said with a wide smile.

'You told me that you felt badly about how you treated Dash Hardy but, of course, he doesn't figure in your work very much. Erich Ackermann does, though. He's where everything begins for you.'

'That's true,' I said. 'But it was all such a long time ago. Quite honestly, I barely think of him at all any more.'

'But you must on occasion. And he's a central part of my thesis, obviously.'

'On occasion,' I agreed. 'What would you like to know?'

'I'd like to *know*,' he said, laying an unexpected stress on the verb, 'what you feel when you look back at those days. And whether you feel that you treated him fairly?'

'Well,' I replied, taking a draught of my pint and considering this, 'I suppose if you want the absolute truth, I can see that I didn't treat him quite as well as I might have. I'll admit that I cultivated his friendship from the start, but I don't think there's any great harm in that. Artists have been doing that since the dawn of time. And, let's face it, you've cultivated mine, after all, haven't you? To get ahead.'

'Well,' he replied, blushing a little, and it seemed as if he was about to say something to justify himself, but I didn't let him.

'Look, on the night that we met I could see how drawn he was to me. It was so obvious it was almost pitiable. Erich had shut down that part of his soul for decades after the death of Oskar Gött and, for whatever reason, I had reawoken him. He was utterly reinvigorated by my presence, as if he'd taken a deep breath after staying underwater for too long. That's why he invited me to visit all those cities with him; it wasn't to help him, it wasn't to be an assistant, it was because he fancied me. And why not? I was a good-looking boy and I brought him back to life. I may have taken advantage of his good nature, but why not? I flirted with him, made sure that I remained sexually ambiguous at all times. Always a possibility but never a certainty. I led him on to the point where he was so overwhelmed with desire that I think there was literally nothing he wouldn't have done for me, had I asked. And then, when I got everything I needed from him, I wrote *Two Germans*.'

'And your friendship ended there?'

'This might seem callous to you, Daniel,' I said. 'Theo, I mean. But once I had what I needed, why would I have stuck around? Are you planning a lifelong relationship with me after you complete your thesis?'

'No, but—'

'I didn't consider him a friend, anyway, and it's impossible to define how he saw me. He was paying me, remember, and you don't pay your friends to travel with you, do you? You pay an assistant. And also, other than a love of books, we had very little in common. Think about it: he was old; I was young. He wanted a lover; I didn't. His career was almost behind him; mine was yet to begin. You could say that I actually did him a favour when I severed the umbilical cord that connected us, even if the cut did produce more blood than either of us had anticipated. No, the time had come to say goodbye. Anything else would have just made Erich look foolish. If he could only have seen that, then he might have thanked me.'

'So you dropped him.'

I shrugged. 'If you want to put it that way, yes.'

'Would it be fair to say that you took his friendship, his mentoring, and all his belief in you and simply threw it back in his face?'

I considered this for a moment. 'Try to look at it from my point of view,' I said. 'What you're describing is a young man utterly calculating and dishonest in his actions. But was Erich honest with me? Let's face it, if I had been two hundred pounds overweight and looked like something that had been washed in on the tides after a particularly brutal storm, do you think he would have asked me to join him for a drink that night in West Berlin? I wasn't the only waiter working that night, you know, but I was the one he chose. It's easy to look at me as the villain of the piece but, really, Erich's actions weren't entirely honourable either.'

'I suppose it comes down to motivation,' said Theo. 'Whatever Erich did was done out of love. And confusion. And regret for a wasted life. While you were just using him. And, really, did he deserve it? An elderly man who, many decades before, while he was still a teenager, had made a single terrible mistake, one that he'd had to live with ever since. How many young men in Germany at that time did something to send people to their death? Oh, it doesn't make it right, of course it doesn't, but he wasn't a monster. Just a bewildered boy who acted without thinking. He spent his entire life punishing himself for that. Did he need that extra suffering at the end?'

I lowered my head, closed my eyes and tried to control my temper. It seemed a little rich to me that, with all the help I was giving this boy, he had the audacity to be so judgemental towards me. I looked up again, ready to say as much, but he was doing that thing again, tapping his index finger quickly against his thumb, just as Daniel had done, and I softened. I needed his forgiveness, not his condemnation.

'Like I said,' I continued quietly, 'it's all a long time ago. And if you don't mind, I'd prefer not to talk about Erich any more. Sometimes it feels as if I've spent half of my life discussing that man and, sooner or later, it has to stop.'

'But—'

'No, Daniel,' I said, placing a hand flat on the table. 'It has to stop.'

He nodded. 'All right.'

The notepad reappeared and he turned to a blank page and started scribbling away, a curious smile on his face. He didn't talk for a long time and I found myself fixated on his hands.

'Do you remember when Miss Willow tried to get you to write with your right hand?' I asked, smiling at the memory.

'I'm sorry?' he said, looking up.

'When you were seven or eight. And Miss Willow said that it would be better if you stopped writing with your left hand. She tried to force you to write with your right and I had to go in to the head, Mrs Lane, and lodge a complaint.'

He said nothing, shook his head, and began scribbling in his notebook again. I ordered some more drinks and drank another neat whisky at the bar, which wasn't like me. I had my strict drinking routine and preferred not to alter it. Somehow, though, I just felt like I needed more. I wanted to fade away.

'Let's move on to something else,' he said, when I sat back down again. He moved his beer to one side, barely glancing at it, while I took a long draught from mine. 'I'd like to ask you about your time in New York. You wrote two books there, am I right?'

'That's right. *The Breach* and *The Broken Ones*. Will they play a big part in your thesis?'

'Of course, but I'm more interested in how you developed the

329

ideas for those books. I've established how you worked on the first three.'

'You're not still angry at what I told you about *The Tribesman*, are you?' I asked with a sigh. 'Really, I think you're making a mountain out of a molehill.'

'You were working for *Storī* at the time?' he asked, ignoring my question.

'Not working for, no. I owned *Storī*. I founded the magazine from scratch. I was the editor. The whole operation was under my control.'

'Of course. Sorry. And what made you set it up in the first place?'

'Well, when I left England I had an idea that it would be worthwhile to do something to help further the careers of new writers. I liked the idea of literary philanthropy. No one had ever helped me, after all, and—'

'Except Erich.'

'Well, yes.'

'And Dash.'

'And Dash, that's true.'

'And Edith.'

'Yes, of course. You see, I wanted the magazine to become a place where writers longed to see their work in print, which is why I only published four editions a year, each with a dozen or so stories. It kept the quality very high. To be published in *Storī*, I felt, should be an honour. An aspiration. Like being published in the *New Yorker*.'

'I've gone through all the old issues.'

'Of the *New Yorker*?'

'No, of course not,' he said, rolling his eyes, and I sat back, astonished that he could behave so disrespectfully towards me. Perhaps he'd had too much to drink. 'Of *Storī*.'

'Oh, of course. What, all of them?'

'Yes. It's important for my thesis to identify where your tastes lay.'

'You're very diligent. You really do want to be a biographer, don't you?'

'There's some pretty brilliant writing in there. Some really wonderful work.'

'Thank you.'

'And you discovered some great talents. Henry Etta James, for one.'

'Oh yes,' I said, laughing a little. 'Not that she ever gives me any credit for launching her career. You know, when she won the Pulitzer for *I Am Dissatisfied with My Boyfriend, My Body and My Career*, I sent her a floral bouquet and she didn't even have the good manners to thank me. She's held a grudge against me for a ridiculously long time.'

'Over that story you refused to publish?'

I stared at him in astonishment.

'How on earth do you know about that?' I asked, trying to control the slight quiver in my voice.

'She told me.'

'Who did?'

'Henry Etta.'

'Henrietta James?'

'Yes.'

I couldn't have been more surprised if he had pulled his face away to reveal hers lying beneath. 'I'm sorry,' I said. 'You'll have to explain. Are you . . . How on earth do you know Henrietta? She can't be a friend of yours, surely?'

'Oh no,' he replied. 'We're not friends as such. I wouldn't even presume. But I went to New York earlier in the year, while I was doing some research for my thesis. I thought it was important to get some idea of where *Storī* fitted into your life. You were there for a long time, after all.'

'All right,' I said doubtfully. 'But how on earth did you find yourself crossing paths with her?'

'I contacted a few of the writers who had begun their careers by being published in your magazine. It wasn't difficult; they're all on social media. Most of them didn't reply, but she did. She was very generous with her time, actually. She took me out for cocktails at the Russian Tea Rooms, which was pretty exciting. She even introduced me to her editor.'

'Did she indeed?' I asked, raising an eyebrow in surprise. 'That was good of her.'

'She was very encouraging.'

'And I suppose she had nothing but bad things to say about me?'

'Not at all. She was very complimentary. She did say that you'd had a small dispute about a story that the *Atlantic* had gone on to publish—'

'She'd completely rewritten it by then,' I protested. 'It wasn't even remotely the same story that she gave me.'

'She wasn't negative, Maurice,' he insisted. 'Settle down.'

'Please don't . . .' I breathed in through my nose again, trying to control my temper. 'Please don't tell me to settle down, all right?'

'Okay. But I promise she wasn't rude about you in any way.'

'Well, all right,' I said, feeling disgruntled anyway.

'I'm sorry if I've upset you.'

'Oh, please,' I said, waving away his concern. 'I have about as much interest in Henrietta's opinion of me as I do the Queen's.'

'Would you like another drink? You look like you could use one.'

'But you've barely touched yours,' I said, seeing how his glass was still three-quarters full while mine was almost empty. 'Have I been drinking quickly or are you drinking slowly?'

'Does it matter? Anyway, I'll get you one if you like.'

'Yes, please,' I said, and he made his way to the bar. It was hard not to feel a little under siege but, when I analysed everything he'd said so far, there seemed no reason for me to feel so.

'She got married last year,' he said when he returned, placing a fresh pint on the table for me, and I took a long draught from it. It irritated me to see that he'd got himself a glass of water. I didn't like drinking alone any more.

'Who did?' I asked.

'Henrietta.'

'Oh,' I said, not caring very much. 'Good for her.'

'I think you know her husband.'

'He's not another writer, is he?' I asked, rolling my eyes. 'What is it with these New Yorkers and their—'

'No, an editor, actually,' said Theo. 'Jarrod Swanson.'

I thought about it, but the name meant nothing to me. 'I don't think so,' I said. 'It doesn't ring a bell.'

'He was an assistant at *Storī* for a time. He was *your* assistant.'

'Jarrod Swanson,' I repeated, racking my memory to recall him and, eventually, I remembered. Jarrod had been classmates with Henrietta at the New School but they'd broken up and, angry with her, he'd rejected one of her stories, the very story that I discovered and went on to publish as her first work. So they'd got back together in the end? And now they were married! Well, good for them, I supposed. It was no skin off my nose.

'Jarrod is actually back working at *Storī* these days,' said Theo. 'He's no longer interested in being a writer, though. He says he got to the point where he realized that he just wasn't good enough and that his calling lay in working with other writers. He has your old job there. Editor. He's making a go of it too. I'm surprised you didn't know any of this.'

I shrugged. 'I haven't paid any attention to the magazine since I sold it,' I said. 'I knew it was still in existence, of course, but other than that . . .' I turned away and checked my watch. The afternoon was turning into a cross-examination and I wasn't enjoying it.

'I'm going to make it a central chapter in my thesis,' said Theo. 'I'm calling it *Storī*time.'

'How inventive.'

'Yes, I thought so. And, if you don't mind, I'd like to ask you about something I discovered while I was over there.'

'Fire away,' I said. 'I get the sense that our foreplay is over at last and, finally, you're about to fuck me.'

'I'm sorry?' he said, sitting back but looking utterly nonplussed by my choice of words.

'Just ask what you want to ask,' I said with a sigh. 'I can see you're itching to do so.'

'All right then,' he said, flicking through his notes. 'The thing is, when Jarrod heard that you were to be the subject of my thesis, he asked whether I'd like to have a look through the *Storī* archives.'

'I sincerely hope that you found more interesting things to do in New York than read through all of them.'

'Actually, I jumped at the opportunity. The magazine's been going a long time now. I thought there was a chance that I might stumble across a lost story by someone who went on to be famous.'

'Famous!' I said, bursting out laughing. 'These are writers we're talking about, Daniel, not movie stars.'

'Maurice, you keep—'

'I keep what?'

He shook his head. 'It doesn't matter,' he said. 'Anyway, of course I couldn't possibly have read everything there. There are thousands of stories in that room.'

'I think you'd abandon reading for ever if you even tried.'

'So instead I decided to focus my attention on two particular periods.'

'Oh yes? Which ones?'

'Spring 2009 and winter 2013.'

'All right,' I said, thinking back, trying to remember what was happening in my life then. 'You were, what, about six years old in 2009 and ten years old in 2013?'

'No, I would have been . . .' He seemed surprised by what I had said. 'I was born in 1996 so I would have been thirteen and then seventeen.'

'Of course,' I said. 'My mistake. So what was so special about those particular periods? Are you going to tell me or do I have to guess?'

'It was when you wrote the first drafts of *The Breach* and *The Broken Ones.*'

I lifted my drink, swallowed almost a third of a pint in one go, then set it back on the table.

'You really are very diligent, aren't you?' I said. 'I feel I may have underestimated you, Theo. And did you find anything good in there? Something that you think I should have published but didn't?'

He took a second notepad from his satchel, a much larger one, and flicked through it, stopping at a particular page and reading it for a long time before speaking.

'There was a story by a woman named Marianne Jilson,' he said finally. 'Called "When the Bough Broke".'

'Awful title,' I said.

'True,' replied Theo. 'And the story wasn't much better, to be honest. Well, the writing wasn't, anyway. Although the plot was sort of interesting.'

'I don't remember it.'

'It was about five brothers living in America in the 1930s, working on their parents' farm. Four join the army but one is left behind because he has flat feet and they won't take him.'

'Flat feet,' I said, laughing. 'I've never really understood what that means, have you?'

'The story is built around how difficult he finds it, being the only young man in town when everyone else has gone away to fight. He feels emasculated, of course.'

'I see,' I said quietly.

'And then there was another story, by Ho Kitson. A Chinese-American writer, if I remember correctly from the accompanying letter.'

'And what did he or she write?'

'He. A story called "A Statement of Intent".'

'Better title.'

335

'Agreed.'

'Oh, I'm so glad.'

'And Ho Kitson's story was about a girl who has abandoned her baby in a railway carriage in California, just as it's about to set off for a cross-country journey.'

I nodded but said nothing.

'You can see where I'm going on this, I presume?' he asked after a lengthy pause.

'*The Breach*,' I said.

'*The Breach*,' he agreed. 'The opening chapter of that novel sees a young woman leaving her unwanted baby in a railway carriage. Another woman boards shortly after, discovers the baby and, being unable to have a child herself, steals him. No one ever knows. She just takes him home and she and her husband raise him as their own. And when the boy turns eighteen, the Vietnam War breaks out and almost all the sons of the families in town go to fight, but when he goes for his medical test—'

'You don't need to recount my own novel to me, Theo,' I said, growing annoyed now by his impertinence. 'I wrote it. I think I remember what it was about.'

'And then there's *The Broken Ones*,' he continued, looking down at his notes again. 'Do I need to go on?'

'Well, you're obviously enjoying yourself,' I said with a shrug. 'So why not?'

'Steven Conway. A story called "The Wedding Anniversary". A husband and wife visit Paris to celebrate twenty years together and, while there, she has a brief affair. And then Anna Smith. A story called "Tuesday". A comic story about life on a university campus where a professor is trying and failing to seduce his students. And if we look at the plot of *The Broken Ones*—'

'All right, Daniel, for fuck's sake,' I said, raising my voice.

'Theo,' he said calmly.

'Just tell me what your fucking point is.'

He looked at me with a certain contempt in his eyes and laughed. 'It's not obvious?'

'Not to me,' I said.

'The ideas. They weren't yours.'

'And?'

'Maurice, I'm not trying to be obtuse—'

'Then you're failing. Tell me this, Theo. Those four stories you read. Were they any good?'

He considered this for a moment and shrugged. 'Not really,' he said. 'I mean, they had some good ideas, story-wise, but the writing was weak and the characters were never fully developed.'

'And if you had been the editor of *Storī* at the time, would you have published them?'

'No. Definitely not.'

'So what's the problem?'

'Your novels – those two novels – they weren't your ideas. They're a blend of other people's stories.'

I smiled. *Other People's Stories*. My new book. My unfinished book. The book that Daniel, the little snoop, had discovered and got so worked up over.

'But their stories weren't any good,' I protested. 'And my novels, the two that we're talking about, were both very well received.'

'Yes, but—'

'Look, Theo. I'm a writer. And what's the most irritating question that a writer can be asked?'

'I don't know. Do you write by hand or on a computer?'

'No, it's *Where do you get your ideas?* And the answer is that no one knows where they come from and nobody *should* know. They evolve in thin air, they float down from some mysterious heaven and we reach out to grab one, to grasp it in our imagination, and to make it our own. One writer might overhear a conversation in a café and a whole novel will build from that moment. Another might see an article in a newspaper and a plot will suggest itself immediately. Another might hear about an unpleasant incident that happened to a friend of a friend at a supermarket. So I took ideas from badly written stories that had been sent to me – unsolicited, I might add – and turned them into something that was not only publishable but sold very well. What's the problem with that?'

'When you express it like that, nothing,' said Theo, looking utterly frustrated by my reply. 'But don't you think—'

'I think what I just said, that's what I think. Are you trying to suggest that no one has ever written a novel about an abandoned child before? For God's sake, Daniel, how does the story of Moses begin? The Pharaoh has condemned all male Hebrew children to death and Jochebed places the baby in an ark, where's he discovered by Bithiah. Are you saying that Ho Kitson stole her idea from the Bible? And, what, a college professor who seduces his students? You've read Updike, I presume? Mailer? Roth?'

'But it's not the same!' he insisted, shaking his head, clearly discombobulated now. 'You're trying to justify your actions and—'

'I'm not trying to justify anything. And if you have an accusation to make, Theo, then perhaps you should just make it. If not, perhaps you should stop fishing for scandal and focus on the work itself. Be a literary biographer, as you say you want to be, and not a tabloid journalist.'

He hesitated and, finally, shook his head. 'I just think it's a little strange that—'

'My boy, you're going to write an extraordinary thesis,' I said. 'I have to compliment you. The level of research you're undertaking is exemplary. I presume you've talked to your father about this. He's still interested in developing this book, I mean? A book about me?'

'Yes,' said Theo, looking down at the table and tapping it with his fingers. The wind had truly been taken out of his sails and I couldn't help but feel a little amused. The poor boy looked crestfallen. He'd thought he was doing a Woodward and Bernstein on me but the truth was, he was very new to this game and I'd been playing it for a long time. It was hardly a contest of equals.

'Are you all right, Theo?' I asked, reaching forward and taking his hand in mine. 'If you don't mind my saying so, you look a little shaken.'

'I'm fine,' he said, checking his watch. 'I should probably go. I have some work I need to do.'

'All right,' I replied. 'But what a great afternoon! If you ask me, I think it's very impressive the lengths you're going to in order to write a strong thesis. It's obvious that you're going to be a great success one day, I'm certain of it. No one's secrets will be safe from you. Are you sure you wouldn't like another drink before you go?' I asked, reaching into my pocket and removing my wallet. 'I feel quite thirsty and I'm so enjoying talking to you.'

6. The Cross Keys, Covent Garden

Sometimes you just know that you've made a mistake. I had put my faith in Theo, had thought that he would be the one to reintroduce me to the literary world, but after our last encounter it began to dawn on me that I had chosen the wrong person. He was hard-working, certainly, an admirable trait in one so young, but simply too naïve. He'd done his research but had utterly failed to understand the value of the information he'd discovered. He'd allowed me to dismiss his concerns and even to make him feel foolish for voicing them at all. Had I been in his place, I would have tightened the screw and made me reveal all, but the poor boy just didn't have the killer instinct. I realized, to my disappointment, that it was time to let him go, just as I'd let Erich go, just as I'd let Dash go, and just as I'd let Edith fall. They'd each served a purpose and, while Theo ultimately hadn't proved as useful to me as I had hoped, at least he'd inspired me to get back to writing and to put the events of the past few years behind me. It was time to stop drinking and begin a novel. If he had done nothing else for me, he had done that.

When I woke that morning, I reached for my phone, intending to text him to say that I would not be available for any further interviews but, just as I lifted it, a message arrived from him, asking whether we could meet later that afternoon in the Cross Keys. I thought, why not? It would be kinder, after all, to tell him face to face that our acquaintance had come to an end and that he would have to finish his thesis without me, than to do so over something so impersonal as a text. And so I replied in the affirmative, saying that I'd meet him there at three o'clock. I hoped there wouldn't be a scene. I've always hated scenes.

It would have been Daniel's birthday that day and I spent most of the morning, and my journey to Covent Garden, thinking about him. His loss lay heavily on me but, just as I was discarding Theo, it was time to discard him too. I couldn't write if I felt guilt. The truth was, I had been wrong all those years when I imagined that I would like to be a father. Perhaps it was the idea rather than the reality that appealed to me most for, in the end, much like my marriage to Edith, the experience hadn't moved me as much as I had expected it to. Certainly, I had formed an attachment to the boy and would have preferred him still to be with me, but a life alone, where I was in control of my own movements and decisions, was my natural state.

Other People's Stories had begun as a rough idea one evening when I was feeling a little dejected from having discovered nothing interesting in the recent pile of *Storī* submissions. It had been almost a year since I'd found anything that I could adapt as my own and so I had started to think about my own life and how I had turned an unpromising beginning into a triumphant career. There were the people who really mattered – my parents, Erich, Dash, Edith and Daniel – and it was true that each had contributed something to my success. I started to make a few rough notes. I thought back over my own actions since I'd first left Yorkshire for the Savoy Hotel in West Berlin and realized the story I was searching for had been there all along.

It wasn't another person's story at all.

It was my own.

Not that I intended to write a memoir. Certainly not. Fiction was my métier and fiction was my comforting home. Also, it wasn't as if I could ever write a *truthful* autobiography. I would be vilified instantly and, one would assume, arrested. No, I couldn't do anything as theatrical as that, but what I could do was write a novel. All I'd ever needed was a story and, once I had that, I still believed that I was one of the best in the game.

And so I did what I had been doing all my life: I started to write.

I began with a boy growing up in Yorkshire who wanted to make something of himself. I kept separate files, taking the truth and re-creating it exactly as I remembered it. I began with my friendship with Henry Rowe, that early conquest of mine and the first person who had made me understand the powerful draw of my beauty. It hadn't worked out, of course, and I'd never managed to finish the story I was writing, but I'd been young at the time and I wasn't going to reproach myself for that. I'd still been learning, after all, and Henry had proved an excellent place to start.

Then there was Erich. And Dash. And Edith. All good stories to tell. To make it easier for myself, my first draft was written exactly as I remembered things, using their real names and using my own. The plan was to write about a person with absolutely no conscience, someone who would use anyone to get ahead, an operator on the very highest level. And then, when my first draft was written, I would get down to the real work. Change the names, of course, and draw much wider distinctions between myself and the characters' real-life counterparts. Also, I had decided that my protagonist would not be an aspiring writer but an actor. Erich and Dash would be great men of the theatre, Edith an ingénue. I had a lovely idea for a section where I and my Dash recreations would spend a night at the home of Laurence Olivier and Joan Plowright, where Olivier, wily old fox that he was, would be the only person who had ever seen through me. I was certain that Gore would appreciate the comparison with perhaps the most handsome and talented actor ever to appear on screen. I had written several drafts of that section and it was my favourite by far because I'd always thought that, if Gore had simply taken the time to get to know me, then we might have got along. It was a shame, I thought, that he was no longer alive to read it.

That day had also been a Saturday, and Daniel had been in a grouchy mood all morning, which I put down to the fact that he was thirteen and was entering puberty. He'd been quite annoying of late and I was starting to dread the two or three years that lay ahead.

I'd gone out that afternoon to the *Storī* offices to catch up on some work and then, not relishing the idea of returning home to a moody teenager, had gone to the Angelika for a screening of *Midnight in Paris*. It had left me in a good mood, and when I got off the subway on my way home, I stopped at a local take-away and picked up some food. His favourite restaurant, I might add, not mine.

When I returned home, however, I was surprised to realize that the apartment was empty. It was designed in such a way that Daniel's bedroom was at one end, near the front door, while mine, and my office, was at the other, the two wings separated by a communal living space and kitchen. I opened the door to his room, but he wasn't there and, as he wasn't lying on the sofa reading or watching television, I assumed that he'd gone out. Perhaps one of his friends had called around and they'd gone to the movies or to wherever boys his age went when there were no adults around to tell them no. I generally didn't ask too many questions. Daniel, after all, was quite responsible and, because of that, I was content to allow him his freedom.

It was only after I put the food in the refrigerator for reheating later and returned to the living room that I heard noises coming from the other end of the apartment. Daniel rarely went down there so I was immediately surprised and a little anxious. I walked down the corridor, opened the door to my office and, to my surprise, discovered my son sitting at my computer. I don't think I'd ever seen him there before, as he knew that he was expressly forbidden from using it.

'What are you doing?' I asked.

He didn't reply, nor did he turn around. His attention was entirely fixed on the screen before him and only when I repeated my question did he slowly turn to look at me. His expression was one I had never seen on his face before, a mixture of disillusionment, fear and hatred.

'I've told you before, Daniel,' I said, slightly disconcerted by this, and I could hear in my voice that I did not sound as stern as I had hoped. 'My office is out of bounds at all times and no exceptions. You have your own computer. Use it.'

'It's broken,' he said, and his tone was rather flat, as if he could barely bring himself to respond to me. 'I dropped it earlier and it's not working.'

'Then we'll get it fixed,' I said. 'Or we can get you a new one on Monday. But don't use mine, all right? That's my work computer. I don't like people messing with it.'

He stared at me for a long time and, despite the fact that he was only thirteen, I couldn't help but feel that I was the child in this situation.

'Was Edith my mother?' he asked finally, and I hesitated, like a chess player calculating a few steps ahead, wondering how he would respond to any reply of mine, and what I would say to him then, and how he would react to that. I turned my attention to the screen before him. A Word document was open but I couldn't make out which one.

'Where did you hear that name?' I asked, and it crossed my mind that I had never talked to him about my marriage. There seemed no reason to, after all, for Edith was already dead before I even met

343

the Italian chambermaid. All Daniel had ever known was he and I, and there had seemed little point in dragging up the past.

'I read your book,' he said. 'The first section, anyway. Everything you've written about your life.'

His voice came in quick gasps; he was obviously upset, and he reached for the Ventolin inhaler on the desk before him and took a quick puff to decongest his lungs.

'Edith wasn't your mother,' I said.

'But you were married to her. It says so here.' He pointed in the direction of the open file.

'She was my wife, yes, but she wasn't your mother. She died a few years before you were born. She had nothing to do with you at all.'

'It says here that you killed her,' he said, his voice filling with emotion, tears starting to fall down his face, and he took another quick puff from his inhaler. His words were coming in staccato rhythm, the syllables broken up between gasps.

'It's just a novel, Daniel,' I said, moving towards him. 'It's not the truth. You know the difference between fiction and real life, right?'

'But you use your name,' he insisted, raising his voice now. 'It's all Maurice this and Maurice that. And you talk about *Two Germans*. And I looked up Edith Camberley on the Internet and it says that she wrote a book too. And this Erich person,' he continued. 'I read that file too. And another man.' He swallowed, looking half embarrassed and half horrified. 'Did you have sex with men? Are you gay?'

'What do you know about sex?' I asked, trying to laugh it off.

'You've written that you killed her,' he said, turning and sliding his finger along the top of the mouse, dragging the screen back to the part where I described our year in Norwich, when I had felt like Edith's eunuch. 'It says that you pushed her down the stairs.'

'Don't be ridiculous,' I said, trying to keep control of my temper. I could see that he was getting more upset now too. His breath was growing even shorter in his throat and I knew from experience that when he got so worked up he needed more and more of his Ventolin. 'She lost her footing, that's all. And she fell. It was an accident.'

'You write that you pushed her. She found out that you'd copied her book and sold it as your own and—'

'It's a novel, Daniel,' I insisted. 'Nothing more. For Christ's sake!'

'It's not!' he cried, and the tears were rolling down his face now, his words difficult to understand. 'I've read all of it. I've read everything you've written here. You didn't even write any of your own books. You stole them all!'

'That's not true,' I said, starting to feel panicked now, for I'd never seen him so upset, nor had I ever found myself so close to discovery. 'I wrote every word.'

'But they weren't your ideas! You're a liar!'

'I'm not,' I told him. 'Look, you shouldn't even be in here. You've broken into my private computer and—'

'Was Edith my mother?' he asked again, and the words were completely disconnected from each other as he tried to catch his breath. I looked to my right. His blue Ventolin inhaler sat between us. 'Did you kill my mother?' he shouted.

'Of course not,' I cried. 'What do you take me for?'

'You did!' he roared. 'You killed my mother! And you stole her book!'

He could barely breathe now, and he reached out for his Ventolin and, without thinking, I reached for it too, grabbing it before he could and wrapping it in my closed fist as I stepped back towards the door.

'Give it to me,' he gasped, and I told myself to hand it over but, somehow, I couldn't. I knew my son, I knew how honest he was, how persistent, and I knew that he would never let this go until he discovered the truth. 'Give it to me, Dad!' he cried, standing up, the words like broken syllables in his throat as he wheezed, his entire body doing all it could to clutch at small breaths of air to clear his increasingly clogged lungs.

'I can't,' I said. My eyes flicked to the clock on the wall of my office. It was eight minutes past two when he fell to the floor, his hand on his chest, his body pulsing up and down as it went into shock. And at that moment I understood only too clearly that it was him or me. If I helped him, my career would be over, and I could not – *I would not* – allow that to happen. I had worked far too long and far too hard to let it go. I was a writer, for fuck's sake. I was born to be a writer. No one would ever take that away from me.

'So, you just let me die?' asked Daniel, and I lifted the pint before me and took a long drink, allowing the alcohol to enter my bloodstream, making everything seem all right, before setting it down on the table once again.

'I let you die,' I admitted.

'I begged you for my inhaler. You wouldn't give it to me.'

'You would have told. I couldn't allow that. I'm sorry.'

'But you're not, though, are you? You're not really sorry.'

'I did what I had to do,' I told him. 'You don't know what it's like to have wanted something your entire life and never be good enough.'

'Of course I don't. I died when I was thirteen. I never got the chance.'

'Jesus.'

I looked up, glanced around. I was surrounded by a blur that gradually began to focus. I was in the Cross Keys. How had I got there? I remembered leaving home earlier but couldn't recall arriving. How long had I been sitting there?

'Daniel?' I asked quietly, but it wasn't Daniel sitting opposite me. It was Theo.

'Your wife?' he said. 'Your own son? I knew you were bad, but this—'

'What are you talking about?' I asked. I felt that disoriented sensation one feels when waking from a mid-afternoon nap, confused about the time of day, uncertain of one's location or whether you've been part of a dream or reality.

'I thought you were just a liar. A manipulator. An operator and a plagiarist. But this? I never even suspected—'

'Who do you think you're talking to?' I said, leaning forward, my entire body shaking now in confusion. 'You can't speak to me like that, you little prick.'

He nodded down towards his phone and tapped the screen. A large red button was visible in the centre.

'You can't act as if you didn't say it. I have it all here.'

'You recorded me?' I asked, frightened now. I couldn't recall ever being frightened in my entire life.

'Of course I did,' he said. 'I've recorded all our conversations. Right from the start. You said I could, remember? When we met that first day in the Queen's Head on Denman Street? I wanted to quote you accurately for my so-called thesis.'

I swallowed, trying to recall. That had been almost a month ago now but, yes, he had asked and I had said yes. He'd put the phone in his pocket so that it wouldn't distract us and I had complimented him on his professionalism. But still, the things he was saying didn't quite make sense to me. 'What are you talking about?' I asked. 'You *are* writing a thesis, aren't you? That's what you told me.'

'No,' he replied. 'I'm writing a book.'

'A thesis that will become a book.'

'No, just a book.'

I shook my head, desperately trying to understand. 'A book about me, though, yes? For your father? At Random House?'

'Oh yes,' he said, nodding. 'That's true. It was his idea, actually. And I do want to be a literary biographer. I know I'm young, but what's wrong with that? You were young when you published your first book. If this works out, and I think it will now, I'd say I have a great career ahead of me.'

'So there's no thesis then,' I said, considering this. 'Just a book.' Well, that wasn't so bad. It cut out the middle man, so to speak. 'You've been writing a book about me all this time.'

He smiled and looked around the bar, the expression on his face suggesting that he couldn't quite believe how slow I was.

'You don't get it, do you?' he asked. 'You're not the subject of the book.'

'I'm not?'

'No.'

'Then who is?'

'You can't guess?'

I thought about it but, no, I couldn't. 'Who?' I asked again.

'Don't you remember when we first met? I told you that books had been my passion since I was a kid? And that my father worked in publishing but that his uncle used to write a little?'

I looked away. Did I remember this? Yes, I did, but I had focussed only on the fact that his father was an editor.

'My great-uncle, that would be,' he said. 'He's the subject. I'm writing about him.'

'And not me?'

'No.'

'But I don't understand,' I said, placing both hands on the edge of the table before me, for I was beginning to feel faint. 'I feel like I'm in a daze.'

'How's your German, Maurice?' he asked.

'Average, I suppose,' I said. 'Enough to get by on. Why?'

'Theo Field,' he said, very slowly, enunciating each syllable as he smiled at me.

'I don't . . .' And then, like a door opening beneath my feet and sending me falling to the rocks below, I felt a sensation that I was no longer part of this world. 'Field,' I said. '*Acker.*'

'*Acker,*' he agreed with a nod.

'Ackermann. You're . . .'

'My father is Georg Ackermann's son. He was killed in a tram crash, remember? You told me so yourself. Erich's younger brother.'

'Erich was your uncle.'

348

'Well, my great-uncle.'

I leaned forward and peered into his face. Did he look like Erich Ackermann? No, he looked like Daniel. He looked like my son.

'I thought you would be more willing to confide in me if I shared some things in common with him,' he said, sensing what I was thinking. 'It wasn't very difficult. There's lots of pictures of him online, so I changed my hair colour to look like his. And he posted pictures on his Instagram account of his bedroom and I saw that band poster on the wall. So I bought a T-shirt to match.'

'No,' I said quietly.

'And he wore a ring on the fourth finger of his right hand. So I got one of those too.'

'Your glasses?'

'There's no prescription,' he said, taking them off and handing them across to me. 'Just frames with glass. The same ones that he wore.'

I put them on. I could see through them without any difficulty.

'He posted videos on Facebook too. That's where I noticed this.' He started to tap his index finger against his thumb rapidly. 'A nervous affliction, was it?'

'Yes,' I said. 'He'd had it all his life. And your asthma?' I asked.

He burst out laughing, reached into his satchel and removed his blue inhaler, handing it across.

'Here,' he said. 'Try it.'

I put it in my mouth, pushed the button and breathed in quickly. Nothing. Just air. It was empty.

'I don't have asthma,' he said. 'I've never had asthma.'

'The picture of Erich and me in Montmartre,' I said. 'You said that you were looking at old photos. I thought you had found it in a newspaper or a book.'

'I never said that,' he replied with a shrug. 'I simply said that I was looking at it. You know that he was dead a week before they discovered the body?'

'I heard that, yes,' I said, looking down at the table. 'Dash told me.'

'He was holding the photograph in his hands when he was found. I suppose he still loved you, despite what you did to him. The coroner passed it on to my father.'

I stared at him. I said nothing for a very long time.

'But why?' I asked finally, when I found my voice again. 'Why would you do this?'

'Why did you do what you did to my great-uncle?'

'Because I wanted to succeed,' I replied, beginning to feel the shame of my actions at last.

'For what it's worth, you've given me more than I ever dreamed of,' he said. 'I don't even know whether the book will be about him now or about you. Or about both of you. But I have a feeling that it's going to be the best start to a literary career since . . .' He broke into a wide smile. 'Well, since yours, I suppose!'

'But what have I given you?' I asked, trying to recall each of the conversations we'd had and all the confidences I'd entrusted him with. Happy to oblige me, he counted them off on his fingers.

'First, Dash. Then Erich. *Storī*, of course. *The Tribesman*, which you didn't even write.'

'I tidied it up.'

'But you didn't write it! Although all of that pales into insignificance compared to what you did to Edith and Daniel. Two murders, Maurice. Two murders. Four, if you count your responsibility for both Erich's death and Dash's.'

'Edith fell,' I said.

'You pushed her.'

'Daniel had an asthma attack.'

'And you withheld his inhaler.' He looked down at his phone, tapped it for a moment, and put it in his pocket before standing up. 'It's all here, Maurice. Every word.'

'No,' I said, shaking my head. 'No, wait. Let's have another drink.'

'I've drunk enough with you. I'll be happy if I never have another pint in my life.'

'Please,' I said, standing up, but he shook his head, lifted his drink from the table and swallowed what was left in one go.

'I'll be in touch, Maurice,' he said.

'Sit down, let me order you another one. Please.'

'No.'

'Surely after everything I've done for you—'

'You haven't done anything for me,' he said, laughing. 'You've bought me a few drinks, that's all. Tried to use me to get what you want. You hoped my father would use his connections to get you a new book deal, right? Well, that's not going to happen. I don't owe you anything, Maurice.'

'No, but—'

'I'm leaving,' he said, walking away.

'Wait!' I shouted, but he was already halfway towards the door. 'Daniel!' I roared at the top of my voice, a desperate cry from the depths of my soul. He stopped as the pub fell silent, every head turning in my direction, eyes staring at me as if I were about to deliver the final monologue in a wonderful tragedy. But it wasn't me who spoke, for I had nothing left to say.

'It's Theo,' he said, looking at me with a mixture of contempt and boredom. 'How many times, Maurice? My name is Theo, not Daniel.'

And with that, he turned his back on me and was gone.

7. HM Prison Belmarsh

Many years ago, at the end of our acquaintance, I suggested to Erich Ackermann that perhaps he had seen me as he wanted me to be and not as who I actually was. I was right then, but the truth is that I made a similar mistake with Theo. Was it an absurd mixture of grief, guilt and alcoholism that allowed me to believe I was confessing everything to Daniel and that he would somehow forgive me and make my world clean again? Or had I always planned on telling Theo the truth? It's difficult to know. I was always in control of everything and it's a curious sensation when that's no longer the case.

But, despite my downfall and disgrace, life has actually been a lot happier since my incarceration. For one thing, I'm able to read more than I have in years. Always new fiction, of course. Young writers on their first, second or third books. I've been making notes of my favourite ones and would love to publicly comment on their work but, sadly, prisoners are not allowed use of the Internet, which seems a little unfair to me. How else are we to get our online law degrees and convince ourselves that we can argue our way out of this place? I'm being facetious, of course. Prison humour.

Recently, I even tortured myself by trawling through Garrett Colby's new novel, which was about an unrequited love affair between a man and a raccoon. What is his issue with animals? Did his puppy get run over when he was a child and he's never got over it since? The whole thing is beyond me. Anyway, the book was awful. True, I've made some questionable choices in my life, but I can honestly say that I've never written or stolen anything as bad as that book. To my astonishment, however, the reviews were ecstatic, and somehow it soared to victory on the night of The Prize this year. That's twice now that his name appears on the honour roll while mine is still absent. It's enough to make one want to throw in the towel, it really is.

Theo finished his book, which he titled *Two Writers: Erich & Maurice*, and he won the Costa Biography Award. He preceded this with an exposé in the *Guardian*, which won him several journalism awards. He seems set up for life. I feel quite proud of him. Truly, I do.

Of course, the response from the writing fraternity to the revelations of my crimes were mixed.

Some claimed that they'd always known I was a charlatan, that no one with such little self-awareness could possibly write as well as I did.

Some said that they admired how I'd blurred the lines between my life and my writing and that my career was the embodiment of a new type of fiction. They even wrote editorial pieces for the newspapers suggesting that I should be applauded, not shunned.

Some said that they'd never read me anyway and didn't care what I did or how I did it because they were the only people worth reading and anyone who spent even a moment on my prose was wasting their life.

One said that literature was more important than human life so what was the problem if a few people had died in the pursuit of excellence?

One declared that he had originally considered *The Tribesman* to be a masterpiece, but now that he knew it had actually been written by a woman, he was revising that opinion and realized that it was just a tedious piece of domestic trivia, driven by sentimentality.

There were interminable debates and discussions on radio, television and in the newspapers about the way my work had been received over the years. For a brief time, I became the most famous writer in the world, which was enormously pleasing and everything I'd ever hoped for. Erich's novels were republished in uniform jackets – his poetry collection too, which he always said was ill advised – each one with an introduction by a famous writer. The general feeling was that he'd been unfairly treated, which was a bit rich, I thought, considering he sent five people to their deaths. But revisionism is revisionism and at least it gave me hope that, long after I'm gone, readers will rediscover me and my reputation will be restored.

I wasn't sure when the original newspaper piece was going to be published and was held in a state of suspense for some time until I received a call one day from someone at the *Guardian*, who had

353

naturally been suspicious of a twenty-year-old arriving in the lobby with such outrageous claims about a famous writer, but then they listened to the conversations recorded on his phone and the evidence was indisputable. I knew there was no point trying to argue – I was *exhausted* by my life at this point – and admitted that his piece was wholly accurate.

I returned home from the pub a few nights later to find a crew of television cameras and radio reporters waiting on my doorstep, each of whom had clearly been tipped off about what was going to be published the next day. As I paid my taxi fare and stepped out to a barrage of questions, I recalled that YouTube clip of Doris Lessing returning home from her local Tesco only to discover a dozen reporters standing outside her house, giving her the wonderful news that she had just been awarded the Nobel Prize in Literature. 'Oh Christ,' she said on that occasion, rolling her eyes in exasperation, a priceless reaction. 'This has been going on for thirty years.' I said nothing quite as amusing as Doris, simply brushing past them while muttering that they were in my way, and stumbling through my door. I was obviously drunk. I giggled when I got inside. So, this was what self-destruction felt like.

The afternoon that the *Guardian* article appeared, the police showed up at my door and arrested me on suspicion of murder. I protested that I had never committed such a heinous crime, that the two most obvious deaths on my conscience had been manslaughter, but my claims were rejected by the CPS and I was sent for trial. The jury didn't believe my story either and sent me down for life. I think that's highly unfair.

Perhaps I should mention that Edith's family, whom I hadn't seen in so long, showed up at the trial. Her mother had died a few years before but Rebecca was there – minus Arjan, who had left her for a much younger actress in Hollywood – along with her sons, Damien and Edward, who had grown into handsome young men and spent every day glaring at me as if they would like to be left alone in a quiet room with me for half an hour. I spotted Robert too, seated in the back row, and wondered how he felt about being back in a courtroom. He'd been released from prison after five years but was forced to be on the sex offenders list, poor man. There was another man sitting near them, one I vaguely recognized from Edith's and my UEA days, but I couldn't recall his name. He became very upset when the details of my wife's death were recounted. I can only assume that they were particularly friendly in some way and I admired him for still caring after all these years.

Of course, my publishers were left in something of a dilemma. What do you do when one of the most famous writers in the world – if not *the* most famous – is in disgrace but everyone is desperate to read the offending books out of a macabre fascination? This is what you do: you reprint all the books in new editions – except *The Tribesman*, of course, which is now only printed under Edith's name – and donate thirty per cent of the royalties to charity. And you pocket the rest.

Now, my health. Naturally, I went through some major withdrawal symptoms from alcohol, and the prison authorities, to their credit, were extremely sympathetic and helpful in this. But the damage had been done. My liver is destroyed and my kidneys are in pretty bad shape too. The doctors say that one more drink would kill me, but that's obviously nonsense. It would be too much of a coincidence if the moment I was forced to give up was exactly the moment that I would have been teetering on the edge of death. Anyway, I drink regularly in here – although obviously not at the same levels as I did during my later London years – in my cell with King Kong, of whom more in a moment. You'd be surprised – or maybe you wouldn't – at how much contraband is available in prison. Everything is banned, of course, but most of the inmates have a phone, a television, cigarettes, drugs, alcohol. There are prostitutes for those who require such services. Men or women.

Whenever there's a big boxing match on television everyone knows whose cell has the subscription services. Honestly, it's not a bad life.

And I have a job! My first real job since I worked in the Savoy Hotel in West Berlin back in 1988. I teach a creative-writing course and conduct a bi-weekly two-hour session with fourteen inmates of varying ability. They're a rough bunch, of course – murderers, for the most part, rapists, violent offenders – and they all like to write about crime. All but one, the aforementioned King Kong, who has been given that name because of an uncanny resemblance he bears to that cinematic simian. For almost a year he was working on a novel about an heiress in nineteenth-century Boston and, quite honestly, it would give Henry James a run for his money. He was too nervous to show it to the other classmates, but he gave it to me and I was amazed by his skill with language, his gift for characterization and his witty dialogue. I encouraged him, mentored him, supported him, and he'd just finished his fourth draft when he got into an altercation with another prisoner, leading to a dust-up in the prison yard where he was stabbed in the neck with a toothbrush that had a Stanley blade taped to its end. He bled out in minutes, poor chap.

Which left me with his manuscript. And it was eminently publishable. Really, the kind of thing that wins awards and hits the bestseller lists. So, I did another draft or two, tidied up some of the language, and sent it to a London publisher, being quite clear who I was and admitting that I would never be able to promote the book in person as I'd been committed to Belmarsh for the rest of my natural but that I had found something to fill the time while I was here, the thing that I had always enjoyed most.

Writing.

And, despite the public outcry, they published it. And, against all the odds, it's been one of the bestselling books of the year. The longlist for this year's Prize is being announced tomorrow and, quite honestly, I think I'm in with a very strong chance.

Acknowledgements

For all their advice and support, many thanks to Bill Scott-Kerr, Larry Finlay, Patsy Irwin, Darcy Nicholson, Fiona Murphy and everyone at Transworld; Simon Trewin, Eric Simonoff, Laura Bonner and the team at WME; and all my publishers around the world, who publish my books with such enthusiasm and commitment.

John Boyne was born in Ireland in 1971. He is the author of eleven novels for adults, five for young readers and a collection of short stories. Perhaps best known for his 2006 multi-award-winning book *The Boy in the Striped Pyjamas*, John's other novels, notably *The Absolutist* and *A History of Loneliness*, have been widely praised and are international bestsellers. Most recently, *The Heart's Invisible Furies* was a Richard & Judy Bookclub word-of-mouth bestseller.

His novels are published in over fifty languages.